LEGENDS II

DRAGON,
SWORD,
AND KING

EDITED BY

ROBERT SILVERBERG

Great!
3-28-13

BALLANTINE BOOKS • NEW YORK

A Del Rey® Book
Published by The Random House Publishing Group

www.delreybooks.com

ISBN 0-345-47578-X

Manufactured in the United States of America

OPM   9   8   7   6   5   4   3   2   1

First Edition: January 2004
First Mass Market Edition: November 2004

*For George R. R. Martin
who baited the trap*

*And Terry Brooks
for valiant help from an unexpected quarter*

CONTENTS

INTRODUCTION

The first *Legends* anthology, which was published in 1998, contained eleven never-before-published short novels by eleven best-selling fantasy writers, each story set in the special universe of the imagination that its author had made famous throughout the world. It was intended as the definitive anthology of modern fantasy, and—judging by the reception the book received from readers worldwide—it succeeded at that.

And now comes *Legends II*. If the first book was definitive, why do another one?

The short answer is that fantasy is inexhaustible. There are always new stories to tell, new writers to tell them; and no theme, no matter how hoary, can ever be depleted.

As I said in the introduction to the first volume, fantasy is the oldest branch of imaginative literature—as old as the human imagination itself. It is not difficult to believe that the same artistic impulse that produced the extraordinary cave paintings of Lascaux and Altamira and Chauvet, fifteen and twenty and even thirty thousand years ago, also probably produced astounding tales of gods and demons, of talismans and spells, of dragons and werewolves, of wondrous lands beyond the horizon—tales that fur-clad shamans recited to fascinated audiences around the campfires of Ice Age Europe. So, too, in torrid Africa, in the China of prehistory, in ancient India, in the Americas: everywhere, in fact, on and on back through time for thousands or even hundreds of thousands of years. I like to think that the storytelling impulse is universal—that there have been storytellers as long as there have been beings in this world that could be spoken of as "human"—and that those storytellers have in particular devoted their skills and energies and talents, throughout our long evolutionary path, to the creation of extraordinary marvels and wonders. The Sumerian epic of Gilgamesh is a tale of fantasy; so, too, is Homer's *Odyssey,* and on and on up through such modern fantasists as E. R. Eddison, A. Merritt, H. P. Lovecraft, and J. R. R. Tolkien, and all the great science-fiction writers from Verne and Wells to our own time. (I include science fiction because science fiction, as I see it, belongs firmly in the fantasy category: It is a specialized branch of fantasy, a technology-oriented kind of visionary literature in which the imagination is given free play for the sake of making the scientifically impossible, or at least the implausible, seem altogether probable.)

Many of the contributors to the first *Legends* were eager to return to their special worlds of fantasy for a second round. Several of them raised the subject of a new anthology so often that finally I began to agree with them that a second book would be a good idea. And here it is. Six writers—Orson Scott Card, George R. R. Martin, Raymond E. Feist,* Anne McCaffrey,* Tad Williams,* and myself*—have returned from the first one. Joining them are four others—Robin Hobb,* Elizabeth Haydon, Diana Gabaldon, and Neil Gaiman*—who have risen to great fame among fantasy enthusiasts since the first anthology was published, and one grand veteran of fantasy, Terry Brooks, who had found himself unable at the last minute to participate in the first volume of *Legends* but who joins us for this one.

My thanks are due once again to my wife, Karen, and to my literary agent, Ralph Vicinanza, both of whom aided me in all sorts of ways in the preparation of this book, and, of course, to all the authors who came through with such splendid stories. I acknowledge also a debt of special gratitude to Betsy Mitchell of Del Rey Books, whose sagacious advice

*These authors appear in *Legends II: Shadows, Gods, and Demons.*

and unfailing good cheer were essential to the project. Without her help this book most literally would not have come into being.

—ROBERT SILVERBERG
    February 2003

A Song of Ice and Fire

George R. R. Martin

A Song of Ice and Fire began life as a trilogy, and has since expanded to six books. As J. R. R. Tolkien once said, the tale grew in the telling.

The setting for the books is the great continent of Westeros, in a world both like and unlike our own, where the seasons last for years and sometimes decades. Standing hard against the sunset sea at the western edge of the known world, Westeros stretches from the red sands of Dorne in the south to the icy mountains and frozen fields of the north, where snow falls even during the long summers.

The children of the forest were the first known inhabitants of Westeros, during the Dawn of Days: a race small of stature who made their homes in the greenwood, and carved strange faces in the bone-white weirwood trees. Then came the First Men, who crossed a land bridge from the larger continent to the east with their bronze swords and horses, and warred against the children for centuries before finally making peace with the older race and adopting their nameless, ancient gods. The Compact marked the beginning of the Age of Heroes, when the First Men and the children shared Westeros, and a hundred petty kingdoms rose and fell.

Other invaders came in turn. The Andals crossed the narrow sea in ships, and with iron and fire they swept across the kingdoms of the First Men, and drove the children from their forests, putting many of the weirwoods to the ax. They brought their own faith, worshiping a god with seven aspects whose symbol was a seven-pointed star. Only in the far north did the First Men, led by the Starks of Winterfell, throw back the newcomers. Elsewhere the Andals triumphed, and raised kingdoms of their own. The children of the forest dwindled and disappeared, while the First Men intermarried with their conquerors.

The Rhoynar arrived some thousands of years after the Andals, and came not as invaders but as refugees, crossing the seas in ten thousand ships to escape the growing might of the Freehold of Valyria. The lords freeholder of Valyria ruled the greater part of the known world; they were sorcerers, great in lore, and alone of all the races of man they had learned to breed dragons and bend them to their will. Four hundred years before the opening of *A Song of Ice and Fire,* however, the Doom descended on Valyria, destroying the city in a single night. Thereafter the great Valyrian empire disintegrated into dissension, barbarism, and war.

Westeros, across the narrow sea, was spared the worst of the chaos that followed. By that time only seven kingdoms remained where once there had been hundreds—but they would not stand for much longer. A scion of lost Valyria named Aegon Targaryen landed at the mouth of the Blackwater with a small army, his two sisters (who were also his wives), and three great dragons. Riding on dragonback, Aegon and his sisters won battle after battle, and subdued six of the seven Westerosi kingdoms by fire, sword, and treaty. The conqueror collected the melted, twisted blades of his fallen foes, and used them to make a monstrous, towering barbed seat: the Iron Throne, from which he ruled henceforth as Aegon, the First of His Name, King of the Andals and the Rhoynar and the First Men, and Lord of the Seven Kingdoms.

The dynasty founded by Aegon and his sisters endured for most of three hundred years. Another Targaryen king, Daeron the Second, later brought Dorne into the realm, uniting all of Westeros under a single ruler. He did so by marriage, not conquest, for the last of the dragons had died half a century before. *The Hedge Knight,* published in the first *Legends,* takes place in the last days of Good King Daeron's reign, about a hundred years before the opening of the first of the *Ice and Fire* novels, with the realm at peace and the

Targaryen dynasty at its height. It tells the story of the first meeting between Dunk, a hedge knight's squire, and Egg, a boy who is rather more than he seems, and of the great tourney at Ashford Meadow. *The Sworn Sword,* the tale that follows, picks up their story a year or so later.

THE SWORN SWORD

A Tale of the Seven Kingdoms

GEORGE R. R. MARTIN

In an iron cage at the crossroads, two dead men were rotting in the summer sun.

Egg stopped below to have a look at them. "Who do you think they were, ser?" His mule Maester, grateful for the respite, began to crop the dry brown devilgrass along the verges, heedless of the two huge wine casks on his back.

"Robbers," Dunk said. Mounted atop Thunder, he was much closer to the dead men. "Rapers. Murderers." Dark circles stained his old green tunic under both arms. The sky was blue and the sun was blazing hot, and he had sweated gallons since breaking camp this morning.

Egg took off his wide-brimmed floppy straw hat. Beneath, his head was bald and shiny. He used the hat to fan away the flies. There were hundreds crawling on the dead men, and more drifting lazily through the still, hot air. "It must have been something bad, for them to be left to die inside a crow cage."

Sometimes Egg could be as wise as any maester, but other times he was still a boy of ten. "There are lords and lords," Dunk said. "Some don't need much reason to put a man to death."

The iron cage was barely big enough to hold one man, yet two had been forced inside it. They stood face to face, with their arms and legs in a tangle and their backs against the hot black iron of the bars. One had tried to eat the other, gnawing at his neck and shoulder. The crows had been at both of them. When Dunk and Egg had come around the hill, the birds had risen like a black cloud, so thick that Maester spooked.

"Whoever they were, they look half starved," Dunk said. *Skeletons in skin, and the skin is green and rotting.* "Might be they stole some bread, or poached a deer in some lord's wood." With the drought entering its second year, most lords had become less tolerant of poaching, and they hadn't been very tolerant to begin with.

"It could be they were in some outlaw band." At Dosk, they'd heard a harper sing "The Day They Hanged Black Robin." Ever since, Egg had been seeing gallant outlaws behind every bush.

Dunk had met a few outlaws while squiring for the old man. He was in no hurry to meet any more. None of the ones he'd known had been especially gallant. He remembered one outlaw Ser Arlan had helped hang, who'd been fond of stealing rings. He would cut off a man's fingers to get at them, but with women he preferred to bite. There were no songs about him that Dunk knew. *Outlaws or poachers, makes no matter. Dead men make poor company.* He walked Thunder slowly around the cage. The empty eyes seemed to follow him. One of the dead men had his head down and his mouth gaping open. *He has no tongue,* Dunk observed. He supposed the crows might have eaten it. Crows always pecked a corpse's eyes out first, he had heard, but maybe the tongue went second. *Or maybe a lord had it torn out, for something that he said.*

Dunk pushed his fingers through his mop of sun-streaked hair. The dead were beyond his help, and they had casks of wine to get to Standfast. "Which way did we come?" he asked, looking from one road to the other. "I'm turned around."

"Standfast is that way, ser." Egg pointed.

"That's for us, then. We could be back by evenfall, but not if we sit here all day counting flies." He touched Thunder with his heels and turned the big destrier toward the left-hand fork. Egg put his floppy hat back on and tugged sharply at Maester's lead. The mule left off cropping at the devilgrass and came along without an argument for once. *He's hot as well,* Dunk thought, *and those wine casks must be heavy.*

The summer sun had baked the road as hard as brick. Its ruts were deep enough to break a horse's leg, so Dunk was careful to keep Thunder to the higher ground between them. He had twisted his own ankle the day they left Dosk, walking in the black of night when it was cooler. A knight had to learn to live with aches and pains, the old man used to say. *Aye, lad, and with broken bones and scars. They're as much a part of knighthood as your swords and shields.* If Thunder was to break a leg, though . . . well, a knight without a horse was no knight at all.

Egg followed five yards behind him, with Maester and the wine casks. The boy was walking with one bare foot in a rut and one out, so he rose and fell with every step. His dagger was sheathed on one hip, his boots slung over his backpack, his ragged brown tunic rolled up and knotted around his waist. Beneath his wide-brimmed straw hat, his face was smudged and dirty, his eyes large and dark. He was ten, not quite five feet tall. Of late he had been sprouting fast, though he had a long long way to grow before he'd be catching up to Dunk. He looked just like the stableboy he wasn't, and not at all like who he really was.

The dead men soon disappeared behind them, but Dunk found himself thinking about them all the same. The realm was full of lawless men these days. The drought showed no signs of ending, and smallfolk by the thousands had taken to the roads, looking for someplace where the rains still fell. Lord Bloodraven had commanded them to return to their own lands and lords, but few obeyed. Many blamed Bloodraven and King Aerys for the drought. It was a judgment from the gods, they said, for the kinslayer is accursed. If they were wise, though, they did not say it loudly. *How many eyes does Lord Bloodraven have?* ran the riddle Egg had heard in Oldtown. *A thousand eyes, and one.*

Six years ago in King's Landing, Dunk had seen him with his own two eyes, as he rode a pale horse up the Street of Steel with fifty Raven's Teeth behind him. That was before

King Aerys had ascended to the Iron Throne and made him the Hand, but even so he cut a striking figure, garbed in smoke and scarlet with Dark Sister on his hip. His pallid skin and bone-white hair made him look a living corpse. Across his cheek and chin spread a wine-stain birthmark that was supposed to resemble a red raven, though Dunk only saw an odd-shaped blotch of discolored skin. He stared so hard that Bloodraven felt it. The king's sorcerer had turned to study him as he went by. He had one eye, and that one red. The other was an empty socket, the gift Bittersteel had given him upon the Redgrass Field. Yet it seemed to Dunk that both eyes had looked right through his skin, down to his very soul.

Despite the heat, the memory made him shiver. "Ser?" Egg called. "Are you unwell?"

"No," said Dunk. "I'm as hot and thirsty as them." He pointed toward the field beyond the road, where rows of melons were shriveling on the vines. Along the verges goatheads and tufts of devilgrass still clung to life, but the crops were not faring near as well. Dunk knew just how the melons felt. Ser Arlan used to say that no hedge knight need ever go thirsty. "Not so long as he has a helm to catch the rain in. Rainwater is the best drink there is, lad." The old man never saw a summer like this one, though. Dunk had left his helm at Standfast. It was too hot and heavy to wear, and there had been precious little rain to catch in it. *What's a hedge knight do when even the hedges are brown and parched and dying?*

Maybe when they reached the stream he'd have a soak. He smiled, thinking how good that would feel, to jump right in and come up sopping wet and grinning, with water cascading down his cheeks and through his tangled hair and his tunic clinging sodden to his skin. Egg might want a soak as well, though the boy looked cool and dry, more dusty than sweaty. He never sweated much. He liked the heat. In Dorne he went about bare-chested, and turned brown as a Dornishman. *It is his dragon blood,* Dunk told himself. *Whoever heard of a sweaty dragon?* He would gladly have pulled his own tunic off, but it would not be fitting. A hedge knight could ride bare naked if he chose; he had no one to shame but himself. It was different when your sword was sworn. *When you accept a lord's meat and mead, all you do reflects on him,* Ser Arlan used to say. *Always do more than he expects of you, never less. Never flinch at any task or hardship. And above all, never shame the lord you serve.* At Standfast, "meat and mead" meant chicken and ale, but Ser Eustace ate the same plain fare himself.

Dunk kept his tunic on, and sweltered.

Ser Bennis of the Brown Shield was waiting at the old plank bridge. "So you come back," he called out. "You were gone so long I thought you run off with the old man's silver." Bennis was sitting on his shaggy garron, chewing a wad of sourleaf that made it look as if his mouth were full of blood.

"We had to go all the way to Dosk to find some wine," Dunk told him. "The krakens raided Little Dosk. They carried off the wealth and women and burned half of what they did not take."

"That Dagon Greyjoy wants for hanging," Bennis said. "Aye, but who's to hang him? You see old Pinchbottom Pate?"

"They told us he was dead. The ironmen killed him when he tried to stop them taking off his daughter."

"Seven bloody hells." Bennis turned his head and spat. "I seen that daughter once. Not worth dying for, you ask me. That fool Pate owed me half a silver." The brown knight looked just as he had when they left; worse, he smelled the same as well. He wore the same garb every day: brown breeches, a shapeless roughspun tunic, horsehide boots. When armored he donned a loose brown surcoat over a shirt of rusted mail. His swordbelt was a cord of boiled leather, and his seamed face might have been made of the same thing. *His head looks like one of those shriveled melons that we passed.* Even his teeth were brown, under the red stains left by the sourleaf he liked to chew. Amidst all that brownness, his eyes stood out; they were a pale green, squinty small, close set, and shiny-bright with malice. "Only two casks," he observed. "Ser Useless wanted four."

"We were lucky to find two," said Dunk. "The drought reached the Arbor, too. We heard the grapes are turning into raisins on the vines, and the ironmen have been pirating—"

"Ser?" Egg broke in. "The water's gone."

Dunk had been so intent on Bennis that he hadn't noticed. Beneath the warped wooden planks of the bridge only sand and stones remained. *That's queer. The stream was running low when we left, but it was running.*

Bennis laughed. He had two sorts of laughs. Sometimes he cackled like a chicken, and sometimes he brayed louder than Egg's mule. This was his chicken laugh. "Dried up while you was gone, I guess. A drought'll do that."

Dunk was dismayed. *Well, I won't be soaking now.* He swung down to the ground. *What's going to happen to the crops?* Half the wells in the Reach had gone dry, and all the rivers were running low, even the Blackwater Rush and the mighty Mander.

"Nasty stuff, water," Bennis said. "Drank some once, and it made me sick as a dog. Wine's better."

"Not for oats. Not for barleycorn. Not for carrots, onions, cabbages. Even grapes need water." Dunk shook his head. "How could it go dry so quick? We've only been six days."

"Wasn't much water in there to start with, Dunk. Time was, I could piss me bigger streams than this one."

"Not *Dunk*," said Dunk. "I told you that." He wondered why he bothered. Bennis was a mean-mouthed man, and it pleased him to make mock. "I'm called Ser Duncan the Tall."

"By who? Your bald pup?" He looked at Egg and laughed his chicken laugh. "You're taller than when you did for Penny-tree, but you still look a proper *Dunk* to me."

Dunk rubbed the back of his neck and stared down at the rocks. "What should we do?"

"Fetch home the wines, and tell Ser Useless his stream's gone dry. The Standfast well still draws, he won't go thirsty."

"Don't call him Useless." Dunk was fond of the old knight. "You sleep beneath his roof, give him some respect."

"You respect him for the both o' us, Dunk," said Bennis. "I'll call him what I will."

The silvery gray planks creaked heavily as Dunk walked out onto the bridge, to frown down at the sand and stones below. A few small brown pools glistened amongst the rocks, he saw, none larger than his hand. "Dead fish, there and there, see?" The smell of them reminded him of the dead men at the crossroads.

"I see them, ser," said Egg.

Dunk hopped down to the streambed, squatted on his heels, and turned over a stone. *Dry and warm on top, moist and muddy underneath.* "The water can't have been gone long." Standing, he flicked the stone sidearm at the bank, where it crashed through a crumbling overhang in a puff of dry brown earth. "The soil's cracked along the banks, but soft and muddy in the middle. Those fish were alive yesterday."

"Dunk the lunk, Pennytree used to call you. I recall." Ser Bennis spat a wad of sourleaf onto the rocks. It glistened red and slimy in the sunlight. "Lunks shouldn't try and think, their heads is too bloody thick for such."

Dunk the lunk, thick as a castle wall. From Ser Arlan the words had been affectionate. He had been a kindly man, even in his scolding. In the mouth of Ser Bennis of the Brown Shield, they sounded different. "Ser Arlan's two years dead," Dunk said, "and I'm called Ser Duncan the Tall." He was sorely tempted to put his fist through the brown knight's face and smash those red and rotten teeth to splinters. Bennis of the Brown Shield might be a nasty piece of work, but Dunk had a good foot and a half on him, and four stone as well. He might be a lunk, but he was big. Sometimes it seemed as though he'd thumped his head on half the doors in Westeros, not to mention every beam in every inn from Dorne up to the Neck. Egg's brother Aemon had measured him in Oldtown and found he lacked an inch of seven feet, but that was half a year ago. He might have grown since. Growing was the one thing that Dunk did really well, the old man used to say.

He went back to Thunder and mounted up again. "Egg, get on back to Standfast with the wine. I'm going to see what's happened to the water."

"Streams dry up all the time," said Bennis.

"I just want to have a look—"

"Like how you looked under that rock? Shouldn't go turning over rocks, lunk. Never know what might crawl out. We got us nice straw pallets back at Standfast. There's eggs more days than not, and not much to do but listen to Ser Useless go on about how great he used to be. Leave it be, I say. The stream went dry, that's all."

Dunk was nothing if not stubborn. "Ser Eustace is waiting on his wine," he told Egg. "Tell him where I went."

"I will, ser." Egg gave a tug on Maester's lead. The mule twitched his ears, but started off again at once. *He wants to get those wine casks off his back.* Dunk could not blame him.

The stream flowed north and east when it was flowing, so he turned Thunder south and west. He had not ridden a dozen yards before Bennis caught him. "I best come see you don't get hanged." He pushed a fresh sourleaf into his mouth. "Past that clump o' sandwillows, the whole right bank is spider land."

"I'll stay on our side." Dunk wanted no trouble with the Lady of the Coldmoat. At Standfast you heard ill things of her. *The Red Widow,* she was called, for the husbands she had put into the ground. Old Sam Stoops said she was a witch, a poisoner, and worse. Two years ago she had sent her knights across the stream to seize an Osgrey man for stealing sheep. "When m'lord rode to Coldmoat to demand him back, he was told to look for him at the bottom of the moat," Sam had said. "She'd sewn poor Dake in a bag o' rocks and sunk him. 'Twas after that Ser Eustace took Ser Bennis into service, to keep them spiders off his lands."

Thunder kept a slow, steady pace beneath the broiling sun. The sky was blue and hard, with no hint of cloud anywhere to be seen. The course of the stream meandered around rocky knolls and forlorn willows, through bare brown hills and fields of dead and dying grain. An hour upstream from the bridge, they found themselves riding on the edge of the small Osgrey forest called Wat's Wood. The greenery looked inviting from afar, and filled Dunk's head with thoughts of shady glens and chuckling brooks, but when they reached the trees they found them thin and scraggly, with drooping limbs. Some of the great oaks were shedding leaves, and half the pines had turned as brown as Ser Bennis, with rings of dead needles girdling their trunks. *Worse and worse,* thought Dunk. *One spark, and this will all go up like tinder.*

For the moment, though, the tangled underbrush along the Chequy Water was still thick with thorny vines, nettles, and tangles of briarwhite and young willow. Rather than fight through it, they crossed the dry streambed to the Coldmoat side, where the trees had been cleared away for pasture. Amongst the parched brown grasses and faded wildflowers, a few black-nosed sheep were grazing. "Never knew an animal stupid as a sheep," Ser Bennis commented. "Think they're kin to you, lunk?" When Dunk did not reply, he laughed his chicken laugh again.

Half a league farther south, they came upon the dam.

It was not large as such things went, but it looked strong. Two stout wooden barricades had been thrown across the stream from bank to bank, made from the trunks of trees with the bark still on. The space between them was filled with rocks and earth and packed down hard. Behind the dam the flow was creeping up the banks and spilling off into a ditch that had been cut through Lady Webber's fields. Dunk stood in his stirrups for a better look. The glint of sun on water betrayed a score of lesser channels, running off in all directions like a spider's web. *They are stealing our stream.* The sight filled him with indignation, especially when it dawned on him that the trees must surely have been taken from Wat's Wood.

"See what you went and did, lunk," said Bennis. "Couldn't have it that the stream dried up, no. Might be this starts with water, but it'll end with blood. Yours and mine, most like."

The brown knight drew his sword. "Well, no help for it now. There's your thrice-damned diggers. Best we put some fear in them." He raked his garron with his spurs and galloped through the grass.

Dunk had no choice but to follow. Ser Arlan's longsword rode his hip, a good straight piece of steel. *If these ditch-diggers have a lick of sense, they'll run.* Thunder's hooves kicked up clods of dirt.

One man dropped his shovel at the sight of the oncoming knights, but that was all. There were a score of the diggers, short and tall, old and young, all baked brown by the sun. They formed a ragged line as Bennis slowed, clutching their spades and picks. "This is Coldmoat land," one shouted.

"And that's an Osgrey stream." Bennis pointed with his longsword. "Who put that damned dam up?"

"Maester Cerrick made it," said one young digger.

"No," an older man insisted. "The gray pup pointed some and said do this and do that, but it were us who made it."

"Then you can bloody well unmake it."

The diggers' eyes were sullen and defiant. One wiped the sweat off his brow with the back of his hand. No one spoke.

"You lot don't hear so good," said Bennis. "Do I need to lop me off an ear or two? Who's first?"

"This is Webber land." The old digger was a scrawny fellow, stooped and stubborn. "You got no right to be here. Lop off any ears and m'lady will drown you in a sack."

Bennis rode closer. "Don't see no ladies here, just some mouthy peasant." He poked the digger's bare brown chest with the point of his sword, just hard enough to draw a bead of blood.

He goes too far. "Put up your steel," Dunk warned him. "This is not his doing. This maester set them to the task."

"It's for the crops, ser," a jug-eared digger said. "The wheat was dying, the maester said. The pear trees, too."

"Well, maybe them pear trees die, or maybe you do."

"Your talk don't frighten us," said the old man.

"No?" Bennis made his longsword whistle, opening the old man's cheek from ear to jaw. "I said, them pear trees die, or you do." The digger's blood ran red down one side of his face.

He should not have done that. Dunk had to swallow his rage. Bennis was on his side in this. "Get away from here," he shouted at the diggers. "Go back to your lady's castle."

"Run," Ser Bennis urged.

Three of them let go of their tools and did just that, sprinting through the grass. But another man, sunburned and brawny, hefted a pick and said, "There's only two of them."

"Shovels against swords is a fool's fight, Jorgen," the old man said, holding his face. Blood trickled through his fingers. "This won't be the end of this. Don't think it will."

"One more word, and I might be the end o' you."

"We meant no harm to you," Dunk said to the old man's bloody face. "All we want is our water. Tell your lady that."

"Oh, we'll tell her, ser," promised the brawny man, still clutching his pick. "That we will."

On the way home they cut through the heart of Wat's Wood, grateful for the small measure of shade provided by the trees. Even so, they cooked. Supposedly there were deer in the wood, but the only living things they saw were flies. They buzzed about Dunk's face as he rode, and crept round Thunder's eyes, irritating the big warhorse no end. The air was still, suffocating. *At least in Dorne the days were dry, and at night it grew so cold I shivered in my cloak.* In the Reach the nights were hardly cooler than the days, even this far north.

When ducking down beneath an overhanging limb, Dunk plucked a leaf and crumpled it between his fingers. It fell apart like thousand-year-old parchment in his hand. "There was no need to cut that man," he told Bennis.

"A tickle on the cheek was all it was, to teach him to mind his tongue. I should of cut his bloody throat for him, only then the rest would of run like rabbits, and we'd of had to ride down the lot o' them."

"You'd kill twenty men?" Dunk said, incredulous.

"Twenty-two. That's two more'n all your fingers and your toes, lunk. You have to kill them all, else they go telling tales." They circled round a deadfall. "We should of told Ser Useless the drought dried up his little pissant stream."

"Ser *Eustace*. You would have lied to him."

"Aye, and why not? Who's to tell him any different? The flies?" Bennis grinned a wet red grin. "Ser Useless never leaves the tower, except to see the boys down in the blackberries."

"A sworn sword owes his lord the truth."

"There's truths and truths, lunk. Some don't serve." He spat. "The gods make droughts. A man can't do a bloody buggering thing about the gods. The Red Widow, though . . . we tell Useless that bitch dog took his water, he'll feel honorbound to take it back. Wait and see. He'll think he's got to *do something*."

"He should. Our smallfolk need that water for their crops."

"*Our* smallfolk?" Ser Bennis brayed his laughter. "Was I off having a squat when Ser Useless made you his heir? How many smallfolk you figure you got? Ten? And that's counting Squinty Jeyne's half-wit son that don't know which end o' the ax to hold. Go make knights o' every one, and we'll have half as many as the Widow, and never mind her squires and her archers and the rest. You'd need both hands and both feet to count all them, and your bald-head boy's fingers and toes, too."

"I don't need toes to count." Dunk was sick of the heat, the flies, and the brown knight's company. *He may have ridden with Ser Arlan once, but that was years and years ago. The man is grown mean and false and craven.* He put his heels into his horse and trotted on ahead, to put the smell behind him.

Standfast was a castle only by courtesy. Though it stood bravely atop a rocky hill and could be seen for leagues around, it was no more than a towerhouse. A partial collapse a few centuries ago had required some rebuilding, so the north and west faces were pale gray stone above the windows, and the old black stone below. Turrets had been added to the roofline during the repair, but only on the sides that were rebuilt; at the other two corners crouched ancient stone grotesques, so badly abraded by wind and weather that it was hard to say what they had been. The pinewood roof was flat, but badly warped and prone to leaks.

A crooked path led from the foot of the hill up to the tower, so narrow it could only be ridden single file. Dunk led the way on the ascent, with Bennis just behind. He could see Egg above them, standing on a jut of rock in his floppy straw hat.

They reined up in front of the little daub-and-wattle stable that nestled at the tower's foot, half hidden under a mis-shapen heap of purple moss. The old man's gray gelding was in one of the stalls, next to Maester. Egg and Sam Stoops had gotten the wine inside, it seemed. Hens were wandering the yard. Egg trotted over. "Did you find what happened to the stream?"

"The Red Widow's dammed it up." Dunk dismounted, and gave Thunder's reins to Egg. "Don't let him drink too much at once."

"No, ser. I won't."

"Boy," Ser Bennis called. "You can take my horse as well."

Egg gave him an insolent look. "I'm not your squire."

That tongue of his will get him hurt one day, Dunk thought. "You'll take his horse, or you'll get a clout in the ear."

Egg made a sullen face, but did as he was bid. As he reached for the bridle, though, Ser Bennis hawked and spat. A glob of glistening red phlegm struck the boy between two toes. He gave the brown knight an icy look. "You spit on my foot, ser."

Bennis clambered to the ground. "Aye. Next time I'll spit in your face. I'll have none o' your bloody tongue."

Dunk could see the anger in the boy's eyes. "Tend to the horses, Egg," he said, before things got any worse. "We need to speak with Ser Eustace."

The only entrance into Standfast was through an oak-and-iron door twenty feet above them. The bottom steps were blocks of smooth black stone, so worn they were bowl-shaped in the middle. Higher up, they gave way to a steep wooden stair that could be swung up like a drawbridge in times of trouble. Dunk shooed the hens aside and climbed two steps at a time.

Standfast was bigger than it appeared. Its deep vaults and cellars occupied a good part of the hill on which it perched. Aboveground, the tower boasted four stories. The upper two had windows and balconies, the lower two only arrow slits. It was cooler inside, but so dim that Dunk had to let his eyes adjust. Sam Stoops' wife was on her knees by the hearth, sweeping out the ashes. "Is Ser Eustace above or below?" Dunk asked her.

"Up, ser." The old woman was so hunched that her head was lower than her shoulders. "He just come back from visiting the boys, down in the blackberries."

The boys were Eustace Osgrey's sons: Edwyn, Harrold, Addam. Edwyn and Harrold had been knights, Addam a young squire. They had died on the Redgrass Field fifteen years ago, at the end of the Blackfyre Rebellion. "They died good deaths, fighting bravely for the king," Ser Eustace told Dunk, "and I brought them home and buried them among the blackberries." His wife was buried there as well. Whenever the old man breached a new cask of wine, he went down the hill to pour each of his boys a libation. "To the king!" he would call out loudly, just before he drank.

Ser Eustace's bedchamber occupied the fourth floor of the tower, with his solar just below. That was where he would be found, Dunk knew, puttering amongst the chests and barrels. The solar's thick gray walls were hung with rusted weaponry and captured banners, prizes from battles fought long centuries ago and now remembered by no one but Ser Eustace. Half the banners were mildewed, and all were badly faded and covered with dust, their once bright colors gone to gray and green.

Ser Eustace was scrubbing the dirt off a ruined shield with a rag when Dunk came up the steps. Bennis followed fragrant at his heels. The old knight's eyes seemed to brighten a little at the sight of Dunk. "My good giant," he declared, "and brave Ser Bennis. Come have a look at this. I found it in the bottom of that chest. A treasure, though fearfully neglected."

It was a shield, or what remained of one. That was little enough. Almost half of it had been hacked away, and the rest was gray and splintered. The iron rim was solid rust, and the wood was full of wormholes. A few flakes of paint still clung to it, but too few to suggest a sigil.

"M'lord," said Dunk. The Osgreys had not been lords for centuries, yet it pleased Ser Eustace to be styled so, echoing as it did the past glories of his House. "What is it?"

"The Little Lion's shield." The old man rubbed at the rim, and some flakes of rust came off. "Ser Wilbert Osgrey bore this at the battle where he died. I am sure you know the tale."

"No, m'lord," said Bennis. "We don't, as it happens. The *Little* Lion, did you say? What, was he a dwarf or some such?"

"Certainly not." The old knight's mustache quivered. "Ser Wilbert was a tall and powerful man, and a great knight. The name was given him in childhood, as the youngest of five brothers. In his day there were still seven kings in the Seven Kingdoms, and Highgarden and the Rock were oft at war. The green kings ruled us then, the Gardeners. They were of the blood of old Garth Greenhand, and a green hand upon a white field was their kingly banner. Gyles the Third took his banners east, to war against the Storm King, and Wilbert's brothers all went with him, for in those days the chequy lion always flew beside the green hand when the King of the Reach went forth to battle.

"Yet it happened that while King Gyles was away, the King of the Rock saw his chance to tear a bite out of the Reach, so he gathered up a host of westermen and came down upon us. The Osgreys were the Marshalls of the Northmarch, so it fell to the Little Lion to meet them. It was the fourth King Lancel who led the Lannisters, it seems to me, or mayhaps the fifth. Ser Wilbert blocked King Lancel's path, and bid him halt. *'Come no farther,'* he said. *'You are not wanted here. I forbid you to set foot upon the Reach.'* But the Lannister ordered all his banners forward.

"They fought for half a day, the gold lion and the chequy. The Lannister was armed with a Valyrian sword that no common steel can match, so the Little Lion was hard pressed, his shield in ruins. In the end, bleeding from a dozen grievous wounds with his own blade broken in his hand, he threw himself headlong at his foe. King Lancel cut him near in half, the singers say, but as he died the Little Lion found the gap in the king's armor beneath his arm, and plunged his dagger home. When their king died, the westermen turned back, and the Reach was saved." The old man stroked the broken shield as tenderly as if it had been a child.

"Aye, m'lord," Bennis croaked, "we could use a man like that today. Dunk and me had a look at your stream, m'lord. Dry as a bone, and not from no drought."

The old man set the shield aside. "Tell me." He took a seat and indicated that they should do the same. As the brown knight launched into the tale, he sat listening intently, with his chin up and his shoulders back, as upright as a lance.

In his youth, Ser Eustace Osgrey must have been the very picture of chivalry, tall and broad and handsome. Time and grief had worked their will on him, but he was still unbent, a big-boned, broad-shouldered, barrel-chested man with features as strong and sharp as some old eagle. His close-cropped hair had gone white as milk, but the thick mustache that hid his mouth remained an ashy gray. His eyebrows were the same color, the eyes beneath a paler shade of gray, and full of sadness.

They seemed to grow sadder still when Bennis touched upon the dam. "That stream has been known as the Chequy Water for a thousand years or more," the old knight said. "I caught fish there as a boy, and my sons all did the same. Alysanne liked to splash in the shallows on hot summer days like this." Alysanne had been his daughter, who had perished in the spring. "It was on the banks of the Chequy Water that I kissed a girl for the first time. A cousin, she was, my uncle's youngest daughter, of the Osgreys of Leafy Lake. They are all gone now, even her." His mustache quivered. "This cannot be borne, sers. The woman will not have my water. She will not have my *chequy* water."

"Dam's built strong, m'lord," Ser Bennis warned. "Too strong for me and Ser Dunk to pull down in an hour, even with the bald-head boy to help. We'll need ropes and picks and axes, and a dozen men. And that's just for the work, not for the fighting."

Ser Eustace stared at the Little Lion's shield.

Dunk cleared his throat. "M'lord, as to that, when we came upon the diggers, well . . ."

"Dunk, don't trouble m'lord with trifles," said Bennis. "I taught one fool a lesson, that was all."

Ser Eustace looked up sharply. "What sort of lesson?"

"With my sword, as it were. A little claret on his cheek, that's all it were, m'lord."

The old knight looked long at him. "That . . . that was ill considered, ser. The woman has a spider's heart. She murdered three of her husbands. And all her brothers died in swaddling clothes. Five, there were. Or six, mayhaps, I don't recall. They stood between her and the castle. She would whip the skin off any peasant who displeased her, I do not doubt, but for *you* to cut one . . . no, she will not suffer such an insult. Make no mistake. She will come for you, as she came for Lem."

"Dake, m'lord," Ser Bennis said. "Begging your lordly pardon, you knew him and I never did, but his name were Dake."

"If it please m'lord, I could go to Goldengrove and tell Lord Rowan of this dam," said Dunk. Rowan was the old knight's liege lord. The Red Widow held her lands of him as well.

"Rowan? No, look for no help there. Lord Rowan's sister wed Lord Wyman's cousin Wendell, so he is kin to the Red Widow. Besides, he loves me not. Ser Duncan, on the morrow you must make the rounds of all my villages, and roust out every able-bodied man of fighting age. I am old, but I am not dead. The woman will soon find that the chequy lion still has claws!"

Two, Dunk thought glumly, *and I am one of them.*

Ser Eustace's lands supported three small villages, none more than a handful of hovels, sheepfolds, and pigs. The largest boasted a thatched one-room sept with crude pictures of the Seven scratched upon the walls in charcoal. Mudge, a stoop-backed old swineherd who'd once been to Oldtown, led devotions there every seventh day. Twice a year a real septon came through to forgive sins in the Mother's name. The smallfolk were glad of the forgiveness, but hated the septon's visits all the same, since they were required to feed him.

They seemed no more pleased by the sight of Dunk and Egg. Dunk was known in the villages, if only as Ser Eustace's new knight, but not so much as a cup of water was offered him. Most of the men were in the fields, so it was largely women and children who crept out of the hovels at their coming, along with a few grandfathers too infirm for work. Egg bore the Osgrey banner, the chequy lion green and gold, rampant upon its field of white. "We come from Standfast with Ser Eustace's summons," Dunk told the villagers. "Every able-bodied man between the ages of fifteen and fifty is commanded to assemble at the tower on the morrow."

"Is it war?" asked one thin woman, with two children hiding behind her skirts and a babe sucking at her breast. "Is the black dragon come again?"

"There are no dragons in this, black or red," Dunk told her. "This is between the chequy lion and the spiders. The Red Widow has taken your water."

The woman nodded, though she looked askance when Egg took off his hat to fan his face. "That boy got no hair. He sick?"

"It's *shaved,*" said Egg. He put the hat back on, turned Maester's head, and rode off slowly.

The boy is in a prickly mood today. He had hardly said a

word since they set out. Dunk gave Thunder a touch of the
spur and soon caught the mule. "Are you angry that I did not
take your part against Ser Bennis yesterday?" he asked his
sullen squire, as they made for the next village. "I like the
man no more than you, but he *is* a knight. You should speak
to him with courtesy."

"I'm your squire, not his," the boy said. "He's dirty and
mean-mouthed, and he pinches me."

*If he had an inkling who you were, he'd piss himself before
he laid a finger on you.* "He used to pinch me, too." Dunk
had forgotten that, till Egg's words brought it back. Ser Bennis and Ser Arlan had been among a party of knights hired
by a Dornish merchant to see him safe from Lannisport to
the Prince's Pass. Dunk had been no older than Egg, though
taller. *He would pinch me under the arm so hard he'd leave a
bruise. His fingers felt like iron pincers, but I never told Ser
Arlan.* One of the other knights had vanished near Stoney
Sept, and it was bruited about that Bennis had gutted him in
a quarrel. "If he pinches you again, tell me and I'll end it.
Till then, it does not cost you much to tend his horse."

"Someone has to," Egg agreed. "Bennis never brushes
him. He never cleans his stall. He hasn't even *named* him!"

"Some knights never name their horses," Dunk told him.
"That way, when they die in battle, the grief is not so hard to
bear. There are always more horses to be had, but it's hard
to lose a faithful friend." *Or so the old man said, but he never
took his own counsel. He named every horse he ever owned.*
So had Dunk. "We'll see how many men turn up at the
tower . . . but whether it's five or fifty, you'll need to do for
them as well."

Egg looked indignant. "I have to serve *smallfolk*?"

"Not serve. Help. We need to turn them into fighters." *If
the Widow gives us time enough.* "If the gods are good, a few
will have done some soldiering before, but most will be
green as summer grass, more used to holding hoes than
spears. Even so, a day may come when our lives depend on
them. How old were you when you first took up a sword?"

"I was little, ser. The sword was made from wood."

"Common boys fight with wooden swords, too, only theirs are sticks and broken branches. Egg, these men may seem fools to you. They won't know the proper names for bits of armor, or the arms of the great Houses, or which king it was who abolished the lord's right to the first night . . . but treat them with respect all the same. You are a squire born of noble blood, but you are still a boy. Most of them will be men grown. A man has his pride, no matter how lowborn he may be. You would seem just as lost and stupid in their villages. And if you doubt that, go hoe a row and shear a sheep, and tell me the names of all the weeds and wildflowers in Wat's Wood."

The boy considered for a moment. "I could teach them the arms of the great Houses, and how Queen Alysanne convinced King Jaehaerys to abolish the first night. And they could teach me which weeds are best for making poisons, and whether those green berries are safe to eat."

"They could," Dunk agreed, "but before you get to King Jaehaerys, you'd best help us teach them how to use a spear. And don't go eating anything that Maester won't."

The next day a dozen would-be warriors found their way to Standfast to assemble among the chickens. One was too old, two were too young, and one skinny boy turned out to be a skinny girl. Those Dunk sent back to their villages, leaving eight: three Wats, two Wills, a Lem, a Pate, and Big Rob the lackwit. *A sorry lot,* he could not help but think. The strapping handsome peasant boys who won the hearts of highborn maidens in the songs were nowhere to be seen. Each man was dirtier than the last. Lem was fifty if he was a day, and Pate had weepy eyes; they were the only two who had ever soldiered before. Both had been gone with Ser Eustace and his sons to fight in the Blackfyre Rebellion. The other six were as green as Dunk had feared. All eight had lice. Two of the Wats were brothers. "Guess your mother didn't know no other name," Bennis said, cackling.

As far as arms went, they brought a scythe, three hoes, an old knife, some stout wooden clubs. Lem had a sharpened stick that might serve for a spear, and one of the Wills allowed that he was good at chucking rocks. "Well and good," Bennis said, "we got us a bloody trebuchet." After that the man was known as Treb.

"Are any of you skilled with a longbow?" Dunk asked them.

The men scuffed at the dirt, while hens pecked the ground around them. Pate of the weepy eyes finally answered. "Begging your pardon, ser, but m'lord don't permit us longbows. Osgrey deers is for the chequy lions, not the likes o' us."

"We will get swords and helms and chainmail?" the youngest of the three Wats wanted to know.

"Why, sure you will," said Bennis, "just as soon as you kill one o' the Widow's knights and strip his bloody corpse. Make sure you stick your arm up his horse's arse, too, that's where you'll find his silver." He pinched young Wat beneath his arm until the lad squealed in pain, then marched the whole lot of them off to Wat's Wood to cut some spears.

When they came back, they had eight fire-hardened spears of wildly unequal length, and crude shields of woven branches. Ser Bennis had made himself a spear as well, and he showed them how to thrust with the point and use the shaft to parry . . . and where to put the point to kill. "The belly and the throat are best, I find." He pounded his fist against his chest. "Right there's the heart, that will do the job as well. Trouble is, the ribs is in the way. The belly's nice and soft. Gutting's slow, but certain. Never knew a man to live when his guts was hanging out. Now if some fool goes and turns his back on you, put your point between his shoulder blades or through his kidney. That's here. They don't live long once you prick 'em in the kidney."

Having three Wats in the company caused confusion when Bennis was trying to tell them what to do. "We should give them village names, ser," Egg suggested, "like Ser Arlan of Pennytree, your old master." That might have worked, only their villages had no names, either. "Well," said Egg, "we could call them for their crops, ser." One village sat amongst bean fields, one planted mostly barleycorn, and the third cultivated rows of cabbages, carrots, onions, turnips, and melons. No one wanted to be a Cabbage or a Turnip, so the last lot became the Melons. They ended up with four Barleycorns, two Melons, and two Beans. As the brothers Wat were both Barleycorns, some further distinction was required. When the younger brother made mention of once having fallen down the village well, Bennis dubbed him "Wet Wat," and that was that. The men were thrilled to have been given "lord's names," save for Big Rob, who could not seem to remember whether he was a Bean or a Barleycorn.

Once all of them had names and spears, Ser Eustace emerged from Standfast to address them. The old knight stood outside the tower door, wearing his mail and plate beneath a long woolen surcoat that age had turned more yellow than white. On front and back it bore the chequy lion, sewn in little squares of green and gold. "Lads," he said, "you all remember Dake. The Red Widow threw him in a sack and drowned him. She took his life, and now she thinks to take our water, too, the Chequy Water that nourishes our crops . . . but she will not!" He raised his sword above his head. "For Osgrey!" he said ringingly. "For Standfast!"

"Osgrey!" Dunk echoed. Egg and the recruits took up the shout. *"Ogsrey! Osgrey! For Standfast!"*

Dunk and Bennis drilled the little company amongst the pigs and chickens, while Ser Eustace watched from the balcony above. Sam Stoops had stuffed some old sacks with soiled straw. Those became their foes. The recruits began practicing their spear work as Bennis bellowed at them. "Stick and twist and rip it free. Stick and twist and rip, but *get the damned thing out!* You'll be wanting it soon enough for the next one. Too slow, Treb, too damned slow. If you can't do it quicker, go back to chucking rocks. Lem, get your weight behind your thrust. There's a boy. And in and out and in and out. Fuck 'em with it, that's the way, in and out, rip 'em, rip 'em, *rip 'em.*"

When the sacks had been torn to pieces by half a thousand spear thrusts and all the straw spilled out onto the ground,

Dunk donned his mail and plate and took up a wooden sword
to see how the men would fare against a livelier foe.

Not too well, was the answer. Only Treb was quick enough
to get a spear past Dunk's shield, and he only did it once.
Dunk turned one clumsy lurching thrust after another,
pushed their spears aside, and bulled in close. If his sword
had been steel instead of pine, he would have slain each of
them half a dozen times. "You're *dead* once I get past your
point," he warned them, hammering at their legs and arms to
drive the lesson home. Treb and Lem and Wet Wat soon
learned how to give ground, at least. Big Rob dropped his
spear and ran, and Bennis had to chase him down and drag
him back in tears. The end of the afternoon saw the lot of
them all bruised and battered, with fresh blisters rising on
their callused hands from where they gripped the spears.
Dunk bore no marks himself, but he was half drowned by
sweat by the time Egg helped him peel his armor off.

As the sun was going down, Dunk marched their little
company down into the cellar and forced them all to have a
bath, even those who'd had one just last winter. Afterward
Sam Stoops' wife had bowls of stew for all, thick with carrots, onions, and barley. The men were bone tired, but to hear
them talk every one would soon be twice as deadly as a
Kingsguard knight. They could hardly wait to prove their
valor. Ser Bennis egged them on by telling them of the joys
of the soldier's life; loot and women, chiefly. The two old
hands agreed with him. Lem had brought back a knife and a
pair of fine boots from the Blackfyre Rebellion, to hear him
tell; the boots were too small for him to wear, but he had
them hanging on his wall. And Pate could not say enough
about some of the camp followers he'd known following the
dragon.

Sam Stoops had set them up with eight straw pallets in the
undercroft, so once their bellies were filled they all went off
to sleep. Bennis lingered long enough to give Dunk a look of
disgust. "Ser Useless should of fucked a few more peasant
wenches while he still had a bit o' sap left in them old sad
balls o' his," he said. "If he'd sown himself a nice crop

o' bastard boys back then, might be we'd have some soldiers now."

"They seem no worse than any other peasant levy." Dunk had marched with a few such while squiring for Ser Arlan.

"Aye," Ser Bennis said. "In a fortnight they might stand their own, 'gainst some other lot o' peasants. Knights, though?" He shook his head, and spat.

Standfast's well was in the undercellar, in a dank chamber walled in stone and earth. It was there that Sam Stoops' wife soaked and scrubbed and beat the clothes before carrying them up to the roof to dry. The big stone washtub was also used for baths. Bathing required drawing water from the well bucket by bucket, heating it over the hearth in a big iron kettle, emptying the kettle into the tub, then starting the whole process once again. It took four buckets to fill the kettle, and three kettles to fill the tub. By the time the last kettle was hot the water from the first had cooled to lukewarm. Ser Bennis had been heard to say that the whole thing was too much bloody bother, which was why he crawled with lice and fleas and smelled like a bad cheese.

Dunk at least had Egg to help him when he felt in dire need of a good wash, as he did tonight. The lad drew the water in a glum silence, and hardly spoke as it was heating. "Egg?" Dunk asked as the last kettle was coming to a boil. "Is aught amiss?" When Egg made no reply, he said, "Help me with the kettle."

Together they wrestled it from hearth to tub, taking care not to splash themselves. "Ser," the boy said, "what do you think Ser Eustace means to do?"

"Tear down the dam, and fight off the Widow's men if they try to stop us." He spoke loudly, so as to be heard above the splashing of the bathwater. Steam rose in a white curtain as they poured, bringing a flush to his face.

"Their shields are woven wood, ser. A lance could punch right through them, or a crossbow bolt."

"We may find some bits of armor for them, when they're ready." That was the best they could hope for.

"They might be killed, ser. Wet Wat is still half a boy. Will Barleycorn is to be married the next time the septon comes. And Big Rob doesn't even know his left foot from his right."

Dunk let the empty kettle thump down onto the hard-packed earthen floor. "Roger of Pennytree was younger than Wet Wat when he died on the Redgrass Field. There were men in your father's host who'd been just been married, too, and other men who'd never even kissed a girl. There were hundreds who didn't know their left foot from their right, maybe thousands."

"That was *different,*" Egg insisted. "That was war."

"So is this. The same thing, only smaller."

"Smaller and *stupider,* ser."

"That's not for you or me to say," Dunk told him. "It's their duty to go to war when Ser Eustace summons them . . . and to die, if need be."

"Then we shouldn't have named them, ser. It will only make the grief harder for us when they die." He screwed up his face. "If we used my boot—"

"No." Dunk stood on one leg to pull his own boot off.

"Yes, but my father—"

"No." The second boot went the way of the first.

"We—"

"No." Dunk pulled his sweat-stained tunic up over his head and tossed it at Egg. "Ask Sam Stoops' wife to wash that for me."

"I will, ser, but—"

"No, I said. Do you need a clout in the ear to help you hear better?" He unlaced his breeches. Underneath was only him; it was too hot for smallclothes. "It's good that you're concerned for Wat and Wat and Wat and the rest of them, but the boot is only meant for dire need." *How many eyes does Lord Bloodraven have? A thousand eyes, and one.* "What did your father tell you, when he sent you off to squire for me?"

"To keep my hair shaved or dyed, and tell no man my true name," the boy said, with obvious reluctance.

Egg had served Dunk for a good year and a half, though some days it seemed like twenty. They had climbed the

Prince's Pass together and crossed the deep sands of Dorne, both red and white. A poleboat had taken them down the Greenblood to the Planky Town, where they took passage for Oldtown on the galleas *White Lady*. They had slept in stables, inns, and ditches, broken bread with holy brothers, whores, and mummers, and chased down a hundred puppet shows. Egg had kept Dunk's horse groomed, his longsword sharp, his mail free of rust. He had been as good a companion as any man could wish for, and the hedge knight had come to think of him almost as a little brother.

He isn't, though. This egg had been hatched of dragons, not of chickens. *Egg* might be a hedge knight's squire, but Aegon of House Targaryen was the fourth and youngest son of Maekar, Prince of Summerhall, himself the fourth son of the late King Daeron the Good, the Second of His Name, who'd sat the Iron Throne for five-and-twenty years until the Great Spring Sickness took him off.

"So far as most folk are concerned, Aegon Targaryen went back to Summerhall with his brother Daeron after the tourney at Ashford Meadow," Dunk reminded the boy. "Your father did not want it known that you were wandering the Seven Kingdoms with some hedge knight. So let's hear no more about your boot."

A look was all the answer that he got. Egg had big eyes, and somehow his shaven head made them look even larger. In the dimness of the lamplit cellar they looked black, but in better light their true color could be seen: deep and dark and purple. *Valyrian eyes,* thought Dunk. In Westeros, few but the blood of the dragon had eyes that color, or hair that shone like beaten gold and strands of silver woven all together.

When they'd been poling down the Greenblood, the orphan girls had made a game of rubbing Egg's shaven head for luck. It made the boy blush redder than a pomegranate. "Girls are so *stupid,*" he would say. "The next one who touches me is going into the river." Dunk had to tell him, "Then *I'll* be touching you. I'll give you such a clout in the ear you'll be hearing bells for a moon's turn." That only goaded the boy to further insolence. "Better bells than stupid *girls,*" he insisted, but he never threw anyone into the river.

Dunk stepped into the tub and eased himself down until the water covered him up to his chin. It was still scalding hot on top, though cooler farther down. He clenched his teeth to keep from yelping. If he did the boy would laugh. Egg *liked* his bathwater scalding hot.

"Do you need more water boiled, ser?"

"This will serve." Dunk rubbed at his arms and watched the dirt come off in long gray clouds. "Fetch me the soap. Oh, and the long-handled scrub brush, too." Thinking about Egg's hair had made him remember that his own was filthy. He took a deep breath and slid down beneath the water to give it a good soak. When he emerged again, sloshing, Egg was standing beside the tub with the soap and long-handled horsehair brush in hand. "You have hairs on your cheek," Dunk observed, as he took the soap from him. "Two of them. There, below your ear. Make sure you get them the next time you shave your head."

"I will, ser." The boy seemed pleased by the discovery.

No doubt he thinks a bit of beard makes him a man. Dunk had thought the same when he first found some fuzz growing on his upper lip. *I tried to shave with my dagger, and almost nicked my nose off.* "Go and get some sleep now," he told Egg. "I won't have any more need of you till morning."

It took a long while to scrub all the dirt and sweat away. Afterward, he put the soap aside, stretched out as much as he was able, and closed his eyes. The water had cooled by then. After the savage heat of the day, it was a welcome relief. He soaked till his feet and fingers were all wrinkled up and the water had gone gray and cold, and only then reluctantly climbed out.

Though he and Egg had been given thick straw pallets down in the cellar, Dunk preferred to sleep up on the roof. The air was fresher there, and sometimes there was a breeze. It was not as though he need have much fear of rain. The next time it rained on them up there would be the first.

Egg was asleep by the time Dunk reached the roof. He lay

on his back with his hands behind his head and stared up at the sky. The stars were everywhere, thousands and thousands of them. It reminded him of a night at Ashford Meadow, before the tourney started. He had seen a falling star that night. Falling stars were supposed to bring you luck, so he'd told Tanselle to paint it on his shield, but Ashford had been anything but lucky for him. Before the tourney ended, he had almost lost a hand and a foot, and three good men had lost their lives. *I gained a squire, though. Egg was with me when I rode away from Ashford. That was the only good thing to come of all that happened.*

He hoped that no stars fell tonight.

There were red mountains in the distance and white sands beneath his feet. Dunk was digging, plunging a spade into the dry hot earth, and flinging the fine sand back over his shoulder. He was making a hole. *A grave,* he thought, *a grave for hope.* A trio of Dornish knights stood watching, making mock of him in quiet voices. Farther off the merchants waited with their mules and wayns and sand sledges. They wanted to be off, but he could not leave until he'd buried Chestnut. He would not leave his old friend to the snakes and scorpions and sand dogs.

The stot had died on the long thirsty crossing between the Prince's Pass and Vaith, with Egg upon his back. His front legs just seemed to fold up under him, and he knelt right down, rolled onto his side, and died. His carcass sprawled beside the hole. Already it was stiff. Soon it would begin to smell.

Dunk was weeping as he dug, to the amusement of the Dornish knights. "Water is precious in the waste," one said, "you ought not to waste it, ser." The other chuckled and said, "Why do you weep? It was only a horse, and a poor one."

Chestnut, Dunk thought, digging, *his name was Chestnut, and he bore me on his back for years, and never bucked or bit.* The old stot had looked a sorry thing beside the sleek sand steeds that the Dornishmen were riding, with their elegant heads, long necks, and flowing manes, but he had given all he had to give.

"Weeping for a swaybacked stot?" Ser Arlan said, in his old man's voice. "Why, lad, you never wept for me, who put you on his back." He gave a little laugh, to show he meant no harm by the reproach. "That's Dunk the lunk, thick as a castle wall."

"He shed no tears for me, either," said Baelor Breakspear from the grave, "Though I was his prince, the hope of Westeros. The gods never meant for me to die so young."

"My father was only nine-and-thirty," said Prince Valarr. "He had it in him to be a great king, the greatest since Aegon the Dragon." He looked at Dunk with cool blue eyes. "Why would the gods take him, and leave *you*?" The Young Prince had his father's light brown hair, but a streak of silver-gold ran through it.

You are dead, Dunk wanted to scream, *you are all three dead, why won't you leave me be?* Ser Arlan had died of a chill, Prince Baelor of the blow his brother dealt him during Dunk's trial of seven, his son Valarr during the Great Spring Sickness. *I am not to blame for that. We were in Dorne, we never even knew.*

"You are mad," the old man told him. "We will dig no hole for you, when you kill yourself with this folly. In the deep sands a man must hoard his water."

"Begone with you, Ser Duncan," Valarr said. "Begone."

Egg helped him with the digging. The boy had no spade, only his hands, and the sand flowed back into the grave as fast as they could fling it out. It was like trying to dig a hole in the sea. *I have to keep digging,* Dunk told himself, though his back and shoulders ached from the effort. *I have to bury him down deep where the sand dogs cannot find him. I have to . . .*

". . . die?" said Big Rob the simpleton from the bottom of the grave. Lying there, so still and cold, with a ragged red wound gaping in his belly, he did not look very big at all.

Dunk stopped and stared at him. "You're not dead. You're

down sleeping in the cellar." He looked to Ser Arlan for help. "Tell him, ser," he pleaded, "tell him to get out of the grave."

Only it was not Ser Arlan of Pennytree standing over him at all, it was Ser Bennis of the Brown Shield. The brown knight only cackled. "Dunk the lunk," he said, "gutting's slow, but certain. Never knew a man to live with his entrails hanging out." Red froth bubbled on his lips. He turned and spat, and the white sands drank it down. Treb was standing behind him with an arrow in his eye, weeping slow red tears. And there was Wet Wat, too, his head cut near in half, with old Lem and red-eyed Pate and all the rest. They had all been chewing sourleaf with Bennis, Dunk thought at first, but then he realized that it was blood trickling from their mouths. *Dead,* he thought, *all dead,* and the brown knight brayed. "Aye, so best get busy. You've more graves to dig, lunk. Eight for them and one for me and one for old Ser Useless, and one last one for your bald-head boy."

The spade slipped from Dunk's hands. "Egg," he cried, "run! We have to *run!*" But the sands were giving way beneath their feet. When the boy tried to scramble from the hole, its crumbling sides gave way and collapsed. Dunk saw the sands wash over Egg, burying him as he opened his mouth to shout. He tried to fight his way to him, but the sands were rising all around him, pulling him down into the grave, filling his mouth, his nose, his eyes . . .

Come the break of day, Ser Bennis set about teaching their recruits to form a shield wall. He lined the eight of them up shoulder to shoulder, with their shields touching and their spear points poking through like long sharp wooden teeth. Then Dunk and Egg mounted up and charged them.

Maester refused to go within ten feet of the spears and stopped abruptly, but Thunder had been trained for this. The big warhorse pounded straight ahead, gathering speed. Hens ran beneath his legs and flapped away screeching. Their panic must have been contagious. Once more Big Rob was the first to drop his spear and run, leaving a gap in the middle of the wall. Instead of closing up, Standfast's other warriors joined the flight. Thunder trod upon their discarded shields before Dunk could rein him up. Woven branches cracked and splintered beneath his iron-shod hooves. Ser Bennis rattled off a pungent string of curses as chickens and peasants scattered in all directions. Egg fought manfully to hold his laughter in, but finally lost the battle.

"Enough of that." Dunk drew Thunder to a halt, unfastened his helm, and tore it off. "If they do that in a battle, it will get the whole lot of them killed." *And you and me as well, most like.* The morning was already hot, and he felt as soiled and sticky as if he'd never bathed at all. His head was pounding, and he could not forget the dream he dreamed the night before. *It never happened that way,* he tried to tell himself. *It wasn't like that.* Chestnut had died on the long dry ride to Vaith, that part was true. He and Egg rode double until Egg's brother gave them Maester. The rest of it, though . . .

I never wept. I might have wanted to, but I never did. He had wanted to bury the horse as well, but the Dornishmen would not wait. "Sand dogs must eat and feed their pups," one of the Dornish knights told him as he helped Dunk strip the stot of saddle and bridle. "His flesh will feed the dogs or feed the sands. In a year, his bones will be scoured clean. This is Dorne, my friend." Remembering, Dunk could not help but wonder who would feed on Wat's flesh, and Wat's, and Wat's. *Maybe there are chequy fish down beneath the Chequy Water.*

He rode Thunder back to the tower and dismounted. "Egg, help Ser Bennis round them up and get them back here." He shoved his helm at Egg and strode to the steps.

Ser Eustace met him in the dimness of his solar. "That was not well done."

"No, m'lord," said Dunk. "They will not serve." *A sworn sword owes his liege service and obedience, but this is madness.*

"It was their first time. Their fathers and brothers were as bad or worse when they began their training. My sons worked with them, before we went to help the king. Every day, for a good fortnight. They made soldiers of them."

"And when the battle came, m'lord?" Dunk asked. "How did they fare then? How many of them came home with you?"

The old knight looked long at him. "Lem," he said at last, "and Pate, and Dake. Dake foraged for us. He was as fine a forager as I ever knew. We never marched on empty bellies. Three came back, ser. Three and me." His mustache quivered. "It may take longer than a fortnight."

"M'lord," said Dunk, "the woman could be here upon the morrow, with all her men." *They are good lads,* he thought, *but they will soon be dead lads, if they go up against the knights of Coldmoat.* "There must be some other way."

"Some other way." Ser Eustace ran his fingers lightly across the Little Lion's shield. "I will have no justice from Lord Rowan, nor this king . . ." He grasped Dunk by the forearm. "It comes to me that in days gone by, when the green kings ruled, you could pay a man a blood price if you had slain one of his animals or peasants."

"A blood price?" Dunk was dubious.

"Some other way, you said. I have some coin laid by. It was only a little claret on the cheek, Ser Bennis says. I could pay the man a silver stag, and three to the woman for the insult. I could, and would . . . if she would take the dam down." The old man frowned. "I cannot go to her, however. Not at Coldmoat." A fat black fly buzzed around his head and lighted on his arm. "The castle was ours once. Did you know that, Ser Duncan?"

"Aye, m'lord." Sam Stoops had told him.

"For a thousand years before the Conquest, we were the Marshalls of the Northmarch. A score of lesser lordlings did us fealty, and a hundred landed knights. We had four castles then, and watchtowers on the hills to warn of the coming of our enemies. Coldmoat was the greatest of our seats. Lord Perwyn Osgrey raised it. Perwyn the Proud, they called him.

"After the Field of Fire, Highgarden passed from kings to stewards, and the Osgreys dwindled and diminished. 'Twas

Aegon's son King Maegor who took Coldmoat from us, when Lord Ormond Osgrey spoke out against his supression of the Stars and Swords, as the Poor Fellows and the Warrior's Sons were called." His voice had grown hoarse. "There is a chequy lion carved into the stone above the gates of Coldmoat. My father showed it to me, the first time he took me with him to call on old Reynard Webber. I showed it to my own sons in turn. Addam . . . Addam served at Coldmoat, as a page and squire, and a . . . a certain . . . fondness grew up between him and Lord Wyman's daughter. So one winter day I donned my richest raiment and went to Lord Wyman to propose a marriage. His refusal was courteous, but as I left I heard him laughing with Ser Lucas Inchfield. I never returned to Coldmoat after that, save once, when that woman presumed to carry off one of mine own. When they told me to seek for poor Lem at the bottom of the moat—"

"Dake," said Dunk. "Bennis says his name was Dake."

"Dake?" The fly was creeping down his sleeve, pausing to rub its legs together the way flies did. Ser Eustace shooed it away, and rubbed his lip beneath his mustache. "Dake. That was what I said. A staunch fellow, I recall him well. He foraged for us, during the war. We never marched on empty bellies. When Ser Lucas informed me of what had been done to my poor Dake, I swore a holy vow that I would never set foot inside that castle again, unless to take possession. So you see, I cannot go there, Ser Duncan. Not to pay the blood price, or for any other reason. I *cannot*."

Dunk understood. "I could go, m'lord. I swore no vows."

"You are a good man, Ser Duncan. A brave knight, and true." Ser Eustace gave Dunk's arm a squeeze. "Would that the gods had spared my Alysanne. You are the sort of man I had always hoped that she might marry. A true knight, Ser Duncan. A true knight."

Dunk was turning red. "I will tell Lady Webber what you said, about the blood price, but . . ."

"You will save Ser Bennis from Dake's fate. I know it. I am no mean judge of men, and you are the true steel. You will give them pause, ser. The very sight of you. When that woman sees that Standfast has such a champion, she may well take down that dam of her own accord."

Dunk did not know what to say to that. He knelt. "M'lord. I will go upon the morrow, and do the best I can."

"On the morrow." The fly came circling back, and lit upon Ser Eustace's left hand. He raised his right and smashed it flat. "Yes. On the morrow."

"*Another* bath?" Egg said, dismayed. "You washed yesterday."

"And then I spent a day in armor, swimming in my sweat. Close your lips and fill the kettle."

"You washed the night Ser Eustace took us into service," Egg pointed out. "And last night, and now. That's *three times, ser*."

"I need to treat with a highborn lady. Do you want me to turn up before her high seat smelling like Ser Bennis?"

"You would have to roll in a tub of Maester's droppings to smell as bad as that, ser." Egg filled the kettle. "Sam Stoops says the castellan at Coldmoat is as big as you are. Lucas Inchfield is his name, but he's called the Longinch for his size. Do you think he's as big as you are, ser?"

"No." It had been years since Dunk had met anyone as tall as he was. He took the kettle and hung it above the fire.

"Will you fight him?"

"No." Dunk almost wished it had been otherwise. He might not be the greatest fighter in the realm, but size and strength could make up for many lacks. *Not for a lack of wits, though.* He was no good with words, and worse with women. This giant Lucas Longinch did not daunt him half so much as the prospect of facing the Red Widow. "I'm going to talk to the Red Widow, that's all."

"What will you tell her, ser?"

"That she has to take the dam down." *You must take down your dam, m'lady, or else . . .* "Ask her to take down the dam, I mean." *Please give back our chequy water.* "If it pleases her." *A little water, m'lady, if it please you.* Ser Eustace would not want him to beg. *How do I say it, then?*

The water soon begun to steam and bubble. "Help me lug this to the tub," Dunk told the boy. Together they lifted the kettle from the hearth and crossed the cellar to the big wooden tub. "I don't know how to talk with highborn ladies," he confessed as they were pouring. "We both might have been killed in Dorne, on account of what I said to Lady Vaith."

"Lady Vaith was mad," Egg reminded him, "but you could have been more gallant. Ladies like it when you're gallant. If you were to rescue the Red Widow the way you rescued that puppet girl from Aerion . . ."

"Aerion's in Lys, and the Widow's not in want of rescuing." He did not want to talk of Tanselle. *Tanselle Too-Tall was her name, but she was not too tall for me.*

"Well," the boy said, "some knights sing gallant songs to their ladies, or play them tunes upon a lute."

"I have no lute." Dunk looked morose. "And that night I drank too much in the Planky Town, you told me I sang like an ox in a mud wallow."

"I had forgotten, ser."

"How could you forget?"

"You told me to forget, ser," said Egg, all innocence. "You told me I'd get a clout in the ear the next time I mentioned it."

"There will be no singing." Even if he had the voice for it, the only song Dunk knew all the way through was "The Bear and the Maiden Fair." He doubted that would do much to win over Lady Webber. The kettle was steaming once again. They wrestled it over to the tub and upended it.

Egg drew water to fill it for the third time, then clambered back onto the well. "You'd best not take any food or drink at Coldmoat, ser. The Red Widow poisoned all her husbands."

"I'm not like to marry her. She's a highborn lady, and I'm Dunk of Flea Bottom, remember?" He frowned. "Just how many husbands has she had, do you know?"

"Four," said Egg, "but no children. Whenever she gives birth, a demon comes by night to carry off the issue. Sam Stoops' wife says she sold her babes unborn to the Lord of the Seven Hells, so he'd teach her his black arts."

"Highborn ladies don't meddle with the black arts. They dance and sing and do embroidery."

"Maybe she dances with demons and embroiders evil spells," Egg said with relish. "And how would you know what highborn ladies do, ser? Lady Vaith is the only one you ever knew."

That was insolent, but true. "Might be I don't know any highborn ladies, but I know a boy who's asking for a good clout in the ear." Dunk rubbed the back of his neck. A day in chainmail always left it hard as wood. "You've known queens and princesses. Did they dance with demons and practice the black arts?"

"Lady Shiera does. Lord Bloodraven's paramour. She bathes in blood to keep her beauty. And once my sister Rhae put a love potion in my drink, so I'd marry her instead of my sister Daella."

Egg spoke as if such incest was the most natural thing in the world. *For him it is.* The Targaryens had been marrying brother to sister for hundreds of years, to keep the blood of the dragon pure. Though the last actual dragon had died before Dunk was born, the dragonkings went on. *Maybe the gods don't mind them marrying their sisters.* "Did the potion work?" Dunk asked.

"It would have," said Egg, "but I spit it out. I don't want a wife, I want to be a knight of the Kingsguard, and live only to serve and defend the king. The Kingsguard are sworn not to wed."

"That's a noble thing, but when you're older you may find you'd sooner have a girl than a white cloak." Dunk was thinking of Tanselle Too-Tall, and the way she'd smiled at him at Ashford. "Ser Eustace said I was the sort of man he'd hoped to have his daughter wed. Her name was Alysanne."

"She's dead, ser."

"I know she's dead," said Dunk, annoyed. "If she was alive, he said. If she was, he'd like her to marry me. Or someone like me. I never had a lord offer me his daughter before."

"His *dead* daughter. And the Osgreys might have been

lords in the old days, but Ser Eustace is only a landed knight."

"I know what he is. Do you want a clout in the ear?"

"Well," said Egg, "I'd sooner have a clout than a *wife*. Especially a dead wife, ser. The kettle's steaming."

They carried the water to the tub, and Dunk pulled his tunic over his head. "I will wear my Dornish tunic to Coldmoat." It was sandsilk, the finest garment that he owned, painted with his elm and falling star.

"If you wear it for the ride it will get all sweaty, ser," Egg said. "Wear the one you wore today. I'll bring the other, and you can change when you reach the castle."

"*Before* I reach the castle. I'd look a fool, changing clothes on the drawbridge. And who said you were coming with me?"

"A knight is more impressive with a squire in attendance."

That was true. The boy had a good sense of such things. *He should. He served two years as a page at King's Landing.* Even so, Dunk was reluctant to take him into danger. He had no notion what sort of welcome awaited him at Coldmoat. If this Red Widow was as dangerous as they said, he could end up in a crow cage, like those two men they had seen upon the road. "You will stay and help Bennis with the smallfolk," he told Egg. "And don't give me that sullen look." He kicked his breeches off, and climbed into the tub of steaming water. "Go on and get to sleep now, and let me have my bath. You're not going, and that's the end of it."

Egg was up and gone when Dunk awoke, with the light of the morning sun in his face. *Gods be good, how can it be so hot so soon?* He sat up and stretched, yawning, then climbed to his feet and stumbled sleepily down to the well, where he lit a fat tallow candle, splashed some cold water on his face, and dressed.

When he stepped out into the sunlight, Thunder was waiting by the stable, saddled and bridled. Egg was waiting, too, with Maester his mule.

The boy had put his boots on. For once he looked a proper

squire, in a handsome doublet of green and gold checks and a pair of tight white woolen breeches. "The breeches were torn in the seat, but Sam Stoops' wife sewed them up for me," he announced.

"The clothes were Addam's," said Ser Eustace, as he led his own gray gelding from his stall. A chequy lion adorned the frayed silk cloak that flowed from the old man's shoulders. "The doublet is a trifle musty from the trunk, but it should serve. A knight is more impressive with a squire in attendance, so I have decided that Egg should accompany you to Coldmoat."

Outwitted by a boy of ten. Dunk looked at Egg and silently mouthed the words *clout in the ear.* The boy grinned.

"I have something for you as well, Ser Duncan. Come." Ser Eustace produced a cloak, and shook it out with a flourish.

It was white wool, bordered with squares of green satin and cloth of gold. A woolen cloak was the last thing he needed in such heat, but when Ser Eustace draped it about his shoulders, Dunk saw the pride on his face, and found himself unable to refuse. "Thank you, m'lord."

"It suits you well. Would that I could give you more." The old man's mustache twitched. "I sent Sam Stoops down into the cellar to search through my sons' things, but Edwyn and Harrold were smaller men, thinner in the chest and much shorter in the leg. None of what they left would fit you, sad to say."

"The cloak is enough, m'lord. I won't shame it."

"I do not doubt that." He gave his horse a pat. "I thought I'd ride with you part of the way, if you have no objection."

"None, m'lord."

Egg led them down the hill, sitting tall on Maester. "Must he wear that floppy straw hat?" Ser Eustace asked Dunk. "He looks a bit foolish, don't you think?"

"Not so foolish as when his head is peeling, m'lord." Even at this hour, with the sun barely above the horizon, it was hot. *By afternoon the saddles will be hot enough to raise blisters.* Egg might look elegant in the dead boy's finery, but he would be a boiled Egg by nightfall. Dunk at least could change; he had his good tunic in his saddlebag, and his old green one on his back.

"We'll take the west way," Ser Eustace announced. "It is little used these past years, but still the shortest way from Standfast to Coldmoat Castle." The path took them around back of the hill, past the graves where the old knight had laid his wife and sons to rest in a thicket of blackberry bushes. "They loved to pick the berries here, my boys. When they were little they would come to me with sticky faces and scratches on their arms, and I'd know just where they'd been." He smiled fondly. "Your Egg reminds me of my Addam. A brave boy, for one so young. Addam was trying to protect his wounded brother Harrold when the battle washed over them. A riverman with six acorns on his shield took his arm off with an ax." His sad gray eyes found Dunk's. "This old master of yours, the knight of Pennytree . . . did he fight in the Blackfyre Rebellion?"

"He did, m'lord. Before he took me on." Dunk had been no more than three or four at the time, running half naked through the alleys of Flea Bottom, more animal than boy.

"Was he for the red dragon or the black?"

Red or black? was a dangerous question, even now. Since the days of Aegon the Conquerer, the arms of House Targaryen had borne a three-headed dragon, red on black. Daemon the Pretender had reversed those colors on his own banners, as many bastards did. *Ser Eustace is my liege lord,* Dunk reminded himself. *He has a right to ask.* "He fought beneath Lord Hayford's banner, m'lord."

"Green fretty over gold, a green pale wavy?"

"It might be, m'lord. Egg would know." The lad could recite the arms of half the knights in Westeros.

"Lord Hayford was a noted *loyalist.* King Daeron made him his Hand just before the battle. Butterwell had done such a dismal job that many questioned his loyalty, but Lord Hayford had been stalwart from the first."

"Ser Arlan was beside him when he fell. A lord with three castles on his shield cut him down."

"Many good men fell that day, on both sides. The grass was not red before the battle. Did your Ser Arlan tell you that?"

"Ser Arlan never liked to speak about the battle. His squire died there, too. Roger of Pennytree was his name, Ser Arlan's sister's son." Even saying the name made Dunk feel vaguely guilty. *I stole his place.* Only princes and great lords had the means to keep two squires. If Aegon the Unworthy had given his sword to his heir Daeron instead of his bastard Daemon, there might never have been a Blackfyre Rebellion, and Roger of Pennytree might be alive today. *He would be a knight someplace, a truer knight than me. I would have ended on the gallows, or been sent off to the Night's Watch to walk the Wall until I died.*

"A great battle is a terrible thing," the old knight said, "but in the midst of blood and carnage, there is sometimes also beauty, beauty that could break your heart. I will never forget the way the sun looked when it set upon the Redgrass Field . . . ten thousand men had died, and the air was thick with moans and lamentations, but above us the sky turned gold and red and orange, so beautiful it made me weep to know that my sons would never see it." He sighed. "It was a closer thing than they would have you believe, these days. If not for Bloodraven . . ."

"I'd always heard that it was Baelor Breakspear who won the battle," said Dunk. "Him and Prince Maekar."

"The hammer and the anvil?" The old man's mustache gave a twitch. "The singers leave out much and more. Daemon was the Warrior himself that day. No man could stand before him. He broke Lord Arryn's van to pieces and slew the Knight of Ninestars and Wild Wyl Waynwood before coming up against Ser Gwayne Corbray of the Kingsguard. For near an hour they danced together on their horses, wheeling and circling and slashing as men died all around them. It's said that whenever Blackfyre and Lady Forlorn clashed, you could hear the sound for a league around. It was half a song and half a scream, they say. But when at last the Lady faltered, Blackfyre clove through Ser Gwayne's helm and left him blind and bleeding. Daemon dismounted to see that his fallen foe was not trampled, and commanded Redtusk to carry him back to the maesters in the rear. And there was his mortal error, for the Raven's Teeth had gained the top of Weeping Ridge, and Bloodraven saw his half brother's royal standard three hundred yards away, and Daemon and his sons beneath it. He slew Aegon first, the elder of the twins, for he knew that Daemon would never leave the boy whilst warmth lingered in his body, though white shafts fell like rain. Nor did he, though seven arrows pierced him, driven as much by sorcery as by Bloodraven's bow. Young Aemon took up Blackfyre when the blade slipped from his dying father's fingers, so Bloodraven slew him, too, the younger of the twins. Thus perished the black dragon and his sons.

"There was much and more afterward, I know. I saw a bit of it myself . . . the rebels running, Bittersteel turning the rout and leading his mad charge . . . his battle with Bloodraven, second only to the one Daemon fought with Gwayne Corbray . . . Prince Baelor's hammerblow against the rebel rear, the Dornishmen all screaming as they filled the air with spears . . . but at the end of the day, it made no matter. The war was done when Daemon died.

"So close a thing . . . if Daemon had ridden over Gwayne Corbray and left him to his fate, he might have broken Maekar's left before Bloodraven could take the ridge. The day would have belonged to the black dragons then, with the Hand slain and the road to King's Landing open before them. Daemon might have been sitting on the Iron Throne by the time Prince Baelor could come up with his stormlords and his Dornishmen.

"The singers can go on about their hammer and their anvil, ser, but it was the kinslayer who turned the tide with a white arrow and a black spell. He rules us now as well, make no mistake. King Aerys is his creature. It would not surprise to learn that Bloodraven had ensorceled His Grace, to bend him to his will. Small wonder we are cursed." Ser Eustace shook his head and lapsed into a brooding silence. Dunk wondered how much Egg had overheard, but there was no way to ask him. *How many eyes does Lord Bloodraven have?* he thought.

Already the day was growing hotter. *Even the flies have fled,* Dunk noted. *Flies have better sense than knights. They stay out of the sun.* He wondered whether he and Egg would be offered hospitality at Coldmoat. A tankard of cool brown ale would go down well. Dunk was considering that prospect with pleasure when he remembered what Egg had said about the Red Widow poisoning her husbands. His thirst fled at once. There were worse things than dry throats.

"There was a time when House Osgrey held all the lands for many leagues around, from Nunny in the east to Cobble Cover," Ser Eustace said. "Coldmoat was ours, and the Horseshoe Hills, the caves at Derring Downs, the villages of Dosk and Little Dosk and Brandybottom, both sides of Leafy Lake . . . Osgrey maids wed Florents, Swanns, and Tarbecks, even Hightowers and Blackwoods."

The edge of Wat's Wood had come in sight. Dunk shielded his eyes with one hand and squinted at the greenery. For once he envied Egg his floppy hat. *At least we'll have some shade.*

"Wat's Wood once extended all the way to Coldmoat," Ser Eustace said. "I do not recall who Wat was. Before the Conquest you could find aurochs in his wood, though, and great elks of twenty hands and more. There were more red deer than any man could take in a lifetime, for none but the king and the chequy lion were allowed to hunt here. Even in my father's day, there were trees on both sides of the stream, but the spiders cleared the woods away to make pasture for their cows and sheep and horses."

A thin finger of sweat crept down Dunk's chest. He found himself wishing devoutly that his liege lord would keep quiet. *It is too hot for talk. It is too hot for riding. It is just too bloody hot.*

In the woods they came upon the carcass of a great brown tree cat, crawling with maggots. "Eew," Egg said, as he walked Maester wide around it, "that stinks worse than Ser Bennis."

Ser Eustace reined up. "A tree cat. I had not known there

were any left in this wood. I wonder what killed him." When no one answered, he said, "I will turn back here. Just continue on the west way and it will take you straight to Coldmoat. You have the coin?" Dunk nodded. "Good. Come home with my water, ser." The old knight trotted off, back the way they'd come.

When he was gone, Egg said, "I thought how you should speak to Lady Webber, ser. You should win her to your side with gallant compliments." The boy looked as cool and crisp in his chequy tunic as Ser Eustace had in his cloak.

Am I the only one who sweats? "Gallant compliments," Dunk echoed. "What sort of gallant compliments?"

"You know, ser. Tell her how fair and beautiful she is."

Dunk had doubts. "She's outlived four husbands, she must be as old as Lady Vaith. If I say she's fair and beautiful when she's old and warty, she will take me for a liar."

"You just need to find something true to say about her. That's what my brother Daeron does. Even ugly old whores can have nice hair or well-shaped ears, he says."

"Well-shaped ears?" Dunk's doubts were growing.

"Or pretty eyes. Tell her that her gown brings out the color of her eyes." The lad reflected for a moment. "Unless she only has the one eye, like Lord Bloodraven."

My lady, that gown brings out the color of your eye. Dunk had heard knights and lordlings mouth such gallantries at other ladies. They never put it quite so baldly, though. *Good lady, that gown is beautiful. It brings out the color of both your lovely eyes.* Some of the ladies had been old and scrawny, or fat and florid, or pox-scarred and homely, but all wore gowns and had two eyes, and as Dunk recalled, they'd been well pleased by the flowery words. *What a lovely gown, my lady. It brings out the lovely beauty of your beautiful colored eyes.* "A hedge knight's life is simpler," Dunk said glumly. "If I say the wrong thing, she's like to sew me in a sack of rocks and throw me in her moat."

"I doubt she'll have that big a sack, ser," said Egg. "We could use my boot instead."

"No," Dunk growled, "we couldn't."

When they emerged from Wat's Wood, they found themselves well upstream of the dam. The waters had risen high enough for Dunk to take that soak he'd dreamed of. *Deep enough to drown a man,* he thought. On the far side, the bank had been cut through and a ditch dug to divert some of the flow westward. The ditch ran along the road, feeding a myriad of smaller channels that snaked off through the fields. *Once we cross the stream, we are in the Widow's power.* Dunk wondered what he was riding into. He was only one man, with a boy of ten to guard his back.

Egg fanned his face. "Ser? Why are we stopped?"

"We're not." Dunk gave his mount his heels and splashed down into the stream. Egg followed on the mule. The water rose as high as Thunder's belly before it began to fall again. They emerged dripping on the Widow's side. Ahead, the ditch ran straight as a spear, shining green and golden in the sun.

When they spied the towers of Coldmoat several hours later, Dunk stopped to change to his good Dornish tunic and loosen his longsword in its scabbard. He did not want the blade sticking should he need to pull it free. Egg gave his dagger's hilt a shake as well, his face solemn beneath his floppy hat. They rode on side by side, Dunk on the big destrier, the boy upon his mule, the Osgrey banner flapping listlessly from its staff.

Coldmoat came as somewhat of a disappointment, after all that Ser Eustace had said of it. Compared to Storm's End or Highgarden and other lordly seats that Dunk had seen, it was a modest castle . . . but it *was* a castle, not a fortified watchtower. Its crenellated outer walls stood thirty feet high, with towers at each corner, each one half again the size of Standfast. From every turret and spire the black banners of Webber hung heavy, each emblazoned with a spotted spider upon a silvery web.

"Ser?" Egg said. "The water. Look where it goes."

The ditch ended under Coldmoat's eastern walls, spilling down into the moat from which the castle took its name. The gurgle of the falling water made Dunk grind his teeth. *She will not have my chequy water.* "Come," he said to Egg.

Over the arch of the main gate a row of spider banners drooped in the still air, above the older sigil carved deep into the stone. Centuries of wind and weather had worn it down, but the shape of it was still distinct: a rampant lion made of checkered squares. The gates beneath were open. As they clattered across the drawbridge, Dunk made note of how low the moat had fallen. *Six feet at least,* he judged.

Two spearman barred their way at the portcullis. One had a big black beard and one did not. The beard demanded to know their purpose here. "My lord of Osgrey sent me to treat with Lady Webber," Dunk told him. "I am called Ser Duncan, the Tall."

"Well, I knew you wasn't Bennis," said the beardless guard. "We would have smelled him coming." He had a missing tooth and a spotted spider badge sewn above his heart.

The beard was squinting suspiciously at Dunk. "No one sees her ladyship unless the Longinch gives his leave. You come with me. Your stableboy can stay with the horses."

"I'm a squire, not a stableboy," Egg insisted. "Are you blind, or only stupid?"

The beardless guard broke into laughter. The beard put the point of his spear to the boy's throat. "Say that again."

Dunk gave Egg a clout in the ear. "No, shut your mouth and tend the horses." He dismounted. "I'll see Ser Lucas now."

The beard lowered his spear. "He's in the yard."

They passed beneath the spiked iron portcullis and under a murder hole before emerging in the outer ward. Hounds were barking in the kennels, and Dunk could hear singing coming from the leaded-glass windows of a seven-sided wooden sept. In front of the smithy, a blacksmith was shoeing a warhorse, with a 'prentice boy assisting. Nearby a squire was loosing shafts at the archery butts, while a freckled girl with a long braid matched him shot for shot. The quintain was spinning, too, as half a dozen knights in quilted padding took their turns knocking it around.

They found Ser Lucas Longinch among the watchers at the quintain, speaking with a great fat septon who was sweating worse than Dunk, a round white pudding of a man in robes as damp as if he'd worn them in his bath. Inchfield was a lance beside him, stiff and straight and very tall . . . though not so tall as Dunk. *Six feet and seven inches,* Dunk judged, *and each inch prouder than the last.* Though he wore black silk and cloth-of-silver, Ser Lucas looked as cool as if he were walking on the Wall.

"My lord," the guard hailed him. "This one comes from the chicken tower for an audience with her ladyship."

The septon turned first, with a hoot of delight that made Dunk wonder if he were drunk. "And what is this? A hedge knight? You have large hedges in the Reach." The septon made a sign of blessing. "May the Warrior fight ever at your side. I am Septon Sefton. An unfortunate name, but mine own. And you?"

"Ser Duncan the Tall."

"A modest fellow, this one," the septon said to Ser Lucas. "Were I as large as him, I'd call myself Ser Sefton the Immense. Ser Sefton the Tower. Ser Sefton with the Clouds About His Ears." His moon face was flushed, and there were wine stains on his robe.

Ser Lucas studied Dunk. He was an older man; forty at the least, perhaps as old as fifty, sinewy rather than muscular, with a remarkably ugly face. His lips were thick, his teeth a yellow tangle, his nose broad and fleshy, his eyes protruding. *And he is angry,* Dunk sensed, even before the man said, "Hedge knights are beggars with blades at best, outlaws at worst. Begone with you. We want none of your sort here."

Dunk's face darkened. "Ser Eustace Osgrey sent me from Standfast to treat with the lady of the castle."

"Osgrey?" The septon glanced at the Longinch. "Osgrey of the chequy lion? I thought House Osgrey was extinguished."

"Near enough as makes no matter. The old man is the last

of them. We let him keep a crumbling towerhouse a few leagues east." Ser Lucas frowned at Dunk. "If Ser Eustace wants to talk with her ladyship, let him come himself." His eyes narrowed. "You were the one with Bennis at the dam. Don't trouble to deny it. I ought to hang you."

"Seven save us." The septon dabbed sweat from his brow with his sleeve. "A brigand, is he? And a big one. Ser, repent your evil ways, and the Mother will have mercy." The septon's pious plea was undercut when he farted. "Oh, dear. Forgive my wind, ser. That's what comes of beans and barley bread."

"I am not a brigand," Dunk told the two of them, with all the dignity that he could muster.

The Longinch was unmoved by the denial. "Do not presume upon my patience, ser . . . if you are a *ser*. Run back to your chicken tower and tell Ser Eustace to deliver up Ser Bennis Brownstench. If he spares us the trouble of winkling him out of Standfast, her ladyship may be more inclined to clemency."

"I will speak with her ladyship about Ser Bennis and the trouble at the dam, and about the stealing of our water, too."

"Stealing?" said Ser Lucas. "Say that to our lady, and you'll be swimming in a sack before the sun has set. Are you quite certain that you wish to see her?"

The only thing that Dunk was certain of was that he wanted to drive his fist through Lucas Inchfield's crooked yellow teeth. "I've told you what I want."

"Oh, let him speak with her," the septon urged. "What harm could it do? Ser Duncan has had a long ride beneath this beastly sun, let the fellow have his say."

Ser Lucas studied Dunk again. "Our septon is a godly man. Come. I will thank you to be brief." He strode across the yard, and Dunk was forced to hurry after him.

The doors of the castle sept had opened, and worshipers were streaming down the steps. There were knights and squires, a dozen children, several old men, three septas in white robes and hoods . . . and one soft, fleshy lady of high birth, garbed in a gown of dark blue damask trimmed with

Myrish lace, so long its hems were trailing in the dirt. Dunk
judged her to be forty. Beneath a spun-silver net her auburn
hair was piled high, but the reddest thing about her was her
face.

"My lady," Ser Lucas said, when they stood before her and
her septas, "this hedge knight claims to bring a message
from Ser Eustace Osgrey. Will you hear it?"

"If you wish it, Ser Lucas." She peered at Dunk so hard
that he could not help but recall Egg's talk of sorcery. *I don't
think this one bathes in blood to keep her beauty.* The Widow
was stout and square, with an oddly pointed head that her
hair could not quite conceal. Her nose was too big, and her
mouth too small. She did have two eyes, he was relieved to
see, but all thought of gallantry had abandoned Dunk by
then. "Ser Eustace bid me talk with you concerning the recent trouble at your dam."

She blinked. "The . . . dam, you say?"

A crowd was gathering about them. Dunk could feel un-
friendly eyes upon him. "The stream," he said, "the Chequy
Water. Your ladyship built a dam across it . . ."

"Oh, I am quite sure I haven't," she replied. "Why, I have
been at my devotions all morning, ser."

Dunk heard Ser Lucas chuckle. "I did not mean to say that
your ladyship built the dam herself, only that . . . without that
water, all our crops will die . . . the smallfolk have beans and
barley in the fields, and melons . . ."

"Truly? I am very fond of melons." Her small mouth
made a happy bow. "What sort of melons are they?"

Dunk glanced uneasily at the ring of faces, and felt his
own face growing hot. *Something is amiss here. The Longinch is playing me for a fool.* "M'lady, could we continue our
discussion in some . . . more private place?"

"A silver says the great oaf means to *bed her!*" someone
japed, and a roar of laughter went up all around him. The
lady cringed away, half in terror, and raised both hands to
shield her face. One of the septas moved quickly to her side
and put a protective arm around her shoulders.

"And what is all this merriment?" The voice cut through

the laughter, cool and firm. "Will no one share the jape? Ser knight, why are you troubling my good-sister?"

It was the girl he had seen earlier at the archery butts. She had a quiver of arrows on one hip, and held a longbow that was just as tall as she was, which wasn't very tall. If Dunk was shy an inch of seven feet, the archer was shy an inch of five. He could have spanned her waist with his two hands. Her red hair was bound up in a braid so long it brushed past her thighs, and she had a dimpled chin, a snub nose, and a light spray of freckles across her cheeks.

"Forgive us, Lady Rohanne." The speaker was a pretty young lord with the Caswell centaur embroidered on his doublet. "This great oaf took the Lady Helicent for you."

Dunk looked from one lady to the other. "*You* are the Red Widow?" he heard himself blurt out. "But you're too—"

"Young?" The girl tossed her longbow to the lanky lad he'd seen her shooting with. "I am five-and-twenty, as it happens. Or was it *small* you meant to say?"

"—pretty. It was *pretty.*" Dunk did not know where that came from, but he was glad it came. He liked her nose, and the strawberry-blond color of her hair, and the small but well-shaped breasts beneath her leather jerkin. "I thought that you'd be . . . I mean . . . they said you were four times a widow, so . . ."

"My first husband died when I was ten. He was twelve, my father's squire, ridden down upon the Redgrass Field. My husbands seldom linger long, I fear. The last died in the spring."

That was what they always said of those who had perished during the Great Spring Sickness two years past. *He died in the spring.* Many tens of thousands had died in the spring, among them a wise old king and two young princes full of promise. "I . . . I am sorry for all your losses, m'lady." *A gallantry, you lunk, give her a gallantry.* "I want to say . . . your gown . . ."

"Gown?" She glanced down at her boots and breeches, loose linen tunic, and leather jerkin. "I wear no gown."

"Your hair, I meant . . . it's soft and . . ."

"And how would you know that, ser? If you had ever touched my hair, I should think that I might remember."

"Not soft," Dunk said miserably. "Red, I meant to say. Your hair is very red."

"*Very* red, ser? Oh, not as red as your face, I hope." She laughed, and the onlookers laughed with her.

All but Ser Lucas Longinch. "My lady," he broke in, "this man is one of Standfast's sellswords. He was with Bennis of the Brown Shield when he attacked your diggers at the dam and carved up Wolmer's face. Old Osgrey sent him to treat with you."

"He did, m'lady. I am called Ser Duncan, the Tall."

"Ser Duncan the Dim, more like," said a bearded knight who wore the threefold thunderbolt of Leygood. More guffaws sounded. Even Lady Helicent had recovered herself enough to give a chuckle.

"Did the courtesy of Coldmoat die with my lord father?" the girl asked. *No, not a girl, a woman grown.* "How did Ser Duncan come to make such an error, I wonder?"

Dunk gave Inchfield an evil look. "The fault was mine."

"Was it?" The Red Widow looked Dunk over from his heels up to his head, though her gaze lingered longest on his chest. "A tree and shooting star. I have never seen those arms before." She touched his tunic, tracing a limb of his elm tree with two fingers. "And painted, not sewn. The Dornish paint their silks, I've heard, but you look too big to be a Dornishman."

"Not all Dornishmen are small, m'lady." Dunk could feel her fingers through the silk. Her hand was freckled, too. *I'll bet she's freckled all over.* His mouth was oddly dry. "I spent a year in Dorne."

"Do all the oaks grow so tall there?" she said, as her fingers traced a tree limb around his heart.

"It's meant to be an elm, m'lady."

"I shall remember." She drew her hand back, solemn. "The ward is too hot and dusty for a conversation. Septon, show Ser Duncan to my audience chamber."

"It would be my great pleasure, good-sister."

"Our guest will have a thirst. You may send for a flagon of wine as well."

"Must I?" The fat man beamed. "Well, if it please you."

"I will join you as soon as I have changed." Unhooking her belt and quiver, she handed them to her companion. "I'll want Maester Cerrick as well. Ser Lucas, go ask him to attend me."

"I will bring him at once, my lady," said Lucas the Longinch.

The look she gave her castellan was cool. "No need. I know you have many duties to perform about the castle. It will suffice if you send Maester Cerrick to my chambers."

"M'lady," Dunk called after her. "My squire was made to wait by the gates. Might he join us as well?"

"Your squire?" When she smiled, she looked a girl of five-and-ten, not a woman five-and-twenty. *A pretty girl full of mischief and laughter.* "If it please you, certainly."

"Don't drink the wine, ser," Egg whispered to him as they waited with the septon in her audience chamber. The stone floors were covered with sweet-smelling rushes, the walls hung with tapestries of tourney scenes and battles.

Dunk snorted. "She has no need to poison me," he whispered back. "She thinks I'm some great lout with pease porridge between his ears, you mean."

"As it happens, my good-sister likes pease porridge," said Septon Sefton, as he reappeared with a flagon of wine, a flagon of water, and three cups. "Yes, yes, I heard. I'm fat, not deaf." He filled two cups with wine and one with water. The third he gave to Egg, who gave it a long dubious look and put it aside. The septon took no notice. "This is an Arbor vintage," he was telling Dunk. "Very fine, and the poison gives it a special piquance." He winked at Egg. "I seldom touch the grape myself, but I have heard." He handed Dunk a cup.

The wine was lush and sweet, but Dunk sipped it gingerly, and only after the septon had quaffed down half of his in three big, lip-smacking gulps. Egg crossed his arms and continued to ignore his water.

"She does like pease porridge," the septon said, "and you as well, ser. I know my own good-sister. When I first saw you in the yard, I half hoped you were some suitor, come from King's Landing to seek my lady's hand."

Dunk furrowed his brow. "How did you know I was from King's Landing, septon?"

"Kingslanders have a certain way of speaking." The septon took a gulp of wine, sloshed it about his mouth, swallowed, and sighed with pleasure. "I have served there many years, attending our High Septon in the Great Sept of Baelor." He sighed. "You would not know the city since the spring. The fires changed it. A quarter of the houses gone, and another quarter empty. The rats are gone as well. That is the queerest thing. I never thought to see a city without rats."

Dunk had heard that, too. "Were you there during the Great Spring Sickness?"

"Oh, indeed. A dreadful time, ser, dreadful. Strong men would wake healthy at the break of day and be dead by evenfall. So many died so quickly there was no time to bury them. They piled them in the Dragonpit instead, and when the corpses were ten feet deep, Lord Rivers commanded the pyromancers to burn them. The light of the fires shone through the windows, as it did of yore when living dragons still nested beneath the dome. By night you could see the glow all through the city, the dark green glow of wildfire. The color green still haunts me to this day. They say the spring was bad in Lannisport and worse in Oldtown, but in King's Landing it cut down four of ten. Neither young nor old were spared, nor rich nor poor, nor great nor humble. Our good High Septon was taken, the gods' own voice on earth, with a third of the Most Devout and near all our silent sisters. His Grace King Daeron, sweet Matarys and bold Valarr, the Hand . . . oh, it was a dreadful time. By the end, half the city was praying to the Stranger." He had another drink. "And where were you, ser?"

"In Dorne," said Dunk.

"Thank the Mother for her mercy, then." The Great Spring Sickness had never come to Dorne, perhaps because the Dornish had closed their borders and their ports, as had the Arryns of the Vale, who had also been spared. "All this talk of death is enough to put a man off wine, but cheer is hard to come by in such times as we are living. The drought endures, for all our prayers. The kingswood is one great tinderbox, and fires rage there night and day. Bittersteel and the sons of Daemon Blackfyre are hatching plots in Tyrosh, and Dagon Greyjoy's krakens prowl the sunset sea like wolves, raiding as far south as the Arbor. They carried off half the wealth of Fair Isle, it's said, and a hundred women, too. Lord Farman is repairing his defenses, though that strikes me as akin to the man who claps his pregnant daughter in a chastity belt when her belly's big as mine. Lord Bracken is dying slowly on the Trident, and his eldest son perished in the spring. That means Ser Otho must succeed. The Blackwoods will never stomach the Brute of Bracken as a neighbor. It will mean war."

Dunk knew about the ancient enmity between the Blackwoods and the Brackens. "Won't their liege lord force a peace?"

"Alas," said Septon Sefton, "Lord Tully is a boy of eight, surrounded by women. Riverrun will do little, and King Aerys will do less. Unless some maester writes a book about it, the whole matter may escape his royal notice. Lord Rivers is not like to let any Brackens in to see him. Pray recall, our Hand was born half Blackwood. If he acts at all, it will be only to help his cousins bring the Brute to bay. The Mother marked Lord Rivers on the day that he was born, and Bittersteel marked him once again upon the Redgrass Field."

Dunk knew he meant Bloodraven. Brynden Rivers was the Hand's true name. His mother had been a Blackwood, his father King Aegon the Fourth.

The fat man drank his wine and rattled on. "As for Aerys, His Grace cares more for old scrolls and dusty prophecies than for lords and laws. He will not even bestir himself to sire an heir. Queen Aelinor prays daily at the Great Sept, beseeching the Mother Above to bless her with a child, yet she remains a maid. Aerys keeps his own apartments, and it is said that he would sooner take a book to bed than any woman." He filled his cup again. "Make no mistake, 'tis Lord Rivers who rules us, with his spells and spies. There is no one to oppose him. Prince Maekar sulks at Summerhall, nursing his grievances against his royal brother. Prince Rhaegal is as meek as he is mad, and his children are . . . well, children. Friends and favorites of Lord Rivers fill every office, the lords of the small council lick his hand, and this new Grand Maester is as steeped in sorcery as he is. The Red Keep is garrisoned by Raven's Teeth, and no man sees the king without his leave."

Dunk shifted uncomfortably in his seat. *How many eyes does Lord Bloodraven have? A thousand eyes, and one.* He hoped the King's Hand did not have a thousand ears and one as well. Some of what Septon Sefton was saying sounded treasonous. He glanced at Egg, to see how he was taking all of this. The boy was struggling with all his might to hold his tongue.

The septon pushed himself to his feet. "My good-sister will be a while yet. As with all great ladies, the first ten gowns she tries will be found not to suit her mood. Will you take more wine?" Without waiting for an answer, he refilled both cups.

"The lady I mistook," said Dunk, anxious to speak of something else, "is she your sister?"

"We are all children of the Seven, ser, but apart from that . . . dear me, no. Lady Helicent was sister to Ser Rolland Uffering, Lady Rohanne's fourth husband, who died in the spring. My brother was his predecessor, Ser Simon Staunton, who had the great misfortune to choke upon a chicken bone. Coldmoat crawls with revenants, it must be said. The husbands die yet their kin remain, to drink my lady's wines and eat her sweetmeats, like a plague of plump pink locusts done up in silk and velvet." He wiped his mouth. "And yet she must wed again, and soon."

"Must?" said Dunk.

"Her lord father's will demands it. Lord Wyman wanted

grandsons to carry on his line. When he sickened he tried to
wed her to the Longinch, so he might die knowing that she
had a strong man to protect her, but Rohanne refused to have
him. His lordship took his vengeance in his will. If she remains
unwed on the second anniversary of her father's passing, Coldmoat and its lands pass to his cousin Wendell. Perhaps you
glimpsed him in the yard. A short man with a goiter on his
neck, much given to flatulence. Though it is small of me to
say so. I am cursed with excess wind myself. Be that as it
may. Ser Wendell is grasping and stupid, but his lady wife is
Lord Rowan's sister . . . and damnably fertile, that cannot be
denied. She whelps as often as he farts. Their sons are quite
as bad as he is, their daughters worse, and all of them have
begun to count the days. Lord Rowan has upheld the will, so
her ladyship has only till the next new moon."

"Why has she waited so long?" Dunk wondered aloud.

The septon shrugged. "If truth be told, there has been a
dearth of suitors. My good-sister is not hard to look upon,
you will have noticed, and a stout castle and broad lands add
to her charms. You would think that younger sons and land-
less knights would swarm about her ladyship like flies. You
would be wrong. The four dead husbands make them wary,
and there are those who will say that she is barren, too . . .
though never in her hearing, unless they yearn to see the inside of a crow cage. She has carried two children to term, a
boy and a girl, but neither lived to see a name day. Those few
who are not put off by talk of poisonings and sorcery want
no part of the Longinch. Lord Wyman charged him on his
deathbed to protect his daughter from unworthy suitors,
which he has taken to mean *all* suitors. Any man who means
to have her hand would need to face his sword first." He finished his wine and set the cup aside. "That is not to say there
has been no one. Cleyton Caswell and Simon Leygood have
been the most persistent, though they seem more interested
in her lands than in her person. Were I given to wagering, I
should place my gold on Gerold Lannister. He has yet to put
in an appearance, but they say he is golden-haired and quick
of wit, and more than six feet tall . . ."

". . . and Lady Webber is much taken with his letters." The lady in question stood in the doorway, beside a homely young maester with a great hooked nose. "You would lose your wager, good-brother. Gerold will never willingly forsake the pleasures of Lannisport and the splendor of Casterly Rock for some little lordship. He has more influence as Lord Tybolt's brother and adviser than he could ever hope for as my husband. As for the others, Ser Simon would need to sell off half my land to pay his debts and Ser Cleyton trembles like a leaf whenever the Longinch deigns to look his way. Besides, he is prettier than I am. And you, septon, have the biggest mouth in Westeros."

"A large belly requires a large mouth," said Septon Sefton, utterly unabashed. "Else it soon becomes a small one."

"Are *you* the Red Widow?" Egg asked, astonished. "I'm near as tall as you are!"

"Another boy made that same observation not half a year ago. I sent him to the rack to make him taller." When Lady Rohanne settled onto the high seat on the dais, she pulled her braid forward over her left shoulder. It was so long that the end of it lay coiled in her lap, like a sleeping cat. "Ser Duncan, I should not have teased you in the yard, when you were trying so hard to be gracious. It was only that you blushed so red . . . was there no girl to tease you, in the village where you grew so tall?"

"The village was King's Landing." He did not mention Flea Bottom. "There were girls, but . . ." The sort of teasing that went on in Flea Bottom sometimes involved cutting off a toe.

"I expect they were afraid to tease you." Lady Rohanne stroked her braid. "No doubt they were frightened of your size. Do not think ill of Lady Helicent, I pray you. My goodsister is a simple creature, but she has no harm in her. For all her piety, she could not dress herself without her septas."

"It was not her doing. The mistake was mine."

"You lie most gallantly. I know it was Ser Lucas. He is a man of cruel humors, and you offended him on sight."

"How?" Dunk said, puzzled. "I never did him any harm."

She smiled a smile that made him wish she were plainer. "I saw you standing with him. You're taller by a hand, or near enough. It has been a long while since Ser Lucas met anyone he could not look down on. How old are you, ser?"

"Near twenty, if it please m'lady." Dunk liked the ring of *twenty,* though most like he was a year younger, maybe two. No one knew for certain, least of all him. He must have had a mother and a father like everybody else, but he'd never known them, not even their names, and no one in Flea Bottom had ever cared much when he'd been born, or to whom.

"Are you as strong as you appear?"

"How strong do I appear, m'lady?"

"Oh, strong enough to annoy Ser Lucas. He is my castellan, though not by choice. Like Coldmoat, he is a legacy of my father. Did you come to knighthood on some battlefield, Ser Duncan? Your speech suggests that you were not born of noble blood, if you will forgive my saying so."

I was born of gutter blood. "A hedge knight named Ser Arlan of Pennytree took me on to squire for him when I was just a boy. He taught me chivalry and the arts of war."

"And this same Ser Arlan knighted you?"

Dunk shuffled his feet. One of his boots was half unlaced, he saw. "No one else was like to do it."

"Where is Ser Arlan now?"

"He died." He raised his eyes. He could lace his boot up later. "I buried him on a hillside."

"Did he fall valiantly in battle?"

"There were rains. He caught a chill."

"Old men are frail, I know. I learned that from my second husband. I was thirteen when we wed. He would have been five-and-fifty on his next name day, had he lived long enough to see it. When he was half a year in the ground, I gave him a little son, but the Stranger came for him as well. The septons said his father wanted him beside him. What do you think, ser?"

"Well," Dunk said hesitantly, "that might be, m'lady."

"Nonsense," she said, "the boy was born too weak. Such a tiny thing. He scarce had strength enough to nurse. Still. The gods gave his father five-and-fifty years. You would think they might have granted more than three days to the son."

"You would." Dunk knew little and less about the gods. He went to sept sometimes, and prayed to the Warrior to lend strength to his arms, but elsewise he let the Seven be.

"I am sorry your Ser Arlan died," she said, "and sorrier still that you took service with Ser Eustace. All old men are not the same, Ser Duncan. You would do well to go home to Pennytree."

"I have no home but where I swear my sword." Dunk had never seen Pennytree; he couldn't even say if it was in the Reach.

"Swear it here, then. The times are uncertain. I have need of knights. You look as though you have a healthy appetite, Ser Duncan. How many chickens can you eat? At Coldmoat you would have your fill of warm pink meat and sweet fruit tarts. Your squire looks in need of sustenance as well. He is so scrawny that all his hair has fallen out. We'll have him share a cell with other boys of his own age. He'll like that. My master-at-arms can train him in all the arts of war."

"I train him," said Dunk defensively.

"And who else? Bennis? Old Osgrey? The chickens?"

There had been days when Dunk had set Egg to chasing chickens. *It helps make him quicker,* he thought, but he knew that if he said it she would laugh. She was distracting him, with her snub nose and her freckles. Dunk had to remind himself of why Ser Eustace had sent him here. "My sword is sworn to my lord of Osgrey, m'lady," he said, "and that's the way it is."

"So be it, ser. Let us speak of less pleasant matters." Lady Rohanne gave her braid a tug. "We do not suffer attacks on Coldmoat or its people. So tell me why I should not have you sewn in a sack."

"I came to parlay," he reminded her, "and I have drunk your wine." The taste still lingered in his mouth, rich and sweet. So far it had not poisoned him. Perhaps it was the wine that made him bold. "And you don't have a sack big enough for me."

To his relief, Egg's jape made her smile. "I have several that are big enough for Bennis, though. Maester Cerrick says Wolmer's face was sliced open almost to the bone."

"Ser Bennis lost his temper with the man, m'lady. Ser Eustace sent me here to pay the blood price."

"The blood price?" She laughed. "He is an old man, I know, but I had not realized that he was so old as that. Does he think we are living in the Age of Heroes, when a man's life was reckoned to be worth no more than a sack of silver?"

"The digger was not killed, m'lady," Dunk reminded her. "No one was killed that I saw. His face was cut, is all."

Her fingers danced idly along her braid. "How much does Ser Eustace reckon Wolmer's cheek to be worth, pray?"

"One silver stag. And three for you, m'lady."

"Ser Eustace sets a niggard's price upon my honor, though three silvers are better than three chickens, I grant you. He would do better to deliver Bennis up to me for chastisement."

"Would this involve that sack you mentioned?"

"It might." She coiled her braid around one hand. "Osgrey can keep his silver. Only blood can pay for blood."

"Well," said Dunk, "it may be as you say, m'lady, but why not send for that man that Bennis cut, and ask him if he'd sooner have a silver stag or Bennis in a sack?"

"Oh, he'd pick the silver, if he couldn't have both. I don't doubt that, ser. It is not his choice to make. This is about the lion and the spider now, not some peasant's cheek. It is Bennis I want, and Bennis I shall have. No one rides onto my lands, does harm to one of mine, and escapes to laugh about it."

"Your ladyship rode onto Standfast land, and did harm of one of Ser Eustace's," Dunk said, before he stopped to think about it.

"Did I?" She tugged her braid again. "If you mean the sheep-stealer, the man was notorious. I had twice complained to Osgrey, yet he did nothing. I do not ask thrice. The king's law grants me the power of pit and gallows."

It was Egg who answered her. "On your own lands," the

boy insisted. "The king's law gives lords the power of pit and gallows on their own lands."

"Clever boy," she said. "If you know that much, you will also know that landed knights have no right to punish without their liege lord's leave. Ser Eustace holds Standfast of Lord Rowan. Bennis broke the king's peace when he drew blood, and must answer for it." She looked to Dunk. "If Ser Eustace will deliver Bennis to me, I'll slit his nose, and that will be the end of it. If I must come and take him, I make no such promise."

Dunk had a sudden sick feeling in the pit of his stomach. "I will tell him, but he won't give up Ser Bennis." He hesitated. "The dam was the cause of all the trouble. If your ladyship would consent to take it down—"

"Impossible," declared the young maester by Lady Rohanne's side. "Coldmoat supports twenty times as many smallfolk as does Standfast. Her ladyship has fields of wheat and corn and barley, all dying from the drought. She has half a dozen orchards, apples and apricots and three kinds of pears. She has cows about to calf, five hundred head of black-nosed sheep, and she breeds the finest horses in the Reach. We have a dozen mares about to foal."

"Ser Eustace has sheep, too," Dunk said. "He has melons in the fields, beans and barleycorn, and . . ."

"You were taking water for the *moat*!" Egg said loudly.

I was getting to the moat, Dunk thought.

"The moat is essential to Coldmoat's defenses," the maester insisted. "Do you suggest that Lady Rohanne leave herself open to attack, in such uncertain times as these?"

"Well," Dunk said slowly, "a dry moat is still a moat. And m'lady has strong walls, with ample men to defend them."

"Ser Duncan," Lady Rohanne said, "I was ten years old when the black dragon rose. I begged my father not to put himself at risk, or at least to leave my husband. Who would protect me, if both my men were gone? So he took me up onto the ramparts, and pointed out Coldmoat's strong points. 'Keep them strong,' he said, 'and they will keep you safe. If you see to your defenses, no man may do you harm.' The first thing he pointed at was the moat." She stroked her cheek with the tail of her braid. "My first husband perished on the Redgrass Field. My father found me others, but the Stranger took them, too. I no longer trust in men, no matter how *ample* they may seem. I trust in stone and steel and water. I trust in moats, ser, and mine will *not* go dry."

"What your father said, that's well and good," said Dunk, "but it doesn't give you the right to take Osgrey water."

She tugged her braid. "I suppose Ser Eustace told you that the stream was his."

"For a thousand years," said Dunk. "It's *named* the Chequy Water. That's plain."

"So it is." She tugged again; once, twice, thrice. "As the river is called the Mander, though the Manderlys were driven from its banks a thousand years ago. Highgarden is still Highgarden, though the last Gardener died on the Field of Fire. Casterly Rock teems with Lannisters, and nowhere a Casterly to be found. The world changes, ser. This Chequy Water rises in the Horseshoe Hills, which were wholly mine when last I looked. The water is mine as well. Maester Cerrick, show him."

The maester descended from the dais. He could not have been much older than Dunk, but in his gray robes and chain collar he had an air of somber wisdom that belied his years. In his hands was an old parchment. "See for yourself, ser," he said as he unrolled it, and offered it to Dunk.

Dunk the lunk, thick as a castle wall. He felt his cheeks reddening again. Gingerly he took the parchment from the maester and scowled at the writing. Not a word of it was intelligible to him, but he knew the wax seal beneath the ornate signature; the three-headed dragon of House Targaryen. *The king's seal.* He was looking at a royal decree of some sort. Dunk moved his head from side to side so they would think that he was reading. "There's a word here I can't make out," he muttered, after a moment. "Egg, come have a look, you have sharper eyes than me."

The boy darted to his side. "Which word, ser?" Dunk

pointed. "That one? Oh." Egg read quickly, then raised his eyes to Dunk's and gave a little nod.

It is her stream. She has a paper. Dunk felt as though he'd been punched in the stomach. *The king's own seal.* "This . . . there must be some mistake. The old man's sons died in service to the king, why would His Grace take his stream away?"

"If King Daeron had been a less forgiving man, he should have lost his head as well."

For half a heartbeat Dunk was lost. "What do you mean?"

"She means," said Maester Cerrick, "that Ser Eustace Osgrey is a rebel and a traitor."

"Ser Eustace chose the black dragon over the red, in the hope that a Blackfyre king might restore the lands and castles that the Osgreys had lost under the Targaryens," Lady Rohanne said. "Chiefly he wanted Coldmoat. His sons paid for his treason with their life's blood. When he brought their bones home and delivered his daughter to the king's men for a hostage, his wife threw herself from the top of Standfast tower. Did Ser Eustace tell you that?" Her smile was sad. "No, I did not think so."

"The black dragon." *You swore your sword to a traitor, lunk. You ate a traitor's bread and slept beneath a rebel's roof.* "M'lady," he said, groping, "the black dragon . . . that was fifteen years ago. This is now, and there's a drought. Even if he was a rebel once, Ser Eustace still needs water."

The Red Widow rose and smoothed her skirts. "He had best pray for rain, then."

That was when Dunk recalled Osgrey's parting words in the wood. "If you will not grant him a share of the water for his own sake, do it for his son."

"His son?"

"Addam. He served here as your father's page and squire."

Lady Rohanne's face was stone. "Come closer."

He did not know what else to do, but to obey. The dais added a good foot to her height, yet even so Dunk towered over her. "Kneel," she said. He did.

The slap she gave him had all her strength behind it, and

she was stronger than she looked. His cheek burned, and he could taste blood in his mouth from a broken lip, but she hadn't truly hurt him. For a moment all Dunk could think of was grabbing her by that long red braid and pulling her across his lap to slap her arse, as you would a spoiled child. *If I do, she'll scream, though, and twenty knights will come bursting in to kill me.*

"You dare appeal to me in *Addam's* name?" Her nostrils flared. "Remove yourself from Coldmoat, ser. At once."

"I never meant—"

"*Go,* or I will find a sack large enough for you, if I have to sew one up myself. Tell Ser Eustace to bring me Bennis of the Brown Shield by the morrow, else I will come for him myself with fire and sword. Do you understand me? *Fire and sword!*"

Septon Sefton took Dunk's arm and pulled him quickly from the room. Egg followed close behind them. "That was most unwise, ser," the fat septon whispered, and he led them to the steps. "*Most* unwise. To mention Addam Osgrey . . ."

"Ser Eustace told me she was fond of the boy."

"Fond?" The septon huffed heavily. "She loved the boy, and him her. It never went beyond a kiss or two, but . . . it was Addam she wept for after the Redgrass Field, not the husband she hardly knew. She blames Ser Eustace for his death, and rightly so. The boy was twelve."

Dunk knew what it was to bear a wound. Whenever someone spoke of Ashford Meadow, he thought of the three good men who'd died to save his foot, and it never failed to hurt. "Tell m'lady that it was not my wish to hurt her. Beg her pardon."

"I shall do all I can, ser," Septon Sefton said, "but tell Ser Eustace to bring her Bennis, and *quickly.* Elsewise it will go hard on him. It will go very hard."

Not until the walls and towers of Coldmoat had vanished in the west behind them did Dunk turn to Egg and say, "What words were written on that paper?"

"It was a grant of rights, ser. To Lord Wyman Webber,

from the king. For his leal service in the late rebellion, Lord Wyman and his descendants were granted all rights to the Chequy Water, from where it rises in the Horseshoe Hills to the shores of Leafy Lake. It also said that Lord Wyman and his descendants should have the right to take red deer and boar and rabbits in Wat's Wood whene'er it pleased them, and to cut twenty trees from the wood each year." The boy cleared his throat. "The grant was only for a time, though. The paper said that if Ser Eustace were to die without a male heir of his body, Standfast would revert to the crown, and Lord Webber's privileges would end."

They were the Marshalls of the Northmarch for a thousand years. "All they left the old man was a tower to die in."

"And his head," said Egg. "His Grace did leave him his head, ser. Even though he was a rebel."

Dunk gave the boy a look. "Would you have taken it?"

Egg had to think about it. "Sometimes at court I would serve the king's small council. They used to fight about it. Uncle Baelor said that clemency was best when dealing with an honorable foe. If a defeated man believes he will be pardoned, he may lay down his sword and bend the knee. Elsewise he will fight on to the death, and slay more loyal men and innocents. But Lord Bloodraven said that when you pardon rebels, you only plant the seeds of the next rebellion." His voice was full of doubts. "Why would Ser Eustace rise against King Daeron? He was a good king, everybody says so. He brought Dorne into the realm and made the Dornishmen our friends."

"You would have to ask Ser Eustace, Egg." Dunk thought he knew the answer, but it was not one the boy would want to hear. *He wanted a castle with a lion on the gatehouse, but all he got were graves among the blackberries.* When you swore a man your sword, you promised to serve and obey, to fight for him at need, not to pry into his affairs and question his allegiances . . . but Ser Eustace had played him for a fool. *He said his sons died fighting for the king, and let me believe the stream was his.*

Night caught them in Wat's Wood.

That was Dunk's fault. He should have gone the straight way home, the way they'd gone, but instead he'd taken them north for another look at the dam. He had half a thought to try and tear the thing apart with his bare hands. But the Seven and Ser Lucas Longinch did not prove so obliging. When they reached the dam they found it guarded by a pair of crossbowmen with spider badges sewn on their jerkins. One sat with his bare feet in the stolen water. Dunk could gladly have throttled him for that alone, but the man heard them coming and was quick to snatch up his bow. His fellow, even quicker, had a quarrel nocked and ready. The best that Dunk could do was scowl at them threateningly.

After that, there was naught to do but retrace their steps. Dunk did not know these lands as well as Ser Bennis did; it would have been humiliating to get lost in a wood as small as Wat's. By the time they splashed across the stream, the sun was low on the horizon and the first stars were coming out, along with clouds of mites. Amongst the tall black trees, Egg found his tongue again. "Ser? That fat septon said my father sulks in Summerhall."

"Words are wind."

"My father doesn't sulk."

"Well," said Dunk, "he might. *You* sulk."

"I do not. Ser." He frowned. "Do I?"

"Some. Not too often, though. Elsewise I'd clout you in the ear more than I do."

"You clouted me in the ear at the gate."

"That was half a clout at best. If I ever give you a whole clout, you'll know it."

"The Red Widow gave *you* a whole clout."

Dunk touched his swollen lip. "You don't need to sound so pleased about it." *No one ever clouted your father in the ear, though. Maybe that's why Prince Maekar is the way he is.* "When the king named Lord Bloodraven his Hand, your lord father refused to be part of his council and departed King's Landing for his own seat," he reminded Egg. "He has been at Summerhall for a year, and half of another. What do you call that, if not sulking?"

"I call it being wroth," Egg declared loftily. "His Grace should have made my father Hand. He's his *brother*, and the finest battle commander in the realm since Uncle Baelor died. Lord Bloodraven's not even a real lord, that's just some stupid *courtesy*. He's a sorcerer, and baseborn besides."

"Bastard born, not baseborn." Bloodraven might not be a real lord, but he was noble on both sides. His mother had been one of the many mistresses of King Aegon the Unworthy. Aegon's bastards had been the bane of the Seven Kingdoms ever since the old king died. He had legitimized the lot upon his deathbed; not only the Great Bastards like Bloodraven, Bittersteel, and Daemon Blackfyre, whose mothers had been ladies, but even the lesser ones he'd fathered on whores and tavern wenches, merchant's daughters, mummer's maidens, and every pretty peasant girl who chanced to catch his eye. *Fire and Blood* were the words of House Targaryen, but Dunk once heard Ser Arlan say that Aegon's should have been *Wash Her and Bring Her to My Bed*.

"King Aegon washed Bloodraven clean of bastardy," he reminded Egg, "the same as he did the rest of them."

"The old High Septon told my father that king's laws are one thing, and the laws of the gods another," the boy said stubbornly. "Trueborn children are made in a marriage bed and blessed by the Father and the Mother, but bastards are born of lust and weakness, he said. King Aegon decreed that his bastards were not bastards, but he could not change their nature. The High Septon said all bastards are born to betrayal . . . Daemon Blackfyre, Bittersteel, even Bloodraven. Lord Rivers was more cunning than the other two, he said, but in the end he would prove himself a traitor, too. The High Septon counseled my father never to put any trust in him, nor in any other bastards, great or small."

Born to betrayal, Dunk thought. *Born of lust and weakness. Never to be trusted, great or small.* "Egg," he said, "didn't you ever think that I might be a bastard?"

"You, ser?" That took the boy aback. "You are not."

"I might be. I never knew my mother, or what became of her. Maybe I was born too big and killed her. Most like she was some whore or tavern girl. You don't find highborn ladies down in Flea Bottom. And if she ever wed my father . . . well, what became of *him,* then?" Dunk did not like to be reminded of his life before Ser Arlan found him. "There was a pot shop in King's Landing where I used to sell them rats and cats and pigeons for the brown. The cook always claimed my father was some thief or cutpurse. 'Most like I saw him hanged,' he used to tell me, 'but maybe they just sent him to the Wall.' When I was squiring for Ser Arlan, I would ask him if we couldn't go up that way someday, to take service at Winterfell or some other northern castle. I had this notion that if I could only reach the Wall, might be I'd come on some old man, a real tall man who looked like me. We never went, though. Ser Arlan said there were no hedges in the north, and all the woods were full of wolves." He shook his head. "The long and short of it is, most like you're squiring for a bastard."

For once Egg had nothing to say. The gloom was deepening around them. Lantern bugs moved slowly through the trees, their little lights like so many drifting stars. There were stars in the sky as well, more stars than any man could ever hope to count, even if he lived to be as old as King Jaehaerys. Dunk need only lift his eyes to find familiar friends: the Stallion and the Sow, the King's Crown and the Crone's Lantern, the Galley, Ghost, and Moonmaid. But there were clouds to the north, and the blue eye of the Ice Dragon was lost to him, the blue eye that pointed north.

The moon had risen by the time they came to Standfast, standing dark and tall atop its hill. A pale yellow light was spilling from the tower's upper windows, he saw. Most nights Ser Eustace sought his bed as soon as he had supped, but not tonight, it seemed. *He is waiting for us,* Dunk knew.

Bennis of the Brown Shield was waiting up as well. They found him sitting on the tower steps, chewing sourleaf and honing his longsword in the moonlight. The slow scrape of stone on steel carried a long way. However much Ser Bennis might neglect his clothes and person, he kept his weapons well.

"The lunk comes back," Bennis said. "Here I was sharpening my steel to go rescue you from that Red Widow."

"Where are the men?"

"Treb and Wet Wat are on the roof standing watch, in case the widow comes to call. The rest crawled into bed whimpering. Sore as sin, they are. I worked them hard. Drew a little blood off that big lackwit, just to make him mad. He fights better when he's mad." He smiled his brown-and-red smile. "Nice bloody lip you got. Next time, don't go turning over rocks. What did the woman say?"

"She means to keep the water, and she wants you as well, for cutting that digger by the dam."

"Thought she might." Bennis spat. "Lot o' bother for some peasant. He ought to thank me. Women like a man with scars."

"You won't mind her slitting your nose, then."

"Bugger that. If I wanted my nose slit I'd slit it for myself." He jerked a thumb up. "You'll find Ser Useless in his chambers, brooding on how great he used to be."

Egg spoke up. "He fought for the black dragon."

Dunk could have given the boy a clout, but the brown knight only laughed. " 'Course he did. Just look at him. He strike you as the kind who picks the winning side?"

"No more than you. Else you wouldn't be here with us." Dunk turned to Egg. "Tend to Thunder and Maester and then come up and join us."

When Dunk came up through the trap, the old knight was sitting by the hearth in his bedrobe, though no fire had been laid. His father's cup was in his hand, a heavy silver cup that had been made for some Lord Osgrey back before the Conquest. A chequy lion adorned the bowl, done in flakes of jade and gold, though some of the jade flakes had gone missing. At the sound of Dunk's footsteps, the old knight looked up and blinked like a man waking from a dream. "Ser Duncan. You are back. Did the sight of you give Lucas Inchfield pause, ser?"

"Not as I saw, m'lord. More like, it made him wroth." Dunk told it all as best he could, though he omitted the part about Lady Helicent, which made him look an utter fool. He would have left out the clout, too, but his broken lip had puffed up twice its normal size, and Ser Eustace could not help but notice.

When he did, he frowned. "Your lip . . ."

Dunk touched it gingerly. "Her ladyship gave me a slap."

"She *struck* you?" His mouth opened and closed. "She struck my envoy, who came to her beneath the chequy lion? She dared lay hands upon your person?"

"Only the one hand, ser. It stopped bleeding before we even left the castle." He made a fist. "She wants Ser Bennis, not your silver, and she won't take down the dam. She showed me a parchment with some writing on it, and the king's own seal. It said the stream is hers. And . . ." He hesitated. "She said that you were . . . that you had . . ."

". . . risen with the black dragon?" Ser Eustace seemed to slump. "I feared she might. If you wish to leave my service, I will not stop you." The old knight gazed into his cup, though what he might be looking for Dunk could not say.

"You told me your sons died fighting for the king."

"And so they did. The *rightful* king, Daemon Blackfyre. The King Who Bore the Sword." The old man's mustache quivered. "The men of the red dragon call themselves the *loyalists,* but we who chose the black were just as loyal, once. Though now . . . all the men who marched beside me to seat Prince Daemon on the Iron Throne have melted away like morning dew. Mayhaps I dreamed them. Or more like, Lord Bloodraven and his Raven's Teeth have put the fear in them. They cannot all be dead."

Dunk could not deny the truth of that. Until this moment, he had never met a man who'd fought for the Pretender. *I must have, though. There were thousands of them. Half the realm was for the red dragon, and half was for the black.* "Both sides fought valiantly, Ser Arlan always said." He thought the old knight would want to hear that.

Ser Eustace cradled his wine cup in both hands. "If Daemon had ridden over Gwayne Corbray . . . if Fireball had not been slain on the eve of battle . . . if Hightower and Tarbeck and Oakheart and Butterwell had lent us their full strength instead of trying to keep one foot in each camp . . . if Manfred Lothston had proved true instead of treacherous . . . if storms had not delayed Lord Bracken's sailing with the Myrish crossbowmen . . . if Quickfinger had not been caught with the stolen dragon's eggs . . . so many *if*s, ser . . . had any one come out differently, it could all have turned t'other way. Then we would called be the loyalists, and the red dragons would be remembered as men who fought to keep the usurper Daeron the Falseborn upon his stolen throne, and failed."

"That's as it may be, m'lord," said Dunk, "but things went the way they went. It was all years ago, and you were pardoned."

"Aye, we were pardoned. So long as we bent the knee and gave him a hostage to ensure our future loyalty, Daeron forgave the traitors and the rebels." His voice was bitter. "I bought my head back with my daughter's life. Alysanne was seven when they took her off to King's Landing and twenty when she died, a silent sister. I went to King's Landing once to see her, and she would not even speak to me, her own father. A king's mercy is a poisoned gift. Daeron Targaryen left me life, but took my pride and dreams and honor." His hand trembled, and wine spilled red upon his lap, but the old man took no notice of it. "I should have gone with Bittersteel into exile, or died beside my sons and my sweet king. That would have been a death worthy of a chequy lion descended from so many proud lords and mighty warriors. Daeron's mercy made me smaller."

In his heart the black dragon never died, Dunk realized.

"My lord?"

It was Egg's voice. The boy had come in as Ser Eustace was speaking of his death. The old knight blinked at him as if he were seeing him for the first time. "Yes, lad? What is it?"

"If it please you . . . the Red Widow says you rebelled to get her castle. That isn't true, is it?"

"The castle?" He seemed confused. "Coldmoat . . .

Coldmoat was promised me by Daemon, yes, but . . . it was
not for gain, no . . ."

"Then why?" asked Egg.

"Why?" Ser Eustace frowned.

"Why were you a traitor? If it wasn't just the castle."

Ser Eustace looked at Egg a long time before replying.
"You are only a young boy. You would not understand."

"Well," said Egg, "I might."

"Treason . . . is only a word. When two princes fight for a
chair where only one may sit, great lords and common men
alike must choose. And when the battle's done, the victors
will be hailed as loyal men and true, whilst those who were
defeated will be known forevermore as rebels and traitors.
That was my fate."

Egg thought about it for a time. "Yes, my lord. Only . . .
King Daeron was a good man. Why would you choose Daemon?"

"Daeron . . ." Ser Eustace almost slurred the word, and
Dunk realized he was half drunk. "Daeron was spindly and
round of shoulder, with a little belly that wobbled when he
walked. Daemon stood straight and proud, and his stomach
was flat and hard as an oaken shield. And he could *fight*.
With ax or lance or flail, he was as good as any knight I ever
saw, but with *the sword* he was the Warrior himself. When
Prince Daemon had Blackfyre in his hand, there was not a
man to equal him . . . not Ulrick Dayne with Dawn, no, nor
even the Dragonknight with Dark Sister.

"You can know a man by his friends, Egg. Daeron surrounded himself with maesters, septons, and singers. Always
there were women whispering in his ear, and his court was
full of Dornishmen. How not, when he had taken a Dornish-
woman into his bed, and sold his own sweet sister to the prince
of Dorne, though it was Daemon that she loved? Daeron bore
the same name as the Young Dragon, but when his Dornish
wife gave him a son he named the child Baelor, after the fee-
blest king who ever sat the Iron Throne.

"Daemon, though . . . Daemon was no more pious than a
king need be, and all the great knights of the realm gathered

to him. It would suit Lord Bloodraven if their names were all forgotten, so he has forbidden us to sing of them, but *I* remember. Robb Reyne, Gareth the Grey, Ser Aubrey Ambrose, Lord Gormon Peake, Black Byren Flowers, Redtusk, Fireball . . . *Bittersteel!* I ask you, has there ever been such a noble company, such a roll of heroes?

"*Why,* lad? You ask me why? Because Daemon was the better man. The old king saw it, too. He gave the sword to Daemon. *Blackfyre,* the sword of Aegon the Conquerer, the blade that every Targaryen king had wielded since the Conquest . . . he put that sword in Daemon's hand the day he knighted him, a boy of twelve."

"My father says that was because Daemon was a swordsman, and Daeron never was," said Egg. "Why give a horse to a man who cannot ride? The sword was not the kingdom, he says."

The old knight's hand jerked so hard that wine spilled from his silver cup. "Your father is a fool."

"He is *not,*" the boy said.

Osgrey's face twisted in anger. "You asked a question and I answered it, but I will not suffer insolence. Ser Duncan, you should beat this boy more often. His courtesy leaves much to be desired. If I must needs do it myself, I will—"

"No," Dunk broke in. "You won't. Ser." He had made up his mind. "It is dark. We will leave at first light."

Ser Eustace stared at him, stricken. "Leave?"

"Standfast. Your service." *You lied to us. Call it what you will, there was no honor in it.* He unfastened his cloak, rolled it up, and put it in the old man's lap.

Osgrey's eyes grew narrow. "Did that woman offer to take you into service? Are you leaving me for that whore's bed?"

"I don't know that she is a whore," Dunk said, "or a witch or a poisoner or none of that. But whatever she may be makes no matter. We're leaving for the hedges, not for Coldmoat."

"The ditches, you mean. You're leaving me to prowl in the woods like wolves, to waylay honest men upon the roads." His hand was shaking. The cup fell from his fingers, spilling

wine as it rolled along the floor. "Go, then. Go. I want none
of you. I should never have taken you on. *Go!*"

"As you say, ser." Dunk beckoned, and Egg followed.

That last night Dunk wanted to be as far from Eustace Osgrey as he could, so they slept down in the cellar, amongst
the rest of Standfast's meager host. It was a restless night.
Lem and red-eyed Pate both snored, the one loudly and the
other constantly. Dank vapors filled the cellar, rising through
the trap from the deeper vaults below. Dunk tossed and
turned on the scratchy bed, drifting off into a half sleep only
to wake suddenly in darkness. The bites he'd gotten in the
woods were itching fiercely, and there were fleas in the straw
as well. *I will be well rid of this place, well rid of the old
man, and Ser Bennis, and the rest of them.* Maybe it was time
that he took Egg back to Summerhall to see his father. He
would ask the boy about that in the morning, when they were
well away.

Morning seemed a long way off, though. Dunk's head was
full of dragons, red and black . . . full of chequy lions, old
shields, battered boots . . . full of streams and moats and
dams, and papers stamped with the king's great seal that he
could not read.

And *she* was there as well, the Red Widow, Rohanne of
the Coldmoat. He could see her freckled face, her slender
arms, her long red braid. It made him feel guilty. *I should be
dreaming of Tanselle. Tanselle Too-Tall, they called her, but
she was not too tall for me.* She had painted arms upon his
shield and he had saved her from the Bright Prince, but she
vanished even before the trial of seven. *She could not bear to
see me die,* Dunk often told himself, but what did he know?
He was as thick as a castle wall. Just thinking of the Red
Widow was proof enough of that. *Tanselle smiled at me, but
we never held each other, never kissed, not even lips to
cheek.* Rohanne at least had touched him; he had the swollen
lip to prove it. *Don't be daft. She's not for the likes of you.
She is too small, too clever, and much too dangerous.*

Drowsing at long last, Dunk dreamed. He was running

through a glade in the heart of Wat's Wood, running toward Rohanne, and she was shooting arrows at him. Each shaft she loosed flew true, and pierced him through the chest, yet the pain was strangely sweet. He should have turned and fled, but he ran toward her instead, running slowly as you always did in dreams, as if the very air had turned to honey. Another arrow came, and yet another. Her quiver seemed to have no end of shafts. Her eyes were gray and green and full of mischief. *Your gown brings out the color of your eyes,* he meant to say to her, but she was not wearing any gown, or any clothes at all. Across her small breasts was a faint spray of freckles, and her nipples were red and hard as little berries. The arrows made him look like some great porcupine as he went stumbling to her feet, but somehow he still found the strength to grab her braid. With one hard yank he pulled her down on top of him and kissed her.

He woke suddenly, at the sound of a shout.

In the darkened cellar, all was confusion. Curses and complaints echoed back and forth, and men were stumbling over one another as they fumbled for their spears or breeches. No one knew what was happening. Egg found the tallow candle and got it lit, to shed some light upon the scene. Dunk was the first one up the steps. He almost collided with Sam Stoops rushing down, puffing like a bellows and babbling incoherently. Dunk had to hold him by both shoulders to keep him from falling. "Sam, what's wrong?"

"The sky," the old man whimpered. "The *sky*!" No more sense could be gotten from him, so they all went up to the roof for a look. Ser Eustace was there before them, standing by the parapets in his bedrobe, staring off into the distance.

The sun was rising in the west.

It was a long moment before Dunk realized what that meant. "Wat's Wood is afire," he said in a hushed voice. From down at the base of the tower came the sound of Bennis cursing, a stream of such surpassing filth that it might have made Aegon the Unworthy blush. Sam Stoops began to pray.

They were too far away to make out flames, but the red

glow engulfed half the western horizon, and above the light the stars were vanishing. The King's Crown was half gone already, obscured behind a veil of the rising smoke.

Fire and sword, she said.

The fire burned until morning. No one in Standfast slept that night. Before long they could smell the smoke, and see flames dancing in the distance like girls in scarlet skirts. They all wondered if the fire would engulf them. Dunk stood behind the parapets, his eyes burning, watching for riders in the night. "Bennis," he said, when the brown knight came up, chewing on his sourleaf, "it's you she wants. Might be you should go."

"What, run?" he brayed. "On *my* horse? Might as well try to fly off on one o' these damned chickens."

"Then give yourself up. She'll only slit your nose."

"I like my nose how it is, lunk. Let her try and take me, we'll see what gets slit open." He sat cross-legged with his back against a merlon and took a whetstone from his pouch to sharpen his sword. Ser Eustace stood above him. In low voices, they spoke of how to fight the war. "The Longinch will expect us at the dam," Dunk heard the old knight say, "so we will burn her crops instead. Fire for fire." Ser Bennis thought that would be just the thing, only maybe they should put her mill to the torch as well. "It's six leagues on t'other side o' the castle, the Longinch won't be looking for us there. Burn the mill and kill the miller, that'll cost her dear."

Egg was listening, too. He coughed, and looked at Dunk with wide white eyes. "Ser, you have to stop them."

"How?" Dunk asked. *The Red Widow will stop them. Her, and that Lucas the Longinch.* "They're only making noise, Egg. It's that, or piss their breeches. And it's naught to do with us now."

Dawn came with hazy gray skies and air that burned the eyes. Dunk meant to make an early start, though after their sleepless night he did not know how far they'd get. He and Egg broke their fast on boiled eggs while Bennis was rousting the others outside for more drill. *They are Osgrey men and we are not,* he told himself. He ate four of the eggs. Ser Eustace owed him that much, as he saw it. Egg ate two. They washed them down with ale.

"We could go to Fair Isle, ser," the boy said as they were gathering up their things. "If they're being raided by the ironmen, Lord Farman might be looking for some swords."

It was a good thought. "Have you ever been to Fair Isle?"

"No, ser," Egg said, "but they say it's fair. Lord Farman's seat is fair, too. It's called Faircastle."

Dunk laughed. "Faircastle it shall be." He felt as if a great weight had been lifted off his shoulders. "I'll see to the horses," he said, when he'd tied his armor up in a bundle, secured with hempen rope. "Go to the roof and get our bed-rolls, squire." The last thing he wanted this morning was another confrontation with the chequy lion. "If you see Ser Eustace, let him be."

"I will, ser."

Outside, Bennis had his recruits lined up with their spears and shields, and was trying to teach them to advance in unison. The brown knight paid Dunk not the slightest heed as he crossed the yard. *He will lead the whole lot of them to death. The Red Widow could be here any moment.* Egg came bursting from the tower door and clattered down the wooden steps with their bedrolls. Above him, Ser Eustace stood stiffly on the balcony, his hands resting on the parapet. When his eyes met Dunk's his mustache quivered, and he quickly turned away. The air was hazy with blowing smoke.

Bennis had his shield slung across his back, a tall kite shield of unpainted wood, dark with countless layers of old varnish and girded all about with iron. It bore no blazon, only a center bosse that reminded Dunk of some great eye, shut tight. *As blind as he is.* "How do you mean to fight her?" Dunk asked.

Ser Bennis looked at his soldiers, his mouth running red with sourleaf. "Can't hold the hill with so few spears. Got to be the tower. We all hole up inside." He nodded at the door. "Only one way in. Haul up them wooden steps, and there's no way they can reach us."

"Until they build some steps of their own. They might bring ropes and grapnels, too, and swarm down on you through the roof. Unless they just stand back with their crossbows and fill you full of quarrels while you're trying to hold the door."

The Melons, Beans, and Barleycorns were listening to all they said. All their brave talk had blown away, though there was no breath of wind. They stood clutching their sharpened sticks, looking at Dunk and Bennis and each other.

"This lot won't do you a lick of good," Dunk said, with a nod at the ragged Osgrey army. "The Red Widow's knights will cut them to pieces if you leave them in the open, and their spears won't be any use inside that tower."

"They can chuck things off the roof," said Bennis. "Treb is good at chucking rocks."

"He could chuck a rock or two, I suppose," said Dunk, "until one of the Widow's crossbowmen puts a bolt through him."

"Ser?" Egg stood beside him. "Ser, if we mean to go, we'd best be gone, in case the Widow comes."

The boy was right. *If we linger, we'll be trapped here.* Yet still Dunk hesitated. "Let them go, Bennis."

"What, lose our valiant lads?" Bennis looked at the peasants, and brayed laughter. "Don't you lot be getting any notions," he warned them. "I'll gut any man who tries to run."

"Try, and I'll gut you." Dunk drew his sword. "Go home, all of you," he told the smallfolk. "Go back to your villages, and see if the fire's spared your homes and crops."

No one moved. The brown knight stared at him, his mouth working. Dunk ignored him. "Go," he told the smallfolk once again. It was as if some god had put the word into his mouth. *Not the Warrior. Is there a god for fools?* "GO!" he said again, roaring it this time. "Take your spears and shields, but *go,* or you won't live to see the morrow. Do you want to kiss your wives again? Do you want to hold your children? *Go home!* Have you all gone deaf?"

They hadn't. A mad scramble ensued amongst the chickens. Big Rob trod on a hen as he made his dash, and Pate came within half a foot of disemboweling Will Bean when his own spear tripped him up, but off they went, running. The Melons went one way, the Beans another, the Barleycorns a third. Ser Eustace was shouting down at them from above, but no one paid him any mind. *They are deaf to him at least,* Dunk thought.

By the time the old knight emerged from his tower and came scrambling down the steps, only Dunk and Egg and Bennis remained among the chickens. "Come back," Ser Eustace shouted at his fast-fleeing host. "You do not have my leave to go. *You do not have my leave!*"

"No use, m'lord," said Bennis. "They're gone."

Ser Eustace rounded on Dunk, his mustache quivering with rage. "You had no right to send them away. *No right!* I told them not to go, I *forbade* it. I *forbade* you to dismiss them."

"We never heard you, my lord." Egg took off his hat to fan away the smoke. "The chickens were cackling too loud."

The old man sank down onto Standfast's lowest step. "What did that woman offer you to deliver me to her?" he asked Dunk in a bleak voice. "How much gold did she give you to betray me, to send my lads away and leave me here alone?"

"You're not alone, m'lord." Dunk sheathed his sword. "I slept beneath your roof, and ate your eggs this morning. I owe you some service still. I won't go slinking off with my tail between my legs. My sword's still here." He touched the hilt.

"One sword." The old knight got slowly to his feet. "What can one sword hope to do against that woman?"

"Try and keep her off your land, to start with." Dunk wished he were as certain as he sounded.

The old knight's mustache trembled every time he took a breath. "Yes," he said at last. "Better to go boldly than hide behind stone walls. Better to die a lion than a rabbit. We were the Marshalls of the Northmarch for a thousand years. I must have my armor." He started up the steps.

Egg was looking up at Dunk. "I never knew you had a tail, ser," the boy said.

"Do you want a clout in the ear?"

"No, ser. Do you want your armor?"

"That," Dunk said, "and one thing more."

There was talk of Ser Bennis coming with them, but in the end Ser Eustace commanded him to stay and hold the tower. His sword would be of little use against the odds that they were like to face, and the sight of him would inflame the Widow further.

The brown knight did not require much convincing. Dunk helped him knock loose the iron pegs that held the upper steps in place. Bennis clambered up them, untied the old gray hempen rope, and hauled on it with all his strength. Creaking and groaning, the wooden stair swung upward, leaving ten feet of air between the top stone step and the tower's only entrance. Sam Stoops and his wife were both inside. The chickens would need to fend for themselves. Sitting below on his gray gelding, Ser Eustace called up to say, "If we have not returned by nightfall . . ."

". . . I'll ride for Highgarden, m'lord, and tell Lord Tyrell how that woman burned your wood and murdered you."

Dunk followed Egg and Maester down the hill. The old man came after, his armor rattling softly. For once a wind was rising, and he could hear the flapping of his cloak.

Where Wat's Wood had stood they found a smoking wasteland. The fire had largely burned itself out by the time they reached the wood, but here and there a few patches were still burning, fiery islands in a sea of ash and cinders. Elsewhere the trunks of burned trees thrust like blackened spears into the sky. Other trees had fallen and lay athwart the west way with limbs charred and broken, dull red fires smoldering inside their hollow hearts. There were hot spots on the forest floor as well, and places where the smoke hung in the air like a hot gray haze. Ser Eustace was stricken with a fit of coughing, and for a few moments Dunk feared the old man would need to turn back, but finally it passed.

They rode past the carcass of a red deer, and later on what

might have been a badger. Nothing lived, except the flies. Flies could live through anything, it seemed.

"The Field of Fire must have looked like this," Ser Eustace said. "It was there our woes began, two hundred years ago. The last of the green kings perished on that field, with the finest flowers of the Reach around him. My father said the dragonfire burned so hot that their swords melted in their hands. Afterward the blades were gathered up, and went to make the Iron Throne. Highgarden passed from kings to stewards, and the Osgreys dwindled and diminished, until the Marshalls of the Northmarch were no more than landed knights bound in fealty to the Rowans."

Dunk had nothing to say to that, so they rode in silence for a time, till Ser Eustace coughed, and said, "Ser Duncan, do you remember the story that I told you?"

"I might, ser," said Dunk. "Which one?"

"The Little Lion."

"I remember. He was the youngest of five sons."

"Good." He coughed again. "When he slew Lancel Lannister, the westermen turned back. Without the king there was no war. Do you understand what I am saying?"

"Aye," Dunk said reluctantly. *Could I kill a woman?* For once Dunk wished he *were* as thick as that castle wall. *It must not come to that. I must not let it come to that.*

A few green trees still stood where the west way crossed the Chequy Water. Their trunks were charred and blackened on one side. Just beyond, the water glimmered darkly. *Blue and green,* Dunk thought, *but all the gold is gone.* The smoke had veiled the sun.

Ser Eustace halted when he reached the water's edge. "I took a holy vow. I will not cross that stream. Not so long as the land beyond is *hers.*" The old knight wore mail and plate beneath his yellowed surcoat. His sword was on his hip.

"What if she never comes, ser?" Egg asked.

With fire and sword, Dunk thought. "She'll come."

She did, and within the hour. They heard her horses first, and then the faint metallic sound of clinking armor, growing louder. The drifting smoke made it hard to tell how far off they were, until her banner bearer pushed through the ragged gray curtain. His staff was crowned by an iron spider painted white and red, with the black banner of the Webbers hanging listlessly beneath. When he saw them across the water, he halted on the bank. Ser Lucas Inchfield appeared half a heartbeat later, armored head to heel.

Only then did Lady Rohanne herself appear, astride a coal-black mare decked out in strands of silverly silk, like unto a spider's web. The Widow's cloak was made of the same stuff. It billowed from her shoulders and her wrists, as light as air. She was armored, too, in a suit of green enamel scale chased with gold and silver. It fit her figure like a glove, and made her look as if she were garbed in summer leaves. Her long red braid hung down behind her, bouncing as she rode. Septon Sefton rode red-faced at her side, atop a big gray gelding. On her other side was her young maester, Cerrick, mounted on a mule.

More knights came after, half a dozen of them, attended by as many esquires. A column of mounted crossbowmen brought up the rear, and fanned out to either side of the road when they reached the Chequy Water and saw Dunk waiting on the other side. There were three-and-thirty fighting men all told, excluding the septon, the maester, and the Widow herself. One of the knights caught Dunk's eye; a squat bald keg of a man in mail and leather, with an angry face and an ugly goiter on his neck.

The Red Widow walked her mare to the edge of the water. "Ser Eustace, Ser Duncan," she called across the stream, "we saw your fire burning in the night."

"Saw it?" Ser Eustace shouted back. "Aye, you saw it . . . after you made it."

"That is a vile accusation."

"For a vile act."

"I was asleep in my bed last night, with my ladies all around me. The shouts from the walls awoke me, as they did almost everyone. Old men climbed up steep tower steps to look, and babes at the breast saw the red light and wept in fear. And that is all I know of your fire, ser."

"It was your fire, woman," insisted Ser Eustace. "My wood is gone. *Gone,* I say!"

Septon Sefton cleared his throat. "Ser Eustace," he boomed, "there are fires in the kingswood too, and even in the rainwood. The drought has turned all our woods to kindling."

Lady Rohanne raised an arm and pointed. "Look at my fields, Osgrey. How dry they are. I would have been a fool to set a fire. Had the wind changed direction, the flames might well have leapt the stream, and burned out half my crops."

"Might have?" Ser Eustace shouted. "It was my woods that burned, and you that burned them. Most like you cast some witch's spell to drive the wind, just as you used your dark arts to slay your husbands and your brothers!"

Lady Rohanne's face grew harder. Dunk had seen that look at Coldmoat, just before she slapped him. "Prattle," she told the old man. "I will waste no more words on you, ser. Produce Bennis of the Brown Shield, or we will come and take him."

"That you shall not do," Ser Eustace declared in ringing tones. "That you shall *never* do." His mustache twitched. "Come no farther. This side of the stream is mine, and you are not wanted here. You shall have no hospitality from me. No bread and salt, not even shade and water. You come as an intruder. I forbid you to set foot on Osgrey land."

Lady Rohanne drew her braid over her shoulder. "Ser Lucas," was all she said. The Longinch made a gesture, the crossbowmen dismounted, winched back their bowstrings with the help of hook and stirrup, and plucked quarrels from their quivers. "Now, ser," her ladyship called out, when every bow was nocked and raised and ready, "what was it you forbade me?"

Dunk had heard enough. "If you cross the stream without leave, you are breaking the king's peace."

Septon Sefton urged his horse forward a step. "The king will neither know nor care," he called. "We are all the Mother's children, ser. For her sake, stand aside."

Dunk frowned. "I don't know much of gods, septon . . .

but aren't we the Warrior's children, too?" He rubbed the back of his neck. "If you try to cross, I'll stop you."

Ser Lucas the Longinch laughed. "Here's a hedge knight who yearns to be a hedgehog, my lady," he said to the Red Widow. "Say the word, and we'll put a dozen quarrels in him. At this distance they will punch through that armor like it was made of spit."

"No. Not yet, ser." Lady Rohanne studied him from across the stream. "You are two men and a boy. We are three-and-thirty. How do you propose to stop us crossing?"

"Well," said Dunk, "I'll tell you. But only you."

"As you wish." She pressed her heels into her horse and rode her out into the stream. When the water reached the mare's belly, she halted, waiting. "Here I am. Come closer, ser. I promise not to sew you in a sack."

Ser Eustace grasped Dunk by the arm before he could respond. "Go to her," the old knight said, "but remember the Little Lion."

"As you say, m'lord." Dunk walked Thunder down into the water. He drew up beside her and said, "M'lady."

"Ser Duncan." She reached up and laid two fingers on his swollen lip. "Did I do this, ser?"

"No one else has slapped my face of late, m'lady."

"That was bad of me. A breach of hospitality. The good septon has been scolding me." She gazed across the water at Ser Eustace. "I scarce remember Addam any longer. It was more than half my life ago. I remember that I loved him, though. I have not loved any of the others."

"His father put him in the blackberries, with his brothers," Dunk said. "He was fond of blackberries."

"I remember. He used to pick them for me, and we'd eat them in a bowl of cream."

"The king pardoned the old man for Daemon," said Dunk. "It is past time you pardoned him for Addam."

"Give me Bennis, and I'll consider that."

"Bennis is not mine to give."

She sighed. "I would as lief not have to kill you."

"I would as lief not die."

"Then give me Bennis. We'll cut his nose off and hand him back, and that will be the end of that."

"It won't, though," Dunk said. "There's still the dam to deal with, and the fire. Will you give us the men who set it?"

"There were lantern bugs in that wood," she said. "It may be they set the fire off, with their little lanterns."

"No more teasing now, m'lady," Dunk warned her. "This is no time for it. Tear down the dam, and let Ser Eustace have the water to make up for the wood. That's fair, is it not?"

"It might be, if I had burned the wood. Which I did not. I was at Coldmoat, safe abed." She looked down at the water. "What is there to prevent us from riding right across the stream? Have you scattered caltrops amongst the rocks? Hidden archers in the ashes? Tell me what you think is going to stop us."

"Me." He pulled one gauntlet off. "In Flea Bottom I was always bigger and stronger than the other boys, so I used to beat them bloody and steal from them. The old man taught me not to do that. It was wrong, he said, and besides, sometimes little boys have great big brothers. Here, have a look at this." Dunk twisted the ring off his finger and held it out to her. She had to let loose of her braid to take it.

"Gold?" she said, when she felt the weight of it. "What is this, ser?" She turned it over in her hand. "A signet. Gold and onyx." Her green eyes narrowed as she studied the seal. "Where did you find this, ser?"

"In a boot. Wrapped in rags and stuffed up in the toe."

Lady Rohanne's fingers closed around it. She glanced at Egg and old Ser Eustace. "You took a great risk in showing me this ring, ser. But how does it avail us? If I should command my men to cross . . ."

"Well," said Dunk, "that would mean I'd have to fight."

"And die."

"Most like," he said, "and then Egg would go back where he comes from, and tell what happened here."

"Not if he died as well."

"I don't think you'd kill a boy of ten," he said, hoping he was right. "Not *this* boy of ten, you wouldn't. You've got three-and-thirty men there, like you said. Men talk. That fat one there especially. No matter how deep you dug the graves, the tale would out. And then, well . . . might be a spotted spider's bite can kill a lion, but a dragon is a different sort of beast."

"I would sooner be the dragon's friend." She tried the ring on her finger. It was too big even for her thumb. "Dragon or no, I must have Bennis of the Brown Shield."

"No."

"You are seven feet of stubborn."

"Less an inch."

She gave him back the ring. "I cannot return to Coldmoat empty-handed. They will say the Red Widow has lost her bite, that she was too weak to do justice, that she could not protect her smallfolk. You do not understand, ser."

"I might." *Better than you know.* "I remember once some little lord in the stormlands took Ser Arlan into service, to help him fight some other little lord. When I asked the old man what they were fighting over, he said, 'Nothing, lad. It's just some pissing contest.' "

Lady Rohanne gave him a shocked look, but could sustain it no more than half a heartbeat before it turned into a grin. "I have heard a thousand empty courtesies in my time, but you are the first knight who ever said *pissing* in my presence." Her freckled face went somber. "Those pissing contests are how lords judge one another's strength, and woe to any man who shows his weakness. A woman must needs piss twice as hard, if she hopes to rule. And if that woman should happen to be *small* . . . Lord Stackhouse covets my Horseshoe Hills, Ser Clifford Conklyn has an old claim to Leafy Lake, those dismal Durwells live by stealing cattle . . . and beneath mine own roof I have the Longinch. Every day I wake wondering if this might be the day he marries me by force." Her hand curled tight around her braid, as hard as if it were a rope, and she was dangling over a precipice. "He wants to, I know. He holds back for fear of my wroth, just as Conklyn and Stackhouse and the Durwells tread carefully

where the Red Widow is concerned. If any of them thought
for a moment that I had turned weak and soft . . ."

Dunk put the ring back on his finger, and drew his dagger.

The widow's eyes went wide at the sight of naked steel.
"What are you doing?" she said. "Have you lost your *wits*?
There are a dozen crossbows trained on you."

"You wanted blood for blood." He laid the dagger against
his cheek. "They told you wrong. It wasn't Bennis cut that
digger, it was me." He pressed the edge of the steel into his
face, slashed downward. When he shook the blood off the
blade, some spattered on her face. *More freckles,* he thought.
"There, the Red Widow has her due. A cheek for a cheek."

"You are quite mad." The smoke had filled her eyes with
tears. "If you were better born, I'd marry you."

"Aye, m'lady. And if pigs had wings and scales and
breathed flame, they'd be as good as dragons." Dunk slid
the knife back in its sheath. His face had begun to throb. The
blood ran down his cheek and dripped onto his gorget. The
smell made Thunder snort, and paw the water. "Give me
the men who burned the wood."

"No one burned the wood," she said, "but if some man of
mine had done so, it must have been to please me. How
could I give such a man to you?" She glanced back at her es-
cort. "It would be best if Ser Eustace were just to withdraw
his accusation."

"Those pigs will be breathing fire first, m'lady."

"In that case, I must assert my innocence before the
eyes of gods and men. Tell Ser Eustace that I demand an
apology . . . or a trial. The choice is his." She wheeled her
horse about to ride back to her men.

The stream would be their battleground.

Septon Sefton waddled out and said a prayer, beseeching the Father Above to look down on these two men and
judge them justly, asking the Warrior to lend his strength to
the man whose cause was just and true, begging the Mother's
mercy for the liar, that he might be forgiven for his sins.
When the praying was over and done with, he turned to Ser

Eustace Osgrey one last time. "Ser," he said, "I beg you once again, withdraw your accusation."

"I will not," the old man said, his mustache trembling.

The fat septon turned to Lady Rohanne. "Good-sister, if you did this thing, confess your guilt, and offer good Ser Eustace some restitution for his wood. Elsewise blood must flow."

"My champion will prove my innocence before the eyes of gods and men."

"Trial by battle is not the only way," said the septon, waist-deep in the water. "Let us go to Goldengrove, I implore you both, and place the matter before Lord Rowan for his judgment."

"Never," said Ser Eustace. The Red Widow shook her head.

Ser Lucas Inchfield looked at Lady Rohanne, his face dark with fury. "You *will* marry me when this mummer's farce is done. As your lord father wished."

"My lord father never knew you as I do," she gave back.

Dunk went to one knee beside Egg, and put the signet back in the boy's hand; four three-headed dragons, two and two, the arms of Maekar, Prince of Summerhall. "Back in the boot," he said, "but if it happens that I die, go to the nearest of your father's friends and have him take you back to Summerhall. Don't try to cross the whole Reach on your own. See you don't forget, or my ghost will come and clout you in the ear."

"Yes, ser," said Egg, "but I'd sooner you didn't die."

"It's too hot to die." Dunk donned his helm, and Egg helped him fasten it tightly to his gorget. The blood was sticky on his face, though Ser Eustace had torn a piece off his cloak to help stop the gash from bleeding. He rose and went to Thunder. Most of the smoke had blown away, he saw as he swung up onto the saddle, but the sky was still dark. *Clouds,* he thought, *dark clouds.* It had been so long. *Maybe it's an omen. But is it his omen, or mine?* Dunk was no good with omens.

Across the stream, Ser Lucas had mounted up as well. His horse was a chestnut courser; a splendid animal, swift and strong, but not as large as Thunder. What the horse lacked in size he made up for in armor, though; he was clad in crinet, chanfron, and a coat of light chain. The Longinch himself wore black enameled plate and silvery ringmail. An onyx spider squatted malignantly atop his helmet, but his shield displayed his own arms: a bend sinister, chequy black and white, on a pale gray field. Dunk watched Ser Lucas hand it to a squire. *He does not mean to use it.* When another squire delivered him a poleax, he knew why. The ax was long and lethal, with a banded haft, a heavy head, and a wicked spike on its back, but it was a two-handed weapon. The Longinch would need to trust in his armor to protect him. *I need to make him rue that choice.*

His own shield was on his left arm, the shield Tanselle had painted with his elm and falling star. A child's rhyme echoed in his head. *Oak and iron, guard me well, or else I'm dead, and doomed to hell.* He slid his longsword from its scabbard. The weight of it felt good in his hands.

He put his heels into Thunder's flanks and walked the big destrier down into the water. Across the stream, Ser Lucas did the same. Dunk pressed right, so as to present the Longinch with his left side, protected by his shield. That was not something Ser Lucas was willing to concede him. He turned his courser quickly, and they came together in a tumult of gray steel and green spray. Ser Lucas struck with his poleax. Dunk had to twist in the saddle to catch it on his shield. The force of it shot down his arm and jarred his teeth together. He swung his sword in answer, a sideways cut that took the other knight beneath his upraised arm. Steel screamed on steel, and it was on.

The Longinch spurred his courser in a circle, trying to get around to Dunk's unprotected side, but Thunder wheeled to meet him, snapping at the other horse. Ser Lucas delivered one crashing blow after another, standing in his stirrups to get all his weight and strength behind the axhead. Dunk shifted his shield to catch each blow as it came. Half crouched beneath its oak, he hacked at Inchfield's arms and side and legs, but his plate turned every stroke. Around they went, and around again, the water lapping at their legs. The Longinch attacked, and Dunk defended, watching for a weakness.

Finally he saw it. Every time Ser Lucas lifted his ax for another blow, a gap appeared beneath his arm. There was mail and leather there, and padding underneath, but no steel plate. Dunk kept his shield up, trying to time his attack. *Soon. Soon.* The ax crashed down, wrenched free, came up. *Now!* He slammed his spurs into Thunder, driving him closer, and thrust with his longsword, to drive his point through the opening.

But the gap vanished as quick as it had appeared. His swordpoint scraped a rondel, and Dunk, overextended, almost lost his seat. The ax descended with a crash, slanting off the iron rim of Dunk's shield, crunching against the side of his helm, and striking Thunder a glancing blow along the neck.

The destrier screamed and reared up on two legs, his eye rolling white in pain as the sharp coppery smell of blood filled the air. He lashed out with his iron hooves just as the Longinch was moving in. One caught Ser Lucas in the face, the other on a shoulder. Then the heavy warhorse came down atop his courser.

It all happened in a heartbeat. The two horses went down in a tangle, kicking and biting at each other, churning up the water and the mud below. Dunk tried to throw himself from the saddle, but one foot tangled in a stirrup. He fell face first, sucking down one desperate gulp of air before the stream came rushing into the helm through the eyeslit. His foot was still caught up, and he felt a savage yank as Thunder's struggles almost pulled his leg out of its socket. Just as quickly he was free, turning, sinking. For a moment he flailed helplessly in the water. The world was blue and green and brown.

The weight of his armor pulled him down until his shoulder bumped the streambed. *If that is down the other way is up.* Dunk's steel-clad hands fumbled at the stones and sands, and somehow he gathered his legs up under him and stood. He was reeling, dripping mud, with water pouring from the

breath holes in his dinted helm, but he was standing. He
sucked down air.

His battered shield still clung to his left arm, but his scabbard was empty and his sword was gone. There was blood inside his helm as well as water. When he tried to shift his
weight, his ankle sent a lance of pain right up his leg. Both
horses had struggled back to their feet, he saw. He turned
his head, squinting one-eyed through a veil of blood, searching for his foe. *Gone,* he thought, *he's drowned, or Thunder
crushed his skull in.*

Ser Lucas burst up out of the water right in front of him,
sword in hand. He struck Dunk's neck a savage blow, and
only the thickness of his gorget kept his head upon his shoulders. He had no blade to answer with, only his shield. He
gave ground, and the Longinch came after, screaming and
slashing. Dunk's upraised arm took a numbing blow above
the elbow. A cut to his hip made him grunt in pain. As he
backed away, a rock turned beneath his foot, and he went
down to one knee, chest-high in the water. He got his shield
up, but this time Ser Lucas struck so hard he split the thick
oak right down the middle, and drove the remnants back into
Dunk's face. His ears were ringing and his mouth was full of
blood, but somewhere far away he heard Egg screaming.
"Get him, ser, get him, get him, *he's right there!*"

Dunk dived forward. Ser Lucas had wrenched his sword
free for another cut. Dunk slammed into him waist-high and
knocked him off his feet. The stream swallowed both of
them again, but this time Dunk was ready. He kept one arm
around the Longinch and forced him to the bottom. Bubbles
came streaming out from behind Inchfield's battered, twisted
visor, but still he fought. He found a rock at the bottom of
the stream and began hammering at Dunk's head and hands.
Dunk fumbled at his swordbelt. *Have I lost the dagger too?*
he wondered. No, there it was. His hand closed around the
hilt and he wrenched it free, and drove it slowly through the
churning water, through the iron rings and boiled leather
beneath the arm of Lucas the Longinch, turning it as he
pushed. Ser Lucas jerked and twisted, and the strength left

him. Dunk shoved away and floated. His chest was on fire. A fish flashed past his face, long and white and slender. *What's that?* he wondered. *What's that? What's that?*

He woke in the wrong castle.

When his eyes opened, he did not know where he was. It was blessedly cool. The taste of blood was in his mouth and he had a cloth across his eyes, a heavy cloth fragrant with some unguent. It smelled of cloves, he thought.

Dunk groped at his face, pulled the cloth away. Above him torchlight played against a high ceiling. Ravens were walking on the rafters overhead, peering down with small black eyes and *quork*ing at him. *I am not blind, at least.* He was in a maester's tower. The walls were lined with racks of herbs and potions in earthen jars and vessels of green glass. A long trestle table nearby was covered with parchments, books, and queer bronze instruments, all spattered with droppings from the ravens in the rafters. He could hear them muttering at one another.

He tried to sit. It proved a bad mistake. His head swam, and his left leg screamed in agony when he put the slightest weight upon it. His ankle was wrapped in linen, he saw, and there were linen strips around his chest and shoulders, too.

"Be still." A face appeared above him, young and pinched, with dark brown eyes on either side of a hooked nose. Dunk knew that face. The man who owned it was all in gray, with a chain collar hanging loose about his neck, a maester's chain of many metals. Dunk grabbed him by the wrist. "Where? . . ."

"Coldmoat," said the maester. "You were too badly injured to return to Standfast, so Lady Rohanne commanded us to bring you here. Drink this." He raised a cup of . . . something . . . to Dunk's lips. The potion had a bitter taste, like vinegar, but at least it washed away the taste of blood.

Dunk made himself drink it all. Afterward he flexed the fingers of his sword hand, and then the other. *At least my hands still work, and my arms.* "What . . . what did I hurt?"

"What not?" The maester snorted. "A broken ankle, a

sprained knee, a broken collarbone, bruising . . . your upper torso is largely green and yellow and your right arm is a purply black. I thought your skull was cracked as well, but it appears not. There is that gash in your face, ser. You will have a scar, I fear. Oh, and you had drowned by the time we pulled you from the water."

"Drowned?" said Dunk.

"I never suspected that one man could swallow so much water, not even a man as large as you, ser. Count yourself fortunate that I am ironborn. The priests of the Drowned God know how to drown a man and bring him back, and I have made a study of their beliefs and customs."

I drowned. Dunk tried to sit again, but the strength was not in him. *I drowned in water that did not even come up to my neck.* He laughed, then groaned in pain. "Ser Lucas?"

"Dead. Did you doubt it?"

No. Dunk doubted many things, but not that. He remembered how the strength had gone out of the Longinch's limbs, all at once. "Egg," he got out. "I want Egg."

"Hunger is a good sign," the maester said, "but it is sleep you need just now, not food."

Dunk shook his head, and regretted it at once. "Egg is my squire . . ."

"Is he? A brave lad, and stronger than he looks. He was the one to pull you from the stream. He helped us get that armor off you, too, and rode with you in the wayn when we brought you here. He would not sleep himself, but sat by your side with your sword across his lap, in case someone tried to do you harm. He even suspected *me,* and insisted that I taste anything I meant to feed you. A queer child, but devoted."

"Where is he?"

"Ser Eustace asked the boy to attend him at the wedding feast. There was no one else on his side. It would have been discourteous for him to refuse."

"Wedding feast?" Dunk did not understand.

"You would not know, of course. Coldmoat and Standfast were reconciled after your battle. Lady Rohanne begged leave of old Ser Eustace to cross his land and visit Addam's grave, and he granted her that right. She knelt before the blackberries and began to weep, and he was so moved that he went to comfort her. They spent the whole night talking of young Addam and my lady's noble father. Lord Wyman and Ser Eustace were fast friends, until the Blackfyre Rebellion. His lordship and my lady were wed this morning, by our good Septon Sefton. Eustace Osgrey is the lord of Cold-moat, and his chequy lion flies beside the Webber spider on every tower and wall."

Dunk's world was spinning slowly all around him. *That potion. He's put me back to sleep.* He closed his eyes, and let all the pain drain out of him. He could hear the ravens *quork*ing and screaming at each other, and the sound of his own breath, and something else as well . . . a softer sound, steady, heavy, somehow soothing. "What's that?" he murmured sleepily. "That sound? . . ."

"That?" The maester listened. "That's just rain."

He did not see her till the day they took their leave.

"This is folly, ser," Septon Sefton complained, as Dunk limped heavily across the yard, swinging his splinted foot and leaning on a crutch. "Maester Cerrick says you are not half healed as yet, and this rain . . . you're like to catch a chill, if you do not drown again. At least wait for the rain to stop."

"That may be years." Dunk was grateful to the fat septon, who had visited him near every day . . . to pray for him, ostensibly, though more time seemed to be taken up with tales and gossip. He would miss his loose and lively tongue and cheerful company, but that changed nothing. "I need to go."

The rain was lashing down around them, a thousand cold gray whips upon his back. His cloak was already sodden. It was the white wool cloak Ser Eustace had given him, with the green-and-gold-checkered border. The old knight had pressed it on him once again, as a parting gift. "For your courage and leal service, ser," he said. The brooch that pinned the cloak at his shoulder was a gift as well; an ivory spider brooch with silver legs. Clusters of crushed garnets made spots upon its back.

"I hope this is not some mad quest to hunt down Bennis," Septon Sefton said. "You are so bruised and battered that I would fear for you, if that one found you in such a state."

Bennis, Dunk thought bitterly, *bloody Bennis.* While Dunk had been making his stand at the stream, Bennis had tied up Sam Stoops and his wife, ransacked Standfast from top to bottom, and made off with every item of value he could find, from candles, clothes, and weaponry to Osgrey's old silver cup and a small cache of coin the old man had hidden in his solar behind a mildewed tapestry. One day Dunk hoped to meet Ser Bennis of the Brown Shield again, and when he did . . . "Bennis will keep."

"Where will you go?" The septon was panting heavily. Even with Dunk on a crutch, he was too fat to match his pace.

"Fair Isle. Harrenhal. The Trident. There are hedges everywhere." He shrugged. "I've always wanted to see the Wall."

"The Wall?" The septon jerked to a stop. "I despair of you, Ser Duncan!" he shouted, standing in the mud with outspread hands as the rain came down around him. "Pray, ser, pray for the Crone to light your way!" Dunk kept walking.

She was waiting for him inside the stables, standing by the yellow bales of hay in a gown as green as summer. "Ser Duncan," she said when he came pushing through the door. Her red braid hung down in front, the end of it brushing against her thighs. "It is good to see you on your feet."

You never saw me on my back, he thought. "M'lady. What brings you to the stables. It's a wet day for a ride."

"I might say the same to you."

"Egg told you?" *I owe him another clout in the ear.*

"Be glad he did, or I would have sent men after you to drag you back. It was cruel of you to try and steal away without so much as a farewell."

She had never come to see him while he was in Maester Cerrick's care, not once. "That green becomes you well, m'lady," he said. "It brings out the color of your eyes." He shifted his weight awkwardly on the crutch. "I'm here for my horse."

"You do not need to go. There is a place for you here, when you're recovered. Captain of my guards. And Egg can join my other squires. No one need ever know who he is."

"Thank you, m'lady, but no." Thunder was in a stall a dozen places down. Dunk hobbled toward him.

"Please reconsider, ser. These are perilous times, even for dragons and their friends. Stay until you've healed." She walked along beside him. "It would please Lord Eustace, too. He is very fond of you."

"Very fond," Dunk agreed. "If his daughter weren't dead, he'd want me to marry her. Then you could be my lady mother. I never had a mother, much less a *lady* mother."

For half a heartbeat Lady Rohanne looked as though she was going to slap him again. *Maybe she'll just kick my crutch away.*

"You are angry with me, ser," she said instead. "You must let me make amends."

"Well," he said, "you could help me saddle Thunder."

"I had something else in mind." She reached out her hand for his, a freckled hand, her fingers strong and slender. *I'll bet she's freckled all over.* "How well do you know horses?"

"I ride one."

"An old destrier bred for battle, slow-footed and ill-tempered. Not a horse to ride from place to place."

"If I need to get from place to place, it's him or these." Dunk pointed at his feet.

"You have large feet," she observed. "Large hands as well. I think you must be large all over. Too large for most palfreys. They'd look like ponies with you perched upon their backs. Still, a swifter mount would serve you well. A big courser, with some Dornish sand steed for endurance." She pointed to the stall across from Thunder's. "A horse like her."

She was a blood bay with a bright eye and a long fiery mane. Lady Rohanne took a carrot from her sleeves and stroked her head as she took it. "The carrot, not the fingers," she told the horse, before she turned again to Dunk. "I call her Flame, but you may name her as you please. Call her Amends, if you like."

For a moment he was speechless. He leaned on the crutch and looked at the blood bay with new eyes. She was magnificent. A better mount than any the old man had ever owned. You had only to look at those long, clean limbs to see how swift she'd be.

"I bred her for beauty, and for speed."

He turned back to Thunder. "I cannot take her."

"Why not?"

"She is too good a horse for me. Just look at her."

A flush crept up Rohanne's face. She clutched her braid, twisting it between her fingers. "I had to marry, you know that. My father's will . . . oh, don't be such a fool."

"What else should I be? I'm thick as a castle wall and bastard born as well."

"Take the horse. I refuse to let you go without something to remember me by."

"I will remember you, m'lady. Have no fear of that."

"Take her!"

Dunk grabbed her braid and pulled her face to his. It was awkward with the crutch and the difference in their heights. He almost fell before he got his lips on hers. He kissed her hard. One of her hands went around his neck, and one around his back. He learned more about kissing in a moment than he had ever known from watching. But when they finally broke apart, he drew his dagger. "I know what I want to remember you by, m'lady."

Egg was waiting for him at the gatehouse, mounted on a handsome new sorrel palfrey and holding Maester's lead. When Dunk trotted up to them on Thunder, the boy looked surprised. "She said she wanted to give you a new horse, ser."

"Even highborn ladies don't get all they want," Dunk said, as they rode out across the drawbridge. "It wasn't a horse I wanted." The moat was so high it was threatening to overflow its banks. "I took something else to remember her by instead. A lock of that red hair." He reached under his cloak, brought out the braid, and smiled.

In the iron cage at the crossroads, the corpses still embraced. They looked lonely, forlorn. Even the flies had abandoned them, and the crows as well. Only some scraps of skin and hair remained upon the dead men's bones.

Dunk halted, frowning. His ankle was hurting from the ride, but it made no matter. Pain was as much a part of knighthood as were swords and shields. "Which way is south?" he asked Egg. It was hard to know, when the world was all rain and mud and the sky was gray as a granite wall.

"That's south, ser." Egg pointed. "That's north."

"Summerhall is south. Your father."

"The Wall is north."

Dunk looked at him. "That's a long way to ride."

"I have a new horse, ser."

"So you do." Dunk had to smile. "And why would you want to see the Wall?"

"Well," said Egg. "I hear it's tall."

THE TALES OF ALVIN MAKER

ORSON SCOTT CARD

THE TALES OF ALVIN MAKER:

In the *Tales of Alvin Maker* series, an alternate-history view of an America that never was, Orson Scott Card postulated what the world might have been like if the Revolutionary War had never happened, and if folk magic actually worked.

America is divided into several provinces, with the Spanish and French still having a strong presence in the New World. The emerging scientific revolution in Europe has led many people with "talent," that is, magical ability, to emigrate to North America, bringing their prevailing magic with them. The books chronicle the life of Alvin, the seventh son of a seventh son—a fact that marks him right away as a person of great power. It is Alvin's ultimate destiny to become a Maker, an adept being of a kind that has not existed for a thousand years. However, there exists an Unmaker for every Maker—a being of great supernatural evil who is Alvin's adversary, and strives to use Alvin's brother Calvin against him.

During the course of his adventures, Alvin explores the world around him and encounters such problems as slavery and the continued enmity between the settlers and the Native Americans who control the western half of the continent. The series appears to be heading toward an ultimate confrontation between Alvin and the Unmaker, with the fate of the entire continent, perhaps even the world, hinging on the outcome.

THE *YAZOO QUEEN*

ORSON SCOTT CARD

Alvin watched as Captain Howard welcomed aboard another group of passengers, a prosperous family with five children and three slaves.

"It's the Nile River of America," said the captain. "But Cleopatra herself never sailed in such splendor as you folks is going to experience on the *Yazoo Queen*."

Splendor for the family, thought Alvin. Not likely to be much splendor for the slaves—though, being house servants, they'd fare better than the two dozen runaways chained together in the blazing sun at dockside all afternoon.

Alvin had been keeping an eye on them since he and Arthur Stuart got here to the Carthage City riverport at eleven. Arthur Stuart was all for exploring, and Alvin let him go. The city that billed itself as the Phoenicia of the West had plenty of sights for a boy Arthur's age, even a half-black boy. Since it was on the north shore of the Hio, there'd be suspicious eyes on him for a runaway. But there was plenty of free blacks in Carthage City, and Arthur Stuart was no fool. He'd keep an eye out.

There was plenty of slaves in Carthage, too. That was the law, that a black slave from the South remained a slave even in a free state. And the greatest shame of all was those chained-up runaways who got themselves all the way across the Hio to freedom, only to be picked up by Finders and dragged back in chains to the whips and other horrors of bondage. Angry owners who'd make an example of them. No wonder there was so many who killed theirselves, or tried to.

Alvin saw wounds on more than a few in this chained-up

group of twenty-five, though many of the wounds could have been made by the slave's own hand. Finders weren't much for injuring the property they were getting paid to bring on home. No, those wounds on wrists and bellies were likely a vote for freedom before life itself.

What Alvin was watching for was to know whether the runaways were going to be loaded on this boat or another. Most often runaways were ferried across the river and made to walk home over land—there was too many stories of slaves jumping overboard and sinking to the bottom with their chains on to make Finders keen on river transportation.

But now and then Alvin had caught a whiff of talking from the slaves—not much, since it could get them a bit of lash, and not loud enough for him to make out the words, but the music of the language didn't sound like English, not northern English, not southern English, not slave English. It wasn't likely to be any African language. With the British waging full-out war on the slave trade, there weren't many new slaves making it across the Atlantic these days.

So it might be Spanish they were talking, or French. Either way, they'd most likely be bound for Nueva Barcelona, or New Orleans, as the French still called it.

Which raised some questions in Alvin's mind. Mostly this one: How could a bunch of Barcelona runaways get themselves to the state of Hio? That would have been a long trek on foot, especially if they didn't speak English. Alvin's wife, Peggy, grew up in an Abolitionist home, with her papa, Horace Guester, smuggling runaways across river. Alvin knew something about how good the Underground Railway was. It had fingers reaching all the way down into the new duchies of Mizzippy and Alabam, but Alvin never heard of any Spanish- or French-speaking slaves taking that long dark road to freedom.

"I'm hungry again," said Arthur Stuart.

Alvin turned to see the boy—no, the young man, he was getting so tall and his voice so low—standing behind him, hands in his pockets, looking at the *Yazoo Queen*.

"I'm a-thinking," said Alvin, "as how instead of just looking at this boat, we ought to get on it and ride a spell."

"How far?" asked Arthur Stuart.

"You asking cause you're hoping it's a long way or a short one?"

"This one goes clear to Barcy."

"It does if the fog on the Mizzippy lets it," said Alvin.

Arthur Stuart made a goofy face at him. "Oh, that's right, cause around you that fog's just bound to close right in."

"It might," said Alvin. "Me and water never did get along."

"When you was a little baby, maybe," said Arthur Stuart. "Fog does what you tell it to do these days."

"You think," said Alvin.

"You showed me your own self."

"I showed you with smoke from a candle," said Alvin, "and just because I *can* do it don't mean that every fog or smoke you see is doing what I say."

"Don't mean it ain't, either," said Arthur Stuart, grinning.

"I'm just waiting to see if this boat's a slave ship or not," said Alvin.

Arthur Stuart looked over where Alvin was looking, at the runaways. "Why don't you just turn them loose?" he asked.

"And where would they go?" said Alvin. "They're being watched."

"Not all that careful," said Arthur Stuart. "Them so-called guards has got jugs that ain't close to full by now."

"The Finders still got their sachets. It wouldn't take long to round them up again, and they'd be in even more trouble."

"So you ain't going to do a thing about it?"

"Arthur Stuart, I can't just pry the manacles off every slave in the South."

"I seen you melt iron like it was butter," said Arthur Stuart.

"So a bunch of slaves run away and leave behind puddles of iron that was once their chains," said Alvin. "What do the authorities think? There was a blacksmith snuck in with a teeny tiny bellows and a ton of coal and lit him a fire that het them chains up? And then he run off after, taking all his coal with him in his pockets?"

Arthur Stuart looked at him defiantly. "So it's all about keeping you safe."

"I reckon so," said Alvin. "You know what a coward I am."

Last year, Arthur Stuart would have blinked and said he was sorry, but now that his voice had changed the word "sorry" didn't come so easy to his lips. "You can't heal everybody, neither," he said, "but that don't stop you from healing *some.*"

"No point in freeing them as can't stay free," said Alvin. "And how many of them would run, do you think, and how many drown themselves in the river?"

"Why would they do that?"

"Because they know as well as I do, there ain't no freedom here in Carthage City for a runaway slave. This town may be the biggest on the Hio, but it's more southern than northern, when it comes to slavery. There's even buying and selling of slaves here, they say, flesh markets hidden in cellars, and the authorities know about it and don't do a thing because there's so much money in it."

"So there's nothing you can do."

"I healed their wrists and ankles where the manacles bite so deep. I cooled them in the sun and cleaned the water they been given to drink so it don't make them sick."

Now, finally, Arthur Stuart looked a bit embarrassed—though still defiant. "I never said you wasn't *nice,*" he said.

"Nice is all I can be," said Alvin. "In this time and place. That and I don't plan to give my money to this captain iffen the slaves are going southbound on his boat. I won't help pay for no slave ship."

"He won't even notice the price of our passage."

"Oh, he'll notice, all right," said Alvin. "This Captain Howard is a fellow what can tell how much money you got in your pocket by the smell of it."

"*You* can't even do that," said Arthur Stuart.

"Money's his knack," said Alvin. "That's my guess. He's got him a pilot to steer the ship, and an engineer to keep that steam engine going, and a carpenter to tend the paddlewheel and such damage as the boat takes passing close to the left bank all the way down the Mizzippy. So why is he captain? It's about the money. He knows who's got it, and he knows how to talk it out of them."

"So how much money's he going to think *you* got?"

"Enough money to own a big young slave, but not enough money to afford one what doesn't have such a mouth on him."

Arthur Stuart glared. "You don't own me."

"I told you, Arthur Stuart, I didn't want you on this trip and I still don't. I hate taking you south because I have to pretend you're my property, and I don't know which is worse, you pretending to be a slave, or me pretending to be the kind of man as would own one."

"I'm going and that's that."

"So you keep on saying," said Alvin.

"And you must not mind because you could force me to stay here iffen you wanted."

"Don't say 'iffen,' it drives Peggy crazy when you do."

"She ain't here and you say it your own self."

"The idea is for the younger generation to be an improvement over the older."

"Well, then, you're a mizzable failure, you got to admit, since I been studying makering with you for lo these many years and I can barely make a candle flicker or a stone crack."

"I think you're doing fine, and you're better than that, anyway, if you just put your mind to it."

"I put my mind to it till my head feels like a cannonball."

"I suppose I should have said, Put your heart in it. It's not about *making* the candle or the stone—or the iron chains, for that matter—it's not about *making* them do what you want, it's about *getting* them to do what you want."

"I don't see you setting down and *talking* no iron into bending or deadwood into sprouting twigs, but they do it."

"You may not see me or hear me do it, but I'm doing it all

the same, only they don't understand words, they understand the plan in my heart."

"Sounds like making wishes to me."

"Only because you haven't learned yourself how to do it yet."

"Which means you ain't much of a teacher."

"Neither is Peggy, what with you still saying 'ain't.' "

"Difference is, I know how *not* to say 'ain't' when she's around to hear it," said Arthur Stuart, "only I can't poke out a dent in a tin cup whether you're there or not."

"Could if you cared enough," said Alvin.

"I want to ride on this boat."

"Even if it's a slave ship?" said Alvin.

"Us staying off ain't going to make it any less a slave ship," said Arthur Stuart.

"Ain't you the idealist."

"You ride this *Yazoo Queen,* Master of mine, and you can keep those slaves comfy all the way back to hell."

The mockery in his tone was annoying, but not misplaced, Alvin decided.

"I could do that," said Alvin. "Small blessings can feel big enough, when they're all you got."

"So buy the ticket, cause this boat's supposed to sail first thing in the morning, and we want to be aboard already, don't we?"

Alvin didn't like the mixture of casualness and eagerness in Arthur Stuart's words. "You don't happen to have some plan to set these poor souls free during the voyage, do you? Because you know they'd jump overboard and there ain't a one of them knows how to swim, you can bet on that, so it'd be plain murder to free them."

"I got no such plan."

"I need your promise you won't free them."

"I won't lift a finger to help them," said Arthur Stuart. "I can make my heart as hard as yours whenever I want."

"I hope you don't think that kind of talk makes me glad to have your company," said Alvin. "Specially because I think you know I don't deserve it."

"You telling me you *don't* make your heart hard, to see such sights and do nothing?"

"If I could make my heart hard," said Alvin, "I'd be a worse man, but a happier one."

Then he went off to the booth where the *Yazoo Queen*'s purser was selling passages. Bought him a cheap ticket all the way to Nueva Barcelona, and a servant's passage for his boy. Made him angry just to have to say the words, but he lied with his face and the tone of his voice and the purser didn't seem to notice anything amiss. Or maybe all slave owners were just a little angry with themselves, so Alvin didn't seem much different from any other.

Plain truth of it was, Alvin was about as excited to make this voyage as a man could get. He loved machinery, all the hinges, pistons, elbows of metal, the fire hot as a smithy, the steam pent up in the boilers. He loved the great paddlewheel, turning like the one he grew up with at his father's mill, except here it was the wheel pushing the water, stead of the water pushing the wheel. He loved feeling the strain on the steel—the torque, the compression, the levering, the flexing and cooling. He sent out his doodlebug and wandered around inside the machines, so he'd know it all like he knew his own body.

The engineer was a good man who cared well for his machine, but there was things he couldn't know. Small cracks in the metal, places where the stress was too much, places where the grease wasn't enough and the friction was a-building up. Soon as he understood how it ought to be, Alvin began to teach the metal how to heal itself, how to seal the tiny fractures, how to smooth itself so the friction was less. That boat wasn't more than two hours out of Carthage before he had the machinery about as perfect as a steam engine could get, and then it was just a matter of riding with it. His body, like everybody else's, riding on the gently shifting deck, and his doodlebug skittering through the machinery to feel it pushing and pulling.

But soon enough it didn't need his attention any more, and so the machinery moved to the back of his mind while he began to take an interest in the goings-on among the passengers.

There was people with money in the first-class cabins, with their servants' quarters close at hand. And then people like Alvin, with only a little coin, but enough for the second-class cabins, where there was four passengers to the room. All *their* servants, them as had any, was forced to sleep below decks like the crew, only even more cramped, not because there wasn't room to do better, but because the crew was bound to get surly iffen their bed was as bad as a blackamoor's.

And finally there was the steerage passengers, who didn't even have no beds, but just benches. Them as was going only a short way, a day's journey or so, it made plain good sense to go steerage. But a good many was just poor folks bound for some far-off destination, like Thebes or Corinth or Barcy itself, and if their butts got sore on the benches, well, it wouldn't be the first pain they suffered in their life, nor would it be their last.

Still, Alvin felt like it was kind of his duty, being as how it took him so little effort, to sort of shape the benches to the butts that sat on them. And it took no great trouble to get the lice and bedbugs to move on up to the first-class cabins. Alvin thought of it as kind of an educational project, to help the bugs get a taste of the high life. Blood so fine must be like fancy likker to a louse, and they ought to get some knowledge of it before their short lives was over.

All this took Alvin's concentration for a good little while. Not that he ever gave it his whole attention—that would be too dangerous, in their world where he had enemies out to kill him, and strangers as would wonder what was in his bag that he kept it always so close at hand. So he kept an eye out for all the heartfires on the boat, and if any seemed coming a-purpose toward him, he'd know it, right enough.

Except it didn't work that way. He didn't sense a soul anywheres near him, and then there was a hand right there on his shoulder, and he like to jumped clean overboard with the shock of it.

"What the devil are you—Arthur Stuart, don't sneak up on a body like that."

"It's hard not to sneak with the steam engine making such a racket," said Arthur, but he was a-grinnin' like old Davy Crockett, he was so proud of himself.

"Why is it the one skill you take the trouble to master is the one that causes me the most grief?" asked Alvin.

"I think it's good to know how to hide my . . . heartfire." He said the last word real soft, on account of it didn't do to talk about makery where others might hear and get too curious.

Alvin taught the skill freely to all who took it serious, but he didn't put on a show of it to inquisitive strangers, especially because there was no shortage of them as would remember hearing tales of the runaway smith's apprentice who stole a magic golden plowshare. Didn't matter that the tale was three-fourths fantasy and nine-tenths lie. It could get Alvin kilt or knocked upside the head and robbed all the same, and the one part that was true was that living plow inside his poke, which he didn't want to lose, specially not after carrying it up and down America for half his life now.

"Ain't nobody on this boat can see your heartfire ceptin' me," said Alvin. "So the only reason for you to learn to hide is to hide from the one person you shouldn't hide from anyhow."

"That's plain dumb," said Arthur Stuart. "If there's one person a slave has to hide from, it's his master."

Alvin glared at him. Arthur grinned back.

A voice boomed out from across the deck. "I like to see a man who's easy with his servants!"

Alvin turned to see a smallish man with a big smile and a face that suggested he had a happy opinion of himself.

"My name's Travis," said the fellow. "William Barret Travis, attorney at law, born, bred, and schooled in the Crown Colonies, and now looking for people as need legal work out here on the edge of civilization."

"The folks on either hand of the Hio like to think of theirselves as mostwise civilized," said Alvin, "but then, they haven't been to Camelot to see the King."

"Was I imagining that I heard you speak to your boy there as 'Arthur Stuart'?"

"It was someone else's joke at the naming of the lad," said Alvin, "but I reckon by now the name suits him." All the time Alvin was thinking, What does this man want, that he'd trouble to speak to a sun-browned, strong-armed, thick-headed-looking wight like me?

He could feel a breath for speech coming up in Arthur Stuart, but the last thing Alvin wanted was to deal with whatever fool thing the boy might take it into his head to say. So he gripped him noticeably on the shoulder and it just kind of squeezed the air right out of him without more than a sigh.

"I noticed you've got shoulders on you," said Travis.

"Most folks do," said Alvin. "Two of 'em, nicely matched, one to an arm."

"I almost thought you might be a smith, except smiths always have one huge shoulder, and the other more like a normal man's."

"Except such smiths as use their left hand exactly as often as their right, just so they keep their balance."

Travis chuckled. "Well, then, that solves the mystery. You *are* a smith."

"When I got me a bellows, and charcoal, and iron, and a good pot."

"I don't reckon you carry that around with you in your poke."

"Sir," said Alvin, "I been to Camelot once, and I don't recollect as how it was good manners there to talk about a man's poke or his shoulders neither, upon such short acquaintance."

"Well, of course, it's bad manners all around the world, I'd say, and I apologize. I meant no disrespect. Only I'm recruiting, you see, them as has skills we need, and yet who don't have a firm place in life. Wandering men, you might say."

"Lots of men a-wanderin'," said Alvin, "and not all of them are what they claim."

"But that's why I've accosted you like this, my friend,"

said Travis. "Because you weren't claiming a blessed thing. And on the river, to meet a man with no brag is a pretty good recommendation."

"Then you're new to the river," said Alvin, "because many a man with no brag is afraid of gettin' recognized."

"Recognized," said Travis. "Not 'reckonize.' So you've had you some schooling."

"Not as much as it would take to turn a smith into a gentleman."

"I'm recruiting," said Travis. "For an expedition."

"Smiths in particular need?"

"Strong men good with tools of all kinds," said Travis.

"Got work already, though," said Alvin. "And an errand in Barcy."

"So you wouldn't be interested in trekking out into new lands, which are now in the hands of bloody savages, awaiting the arrival of Christian men to cleanse the land of their awful sacrifices?"

Alvin instantly felt a flush of anger mixed with fear, and as he did whenever so strong a feeling came over him, he smiled brighter than ever and kept hisself as calm as could be. "I reckon you'd have to brave the fog and cross to the west bank of the river for that," said Alvin. "And I hear the reds on that side of the river has some pretty powerful eyes and ears, just watching for whites as think they can take war into peaceable places."

"Oh, you misunderstood me, my friend," said Travis. "I'm not talking about the prairies where one time trappers used to wander and now the reds won't let no white man pass."

"So what savages did you have in mind?"

"South, my friend, south and west. The evil Mexica tribes, that vile race that tears the heart out of a living man upon the tops of their ziggurats."

"That's a long trek indeed," said Alvin. "And a foolish one. What the might of Spain couldn't rule, you think a few Englishmen with a lawyer at their head can conquer?"

By now Travis was leaning on the rail beside Alvin, looking out over the water. "The Mexica have become rotten.

Hated by the other reds they rule, dependent on trade with Spain for second-rate weaponry—I tell you it's ripe for conquest. Besides, how big an army can they put in the field, after killing so many men on their altars for all these centuries?"

"It's a fool as goes looking for a war that no one brought to him."

"Aye, a fool, a whole passel of fools. The kind of fools as wants to be as rich as Pizarro, who conquered the great Inca with a handful of men."

"Or as dead as Cortés?"

"They're all dead now," said Travis. "Or did you think to live forever?"

Alvin was torn between telling the fellow to go pester someone else and leading him on so he could find out more about what he was planning. But in the long run, it wouldn't do to become too familiar with this fellow, Alvin decided. "I reckon I've wasted your time up to now, Mr. Travis. There's others are bound to be more interested than I am, since I got no interest at all."

Travis smiled all the more broadly, but Alvin saw how his pulse leapt up and his heartfire blazed. A man who didn't like being told no, but hid it behind a smile.

"Well, it's good to make a friend all the same," said Travis, sticking out his hand.

"No hard feelings," said Alvin, "and thanks for thinking of me as a man you might want at your side."

"No hard feelings indeed," said Travis, "and though I won't ask you again, if you change your mind I'll greet you with a ready heart and hand."

They shook on it, clapped shoulders, and Travis went on his way without a backward glance.

"Well, well," said Arthur Stuart. "What do you want to bet it isn't no invasion or war, but just a raiding party bent on getting some of that Mexica gold?"

"Hard to guess," said Alvin. "But he talks free enough, for a man proposing to do something forbidden by King and by

Congress. Neither the Crown Colonies nor the United States would have much patience with him if he was caught."

"Oh, I don't know," said Arthur Stuart. "The law's one thing, but what if King Arthur got it in his head that he needed more land and more slaves and didn't want a war with the U.S.A. to get it?"

"Now there's a thought," said Alvin.

"A pretty smart thought, I think," said Arthur Stuart.

"It's doing you good, traveling with me," said Alvin. "Finally getting some sense into your head."

"I thought of it first," said Arthur Stuart.

In answer, Alvin took a letter out of his pocket and showed it to the boy.

"It's from Miz Peggy," said Arthur. He read for a moment. "Oh, now, don't tell me you knew this fellow was going to be on the boat."

"I most certainly did not have any idea," said Alvin. "I figured my inquiries would begin in Nueva Barcelona. But now I've got a good idea *whom* to watch when we get there."

"She talks about a man named Austin," said Arthur Stuart.

"But he'd have men under him," said Alvin. "Men to go out recruiting for him, iffen he hopes to raise an army."

"And he just happened to walk right up to you."

"He just happened to listen to you sassing me," said Alvin, "and figured I wasn't much of a master, so maybe I'd be a natural follower."

Arthur Stuart folded up the letter and handed it back to Alvin. "So if the King *is* putting together an invasion of Mexico, what of it?"

"Iffen he's fighting the Mexica," said Alvin, "he can't be fighting the free states, now, can he?"

"So maybe the slave states won't be so eager to pick a fight," said Arthur Stuart.

"But someday the war with Mexico will end," said Alvin. "Iffen there is a war, that is. And when it ends, either the King lost, in which case he'll be mad and ashamed and spoilin' for trouble, or he won, in which case he'll have a treasury full of Mexica gold, able to buy him a whole navy iffen he wants."

"Miz Peggy wouldn't be too happy to hear you sayin' 'iffen' so much."

"War's a bad thing, when you take after them as haven't done you no harm, and don't mean to."

"But wouldn't it be good to stop all that human sacrifice?"

"I think the reds as are prayin' for relief from the Mexica don't exactly have slavers in mind as their new masters."

"But slavery's better than death, ain't it?"

"Your mother didn't think so," said Alvin. "And now let's have done with such talk. It just makes me sad."

"To think of human sacrifice? Or slavery?"

"No. To hear you talk as if one was better than the other." And with that dark mood on him, Alvin walked to the room that so far he had all to himself, set the golden plow upon the bunk, and curled up around it to think and doze and dream a little and see if he could understand what it all meant, to have this Travis fellow acting so bold about his project, and to have Arthur Stuart be so blind, when so many people had sacrificed so much to keep him free.

It wasn't till they got to Thebes that another passenger was assigned to Alvin's cabin. He'd gone ashore to see the town—which was being touted as the greatest city on the American Nile—and when he came back, there was a man asleep on the very bunk where Alvin had been sleeping.

Which was irksome, but understandable. It was the best bed, being the lower bunk on the side that got sunshine in the cool of the morning instead of the heat of the afternoon. And it's not as if Alvin had left any possessions in the cabin to mark the bed as his own. He carried his poke with him when he left the boat, and all his worldly goods was in it. Lessen you counted the baby that his wife carried inside her—which, come to think of it, she carried around with her about as constantly as Alvin carried the golden plow.

So Alvin didn't wake the fellow up. He just turned and left, looking for Arthur Stuart or a quiet place to eat the

supper he'd brought on board. Arthur had insisted he wanted
to stay aboard, and that was fine with Alvin, but he was
blamed if he was going to hunt him down before eating. It
wasn't no secret that the whistle had blowed the signal for
everyone to come aboard. So Arthur Stuart should have been
watching for Alvin, and he wasn't.

Not that Alvin doubted where he was. He could key right
in on Arthur's heartfire most of the time, and he doubted the
boy could hide from him if Alvin was actually seeking him
out. Right now he knew that the boy was down below in the
slave quarters, a place where no one would ask him his business or wonder where his master was. What he was about
was another matter.

Almost as soon as Alvin opened up his poke to take out
the cornbread and cheese and cider he'd brought in from
town, he could see Arthur start moving up the ladderway to
the deck. Not for the first time, Alvin wondered just how
much the boy really understood of makering.

Arthur Stuart wasn't a liar by nature, but he could keep a
secret, more or less, and wasn't it just possible that he hadn't
quite got around to telling Alvin all that he'd learned how to
do? Was there a chance the boy picked that moment to come
up because he *knew* Alvin was back from town, and *knew* he
was setting hisself down to eat?

Sure enough, Alvin hadn't got but one bite into his first
slice of bread and cheese when Arthur Stuart plunked himself down beside him on the bench. Alvin could've eaten in
the dining room, but there it would have given offense for
him to let his "servant" set beside him. Out on the deck, it
was nobody's business. Might make him look low class, in
the eyes of some slaveowners, but Alvin didn't much mind
what slaveowners thought of him.

"What was it like?" asked Arthur Stuart.

"Bread tastes like bread."

"I didn't mean the bread, for pity's sake!"

"Cheese is pretty good, despite being made from milk that
come from the most measly, mangy, scrawny, fly-bit, swaybacked, half-blind, bony-hipped, ill-tempered, cud-pukin',

sawdust-fed bunch of cattle as ever teetered on the edge of the grave."

"So they don't specialize in fine dairy, is what you're saying."

"I'm saying that if Thebes is spose to be the greatest city on the American Nile, they might oughta start by draining the swamp. I mean, the reason the Hio and the Mizzippy come together here is because it's low ground, and being low ground it gets flooded a lot. It didn't take no scholar to figure that out."

"Never heard of a scholar who knowed low ground from high, anyhow."

"Now, Arthur Stuart, it's not a requirement that scholars be dumb as mud about . . . well, mud."

"Oh, I know. Somewhere there's bound to be a scholar who's got book learnin' *and* common sense, both. He just hasn't come to America."

"Which I spose is proof of the common sense part, bein' as this is the sort of country where they build a great city in the middle of a bog."

They chuckled together and then filled up their mouths too much for talking.

When the food was gone—and Arthur had et more than half of it, and looked like he was wishing for more—Alvin asked him, pretending to be all casual about it, "So what was so interesting down with the servants in the hold?"

"The slaves, you mean?"

"I'm trying to talk like the kind of person as would own one," said Alvin very softly. "And you ought to try to talk like the kind of person as was owned. Or don't come along on trips south."

"I was trying to find out what language those score-and-a-quarter chained-up runaways was talking."

"And?"

"Ain't French, cause there's a Cajun what says not. Ain't Spanish, cause there's a fellow grew up in Cuba what says not. Nary a soul knew their talk."

"Well, at least we know what they're not."

"I know more than that," said Arthur Stuart.

"I'm listening."

"The Cuba fellow, he takes me aside and he says, Tell you what, boy, I think I hear me their kind talk afore, and I says, what's their language, and he says, I think they be no kind runaway."

"Why's he think that?" said Alvin. But inside, he's noticing the way Arthur Stuart picks up exactly the words the fellow said, and the accent, and he remembers how it used to be when Arthur Stuart could do any voice he heard, a perfect mimic. And not just human voices, neither, but birdcalls and animal cries, and a baby crying, and the wind in the trees or the scrape of a shoe on dirt. But that was before Alvin changed him, deep inside, changed the very smell of him so that the Finders couldn't match him up to his sachet no more. He had to change him in the smallest, most hidden parts of him. Cost him part of his knack, it did, and that was a harsh thing to do to a child. But it also saved his freedom. Alvin couldn't regret doing it. But he could regret the cost.

"He says, I hear me their kind talk aforeday, long day ago, when I belong a massuh go Mexico."

Alvin nodded wisely, though he had no idea what this might mean.

"And I says to him, How come black folk be learning Mexica talk? And he says, They be black folk all over Mexico, from aforeday."

"That would make sense," said Alvin. "The Mexica only threw the Spanish out fifty years ago. I reckon they was inspired by Tom Jefferson getting Cherriky free from the King. Spanish must've brought plenty of slaves to Mexico up to then."

"Well, sure," said Arthur Stuart. "So I was wondering, if the Mexica kill so many sacrifices, why didn't they use up these African slaves first? And he says, Black man dirty, Mexica no can cook him up for Mexica god. And then he just laughed and laughed."

"I guess there's advantages to having folks think you're impure by nature."

"Heard a lot of preachers in America say that God thinks *all* men is filthy at heart."

"Arthur Stuart, I know that's a falsehood, because in your life you never been to hear a *lot* of preachers says a blame thing."

"Well, I heard *of* preachers saying such things. Which explains why our God don't hold with human sacrifice. Ain't none of us worthy, white or black."

"Except I don't think that's the opinion God has of his children," said Alvin, "and neither do you."

"I think what I think," said Arthur Stuart. "Ain't always the same thing as you."

"I'm just happy you've taken up thinkin' at all," said Alvin.

"As a hobby," said Arthur Stuart. "I ain't thinkin' of takin' it up as a trade or nothin'."

Alvin gave a chuckle, and Arthur Stuart settled back to enjoy it.

Alvin got to thinking out loud. "So. We got us twenty-five slaves who used to belong to the Mexica. Only now they're going down the Mizzippy on the very same boat as a man recruiting soldiers for an expedition *against* Mexica. That's a downright miraculous coincidence."

"Guides?" said Arthur Stuart.

"I reckon that's likely. Maybe they're wearing chains for the same reason you're pretending to be a slave. So people will think they're one thing, when actually they're another."

"Or maybe somebody's so dumb he thinks that chained-up slaves will be good guides through uncharted land."

"So you're saying maybe they won't be reliable."

"I'm saying maybe they think starving to death all lost in the desert ain't a bad way to die, if they can take some white slaveowners with them."

Alvin nodded. The boy did understand that slaves might prefer death, after all. "Well, I don't speak Mexica, and neither do you."

"Yet," said Arthur Stuart.

"Don't see how you'll learn it," said Alvin. "They don't let nobody near 'em."

"Yet," said Arthur Stuart.

"I hope you ain't got some damn fool plan going on in your head that you're not going to tell me about."

"Don't mind telling you. I already got me a turn feeding them and picking up their slop bucket. The pre-dawn turn, which nobody belowdecks is hankering to do."

"They're guarded day and night. How you going to start talking to them anyway?"

"Come on now, Alvin, you know there must be at least one of them speaks English, or how would they be able to guide anybody anywhere?"

"Or one of them speaks Spanish, and one of the slave-owners speaks it too, you ever think of that?"

"That's why I got the Cuba fellow to teach me Spanish."

That was brag. "I was only gone into town for six hours, Arthur Stuart."

"Well, he didn't teach me *all* of it."

That set Alvin to wondering once again if Arthur Stuart had more of his knack left than he ever let on. Learn a language in six hours? Of course, there was no guarantee that the Cuban slave knew all that much Spanish, any more than he knew all that much English. But what if Arthur Stuart had him a knack for languages? What if he'd never been a mimic at all, but instead a natural speaker-of-all-tongues? There was tales of such—of men and women who could hear a language and speak it like a native right from the start.

Did Arthur Stuart have such a knack? Now that the boy was becoming a man, was he getting a real grasp of it? For a moment Alvin caught himself being envious. And then he had to laugh at himself—imagine a fellow with *his* knack, envying somebody else. I can make rock flow like water, I can make water as strong as steel and as clear as glass, I can turn iron into living gold, and I'm jealous because I can't also learn languages the way a cat learns to land on its feet? The sin of ingratitude, just one of many that's going to get me sent to hell.

"What're you laughing at?" asked Arthur Stuart.

"Just appreciating that you're not a mere boy any more. I trust that if you need any help from me—like somebody catches you talking to them Mexica slaves and starts whipping you—you'll contrive some way to let me know that you need some help?"

"Sure. And if that knife-wielding killer who's sleeping in your bed gets troublesome, I expect you'll find some way to let me know what you want written on your tombstone?" Arthur Stuart grinned at him.

"Knife-wielding killer?" Alvin asked.

"That's the talk belowdecks. But I reckon you'll just ask him yourself, and he'll tell you all about it. That's how you usually do things, isn't it?"

Alvin nodded. "I spose I do start out asking pretty direct what I want to know."

"And so far you mostly haven't got yourself killed," said Arthur Stuart.

"My average is pretty good so far," said Alvin modestly.

"Haven't always found out what you wanted to know, though," said Arthur Stuart.

"But I always find out something useful," said Alvin. "Like, how easy it is to get some folks riled."

"If I didn't know you had another, I'd say that *was* your knack."

"Rilin' folks."

"They do get mad at you pretty much when you say hello, sometimes," said Arthur Stuart.

"Whereas nobody ever gets mad at you."

"I'm a likable fellow," said Arthur Stuart.

"Not always," said Alvin. "You got a bit of brag in you that can be annoying sometimes."

"Not to my friends," said Arthur, grinning.

"No," Alvin conceded. "But it drives your family insane."

By the time Alvin got to his room, the "knife-wielding killer" had woke up from his nap and was somewhere else. Alvin toyed with sleeping in the very same bed, which had been his first, after all. But that was likely to start a fight, and

Alvin just plain didn't care all that much. He was glad to
have a bed at all, come to think of it, and with four bunks in
the room to share between two men, there was no call to be
provoking anybody over who got to which one first.

Drifting off to sleep, Alvin reached out as he always did,
seeking Peggy, making sure from her heartfire that she was
all right. And then the baby, growing fine inside her, had a
heartbeat now. Not going to end like the first pregnancy, with
a baby born too soon so it couldn't get its breath. Not going
to watch it gasp its little life away in a couple of desperate
minutes, turning blue and dying in his arms while he frantically searched inside it for some way to fix it so's it could
live. What good is it to be a seventh son of a seventh son if
the one person you can't heal is your own firstborn baby?

Alvin and Peggy clung together for the first days after that,
but then over the weeks to follow she began to grow apart
from him, to avoid him, until he finally realized that she was
keeping him from being with her to make another baby. He
talked with her then, about how you couldn't hide from it,
lots of folks lost babies, and half-growed children, too, the
thing to do was try again, have another, and another, to comfort you when you thought about the little body in the grave.

"I grew up with two graves before my eyes," she said,
"and knowing how my parents looked at me and saw my
dead sisters with the same name as me."

"Well, you was a torch, so you knew more than children
ought to know about what goes on inside folks. Our baby
most likely won't be a torch. All she'll know is how much we
love her and how much we wanted her."

He wasn't sure he so much persuaded her to want another
baby as she decided to try again just to make him happy. And
during this pregnancy, just like last time, she kept gallivant-
ing up and down the country, working for Abolition even as
she tried to find some way to bring about freedom short of
war. While Alvin stayed in Vigor Church or Hatrack River,
teaching them as wanted to learn the rudiments of makery.

Until she had an errand for him, like now. Sending him
downriver on a steamboat to Nueva Barcelona, when in his

secret heart he just wished she'd stay home with him and let him take care of her.

Course, being a torch she knew perfectly well that was what he wished for, it was no secret at all. So she must need to be apart from him more than he needed to be with her, and he could live with that.

Couldn't stop him from looking for her on the skirts of sleep, and dozing off with her heartfire and the baby's, so bright in his mind.

He woke in the dark, knowing something was wrong. It was a heartfire right up close to him; then he heard the soft breath of a stealthy man. With his doodlebug he got inside the man and felt what he was doing—reaching across Alvin toward the poke that was tucked in the crook of his arm.

Robbery? On board a riverboat was a blame foolish time for it, if that was what the man had in mind. Unless he was a good enough swimmer to get to shore carrying a heavy golden plowshare.

The man carried a knife in a sheath at his belt, but his hand wasn't on it, so he wasn't looking for trouble.

So Alvin spoke up soft as could be. "If you're looking for food, the door's on the other side of the room."

Oh, the man's heart gave a jolt at that! And his first instinct was for his hand to fly to that knife—he was quick at it, too, Alvin could see that it didn't much matter whether his hand was on the knife or not, he was always ready with that blade.

But in a moment the fellow got a hold of hisself, and Alvin could pretty much guess at his reasoning. It was a dark night, and as far as this fellow knew, Alvin couldn't see any better than him.

"You was snoring," said the man. "I was looking to jostle you to get you to roll over."

Alvin knew that was a flat lie. When Peggy had mentioned a snoring problem to him years ago, he studied out what made people snore and fixed his palate so it didn't make that noise any more. He had a rule about not using his knack to benefit himself, but he figured curing his snore was a gift to other people. *He* always slept through it.

Still, he'd let the lie ride. "Why, thank you," said Alvin. "I sleep pretty light, though, so all it takes is you sayin' 'roll over' and I'll do it. Or so my wife tells me."

And then, bold as brass, the fellow as much as confesses what he was doing. "You know, stranger, whatever you got in that sack, you hug it so close to you that somebody might get curious about what's so valuable."

"I've learned that folks get just as curious when I *don't* hug it close, and they feel a mite freer about groping in the dark to get a closer look."

The man chuckled. "So I reckon you ain't planning to tell me much about it."

"I always answer a well-mannered question," said Alvin.

"But since it ain't good manners to ask about what's in your sack," said the man, "I reckon you don't answer such questions at all."

"I'm glad to meet a man who knows good manners."

"Good manners and a knife that don't break off at the stem, that's what keeps me at peace with the world."

"Good manners has always been enough for me," said Alvin. "Though I admit I would have liked that knife better back when it was still a file."

With a bound the man was at the door, his knife drawn. "Who are you, and what do you know about me?"

"I don't know nothing about you, sir," said Alvin. "But I'm a blacksmith, and I know a file that's been made over into a knife. More like a sword, if you ask me."

"I haven't drawn my knife aboard this boat."

"I'm glad to hear it. But when I walked in on *you* asleep, it was still daylight enough to see the size and shape of the sheath you keep it in. Nobody makes a knife that thick at the haft, but it was right proportioned for a file."

"You can't tell something like that just from looking," said the man. "You heard something. Somebody's been talking."

"People are always talking, but not about you," said Alvin.

"I know my trade, as I reckon you know yours. My name's Alvin."

"Alvin Smith, eh?"

"I count myself lucky to have a name. I'd lay good odds that you've got one, too."

The man chuckled and put his knife away. "Jim Bowie."

"Don't sound like a trade name to me."

"It's a Scotch word. Means 'light-haired.' "

"Your hair is dark."

"But I reckon the first Bowie was a blond Viking who liked what he saw while he was busy raping and pillaging in Scotland, and so he stayed."

"One of his children must have got that Viking spirit again and found his way across another sea."

"I'm a Viking through and through," said Bowie. "You guessed right about this knife. I was witness at a duel at a smithy just outside Natchez a few years ago. Things got out of hand when they both missed—I reckon folks came to see blood and didn't want to be disappointed. One fellow managed to put a bullet through my leg, so I thought I was well out of it, until I saw Major Norris Wright setting on a boy half his size and half his age, and that riled me up. Riled me so bad that I clean forgot I was wounded and bleeding like a slaughtered pig. I went berserk and snatched up a blacksmith's file and stuck it clean through his heart."

"You got to be a strong man to do that."

"Oh, it's more than that. I didn't slip it between no ribs. I jammed it right *through* a rib. We Vikings get the strength of giants when we go berserk."

"Am I right to guess that the knife you carry is that very same file?"

"A cutler in Philadelphia reshaped it for me."

"Did it by grinding, not forging," said Alvin.

"That's right."

"Your lucky knife."

"I ain't dead yet."

"Reckon that takes a lot of luck, if you got the habit of reaching over sleeping men to get at their poke."

The smile died on Bowie's face. "Can't help it if I'm curious."

"Oh, I know, I got me the same fault."

"So now it's your turn," said Bowie.

"My turn for what?"

"To tell your story."

"Me? Oh, all I got's a common skinning knife, but I've done my share of wandering in wild lands and it's come in handy."

"You know that's not what I'm asking."

"That's what I'm telling, though."

"I told you about my knife, so you tell me about your sack."

"You tell everybody about your knife," said Alvin, "which makes it so you don't have to use it so much. But I don't tell nobody about my sack."

"That just makes folks more curious," said Bowie. "And some folks might even get suspicious."

"From time to time that happens," said Alvin. He sat up and swung his legs over the side of his bunk and stood. He had already sized up this Bowie fellow and knew that he'd be at least four inches taller, with longer arms and the massive shoulders of a blacksmith. "But I smile so nice their suspicions just go away."

Bowie laughed out loud at that. "You're a big fellow, all right! And you ain't afeared of nobody."

"I'm afraid of lots of folks," said Alvin. "Especially a man can shove a file through a man's rib and ream out his heart."

Bowie nodded at that. "Well, now, ain't that peculiar. Lots of folks been afraid of me in my time. But the more scared they was, the less likely they was to admit it. You're the first one actually said he was afraid of me. So does that make you the *most* scared? Or the least?"

"Tell you what," said Alvin. "You keep your hands off my poke, and we'll never have to find out."

Bowie laughed again—but his grin looked more like a

wildcat snarling at its prey than like an actual smile. "I like you, Alvin Smith."

"I'm glad to hear it," said Alvin.

"I know a man who's looking for fellows like you."

So this Bowie was part of Travis's company. "If you're talking about Mr. Travis, he and I already agreed that he'll go his way and I'll go mine."

"Ah," said Bowie.

"Did you just join up with him in Thebes?"

"I'll tell you about my knife," said Bowie, "but I won't tell you about my business."

"I'll tell you mine," said Alvin. "My business right now is to get back to sleep and see if I can find the dream I was in before you decided to stop me snoring."

"Well, that's a good idea," said Bowie. "And since I haven't been to sleep at all yet tonight, on account of your snoring, I reckon I'll give it a go before the sun comes up."

Alvin lay back down and curled himself around his poke. His back was to Bowie, but of course he kept his doodlebug in him and knew every move he made. The man stood there watching Alvin for a long time, and from the way his heart was beating and the blood rushed around in him, Alvin could tell he was upset. Angry? Afraid? Hard to tell when you couldn't look at a man's face, and not so easy even then. But his heartfire blazed and Alvin figured the fellow was making some kind of decision about him.

Won't get to sleep very soon if he keeps himself all agitated like that, thought Alvin. So he reached inside the fellow and gradually calmed him down, got his heart beating slower, steadied his breathing. Most folks thought that their emotions caused their bodies to get all agitated, but it was the other way around, Alvin knew. The body leads, and the emotions follow.

In a couple of minutes Bowie was relaxed enough to yawn. And soon after, he was fast asleep. With his knife still strapped on, and his hand never far from it.

This Travis fellow had him some interesting friends.

* * *

Arthur Stuart was feeling way too cocky. But if you *know*
you feel too cocky, and you compensate for it by being extra
careful, then being cocky does you no harm, right? Except
maybe it's your cockiness makes you feel like you're safer
than you really are.

That's what Miz Peggy called "circular reasoning" and it
wouldn't get him nowhere. Anywhere. One of them words.
Whatever the rule was. Thinking about Miz Peggy always
got him listening to the way he talked and finding fault with
himself. Only what good would it do him to talk right? All
he'd be is a half-black man who somehow learned to talk like
a gentleman—a kind of trained monkey, that's how they'd
see him. A dog walking on its hind legs. Not an *actual* gentleman.

Which was why he got so cocky, probably. Always wanting to prove something. Not to Alvin, really.

No, *especially* to Alvin. Cause it was Alvin still treated
him like a boy when he was a man now. Treated him like a
son, but he was no man's son.

All this thinking was, of course, doing him no good at all,
when his job was to pick up the foul-smelling slop bucket
and make a slow and lazy job of it so's he'd have time to find
out which of them spoke English or Spanish.

"Quien me compreende?" he whispered. "Who under-
stands me?"

"Todos te compreendemos, pero calle la boca," whispered
the third man. We all understand you, but shut your mouth.
"Los blancos piensan que hay solo uno que hable un poco de
ingles."

Boy howdy, he talked fast, with nothing like the accent the
Cuban had. But still, when Arthur got the feel of a language
in his mind, it wasn't that hard to sort it out. They all spoke
Spanish, but they were pretending that only one of them
spoke a bit of English.

"Quieren fugir de ser esclavos?" Do you want to escape
from slavery?

"La unica puerta es la muerta." The only door is death.

"Al otro lado del rio," said Arthur, "hay rojos que son

amigos nuestros." On the other side of the river there are reds who are friends of ours.

"Sus amigos no son nuestros," answered the man. Your friends aren't ours.

Another man near enough to hear nodded in agreement. "Y ya no puedo nadar." And I can't swim anyway.

"Los blancos, que van a hacer?" What are the whites going to do?

"Piensan en ser conquistadores." Clearly these men didn't think much of their masters' plans. "Los Mexicos van comer sus corazones." The Mexica will eat their hearts.

Another man chimed in. "Tu hablas como cubano." You talk like a Cuban.

"Soy americano," said Arthur Stuart. "Soy libre. Soy . . ." He hadn't learned the Spanish for "citizen." "Soy igual." I'm equal. But not really, he thought. Still, I'm more equal than you.

Several of the Mexica blacks sniffed at that. "Ya hay visto, tu dueño." All Arthur understood was "dueño," owner.

"Es amigo, no dueño." He's my friend, not my master.

Oh, they thought that was hilarious. But of course their laughter was silent, and a few of them glanced at the guard, who was dozing as he leaned against the wall.

"Me de promesa." Promise me. "Cuando el ferro quiebra, no se maten. No salguen sin ayuda." When the iron breaks, don't kill yourselves. Or maybe it meant don't get killed. Anyway, don't leave without help. Or that's what Arthur thought he was saying. They looked at him with total incomprehension.

"Voy quebrar el ferro," Arthur repeated.

One of them mockingly held out his hands. The chains made a noise. Several looked again at the guard.

"No con la mano," said Arthur. "Con la cabeza."

They looked at each other with obvious disappointment. Arthur knew what they were thinking—This boy is crazy. Thinks he can break iron with his head. But he didn't know how to explain it any better.

"Mañana," he said.

They nodded wisely. Not a one of them believed him.

So much for the hours he'd spent learning Spanish. Though maybe the problem was that they just didn't know about makery and couldn't think of a man breaking iron with his mind.

Arthur Stuart knew he could do it. It was one of Alvin's earliest lessons, but it was only on this trip that Arthur had finally understood what Alvin meant. About getting inside the metal. All this time, Arthur had thought it was something he could do by straining real hard with his mind. But it wasn't like that at all. It was easy. Just a sort of turn of his mind. Kind of the way language worked for him. Getting the taste of the language on his tongue, and then trusting how it felt. Like knowing somehow that even though "mano" ended in "o," it still needed "la" in front of it instead of "el." He just knew how it ought to be.

Back in Carthage City, he gave two bits to a man selling sweet bread, and the man was trying to get away with not giving him change. Instead of yelling at him—what good would that do, there on the levee, a half-black boy yelling at a white man?—Arthur just thought about the coin he'd been holding in his hand all morning, how *warm* it was, how right it felt in his own hand. It was like he understood the metal of it, the way he understood the music of language. And thinking of it warm like that, he could see in his mind that it was getting warmer.

He encouraged it, thought of it getting warmer and warmer, and all of a sudden the man cried out and started slapping at the pocket into which he'd dropped the quarter.

It was burning him.

He tried to get it out of his pocket, but it burned his fingers and finally he flung off his coat, flipped down his suspenders, and dropped his trousers, right in front of everybody. Tipped the coin out of his pocket onto the sidewalk, where it sizzled and made the wood start smoking.

Then all the man could think about was the sore place on his leg where the coin had burned him. Arthur Stuart walked up to him, all the time thinking the coin cool again. He reached down and picked it up off the sidewalk. "Reckon you oughta give me my change," he said.

"You get away from me, you black devil," said the man. "You're a wizard, that's what you are. Cursing a man's coin, that's the same as thievin'!"

"That's awful funny, coming from a man who charged me two bits for a five-cent hunk of bread."

Several passersby chimed in.

"Trying to keep the boy's quarter, was you?"

"There's laws against that, even if the boy is black."

"Stealin' from them as can't fight back."

"Pull up your trousers, fool."

A little later, Arthur Stuart got change for his quarter and tried to give the man his nickel, but he wouldn't let Arthur get near him.

Well, I tried, thought Arthur. I'm not a thief.

What I am is, I'm a maker.

No great shakes at it like Alvin, but dadgummit, I thought a quarter hot and it dang near burned its way out of the man's pocket.

If I can do that, then I can learn to do it all, that's what he thought, and that's why he was feeling cocky tonight. Because he'd been practicing every day on anything metal he could get his hands on. Wouldn't do no good to turn the iron hot enough to melt, of course—these slaves wouldn't thank him if he burned their wrists and ankles up in the process of getting their chains off.

No, his project was to make the metal soft without getting it hot. That was a lot harder than hetting it up. Lots of times he'd caught himself straining again, trying to *push* softness onto the metal. But when he relaxed into it again and got the feel of the metal into his head like a song, he gradually began to get the knack of it again. Turned his own belt buckle so soft he could bend it into any shape he wanted. Though after a few minutes he realized the shape he wanted it in was like a belt buckle, since he still needed it to hold his pants up.

Brass was easier than iron, since it was softer in the first

place. And it's not like Arthur Stuart was fast. He'd seen
Alvin turn a gun barrel soft while a man was in the process
of shooting it at him, that's how quick *he* was. But Arthur
Stuart had to ponder on it first. Twenty-five slaves, each with
an iron band at his ankle and another at his wrist. He had to
make sure they all waited till the last one was free. If any of
them bolted early, they'd all be caught.

Course, he could ask Alvin to help him. But he already
had Alvin's answer. Leave 'em slaves, that's what Alvin had
decided. But Arthur wouldn't do it. These men were in his
hands. He was a maker now, after his own fashion, and it was
up to him to decide for himself when it was right to act and
right to let be. He couldn't do what Alvin did, healing folks
and getting animals to do his bidding and turning water into
glass. But he could soften iron, by damn, and so he'd set
these men free.

Tomorrow night.

Next morning they passed from the Hio into the Mizzippy,
and for the first time in years Alvin got a look at Tenskwa
Tawa's fog on the river.

It was like moving into a wall. Sunny sky, not a cloud, and
when you look ahead it really didn't look like much, just a
little mist on the river. But all of a sudden you couldn't see
more than a hundred yards ahead of you—and that was only
if you were headed up or down the river. If you kept going
straight across to the right bank, it was like you went blind,
you couldn't even see the front of your own boat.

It was the fence that Tenskwa Tawa had built to protect the
reds who moved west after the failure of Ta-Kumsaw's war.
All the reds who didn't want to live under white man's law, all
the reds who were done with war, they crossed over the water
into the West, and then Tenskwa Tawa . . . closed the door behind them.

Alvin had heard tales of the West from trappers who used
to go there. They talked of mountains so sharp with stone, so
rugged and high that they had snow on them clear into June.
Places where the ground itself spat hot water fifty feet into

the sky, or higher. Herds of buffalo so big they could pass by you all day and night, and next morning it still looked like there was just as many as yesterday. Grassland and desert, pine forest and lakes like jewels nestled among mountains so high that if you climbed to the top you ran out of air.

And all that was now red land, where whites would never go again. That's what this fog was all about.

Except for Alvin. He knew that if he wanted to, he could dispel that fog and cross over. Not only that, but he wouldn't be killed, neither. Tenskwa Tawa had said so, and there'd be no red man who'd go against the Prophet's law.

A part of him wanted to put to shore, wait for the riverboat to move on, and then get him a canoe and paddle across the river and look for his old friend and teacher. It would be good to talk to him about all that was going on in the world. About the rumors of war coming, between the United States and the Crown Colonies—or maybe between the free states and slave states within the U.S.A. About rumors of war with Spain to get control of the mouth of the Mizzippy, or war between the Crown Colonies and England.

And now this rumor of war with the Mexica. What would Tenskwa Tawa make of that? Maybe he had troubles of his own—maybe he was working even now to make an alliance of reds to head south and defend their lands against men who dragged their captives to the tops of their ziggurats and tore their hearts out to satisfy their god.

Anyway, that's the kind of thing going through Alvin's mind as he leaned on the rail on the right side of the boat— the stabberd side, that was, though why boatmen should have different words for "right" and "left" made no sense to him. He was just standing there looking out into the fog and seeing no more than any other man, when he noticed something, not with his eyes, but with that inward vision that saw heart-fires.

There was a couple of men out on the water, right out in the middle where they wouldn't be able to tell up from down. Spinning round and round, they were, and scared. It took only a moment to get the sense of it. Two men on a raft, only they didn't have drags under the raft and had it loaded front-heavy. Not boatmen, then. Had to be a homemade raft, and when their tiller broke they didn't know how to get the raft to keep its head straight downriver. At the mercy of the current, that's what, and no way of knowing what was happening five feet away.

Though it wasn't as if the *Yazoo Queen* was quiet. Still, fog had a way of damping down sounds. And even if they heard the riverboat, would they know what the sound was? To terrified men, it might sound like some kind of monster moving along the river.

Well, what could Alvin do about it? How could he claim to see what no one else could make out? And the flow of the river was too strong and complicated for him to get control of it, to steer the raft closer.

Time for some lying. Alvin turned around and shouted. "Did you hear that? Did you see them? Raft out of control on the river! Men on a raft, they were calling for help, spinning around out there!"

In no time the pilot and captain both were leaning over the rail of the pilot's deck. "I don't see a thing!" shouted the pilot.

"Not *now*," said Alvin. "But I saw 'em plain just a second ago, they're not far."

Captain Howard could see the drift of things and he didn't like it. "I'm not taking the *Yazoo Queen* any deeper into this fog than she already is! No sir! They'll fetch up on the bank farther downriver, it's no business of ours!"

"Law of the river!" shouted Alvin. "Men in distress!"

That gave the pilot pause. It *was* the law. You had to give aid.

"I don't see no men in distress!" shouted Captain Howard.

"So don't turn the big boat," said Alvin. "Let me take that little rowboat and I'll go fetch 'em."

Captain didn't like that either, but the pilot was a decent man and pretty soon Alvin was in the water with his hands on the oars.

But before he could fair get away, there was Arthur Stuart,

leaping over the gap and sprawling into the little boat. "That was about as clumsy a move as I ever saw," said Alvin.

"I ain't gonna miss this," said Arthur Stuart.

There was another man at the rail, hailing him. "Don't be in such a hurry, Mr. Smith!" shouted Jim Bowie. "Two strong men is better than one on a job like this!" And then he, too, was leaping—a fair job of it, too, considering he must be at least ten years older than Alvin and a good twenty years older than Arthur Stuart. But when he landed, there was no sprawl about it, and Alvin wondered what this man's knack was. He had supposed it was killing, but maybe the killing was just a sideline. The man fair to flew.

So there they were, each of them at a set of oars while Arthur Stuart sat in the stern and kept his eye peeled.

"How far are they?" he kept asking.

"The current might of took them farther out," said Alvin. "But they're there."

And when Arthur started looking downright skeptical, Alvin fixed him with such a glare that Arthur Stuart finally got it. "I think I see 'em," he said, giving Alvin's lie a boost.

"You ain't trying to cross this whole river and get us kilt by reds," said Jim Bowie.

"No sir," said Alvin. "Got no such plan. I saw those boys, plain as day, and I don't want their death on my conscience."

"Well where are they now?"

Of course Alvin knew, and he was rowing toward them as best he could. Trouble was that Jim Bowie didn't know where they were, and he was rowing too, only not quite in the same direction as Alvin. And seeing as how both of them had their backs to where the raft was, Alvin couldn't even pretend to see them. He could only try to row stronger than Bowie in the direction he wanted to go.

Until Arthur Stuart rolled his eyes and said, "Would you two just stop pretending that anybody believes anybody, and row in the right direction?"

Bowie laughed. Alvin sighed.

"You didn't see nothin'," said Bowie. "Cause I was watching you looking out into the fog."

"Which is why you came along."

"Had to find out what you wanted to do with this boat."

"I want to rescue two lads on a flatboat that's spinning out of control on the current."

"You mean that's *true*?"

Alvin nodded, and Bowie laughed again. "Well I'm jiggered."

"That's between you and your jig," said Alvin. "More downstream, please."

"So what's your knack, man?" said Bowie. "Seeing through fog?"

"Looks like, don't it?"

"I think not," said Bowie. "I think there's a lot more to you than meets the eye."

Arthur Stuart looked Alvin's massive blacksmith's body up and down. "Is that *possible*?"

"And you're no slave," said Bowie.

There was no laugh when he said *that*. That was dangerous for any man to know.

"Am so," said Arthur Stuart.

"No slave would answer back like that, you poor fool," said Bowie. "You got such a mouth on you, there's no way you ever had a taste of the lash."

"Oh, it's a *good* idea for you to come with me on this trip," said Alvin.

"Don't worry," said Bowie. "I got secrets of my own. I can keep yours."

Can—but will you? "Not much of a secret," said Alvin. "I'll just have to take him back north and come down later on another steamboat."

"Your arms and shoulders tell me you really are a smith," said Bowie. "But. Ain't no smith alive can look at a knife in its sheath and say it used to be a file."

"I'm good at what I do," said Alvin.

"Alvin Smith. You really ought to start traveling under another name."

"Why?"

"You're the smith what killed a couple of Finders a few years back."

"Finders who murdered my wife's mother."

"Oh, no jury would convict you," said Bowie. "No more than I got convicted for *my* killing. Looks to me like we got a lot in common."

"Less than you might think."

"Same Alvin Smith who absconded from his master with a particular item."

"A lie," said Alvin. "And he knows it."

"Oh, I'm sure it is. But so the story goes."

"You can't believe these tales."

"Oh, I know," said Bowie. "You aren't slacking off in your rowing, are you?"

"I'm not sure I want to overtake that raft while we're still having this conversation."

"I was just telling you, in my own quiet way, that I think I know what you got in that sack of yours. Some powerful knack you got, if the rumors are true."

"What do they say, that I can fly?"

"You can turn iron to gold, they say."

"Wouldn't that be nice," said Alvin.

"But you didn't deny it, did you?"

"I can't make iron into anything but horseshoes and hinges."

"You did it once, though, didn't you?"

"No sir," said Alvin. "I told you those stories were lies."

"I don't believe you."

"Then you're calling me a liar, sir," said Alvin.

"Oh, you're not going to take offense, are you? Because I have a way of winning all my duels."

Alvin didn't answer, and Bowie looked long and hard at Arthur Stuart. "Ah," said Bowie. "That's the way of it."

"What?" said Arthur Stuart.

"You ain't askeered of me," said Bowie, exaggerating his accent.

"Am so," said Arthur Stuart.

"You're scared of what I know, but you ain't a-scared of me taking down your 'master' in a duel."

"Terrified," said Arthur Stuart.

It was only a split second, but there were Bowie's oars a-dangling, and his knife out of its sheath and his body twisted around with his knife right at Alvin's throat.

Except that it wasn't a knife anymore. Just a handle.

The smile left Bowie's face pretty slow when he realized that his precious knife-made-from-a-file no longer had any iron in it.

"What did you do?" he asked.

"That's a pretty funny question," said Alvin, "coming from a man who meant to kill me."

"Meant to scare you is all," said Bowie. "You didn't have to do that to my knife."

"I got no knack for knowing a man's intentions," said Alvin. "Now turn around and row."

Bowie turned around and took hold of the oars again. "That knife was my luck."

"Then I reckon you just run out of it," said Alvin.

Arthur Stuart shook his head. "You oughta take more care about who you draw against, Mr. Bowie."

"You're the man we want," said Bowie. "That's all I wanted to say. Didn't have to wreck my knife."

"Next time you look to get a man on your team," said Alvin, "don't draw a knife on him."

"And don't threaten to tell his secrets," said Arthur Stuart.

And now, for the first time, Bowie looked more worried than peeved. "Now, I never said I *knew* your secrets. I just had some guesses, that's all."

"Well, Arthur Stuart, Mr. Bowie just noticed he's out here in the middle of the river, in the fog, on a dangerous rescue mission, with a couple of people whose secrets he threatened to tell."

"It's a position to give a man pause," said Arthur Stuart.

"I won't go out of this boat without a struggle," said Bowie.

"I don't plan to hurt you," said Alvin. "Because we're not alike, you and me. I killed a man once, in grief and rage, and I've regretted it ever since."

"Me too," said Bowie.

"It's the proudest moment of your life. You saved the weapon and called it your luck. We're not alike at all."

"I reckon not."

"And if I want you dead," said Alvin, "I don't have to throw you out of no boat."

Bowie nodded. And then took his hands off the oars. His hands began to flutter around his cheeks, around his mouth.

"Can't breathe, can you?" said Alvin. "Nobody's blocking you. Just do it, man. Breathe in, breathe out. You been doing it all your life."

It wasn't like Bowie was choking. He just couldn't get his body to do his will.

Alvin didn't keep it going till the man turned blue or nothing. Just long enough for Bowie to feel real helpless. And then he remembered how to breathe, just like that, and sucked in the air.

"So now that we've settled the fact that you're in no danger from me here on this boat," said Alvin, "let's rescue a couple of fellows got themselves on a homemade raft that got no drag."

And at that moment, the whiteness of the fog before them turned into a flatboat not five feet away. Another pull on the oars and they bumped it. Which was the first time the men on the raft had any idea that anybody was coming after them.

Arthur Stuart was already clambering to the bow of the boat, holding onto the stern rope and leaping onto the raft to make it fast.

"Lord be praised," said the smaller of the two men.

"You come at a right handy time," said the tall one, helping Arthur make the line fast. "Got us an unreliable raft here, and in this fog we wasn't even seeing that much of the countryside. A second-rate voyage by any reckoning."

Alvin laughed at that. "Glad to see you've kept your spirits up."

"Oh, we was both praying and singing hymns," said the lanky man.

"How tall *are* you?" said Arthur Stuart as the man loomed over him.

"About a head higher than my shoulders," said the man, "but not quite long enough for my suspenders."

The fellow had a way about him, right enough. You just couldn't help but like him.

Which made Alvin suspicious right off. If that was the man's knack, then he couldn't be trusted. And yet the most cussed thing about it was, even while you wasn't trusting him, you still had to like him.

"What are you, a lawyer?" asked Alvin.

By now they had maneuvered the boat to the front of the raft, ready to tug it along behind them as they rejoined the riverboat.

The man stood to his full height and then bowed, as awkward looking a maneuver as Alvin had ever seen. He was all knees and elbows, angles everywhere, even his face, nothing soft about him, as bony a fellow as could be. No doubt about it, he was ugly. Eyebrows like an ape's, they protruded so far out over his yes. And yet . . . he wasn't bad to look at. Made you feel warm and welcome, when he smiled.

"Abraham Lincoln of Springfield, at your service, gentlemen," he said.

"And I'm Cuz Johnston of Springfield," said the other man.

"Cuz for 'Cousin,' " said Abraham. "Everybody calls him that."

"They do *now*," said Cuz.

"*Whose* cousin?" asked Arthur Stuart.

"Not mine," said Abraham. "But he looks like a cousin, don't he? He's the epitome of cousinhood, the quintessence of cousiniferosity. So when I started calling him Cuz, it was just stating the obvious."

"Actually, I'm his father's second wife's son by her first husband," said Cuz.

"Which makes us step-strangers," said Abraham. "In-law."

"I'm particularly grateful to you boys for pickin' us up,"

said Cuz, "on account of now old Abe here won't have to finish the most obnoxious tall tale I ever heard."

"It wasn't no tall tale," said old Abe. "I heard it from a man named Taleswapper. He had it in his book, and he didn't never put anything in it lessen it was true."

Old Abe—who couldn't have been more than thirty—was quick of eye. He saw the glance that passed between Alvin and Arthur Stuart.

"So you know him?" asked Abe.

"A truthful man, he is indeed," said Alvin. "What tale did he tell you?"

"Of a child born many years ago," said Abe. "A tragic tale of a brother who got kilt by a tree trunk carried downstream by a flood, which hit him while he was a-saving his mother, who was in a wagon in the middle of the stream, giving birth. But doomed as he was, he stayed alive long enough on that river that when the baby was born, it was the seventh son of a seventh son, and all the sons alive."

"A noble tale," said Alvin. "I've seen that one in his book my own self."

"And you believe it?"

"I do," said Alvin.

"I never said it wasn't true," said Cuz. "I just said it wasn't the tale a man wants to hear when he's spinning downstream on a flapdoodle flatboat in the midst of the Mizzippy mist."

Abe Lincoln ignored the near-poetic language of his companion. "So I was telling Cuz here that the river hadn't treated us half bad, compared to what a much smaller stream done to the folks in that story. And now here *you* are, saving us—so the river's been downright kind to a couple of second-rate raftmakers."

"Made this one yourself, eh?" said Alvin.

"Tiller broke," said Abe.

"Didn't have no spare?" said Alvin.

"Didn't know I'd need one. But if we ever once fetched up on shore, I could have made another."

"Good with your hands?"

"Not really," said Abe. "But I'm willing to do it over till it's right."

Alvin laughed. "Well, time to do this raft over."

"I'd welcome it if you'd show me what we done wrong. I can't see a blame thing here that isn't good raftmaking."

"It's what's under the raft that's missing. Or rather, what ought to be there but ain't. You need a drag at the stern, to keep the back in back. And on top of that you've got it heavy-loaded in front, so it's bound to turn around any old way."

"Well I'm blamed," said Abe. "No doubt about it, I'm not cut out to be a boatman."

"Most folks aren't," said Alvin. "Except my friend Mr. Bowie here. He's just can't keep away from a boat, when he gets a chance to row."

Bowie gave a tight little smile and a nod to Abe and his companion. By now the raft was slogging along behind them in the water, and it was all Alvin and Bowie could do to move it forward.

"Maybe," said Arthur Stuart, "the two of you could stand at the *back* of the raft so it didn't dig so deep in front and make it such a hard pull."

Embarrassed, Abe and Cuz did so at once. And in the thick fog of midstream, it made them mostly invisible and damped down any sound they made so that conversation was nigh impossible.

It took a good while to overtake the steamboat, but the pilot, being a good man, had taken it slow, despite Captain Howard's ire over time lost, and all of a sudden the fog thinned and the noise of the paddlewheel was right beside them as the *Yazoo Queen* loomed out of the fog.

"I'll be plucked and roasted," shouted Abe. "That's a right fine steamboat you got here."

" 'Tain't our'n," said Alvin.

Arthur Stuart noticed how little time it took Bowie to get himself up on deck and away from the boat, shrugging off all the hands clapping at his shoulder like he was a hero. Well, Arthur couldn't blame him. But it was a sure thing that however Alvin might have scared him out on the water, Bowie was still a danger to them both.

Once the dinghy was tied to the *Yazoo Queen,* and the raft lashed alongside as well, there was all kinds of chatter from passengers wanting to know obvious things like how they ever managed to find each other in the famous Mizzippy fog.

"It's like I said," Alvin told them. "They was right close, and even then, we still had to search."

Abe Lincoln heard it with a grin, and didn't say a word to contradict him, but he was no fool, Arthur Stuart could see that. He knew that the raft had been nowheres near the riverboat. He also knew that Alvin had steered straight for the *Yazoo Queen* as if he could see it.

But what was that to him? In no time he was telling all who cared to listen about what a blame fool job he'd done a-making the raft, and how dizzy they got spinning round and round in the fog. "It twisted me up into such a knot that it took the two of us half a day to figure out how to untie my arms from my legs and get my head back out from my armpit." It wasn't all that funny, really, but the way he told it, he got such a laugh. Even though the story wasn't likely to end up in Taleswapper's book.

Well, that night they put to shore at a built-up rivertown and there was so much coming and going on the *Yazoo Queen* that Arthur Stuart gave up on his plan to set the twenty-five Mexica slaves free that night.

Instead, he and Alvin went to a lecture being held in the dining room of the riverboat. The speaker was none other than Cassius Marcellus Clay, the noted antislavery orator, who persisted in his mad course of lecturing against slavery right in the midst of slave country. But listening to him, Arthur Stuart could see how the man got away with it. He didn't call names or declare slavery to be a terrible sin. Instead he talked about how much harm slavery did to the owners and their families.

"What does it do to a man, to raise up his children to believe that their own hands never have to be set to labor? What will happen when he's old, and these children who never learned to work freely spend his money without heed for the morrow?

"And when these same children have seen their fellow human, however dusky of hue his skin might be, treated with disdain, their labor dispraised and their freedom treated as naught—will they hesitate to treat their aging father as a thing of no value, to be discarded when he is no longer useful? For when one human being is treated as a commodity, why should children not learn to think of all humans as either useful or useless, and discard all those in the latter category?"

Arthur Stuart had heard plenty of Abolitionists speak over the years, but this one took the cake. Cause instead of stirring up a mob of slaveowners wanting to tar and feather him, or worse, he got them looking all thoughtful and glancing at each other uneasily, probably thinking on their own children and what a useless set of grubs they no doubt were.

In the end, though, it wasn't likely Clay was doing all that much good. What were they going to do, set their slaves free and move north? That would be like the story in the Bible, where Jesus told the rich young man, Sell all you got and give it unto the poor and come follow me. The wealth of these men was measured in slaves. To give them up was to become poor, or at least to join the middling sort of men who have to pay for what labor they hire. Renting a man's back, so to speak, instead of owning it. None of them had the courage to do it, at least not that Arthur Stuart saw.

But he noticed that Abe Lincoln seemed to be listening real close to everything Clay said, eyes shining. Especially when Clay talked about them as wanted to send black folks back to Africa. "How many of you would be glad to hear of a plan to send *you* back to England or Scotland or Germany or whatever place your ancestors came from? Rich or poor, bond or free, we're Americans now, and slaves whose grandparents were born on this soil can't be sent *back* to Africa, for it's no more their home than China is, or India."

Abe nodded at that, and Arthur Stuart got the impression

that up to now, the lanky fellow probably thought that the way to solve the black problem was exactly that, to ship 'em back to Africa.

"And what of the mulatto? The light-skinned black man who partakes of the blood of Europe and Africa in equal parts? Shall such folk be split in two like a rail, and the pieces divvied up between the lands of their ancestry? No, like it or not we're all bound together in this land, yoked together. When you enslave a black man, you enslave yourself as well, for now you are bound to him as surely as he is bound to you, and your character is shaped by his bondage as surely as his own is. Make the black man servile, and in the same process you make yourself tyrannical. Make the black man quiver in fear before you, and you make yourself a monster of terror. Do you think your children will not see you in that state, and fear you, too? You cannot wear one face to the slave and another face to your family, and expect either face to be believed."

When the talk was over, and before Arthur and Alvin separated to their sleeping places, they had a moment together at the rail overlooking the flatboat. "How can anybody hear that talk," said Arthur Stuart, "and go home to their slaves, and not set them free?"

"Well, for one thing," said Alvin, "I'm not setting *you* free."

"Because you're only pretending I'm a slave," whispered Arthur.

"Then I *could* pretend to set you free, and be a good example for the others."

"No you can't," said Arthur Stuart, "because then what would you do with me?"

Alvin just smiled a little and nodded, and Arthur Stuart got his point. "I didn't say it would be easy. But if everybody would do it—"

"But everybody won't do it," said Alvin. "So them as free their slaves, they're suddenly poor, while them as don't free them, they stay rich. So now who has all the power in slavery country? Them as keep their slaves."

"So there's no hope."

"It has to be all at once, by law, not bit by bit. As long as it's permitted to keep slaves anywhere, then bad men will own them and get advantage from it. You have to ban it outright. That's what I can't get Peggy to understand. All her persuasion in the end will come to nothing, because the moment somebody stops being a slaveowner, he loses all his influence among those who have kept their slaves."

"Congress can't ban slavery in the Crown Colonies, and the King can't ban it in the States. So no matter what you do, you're gonna have one place that's got slaves and the other that doesn't."

"It's going to be war," said Alvin. "Sooner or later, as the free states get sick of slavery and the slave states get more dependent on it, there'll be a revolution on one side of the line or the other. I think there won't be freedom until the King falls and his Crown Colonies become states in the Union."

"That'll never happen."

"I think it will," said Alvin. "But the bloodshed will be terrible. Because people fight most fiercely when they dare not admit even to themselves that their cause is unjust." He spat into the water. "Go to bed, Arthur Stuart."

But Arthur couldn't sleep. Having Cassius Clay speaking on the riverboat had got the belowdecks folks into a state, and some of them were quite angry at Clay for making white folks feel guilty. "Mark my words," said a fellow from Kenituck. "When they get feelin' guilty, then the only way to feel better is to talk theirself into believing we *deserve* to be slaves, and if we deserve to be slaves, we must be very bad and need to be punished all the time."

It sounded pretty convoluted to Arthur Stuart, but then he was only a baby when his mother carried him to freedom, so it's not like he knew what he was talking about in an argument about what slavery was really like.

Even when things finally quieted down, though, Arthur couldn't sleep, until finally he got up and crept up the ladderway to the deck.

It was a moonlit night, here on the east bank, where the fog was only a low mist and you could look up and see stars.

The twenty-five Mexica slaves were asleep on the stern deck, some of them mumbling softly in their sleep. The guard was asleep, too.

I meant to free you tonight, thought Arthur. But it would take too long now. I'd never be done by morning.

And then it occurred to him that maybe it wasn't so. Maybe he could do it faster than he thought.

So he sat down in a shadow and after a couple of false starts, he got the nearest slave's ankle iron into his mind and began to sense the metal the way he had that coin. Began to soften it as he had softened his belt buckle.

Trouble was, the iron ring was thicker and had more metal in it than either the coin or the buckle had had. By the time he got one part softened up, another part was hard again, and so it went. It began to feel like the story Peggy read them about Sisyphus, whose time in Hades was spent pushing a stone up a mountain, but for every step up, he slid two steps back, so after working all day he was farther from the top than he was when he began.

And then he almost cussed out loud at how stupid he had been.

He didn't have to soften the whole ring. What were they going to do, slide it off like a sleeve? All he had to do was soften it at the hinge, where the metal was thinnest and weakest.

He gave it a try and it was getting all nice and soft when he realized something.

The hinges weren't connected. The one side wasn't joined to the other. The pin was gone.

He took one fetter after another into his mind and discovered they were all the same. Every single hinge pin was missing. Every single slave was already free.

He got up from the shadows and walked out to stand among the slaves.

They weren't asleep. They made tiny hand gestures to tell Arthur to go away, to get out of sight.

So he went back into the shadows.

As if at a signal, they all opened their fetters and set the chains gently on the deck. It made a bit of a racket, of course, but the guard didn't stir. Nor did anyone else in the silent boat.

Then the black men arose and swung themselves over the side away from shore.

They're going to drown. Nobody taught slaves to swim, or let them learn it on their own. They were choosing death.

Except that, come to think of it, Arthur didn't hear a single splash.

He stood up when all the slaves were gone from the deck and walked to another part of the rail. Sure enough, they were overboard all right—all gathered on the raft. And now they were carefully loading Abe Lincoln's cargo into the dinghy. It wasn't much of a dinghy, but it wasn't much of a cargo, either, and it didn't take long.

What difference did it make, not to steal Abe's stuff? They were all thieves, anyway, since they were stealing themselves by running away. Or that was the theory, anyway. As if a man, by being free, thereby stole something from someone else.

They laid themselves down on the raft, all twenty-five, making a veritable pile of humanity, and with those at the edges using their hands as paddles, they began to pull away out into the current. Heading out into the fog, toward the red man's shore.

Someone laid a hand on his shoulder and he near jumped out of his skin.

It was Alvin, of course.

"Let's not be seen here," Alvin said softly. "Let's go below."

So Arthur Stuart led the way down into the slave quarters, and soon they were in whispered conversation in the kitchen, which was dark but for a single lantern that Alvin kept trimmed low.

"I figured you'd have some blame fool plan like that," said Alvin.

"And I thought you was going to let them go on as slaves like you didn't care, but I should've knowed better," said Arthur Stuart.

"I thought so, too," said Alvin. "But I don't know if it was having Jim Bowie guess too much, or him trying to kill me with that knife—and no, Arthur Stuart, he did *not* stop in time, if there'd been a blade in that knife it would have cut right through my throat. Could have been the fear of death made me think that I didn't want to face God knowing I could have freed twenty-five men, but chose to leave them slaves. Then again, it might of been Mr. Clay's sermon tonight. Converted me as neat as you please."

"Converted Mr. Lincoln," said Arthur Stuart.

"Might be," said Alvin. "Though he doesn't look like the sort who ever sought to own another man."

"I know why you had to do it," said Arthur Stuart.

"Why is that?"

"Because you knew that if you didn't, I would."

Alvin shrugged. "Well, I knew you'd made up your mind to try."

"I could have done it."

"Very slowly."

"It was working, once I realized I only had to go after the hinge."

"I reckon so," said Alvin. "But the real reason I chose tonight was that the raft was here. A gift to us, don't you think? Woulda been a shame not to use it."

"So what happens when they get to the red man's shore?"

"Tenskwa Tawa will see to them. I gave them a token to show to the first red they meet. When they see it, they'll get escorted straight to the Prophet, wherever he might be. And when *he* sees it, he'll give them safe passage. Or maybe let them dwell there."

"Or maybe he'll need them, to help him fight the Mexica. If they're moving north."

"Maybe."

"What was the token?" asked Arthur Stuart.

"A couple of these," said Alvin. He held up a tiny

shimmering cube that looked like the clearest ice that had ever been, or maybe glass, but no glass had ever shimmered.

Arthur Stuart took it in his hand and realized what it was. "This is water. A box of water."

"More like a block of water. I decided to make it today out on the river, when I came so close to having my blood spill into the water. That's partly how they're made. A bit of my own self has to go into the water to make it strong as steel. You know the law. 'The maker is the one . . .' "

"The maker is the one who is part of what he makes," said Arthur Stuart.

"Get to sleep," said Alvin. "We can't let nobody know we was up tonight. I can't keep them all asleep forever."

"Can I keep this?" said Arthur Stuart. "I think I see something in it."

"You can see everything in it, if you look long enough," said Alvin. "But no, you can't keep it. If you think what I got in my poke is valuable, think what folks would do to have a solid block of water that showed them true visions of things far and near, past and present."

Arthur reached out and offered the cube to Alvin.

But instead of taking it, Alvin only smiled, and the cube went liquid all at once and dribbled through Arthur Stuart's fingers. Arthur looked at the puddle on the table, feeling as forlorn as he ever had.

"It's just water," said Alvin.

"And a little bit of blood."

"Naw," said Alvin. "I took that back."

"Good night," said Arthur Stuart. "And . . . thank you for setting them free."

"Once you set your heart on it, Arthur, what else could I do? I looked at them and thought, Somebody loved them once as much as your mamma loved you. She died to set you free. I didn't have to do that. Just inconvenience myself a little. Put myself at risk, but not by much."

"But you saw what I did, didn't you? I made it soft without getting it hot."

"You done good, Arthur Stuart. There's no denying it. You're a maker now."

"Not much of one."

"Whenever you got two makers, one's going to be more of a maker than the other. But lessen that one starts gettin' uppity, it's good to remember that there's always a third one who's better than both of them."

"Who's better than you?" asked Arthur Stuart.

"You," said Alvin. "Because I'll take an ounce of compassion over a pound of tricks any day. Now go to sleep."

Only then did Arthur let himself feel how very, very tired he was. Whatever had kept him awake before, it was gone now. He barely made it to his cot before he fell asleep.

Oh, there was a hullabaloo in the morning. Suspicions flew every which way. Some folks thought it was the boys from the raft, because why else would the slaves have left their cargo behind? Until somebody pointed out that with the cargo still on the raft, there wouldn't have been room for all the runaways.

Then suspicion fell on the guard who had slept, but most folks knew that was wrong, because if he had done it then why didn't he run off, instead of lying there asleep on the deck till a crewman noticed the slaves was gone and raised the alarm?

Only now, when they were gone, did the ownership of the slaves become clear. Alvin had figured Mr. Travis to have a hand in it, but the man most livid at their loss was Captain Howard hisself. That was a surprise. But it explained why the men bound for Mexico had chosen this boat to make their journey downriver.

To Alvin's surprise, though, Travis and Howard both kept glancing at him and young Arthur Stuart as if they suspected the truth. Well, he shouldn't have been surprised, he realized. If Bowie told them what had happened to his knife out on the water, they'd naturally wonder if a man with such power over iron might have been the one to slip the hinge pins out of all the fetters.

Slowly the crowd dispersed. But not Captain Howard, not Travis. And when Alvin and Arthur made as if to go, Howard headed straight for them. "I want to talk to you," he said, and he didn't sound friendly.

"What about?" said Alvin.

"That boy of yours," said Howard. "I saw how he was doing their slops on the morning watch. I saw him talking to them. That made me suspicious, all right, since not one of them spoke English."

"Pero todos hablaban español," said Arthur Stuart.

Travis apparently understood him, and looked chagrined. "They *all* of them spoke Spanish? Lying skunks."

Oh, right, as if slaves owed you some kind of honesty.

"That's as good as a confession," said Captain Howard. "He just admitted he speaks their language and learned things from them that even their master didn't know."

Arthur was going to protest, but Alvin put a hand on his shoulder. He did *not,* however, stop his mouth. "My boy here," said Alvin, "only just learned to speak Spanish, so naturally he seized on an opportunity to practice. Unless you got some evidence that those fetters was opened by use of a slop bucket, then I think you can safely leave this boy out of it."

"No, I expect he *wasn't* the one who popped them hinge pins," said Captain Howard. "I expect he was somebody's spy to tell them blacks about the plan."

"I didn't tell nobody no plan," said Arthur Stuart hotly.

Alvin clamped his grip tighter. No slave would talk to a white man like that, least of all a boat captain.

Then from behind Travis and Howard came another voice. "It's all right, boy," said Bowie. "You can tell them. No need to keep it secret any more."

And with a sinking feeling, Alvin wondered what kind of pyrotechnics he'd have to go through to distract everybody long enough for him and Arthur Stuart to get away.

But Bowie didn't say at all what Alvin expected. "I got the boy to tell me what he learned from them. They were cooking up some evil Mexica ritual. Something about tearing out somebody's heart one night when they were pretending to be our guides. A treacherous bunch, and so I decided we'd be better off without them."

"*You* decided!" Captain Howard growled. "What right did *you* have to decide?"

"Safety," said Bowie. "You put me in charge of the scouts, and that's what these were supposed to be. But it was a blame fool idea from the start. Why do you think them Mexica left those boys alive instead of taking their beating hearts out of their chests? It was a trap. All along, it was a trap. Well, we didn't fall into it."

"Do you know how much they cost?" demanded Captain Howard.

"They didn't cost *you* anything," said Travis.

That reminder took a bit of the dudgeon out of Captain Howard. "It's the principle of the thing. Just setting them free."

"But I didn't," said Bowie. "I sent them across the river. What do you think will happen to them there—*if* they make it through the fog?"

There was a bit more grumbling, but some laughter, too, and the matter was closed.

Back in his room, Alvin waited for Bowie to return.

"Why?" he demanded.

"I told you I could keep a secret," said Bowie. "I watched you and the boy do it, and I have to say, it was worth it to see how you broke their irons without ever laying a hand on them. To think I'd ever see a knack like that. Oh, you're a maker all right."

"Then come with me," said Alvin. "Leave these men behind. Don't you know the doom that lies over their heads? The Mexica aren't fools. These are dead men you're traveling with."

"Might be so," said Bowie, "but they need what I can do, and you don't."

"I do so," said Alvin. "Because I don't know many men in this world can hide their heartfire from me. It's your knack, isn't it? To disappear from all men's sight, when you want to. Because I never saw you watching us."

"And yet I woke you up just reaching for your poke the other night," said Bowie with a grin.

"Reaching for it?" said Alvin. "Or putting it back?"

Bowie shrugged.

"I thank you for protecting us and taking the blame on yourself."

Bowie chuckled. "Not much blame there. Truth is, Travis was getting sick of all the trouble of taking care of them blacks. It was only Howard who was so dead set on having them, and he ain't even going with us, once he drops us off on the Mexica coast."

"I could teach you. The way Arthur Stuart's been learning."

"I don't think so," said Bowie. "It's like you said. We're different kind of men."

"Not so different but what you can't change iffen you've a mind to."

Bowie only shook his head.

"Well, then, I'll thank you the only way that's useful to you," said Alvin.

Bowie waited. "Well?"

"I just did it," said Alvin. "I just put it back."

Bowie reached down to the sheath at his waist. It wasn't empty. He drew out the knife. There was the blade, plain as day, not a whit changed.

You'd've thought Bowie was handling his long-lost baby.

"How'd you get the blade back on it?" he asked. "You never touched it."

"It was there all along," said Alvin. "I just kind of spread it out a little."

"So I couldn't see it?"

"And so it wouldn't cut nothing."

"But now it will?"

"I think you're bound to die, when you take on them Mexica, Mr. Bowie. But I want you to take some human sacrificers with you on the way."

"I'll do that," said Bowie. "Except for the part about me dying."

"I hope I'm wrong and you're right, Mr. Bowie," said Alvin.

"And I hope you live forever, Alvin Maker," said the knife-wielding killer.

That morning Alvin and Arthur Stuart left the boat, as did Abe Lincoln and Cuz, and they made their journey down to Nueva Barcelona together, all four of them, swapping impossible stories all the way. But that's another tale, not this one.

OUTLANDER

DIANA GABALDON

In 1946, just after World War II, a young woman named
Claire Beauchamp Randall goes to the Scottish Highlands
on a second honeymoon. She and her husband, Frank, have
been separated by the war, he as a British army officer, she as
a combat nurse, and are now becoming reacquainted, rekin-
dling their marriage, and thinking of starting a family. These
plans hit a snag when Claire, walking by herself one afternoon, walks through a circle of standing stones and disap-
pears.

The first person she meets, upon regaining possession of her
faculties, is a man in the uniform of an eighteenth-century
English army officer—a man who bears a startling resemblance to her husband, Frank. This is not terribly surprising,
as Captain Johnathan Randall is her husband's six-times-
great-grandfather. However, Black Jack, as he's called, does
not resemble his descendant in terms of personality, being
a sadistic bisexual pervert, and while attempting to escape
from him, Claire falls into the hands of a group of Highland
Scots, who are also eager to avoid the Captain for reasons of
their own.

Events culminate in Claire's being obliged to marry Jamie
Fraser, a young Highlander, in order to stay out of the hands

* All dates are first U.S. hardcover publication, unless otherwise noted.

of Black Jack Randall. Hoping to escape from the Scots long enough to get back to the stone circle and Frank, Claire agrees—only to find herself gradually falling in love with Jamie.

The *Outlander* books are the story of Claire, Jamie, and Frank, and a complicated double marriage that occupies two separate centuries. They are also the story of the Jacobite Rising under Bonnie Prince Charlie, the end of the Highland clans, and the flight of the Highlanders, after the slaughter of Culloden, to the refuge and promise of the New World—a world that promises to be just as dangerous as the old one. And along the way, the *Outlander* series is an exploration of the nuances, operation, and moral complexities of time travel—and history.

The series encompasses hundreds of characters, both real and fictional. Among these, one of the most complex and interesting is Lord John Grey, whom we meet originally in *Dragonfly in Amber,* and who appears again in the succeeding books of the series. A gay man in a time when that particular predilection could get one hanged, Lord John is a man accustomed to keeping secrets. He's also a man of honor and deep affections—whether returned or not.

Lord John's adventures are interpolations within the story line of the main *Outlander* novels—following the same timeline (complex as that may be), and involving the same universe and people—but focused on the character of Lord John Grey.

LORD JOHN
AND THE SUCCUBUS

DIANA GABALDON

Historical note: Between 1756 and 1763, Great Britain joined with her allies, Prussia and Hanover, to fight against the combined forces of Austria, Saxony—and England's ancient foe, France. In the autumn of 1757, the Duke of Cumberland was obliged to surrender at Kloster-Zeven, leaving the allied armies temporarily shattered and the forces of Frederick the Great of Prussia encircled by French and Austrian troops.

CHAPTER 1
DEATH RIDES A PALE HORSE

Grey's spoken German was improving by leaps and bounds, but found itself barely equal to the present task.

After a long, boring day of rain and paperwork, there had come the sound of loud dispute in the corridor outside his office, and the head of Lance-Korporal Helwig appeared in his doorway wearing an apologetic expression.

"Major Grey?" he said, *"Ich habe ein kleines Englisch-problem."*

A moment later, Lance-Korporal Helwig had disappeared down the corridor like an eel sliding into mud, and Major John Grey, English liaison to the First Regiment of Hanoverian Foot, found himself adjudicating a three-way dispute among an English private, a gypsy prostitute, and a Prussian tavern owner.

"A little English problem," Helwig had described it as. The problem, as Grey saw it, was rather the *lack* of English.

The tavern owner spoke the local dialect with such fluency and speed that Grey grasped no more than one word in ten. The English private, who normally probably knew no more German than *"Ja," "Nein,"* and the two or three crude phrases necessary to accomplish immoral transactions, was so stricken with fury that he was all but speechless in his own tongue as well.

The gypsy, whose abundant charms were scarcely impaired by a missing tooth, had German that most nearly matched Grey's own in terms of grammar—though her vocabulary was immensely more colorful and detailed.

Using alternate hands to quell the sputterings of the private and the torrents of the Prussian, Grey concentrated his attention carefully on the gypsy's explanations—meanwhile taking care to consider the source, which meant discounting the factual basis of most of what she said.

". . . and then the disgusting pig of an Englishman, he put his [incomprehensible colloquial expression] into my [unknown Gypsy word]! And then . . ."

"She said, she said, she'd do it for sixpence, sir! She did, she said so—but, but, but then . . ."

"These-barbarian-pig-dogs-did-revolting-things-under-the-table-and-made-it-fall-over-so-the-leg-of-the-table-was-broken-and-the-dishes-broken-too-even-my-large-platter-which-cost-six-thalers-at-St.-Martin's-Fair-and-the-meat-was-ruined-by-falling-on-the-floor-and-even-if-it-was-not-the-dogs-fell-upon-it-snarling-so-that-I-was-bitten-when-I-tried-to-seize-it-away-from-them-and-all-the-time-these-vile-persons-were-copulating-like-filthy-foxes-on-the-floor-and-THEN . . ."

At length, an accommodation was reached, by means of Grey's demanding that all three parties produce what money was presently in their possession. A certain amount of shifty-eyed reluctance and dramatic pantomimes of purse and pocket searching having resulted in three small heaps of silver and copper, he firmly rearranged these in terms of size and metal value, without reference as to the actual coinage involved, as these appeared to include the currency of at least six different principalities.

Eyeing the gypsy's ensemble, which included both gold earrings and a crude but broad gold band around her finger, he assigned roughly equitable heaps to her and to the private, whose name, when asked, proved to be Bodger.

Assigning a slightly larger heap to the tavern owner, he then scowled fiercely at the three combatants, jabbed a finger at the money, and jerked a thumb over his shoulder, indicating that they should take the coins and leave while he was still in possession of his temper.

This they did, and storing away a most interesting gypsy curse for future reference, Grey returned tranquilly to his interrupted correspondence.

26 September 1757
To Harold, Earl of Melton
From Lord John Grey
The Township of Gundwitz,
Kingdom of Prussia

My Lord—

In reply to your request for information regarding my situation, I beg to say that I am well suited. My duties are . . . He paused, considering, then wrote, *interesting,* smiling slightly to himself at thought of what interpretation Hal might put upon that, . . . *and the conditions comfortable. I am quartered with several other English and German officers in the house of a Princess von Lowenstein, the widow of a minor Prussian noble, who possesses a fine estate near the town.*

We have two English regiments quartered here; Sir Peter Hicks's 35th, and half of the 52nd—I am told Colonel Ruysdale is in command, but have not yet met him, the 52nd having arrived only days ago. As the Hanoverians to whom I am attached and a number of Prussian troops are occupying all the suitable quarters in the town, Hicks's men are encamped some way to the south; Ruysdale to the north.

French forces are reported to be within twenty miles, but we expect no immediate trouble. Still, so late in the year, the snow will come soon, and put an end to the fighting; they may try for a final thrust before the winter sets in. Sir Peter begs me send his regards.

He dipped his quill again, and changed tacks.

My grateful thanks to your good wife for the smallclothes, which are superior in quality to what is available here.

At this point, he was obliged to transfer the pen to his left hand in order to scratch ferociously at the inside of his left thigh. He was wearing a pair of the local German product under his breeches, and while they were well laundered and not infested with vermin, they were made of coarse linen and appeared to have been starched with some substance derived from potatoes, which was irritating in the extreme.

Tell Mother I am still intact, and not starving, he concluded, transferring the pen back to his right hand. *Quite the reverse, in fact; Princess von Lowenstein has an excellent cook.*

Your Most Affec't. Brother,
J.

Sealing this with a brisk stamp of his half-moon signet, he then took down one of the ledgers and a stack of reports, and began the mechanical work of recording deaths and desertions. There was an outbreak of bloody flux among the men; more than a score lost to it in the last two weeks.

The thought brought the gypsy woman's last remarks to mind. Blood and bowels had both come into that, though he feared he had missed some of the refinements. Perhaps she had merely been trying to curse him with the flux?

He paused for a moment, twiddling the quill. It was rather unusual for the flux to occur in cold weather; it was more commonly a disease of hot summer, while winter was the season for consumption, catarrh, influenza, and fever.

He was not at all inclined to believe in curses, but did believe in poison. A whore would have ample opportunity to administer poison to her customers . . . but to what end? He turned to another folder of reports and shuffled through them, but saw no increase in the report of robbery or missing items—and the dead soldiers' comrades would certainly have noted anything of the kind. A man's belongings were sold by auction at his death, the money used to pay his debts and—if anything was left—to be sent to his family.

He put back the folder and shrugged, dismissing it. Illness and death trod closely in a soldier's footsteps, regardless of season or gypsy curse. Still, it might be worth warning Private Bodger to be wary of what he ate, particularly in the company of light-frigates and other dubious women.

A gentle rain had begun to fall again outside, and the sound of it against the windowpanes combined with the soothing shuffle of paper and scratch of quill to induce a pleasant sense of mindless drowsiness. He was disturbed from this trancelike state by the sound of footsteps on the wooden stair.

Captain Stephan von Namtzen, Landgrave von Erdberg, poked his handsome blond head through the doorway, ducking automatically to avoid braining himself on the lintel. The gentleman following him had no such difficulty, being a foot or so shorter.

"Captain von Namtzen," Grey said, standing politely. "May I be of assistance?"

"I have here Herr Blomberg," Stephen said in English, indicating the small, round, nervous-looking individual who accompanied him. "He wishes to borrow your horse."

Grey was sufficiently startled by this that he merely said,

"Which one?" rather than *Who is Herr Blomberg?* or *What does he want with a horse?*

The first of these questions was largely academic in any case; Herr Blomberg wore an elaborate chain of office about his neck, done in broad, flat links of enamel and chased gold, from which depended a seven-pointed starburst, enclosing a plaque of enamel on which was painted some scene of historical interest. Herr Blomberg's engraved silver coat buttons and shoe buckles were sufficient to proclaim his wealth; the chain of office merely confirmed his importance as being secular, rather than noble.

"Herr Blomberg is Buergermeister of the town," Stephan explained, taking matters in a strictly logical order of importance, as was his habit. "He requires a white stallion, in order that he shall discover and destroy a succubus. Someone has told him that you possess such a horse," he concluded, frowning at the temerity of whoever had been bandying such information.

"A succubus?" Grey asked, automatically rearranging the logical order of this speech, as was *his* habit.

Herr Blomberg had no English but evidently recognized the word, for he nodded vigorously, his old-fashioned wig bobbing, and launched into impassioned speech, accompanied by much gesticulation.

With Stephan's assistance, Grey gathered that the town of Gundwitz had recently suffered a series of mysterious and disturbing events, involving a number of men who claimed to have been victimized in their sleep by a young woman of demonic aspect. By the time these events had made their way to the attention of Herr Blomberg, the situation was serious; a man had died.

"Unfortunately," Stephan added, still in English, "the dead man is ours." He pressed his lips tightly together, conveying his dislike of the situation.

"Ours?" Grey asked, unsure what this usage implied, other than that the victim had been a soldier.

"Mine," Stephan clarified, looking further displeased. "One of the Prussians."

The Landgrave von Erdberg had three hundred Hanoverian foot-troops, raised from his own lands, equipped and funded from his personal fortune. In addition, Captain von Namtzen commanded two further companies of Prussian horse, and was in temporary command of the fragments of an artillery company whose officers had all died in an outbreak of the bloody flux.

Grey wished to hear more details regarding both the immediate death and—most particularly—the demoniac visitations, but his questions along these lines were interrupted by Herr Blomberg, who had been growing more restive by the moment.

"It grows soon dark," the Buergermeister pointed out in German. "We do not wish to fall into an open grave, so wet as it is."

"Ein offenes Grab?" Grey repeated, feeling a sudden chill draft on the back of his neck.

"This is true," Stephan said, with a nod of moody acquiescence. "It would be a terrible thing if your horse were to break his leg; he is a splendid creature. Come then, let us go."

"What *is* a s-succubus, me lord?" Tom Byrd's teeth were chattering, mostly from chill. The sun had long since set, and it was raining much harder. Grey could feel the wet seeping through the shoulders of his officer's greatcoat; Byrd's thin jacket was already soaked through, pasted to the young valet's stubby torso like butcher's paper around a joint of beef.

"I believe it is a sort of female . . . spirit," Grey said, carefully avoiding the more evocative term, "demon." The churchyard gates yawned before them like open jaws, and the darkness beyond seemed sinister in the extreme. No need to terrify the boy unnecessarily.

"Horses don't like ghosts," Byrd said, sounding truculent. "Everybody knows that, me lord."

He wrapped his arms around himself, shivering, and

huddled closer to Karolus, who shook his mane as though in agreement, showering water liberally over both Grey and Byrd.

"Surely you don't believe in ghosts, Tom?" Grey said, trying to be jocularly reassuring. He swiped a strand of wet fair hair out of his face, wishing Stephan would hurry.

" 'Tisn't a matter what *I* don't believe in, me lord," Byrd replied, "What if this lady's ghost believes in *us*? Who is she, anyway?" The lantern he carried was sputtering fitfully in the wet, despite its shield. Its dim light failed to illumine more than a vague outline of boy and horse, but perversely caught the shine of their eyes, lending them a disturbingly supernatural appearance, like staring wraiths.

Grey glanced aside, keeping an eye out for Stephan and the Buergermeister, who had gone to assemble a digging party. There was some movement outside the tavern, just visible at the far end of the street. That was sensible of Stephan. Men with a fair amount of beer on board were much more likely to be enthusiastic about the current prospect than were sober ones.

"Well, I do not believe that it is precisely a matter of ghosts," he said. "The German belief, however, seems to be that the succubus . . . er . . . the feminine spirit . . . may possess the body of a recently dead person."

Tom cast a look into the inky depths of the churchyard, and glanced back at Grey.

"Oh?" he said.

"Ah," Grey replied.

Byrd pulled the slouch hat low on his forehead and hunched his collar up around his ears, clutching the horse's halter rope close to his chest. Nothing of his round face now showed save a downturned mouth, but that was eloquent.

Karolus stamped one foot and shifted his weight, tossing his head a little. He didn't seem to mind either rain or churchyard, but was growing restive. Grey patted the stallion's thick neck, taking comfort from the solid feel of the cold firm hide and massive body. Karolus turned his head and blew hot breath affectionately into his ear.

"Almost ready," he said soothingly, twining a fist in the horse's soggy mane. "Now, Tom. When Captain von Namtzen arrives with his men, you and Karolus will walk forward very slowly. You are to lead him back and forth across the church-yard. Keep a few feet in front of him, but leave some slack in the rope."

The point of this procedure, of course, was to keep Karo-lus from stumbling over a gravestone or falling into any open graves, by allowing Tom to do it first. Ideally, Grey had been given to understand, the horse should be turned into the churchyard and allowed to wander over the graves at his own will, but neither he nor Stephan were willing to risk Karo-lus's valuable legs in the dark.

He had suggested waiting until the morning, but Herr Blomberg was insistent. The succubus must be found, with-out delay. Grey was more than curious to hear the details of the attacks, but had so far been told little more than that a Private Koenig had been found dead in the barracks, the body bearing marks that made his manner of death clear. What marks? Grey wondered.

Classically educated, he had read of succubi and incubi, but had been taught to regard such references as quaintly su-perstitious, of a piece with other medieval Popish nonsense like saints who strolled about with their heads in their hands or statues of the Virgin whose tears healed the sick. His fa-ther had been a rationalist, an observer of the ways of nature and a firm believer in the logic of phenomena.

His two months' acquaintance with the Germans, though, had shown him that they were deeply superstitious; more so even than the English common soldiers. Even Stephan kept a small carved image of some pagan deity about his person at all times, to guard against being struck by lightning, and the Prussians seemed to harbor similar notions, judging from Herr Blomberg's behavior.

The digging party was making its way up the street now, bright with sputtering torches and emitting snatches of song. Karolus snorted and pricked his ears; Karolus, Grey had been told, was fond of parades.

"Well, then." Stephan loomed suddenly out of the murk at his side, looking pleased with himself under the broad shelf of his hat. "All is ready, Major?"

"Yes. Go ahead then, Tom."

The diggers—mostly laborers, armed with spades, hoes, and mattocks—stood back, lurching tipsily and stepping on each other's shoes. Tom, lantern held delicately before him in the manner of an insect's feeler, took several steps forward—then stopped. He turned, tugging on the rope.

Karolus stood solidly, declining to move.

"I told you, me lord," Byrd said, sounding more cheerful. "Horses don't like ghosts. Me uncle had an old cart horse once, wouldn't take a step past a churchyard. We had to take him clear round two streets to get him past."

Stephan made a noise of disgust.

"It is not a ghost," he said, striding forward, prominent chin held high. "It is a succubus. A demon. That is quite different."

"Daemon?" one of the diggers said, catching the English word and looking suddenly dubious. *"Ein Teufel?"*

"Demon?" said Tom Byrd, and gave Grey a look of profound betrayal.

"Something of the kind, I believe," Grey said, and coughed. "If such a thing should exist, which I doubt it does."

A chill of uncertainty seemed to have overtaken the party with this demonstration of the horse's reluctance. There was shuffling and murmuring, and heads turned to glance back in the direction of the tavern.

Stephan, magnificently disregarding this tendency to pusillanimity in his troops, clapped Karolus on the neck and spoke to him encouragingly in German. The horse snorted and arched his neck, but still resisted Tom Byrd's tentative yanks on his halter. Instead, he swiveled his enormous head toward Grey, jerking Byrd off his feet. The boy lost his grip on the rope, staggered off balance, trying vainly to keep hold of the lantern, and finally slipped on a stone submerged in the mud, landing on his buttocks with a rude splat.

This mishap had the salutary effect of causing the diggers to roar with laughter, restoring their spirits. Several of the torches had by now been extinguished by the rain, and everyone was thoroughly wet, but goatskin flasks and pottery jugs were produced from a number of pockets and offered to Tom Byrd by way of restorative, being then passed around the company in sociable fashion.

Grey took a deep swig of the fiery plum liquor himself, handed back the jug, and came to a decision.

"I'll ride him."

Before Stephan could protest, Grey had taken a firm grip on Karolus's mane and swung himself up on the stallion's broad back. Karolus appeared to find Grey's familiar weight soothing; the broad white ears, which had been pointing to either side in suspicion, rose upright again, and the horse started forward willingly enough at Grey's nudge against his sides.

Tom, too, seemed heartened, and ran to pick up the trailing halter rope. There was a ragged cheer from the diggers, and the party moved awkwardly after them, through the yawning gates.

It seemed much darker in the churchyard than it had looked from outside. Much quieter, too; the jokes and chatter of the men died away into an uneasy silence, broken only by an occasional curse as someone knocked against a tombstone in the dark. Grey could hear the patter of rain on the brim of his hat, and the suck and thump of Karolus's hooves as he plodded obediently through the mud.

He strained his eyes to see what lay ahead, beyond the feeble circle of light cast by Tom's lantern. It was black-dark, and he felt cold, despite the shelter of his greatcoat. The damp was rising, mist coming up out of the ground; he could see wisps of it purling away from Tom's boots, disappearing in the lantern light. More of it drifted in an eerie fog around the mossy tombstones of neglected graves, leaning like rotted teeth in their sockets.

The notion, as it had been explained to him, was that a

white stallion had the power to detect the presence of the supernatural. The horse would stop at the grave of the succubus, which could then be opened, and steps taken to destroy the creature.

Grey found a number of logical assumptions wanting in this proposal, chief among which—putting aside the question of the existence of succubi, and why a sensible horse should choose to have anything to do with one—was that Karolus was not choosing his own path. Tom was doing his best to keep slack in the rope, but as long as he held it, the horse was plainly going to follow him.

On the other hand, he reflected, Karolus was unlikely to stop *anywhere* so long as Tom kept walking. That being true, the end result of this exercise would be merely to cause them all to miss their suppers and to render them thoroughly wet and chilled. Still, he supposed they would be yet more wet and chilled if obliged actually to open graves and perform whatever ritual might follow—

A hand clamped itself on his calf, and he bit his tongue— luckily, as it kept him from crying out.

"You are all right, Major?" It was Stephan, looming up beside him, tall and dark in a woolen cloak. He had left aside his plumed helmet, and wore a soft-brimmed wide hat against the rain, which made him look both less impressive and more approachable.

"Certainly," Grey said, mastering his temper. "How long must we do this?"

Von Namtzen lifted one shoulder in a shrug.

"Until the horse stops, or until Herr Blomberg is satisfied."

"Until Herr Blomberg begins wanting his supper, you mean." He could hear the Buergermeister's voice at a distance behind them, lifted in exhortation and reassurance.

A white plume of breath floated out from under the brim of von Namtzen's hat, the laugh behind it barely audible.

"He is more . . . resolute? . . . than you might suppose. It is his duty, the welfare of the village. He will endure as long as you will, I assure you."

Grey pressed his bitten tongue against the roof of his mouth, to prevent any injudicious remarks.

Stephan's hand was still curled about his leg, just above the edge of his boot. Cold as it was, he felt no warmth from the grasp, but the pressure of the big hand was both a comfort and something more.

"The horse—he goes well, *nicht wahr*?"

"He is wonderful," Grey said, with complete sincerity. "I thank you again."

Von Namtzen flicked his free hand in dismissal, but made a pleased sound, deep in his throat. He had—against Grey's protests—insisted upon making the stallion a gift to Grey, "in token of our alliance and our friendship," he had said firmly, clapping Grey upon both shoulders and then seizing him in fraternal embrace, kissing him formally upon both cheeks and mouth. At least Grey was obliged to consider it a fraternal embrace, unless and until circumstances might prove it otherwise.

But Stephan's hand still curled around his calf, hidden under the skirt of his greatcoat.

Grey glanced toward the squat bulk of the church, a black mass that loomed beyond the churchyard.

"I am surprised that the minister is not with us. Does he disapprove of this—excursion?"

"The minister is dead. A fever of some kind, *die rote Ruhn,* more than a month since. They will send another, from Strausberg, but he has not come yet." Little wonder; a large number of French troops lay between Strausberg and the town; travel would be difficult, if not impossible.

"I see." Grey glanced back over his shoulder. The diggers had paused to open a fresh jug, torches tilting in momentary distraction.

"Do you believe in this—this succubus?" he asked, careful to keep his voice low.

Rather to his surprise, von Namtzen didn't reply at once. At last, the Hanoverian took a deep breath and hunched his broad shoulders in a gesture not quite a shrug.

"I have seen . . . strange things from time to time," von Namtzen said at last, very quietly. "In this country, particularly. And a man is dead, after all."

The hand on his leg squeezed briefly and dropped away, sending a small flutter of sensation up Grey's back.

He took a deep breath of cold, heavy air, tinged with smoke, and coughed. It was like the smell of grave-dirt, he thought, and then wished the thought had not occurred to him.

"One thing I confess I do not quite understand," he said, straightening himself in the saddle. "A succubus is a demon, if I am not mistaken. How is it, then, that such a creature should take refuge in a churchyard, in consecrated ground?"

"Oh," von Namtzen said, sounding surprised that this was not obvious. "The succubus takes possession of the body of a dead person, and rests within it by day. Such a person must of course be a corrupt and wicked sort, filled with depravity and perversion. So that even within the churchyard the succubus will suitable refuge find."

"How recently must the person have died?" Grey asked. Surely it would make their perambulations more efficient were they to go directly to the more recent graves. From the little he could see in the swaying light of Tom's lantern, most of the stones nearby had stood where they were for decades, if not centuries.

"That I do not know," von Namtzen admitted. "Some people say that the body itself rises with the succubus; others say that the body remains in the grave, and by night the demon rides the air as a dream, seeking men in their sleep."

Tom Byrd's figure was indistinct in the gathering fog, but Grey saw his shoulders rise, nearly touching the brim of his hat. He coughed again, and cleared his throat.

"I see. And . . . er . . . what, precisely, do you intend to do, should a suitable body be located?"

Here von Namtzen was on surer ground.

"Oh, that is simple," he assured Grey. "We will open the coffin, and drive an iron rod through the corpse's heart. Herr Blomberg has brought one."

Tom Byrd made an inarticulate noise, which Grey thought it wiser to ignore.

"I see," he said. His nose had begun to run with the cold, and he wiped it on his sleeve. At least he no longer felt hungry.

They paced for a little in silence. The Buergermeister had fallen silent, too, though the distant sounds of squelching and glugging behind them indicated that the digging party was loyally persevering, with the aid of more plum brandy.

"The dead man," Grey said at last. "Private Koenig. Where was he found? And you mentioned marks upon the body—what sort of marks?"

Von Namtzen opened his mouth to answer, but was forestalled. Karolus glanced suddenly to the side, nostrils flaring. Then he flung up his head with a great "Harrumph!" of startlement, nearly hitting Grey in the face. At the same moment, Tom Byrd uttered a high, thin scream, dropped the rope, and ran.

The big horse flexed his hindquarters, slewed round, and took off, leaping a small stone angel that stood in his path; Grey saw it as a looming pale blur, but had no time to worry about it before it passed beneath the stallion's outstretched hooves, its stone mouth gaping as though in astonishment.

Lacking reins and unable to seize the halter rope, Grey had no recourse but to grip the stallion's mane in both hands, clamp his knees, and stick like a burr. There were shouts and screams behind him, but he had no attention to spare for anything but the wind in his ears and the elemental force between his thighs.

They bounded like a skipping cannonball through the dark, striking the ground and rocketing upward, seeming to cover leagues at a stride. He leaned low and held on, the stallion's mane whipping like stinging nettles across his face, the horse's breath loud in his ears—or was it his own?

Through streaming eyes, he glimpsed light flickering in the distance, and realized they were heading now for the village. There was a six-foot stone wall in the way; he could only hope the horse noticed it in time.

He did; Karolus skidded to a stop, divots of mud and withered grass shooting up around him, sending Grey lurching up onto his neck. The horse reared, came down, then turned sharply, trotted several yards, and slowed to a walk, shaking his head as though to try to free himself of the flapping rope.

Legs quivering as with ague, Grey slid off, and, with cold-stiff fingers, grasped the rope.

"You big white *bastard*," he said, filled with the joy of survival, and laughed. "You're bloody marvelous!"

Karolus took this compliment with tolerant grace, and shoved at him, whickering softly. The horse seemed largely over his fright, whatever had caused it; he could but hope Tom Byrd fared as well.

Grey leaned against the wall, panting until his breath came back and his heart slowed a bit. The exhilaration of the ride was still with him, but he had now a moment's heed to spare for other things.

At the far side of the churchyard, the torches were clustered close together, lighting the fog with a reddish glow. He could see the digging party, standing in a knot shoulder to shoulder, all in attitudes of the most extreme interest. And toward him, a tall black figure came through the mist, silhouetted by the torch glow behind him. He had a moment's turn, for the figure looked sinister, dark cloak swirling about it—but it was, of course, merely Captain von Namtzen.

"Major Grey!" von Namtzen called. "Major Grey!"

"Here!" Grey shouted, finding breath. The figure altered course slightly, hurrying toward him with long, stilted strides that zigged and zagged to avoid obstacles in the path. How in God's name had Karolus managed on that ground, he wondered, without breaking a leg or both their necks?

"Major Grey," Stephan said, grasping both his hands tightly. "John. You are all right?"

"Yes," he said, gripping back. "Yes, of course. What has happened? My valet—Mr. Byrd—is he all right?"

"He has into a hole fallen, but he is not hurt. We have found a body. A dead man."

Grey felt a sudden lurch of the heart.

"What—"

"Not in a grave," the Captain hastened to assure him. "Lying on the ground, leaning against one of the tombstones. Your valet saw the corpse's face most suddenly in the light of his lantern, and was frightened."

"I am not surprised. Is he one of yours?"

"No. One of yours."

"What?" Grey stared up at the Hanoverian. Stephan's face was no more than a black oval in the dark. He squeezed Grey's hands gently and let them go.

"An English soldier. You will come?"

He nodded, feeling the cold air heavy in his chest. It was not impossible; there were English regiments to north and to south of the town, no more than an hour's ride away. Men off duty would often come into town in search of drink, dice, and women. It was, after all, the reason for his own presence here—to act as liaison between the English regiments and their German allies.

The body was less horrible in appearance than he might have supposed; while plainly dead, the man seemed quite peaceful, slumped half sitting against the knee of a stern stone matron holding a book. There was no blood nor wound apparent, and yet Grey felt his stomach clench with shock.

"You know him?" Stephan was watching him intently, his own face stern and clean as those of the stone memorials about them.

"Yes." Grey knelt by the body. "I spoke to him only a few hours ago."

He put the backs of his fingers delicately against the dead man's throat—the slack flesh was clammy, slick with rain, but still warm. Unpleasantly warm. He glanced down, and saw that Private Bodger's breeches were opened, the stuff of his shirttail sticking out, rumpled over the man's thighs.

"Does he still have his dick, or did the she-thing eat it?" said a low voice in German. A faint, shocked snigger ran through the men. Grey pressed his lips tight together and jerked up the soggy shirttail. Private Bodger was somewhat more than intact, he was glad to see. So were the diggers; there was an audible sigh of mass relief behind him.

Grey stood, conscious all at once of tiredness and hunger, and of the rain pattering on his back.

"Wrap him in a canvas; bring him . . ." Where? The dead man must be returned to his own regiment, but not tonight. "Bring him to the Schloss. Tom? Show them the way; ask the gardener to find you a suitable shed."

"Yes, me lord." Tom Byrd was nearly as pale as the dead man, and covered with mud, but once more in control of himself. "Will I take the horse, me lord? Or will you ride him?"

Grey had forgotten entirely about Karolus, and looked blankly about. Where had he gone?

One of the diggers had evidently caught the word "horse" and understood it, for a murmur of *"Das Pferd"* rippled through the group, and the men began to look around, lifting the torches high and craning their necks.

One man gave an excited shout, pointing into the dark. A large white blur stood a little distance away.

"He's on a grave! He's standing still! He's found it!"

This caused a stir of sudden excitement; everyone pressed forward together, and Grey feared lest the horse should take alarm and run again.

No such danger; Karolus was absorbed in nibbling at the soggy remnants of several wreaths, piled at the foot of an imposing tombstone. This stood guard over a small group of family graves—one very recent, as the wreaths and raw earth showed. As the torchlight fell upon the scene, Grey could easily read the name chiseled black into the stone.

BLOMBERG, it read.

CHAPTER 2
BUT WHAT, EXACTLY, DOES A SUCCUBUS *DO?*

They found Schloss Lowenstein alight with candles and wel-
coming fires, despite the late hour of their return. They were
far past the time for dinner, but there was food in abundance
on the sideboard, and Grey and von Namtzen refreshed themselves thoroughly, interrupting their impromptu feast peri-
odically to give particulars of the evening's adventures to the
house's other inhabitants, who were agog with curiosity.

"No! Herr Blomberg's *mother*?" The Princess von Lowenstein pressed fingers to her mouth, eyes wide in delighted
shock. "Old Agathe? I don't believe it!"

"Nor does Herr Blomberg," von Namtzen assured her,
reaching for a leg of roast pheasant. "He was most . . . vehement?" He turned toward Grey, eyebrows raised, then turned
back to the Princess, nodding with assurance. "Vehement."

He had been. Grey would have chosen "apoplectic" as the
better description, but was reasonably sure that none of the
Germans present would know the term, and he had no idea
how to translate it. They were all speaking English, as a courtesy to the British officers present, who included a Captain of
Horse named Billman, Colonel Sir Peter Hicks, and a Lieutenant Dundas, a young Scottish officer in charge of an ord-
nance survey party.

"The old woman was a saint, absolutely a saint!" protested
the Dowager Princess Lowenstein, crossing herself piously.
"I do not believe it, I cannot!"

The younger Princess cast a brief glance at her mother-in-
law, then away—meeting Grey's eyes. The Princess had
bright blue eyes, all the brighter for candlelight, brandy—
and mischief.

The Princess was a widow of a year's standing. Grey
judged from the large portrait over the mantelpiece in the
drawing room that the late Prince had been roughly thirty
years older than his wife; she bore her loss bravely.

"Dear me," she said, contriving to look winsome, despite

her anxiety. "As if the French were not enough! Now we are to be threatened with nightmare demons?"

"Oh, you will be quite safe, madam, I assure you," Sir Peter assured her. "What-what? With so many gallant gentlemen in the house?"

The ancient Dowager glanced at Grey, and said something about gentlemen in highly accented German that Grey didn't quite catch, but the Princess flushed like a peony in bloom, and von Namtzen, within earshot, choked on a swallow of wine.

Captain Billman smote the Hanoverian helpfully on the back.

"Is there news of the French?" Grey asked, thinking that perhaps the conversation should be guided back to more earthly concerns before the party retired to bed.

"Look to be a few of the bastards milling round," Billman said casually, cutting his eyes at the women in a manner suggesting that the word "few" was a highly discreet euphemism. "Expect they'll be moving on, heading for the west within a day or so."

Or heading for Strausberg, to join with the French regiment reported there, Grey thought. He returned Billman's meaningful look. Gundwitz lay in the bottom of a river valley—directly between the French position and Strausberg.

"So," Billman said, changing the subject with a heavy jocularity, "your succubus got away, did she?"

Von Namtzen cleared his throat.

"I would not say that, particularly," he said. "Herr Blomberg refused to allow the men to disturb the grave, of course, but I have men ordered to guard it."

"That'll be popular duty, I shouldn't think," said Sir Peter, with a glance at a nearby window, where even multiple thicknesses of silk and woolen draperies and heavy shutters failed to muffle the thrum of rain and the occasional distant boom of thunder.

"A good idea," one of the German officers said, in heavily accented but very correct English. "We do not wish to have rumors fly about, that there is a succubus behaving badly in the vicinity of the soldiers."

"But what, exactly, does a succubus *do*?" the Princess inquired, looking expectantly from face to face.

There was a sudden massive clearing of throats and gulping of wine as all the men present tried to avoid her eye. An explosive snort from the Dowager indicated what *she* thought of this cowardly behavior.

"A succubus is a she-demon," the old lady said, precisely. "It comes to men in dreams, and has congress with them, in order to extract from them their seed."

The Princess's eyes went perfectly round. She *hadn't* known, Grey observed.

"Why?" she asked. "What does she do with it? Demons do not give birth, do they?"

Grey felt a laugh trying to force its way up under his breastbone, and hastily took another drink.

"Well, no," said Stephan von Namtzen, somewhat flushed, but still self-possessed. "Not exactly. The succubus procures the . . . er . . . essence," he gave a slight bow of apology to the Dowager at this, "and then will mate with an incubus—this being a male demon, you see?"

The old lady looked grim, and placed a hand upon the religious medal she wore pinned to her gown.

Von Namtzen took a deep breath, seeing that everyone was hanging upon his words, and fixed his gaze upon the portrait of the late Prince.

"The incubus then will seek out a human woman by night, couple with her, and impregnate her with the stolen seed—thus producing demon-spawn."

Lieutenant Dundas, who was very young and likely a Presbyterian, looked as though he were being strangled by his stock. The other men, all rather red in the face, attempted to look as though they were entirely familiar with the phenomenon under discussion and thought little of it. The Dowager looked thoughtfully at her daughter-in-law, then upward at the picture of her deceased son, eyebrows raised as though in silent conversation.

"Ooh!" Despite the late hour and the informality of the gathering, the Princess had a fan, which she spread now before her face in shock, big blue eyes wide above it. These eyes swung toward Grey, and blinked in pretty supplication.

"And do you really think, Lord John, that there is such a creature . . ." she shuddered, with an alluring quiver of the bosom, ". . . prowling near?"

Neither eyes nor bosom swayed him, and it was clear to him that the Princess found considerably more excitement than fear in the notion, but he smiled reassuringly, an Englishman secure in his rationality.

"No," he said. "I don't."

As though in instant contradiction of this stout opinion, a blast of wind struck the Schloss, carrying with it a burst of hail that rattled off the shutters and fell hissing down the chimney. The thunder of the hailstorm upon roof and walls and outbuildings was so great that for a moment it drowned all possibility of conversation.

The party stood as though paralyzed, listening to the roar of the elements. Grey's eyes met Stephan's; the Hanoverian lifted his chin a little in defiance of the storm, and gave him a small, private smile. Grey smiled back, then glanced away—just in time to see a dark shape fall from the chimney and plunge into the flames with a piercing shriek.

The shriek was echoed at once by the women—and possibly by Lieutenant Dundas, though Grey could not quite swear to it.

Something was struggling in the fire, flapping and writhing, and the stink of scorched skin came sharp and acrid in the nose. Acting by sheer instinct, Grey seized a poker and swept the thing out of the fire and onto the hearth, where it skittered crazily, emitting sounds that pierced his eardrums.

Stephan lunged forward and stamped on the thing, putting an end to the unnerving display.

"A bat," he said calmly, removing his boot. "Take it away."

The footman to whom he addressed this command came hastily and, flinging a napkin over the blackened corpse, scooped it up and carried it out on a tray, this ceremonial disposal giving Grey a highly inappropriate vision of the bat making a second appearance at breakfast, roasted and garnished with stewed prunes.

A sudden silence had fallen upon the party. This was broken by the sudden chiming of the clock, which made everyone jump, then laugh nervously.

The party broke up, the men standing politely as the women withdrew, then pausing for a few moments' conversation as they finished their wine and brandy. With no particular sense of surprise, Grey found Sir Peter at his elbow.

"A word with you, Major?" Sir Peter said quietly.

"Of course, sir."

The group had fragmented into twos and threes; it was not difficult to draw aside a little, under the pretext of examining a small, exquisite statue of Eros that stood on one of the tables.

"You'll be taking the body back to the Fifty-second in the morning, I expect?" The English officers had all had a look at Private Bodger, declaring that he was none of theirs; by elimination, he must belong to Colonel Ruysdale's Fifty-second Foot, presently encamped on the other side of Gundwitz.

Without waiting for Grey's nod, Sir Peter went on, touching the statue abstractedly.

"The French are up to something; had a scout's report this afternoon, great deal of movement among the troops. They're preparing to move, but we don't yet know where or when. I should feel happier if a few more of Ruysdale's troops were to move to defend the bridge at Aschenwald, just in case."

"I see," Grey said cautiously. "And you wish me to carry a message to that effect to Colonel Ruysdale."

Sir Peter made a slight grimace.

"I've sent one. I think it might be helpful, though, if you were to suggest that von Namtzen wished it, as well."

Grey made a noncommittal noise. It was common knowledge that Sir Peter and Ruysdale were not on good terms. The Colonel might well be more inclined to oblige a German ally.

"I will mention it to Captain von Namtzen," he said, "though I expect he will be agreeable." He would have taken his leave then, but Sir Peter hesitated, indicating that there was something further.

"Sir?" Grey said.

"I think . . ." Sir Peter said, glancing around and lowering his voice still further, ". . . that perhaps the Princess should be advised—cautiously; no need to give alarm—that there is some slight possibility . . . if the French *were* in fact to cross the valley . . ." He rested a hand thoughtfully upon the head of Eros and glanced at the other furnishings of the room, which included a number of rare and costly items. "She might wish to withdraw her family to a place of safety. Not amiss to suggest a few things be put safely away in the meantime. Shouldn't like to see a thing like that decorating a French general's desk, eh?"

"That" was the skull of an enormous bear—an ancient cave-bear, the Princess had informed the party earlier—that stood by itself upon a small, draped table. The skull was covered with gold, hammered flat and etched in primitive designs, with a row of semiprecious stones running up the length of the snout, then diverging to encircle the empty eye sockets. It was a striking object.

"Yes," Grey said, "I quite . . . oh. You wish me to speak with the Princess?"

Sir Peter relaxed a little, having accomplished his goal.

"She seems quite taken by you, Grey," he said, his original joviality returning. "Advice might be better received from you, eh? Besides, you're a liaison, aren't you?"

"To be sure," Grey said, less than pleased, but aware that he had received a direct order. "I shall attend to it as soon as I may, sir." He took leave of the others remaining in the drawing room, and made his way to the staircase that led to the upper floors.

The Princess von Lowenstein *did* seem most taken with him; he wasn't surprised that Sir Peter had noticed her smiles and languishings. Fortunately, she seemed equally taken with Stephan von Namtzen, going so far as to have Hanoverian delicacies served regularly at dinner in his honor.

At the top of the stair, he hesitated. There were three corridors opening off the landing, and it always took a moment to be sure which of the stone-floored halls led to his own chamber. A flicker of movement to the left attracted his eye, and he turned that way, to see someone dodge out of sight behind a tall armoire that stood against the wall.

"Wo ist das?" he asked sharply, and got a stifled gasp in reply.

Moving cautiously, he went and peered around the edge of the armoire, to find a small, dark-haired boy pressed against the wall, both hands clasped over his mouth and eyes round as saucers. The boy wore a nightshirt and cap, and had plainly escaped from his nursery. He recognized the child, though he had seen him only once or twice before; it was the Princess's young son—what was the boy's name? Heinrich? Reinhardt?

"Don't be afraid," he said gently to the boy, in his slow, careful German. "I am your mother's friend. Where is your room?"

The boy didn't reply, but his eyes flicked down the hallway and back. Grey saw no open doors, but held out a hand to the boy.

"It is very late," he said. "Shall we find your bed?"

The boy shook his head so hard that the tassel of his nightcap slapped against the wall.

"I don't want to go to bed. There is a bad woman there. *Eine Hexe.*"

"A witch?" Grey repeated, and felt an odd frisson run down his back, as though someone had touched his nape with a cold finger. "What did this witch look like?"

The child stared back at him, uncomprehending.

"Like a witch," he said.

"Oh," said Grey, momentarily stymied. He rallied, though, and beckoned, curling his fingers at the boy. "Come, then; show me. I am a soldier, I am not afraid of a witch."

"You will kill her and cut out her heart and fry it over the fire?" the boy asked eagerly, peeling himself off the wall. He reached out to touch the hilt of Grey's dagger, still on his belt.

"Well, perhaps," Grey temporized. "Let us go find her first." He picked the boy up under the arms and swung him up; the child came willingly enough, curling his legs around Grey's waist and cuddling close to him for warmth.

The hallway was dark; only a rush-light sputtered in a sconce near the farther end, and the stones emanated a chill that made the child's own warmth more than welcome. Rain was still coming down hard; a small dribble of moisture had seeped in through the shutters at the end of the hall, and the flickering light shone on the puddle.

Thunder boomed in the distance, and the child threw his arms around Grey's neck with a gasp.

"It is all right." Grey patted the small back soothingly, though his own heart had leapt convulsively at the sound. No doubt the noise of the storm had wakened the boy.

"Where is your chamber?"

"Upstairs." The boy pointed vaguely toward the far end of the hallway; presumably there was a back stair somewhere near. The Schloss was immense and sprawling; Grey had learned no more of its geography than what was necessary to reach his own quarters. He hoped that the boy knew the place better, so they were not obliged to wander the chilly hallways all night.

As he approached the end of the hall, the lightning flashed again, a vivid line of white that outlined the window—and showed him clearly that the window was open, the shutters unfastened. With the boom of thunder came a gust of wind, and one loose shutter flung back suddenly, admitting a freezing gust of rain.

"Oooh!" The boy clutched him tightly around the neck, nearly choking him.

"It is all right," he said, as calmly as possible, shifting his burden in order to free one hand.

He leaned out to seize the shutter, trying at the same time to shelter the boy with his body. A soundless flash lit up the world in a burst of black and white, and he blinked, dazzled, a pinwheel of stark images whirling at the back of his eyes. Thunder rolled past, with a sound so like an oxcart full of stones that he glanced up involuntarily, half expecting to see one of the old German gods go past, driving gleefully through the clouds.

The image he saw was not of the storm-tossed sky, though, but of something glimpsed when the lightning flashed. He blinked hard, clearing his sight, and then looked down. It *was* there. A ladder, leaning against the wall of the house. Well, then. Perhaps the child *had* seen someone strange in his room.

"Here," he said to the boy, turning to set him down. "Stay out of the rain while I fasten the shutter."

He turned back, and, leaning out into the storm, pushed the ladder off so that it fell away into the dark. Then he closed and fastened the shutters, and picked up the shivering boy again. The wind had blown out the rush-light, and he was obliged to feel his way into the turning of the hall.

"It's very dark," said the boy, with a tremor in his voice.

"Soldiers are not afraid of the dark," he reassured the child, thinking of the graveyard.

"I'm not afraid!" The little boy's cheek was pressed against his neck.

"Of course you are not. How are you called, young sir?" he asked, in hopes of distracting the boy.

"Siggy."

"Siggy," he repeated, feeling his way along the wall with one hand. "I am John. Johannes, in your tongue."

"I know," said the boy, surprising him. "The servant girls think you are good looking. Not so big as Landgrave Stephan, but prettier. Are you rich? The Landgrave is very rich."

"I won't starve," Grey said, wondering how long the blasted hallway was, and whether he might discover the staircase by falling down it in the dark.

At least the boy seemed to have lost some of his fear; he cuddled close, rubbing his head under Grey's chin. There was a distinct smell about him; nothing unpleasant—rather like the smell of a month-old litter of puppies, Grey thought; warmly animal.

Something occurred to him, then; something he should have thought to ask at once.

"Where is your nurse?" A boy of this age would surely not sleep alone.

"I don't know. Maybe the witch ate her."

This cheering suggestion coincided with a welcome flicker of light in the distance, and the sound of voices. Hastening toward these, Grey at last found the nursery stair, just as a wild-eyed woman in nightgown, cap, and shawl popped out, holding a pottery candlestick.

"Siegfried!" she cried. "Master Siggy, where have you been? What has—oh!" At this point, she realized that Grey was there, and reared back as though struck forcibly in the chest.

"Guten Abend, Madam," he said, politely. "Is this your nurse, Siggy?"

"No," said Siggy, scornful of such ignorance. "That's just Hetty. Mama's maid."

"Siggy? Siegfried, is it you? Oh, my boy, my boy!" The light from above dimmed as a fluttering body hurtled down the stair, and the Princess von Lowenstein seized the boy from Grey's arms, hugging her son and kissing him so passionately that his nightcap fell off.

More servants were coming downstairs, less precipitously. Two footmen and a woman who might be a parlor maid, all in varying degrees of undress, but equipped with candles or rush-lights. Evidently, Grey had had the good fortune to encounter a search party.

There was a good deal of confused conversation, as Grey's attempt at explanation was interrupted by Siggy's own rather disjointed account of his adventures, punctuated by exclamations of horror and surprise from the Princess and Hetty.

"Witch?" the Princess was saying, looking down at her son in alarm. "You saw a witch? Did you have an evil dream, child?"

"No. I just woke up and there was a witch in my room. Can I have some marzipan?"

"Perhaps it would be a good idea to search the house," Grey managed to get in. "It is possible that the . . . witch . . . is still inside."

The Princess had very fine, pale skin, radiant in the candlelight, but at this, it went a sickly color, like toadstools. Grey glanced meaningfully at Siggy, and the Princess at once gave the child to Hetty, telling the maid to take him to his nursery.

"Tell me what is happening," she said, gripping Grey's arm, and he did, finishing the account with a question of his own.

"The child's nurse? Where is she?"

"We don't know. I went to the nursery to look at Siegfried before retiring—" The Princess's hand fluttered to her bosom as she became aware that she was wearing a rather unbecoming woolen nightgown and cap, with a heavy shawl and thick, fuzzy stockings. "He wasn't there; neither was the nurse. Jakob, Thomas—" She turned to the footmen, suddenly taking charge. "Search! The house first, then the grounds."

A distant rumbling of thunder reminded everyone that it was still pouring with rain outside, but the footmen vanished with speed.

The sudden silence left in the wake of their departure gave Grey a slightly eerie feeling, as though the thick stone walls had moved subtly closer. A solitary candle burned, left behind on the stairs.

"Who would do this?" said the Princess, her voice suddenly small and frightened. "Did they mean to take Siegfried? Why?"

It looked very much to Grey as though kidnapping had been the plan; no other possibility had entered his mind, until the Princess seized him by the arm again.

"Do you think—do you think it was . . . her?" she whispered, eyes dilated to pools of horror. "The succubus?"

"I think not," Grey said, taking hold of her hands for reassurance. They were cold as ice—hardly surprising, in view of the temperature inside the Schloss. He smiled at her, squeezing her fingers gently. "A succubus would not require a ladder, surely?" He forebore to add that a boy of Siggy's age was unlikely to have much that a succubus would want, if he had correctly understood the nature of such a creature.

A little color came back into the Princess's face, as she saw the logic in this.

"No, that's true." The edge of her mouth twitched, in an attempt at a smile, though her eyes were still fearful.

"It might be advisable to set a guard near your son's room," Grey suggested. "Though I expect the . . . person . . . has been frightened off by now."

She shuddered, whether from cold or at the thought of roving intruders, he couldn't tell. Still, she was clearly steadier at the thought of action, and that being so, he rather reluctantly took the opportunity to share with her Sir Peter Hicks's cautions, feeling that perhaps a solid enemy such as the French would be preferable to phantasms and shadowy threats.

"Ha, those frog-eaters," she said, proving his supposition by drawing herself up with a touch of scorn in her voice. "They have tried before, the Schloss to take. They have never done it; they will not do it now." She gestured briefly at the stone walls surrounding them, by way of justification in this opinion. "My husband's great-great-great-grandfather built the Schloss; we have a well inside the house, a stable, food stores. This place was built to withstand siege."

"I am sure you are right," Grey said, smiling. "But you will perhaps take some care?" He let go her hands, willing her to draw the interview to a close. Excitement over, he was very much aware that it had been a long day, and that he was freezing.

"I will," she promised him. She hesitated a moment, not quite sure how to take her leave gracefully, then stepped forward, rose onto her toes, and, with her hands on his shoulders, kissed him on the mouth.

"Good night, Lord John," she said softly, in English. *"Danke."* She turned and hurried up the stairs, picking up her skirts as she went.

Grey stood for a startled moment looking after her, the disconcerting feel of her uncorseted breasts still imprinted on his chest, then shook his head and went to pick up the candlestick she had left on the stair for him.

Straightening up, he was overtaken by a massive yawn, the fatigues of the day coming down upon him like a thousandweight of grapeshot. He only hoped he could find his own chamber again, in this ancient labyrinth. Perhaps he should have asked the Princess for direction.

He made his way back down the hallway, his candle flame seeming puny and insignificant in the oppressive darkness cast by the great stone blocks of Schloss Lowenstein. It was only when the light gleamed on the puddle on the floor that the thought suddenly occurred to him: Someone had to have opened the shutters—from the inside.

Grey made his way back as far as the head of the main stair, only to find Stephan von Namtzen coming up it. The Hanoverian was a little flushed with brandy, but still clearheaded, and listened to Grey's account of events with consternation.

"Dreckskerle!" he said, and spat on the floor to emphasize his opinion of kidnappers. "The servants are searching, you say—but you think they will find nothing?"

"Perhaps they will find the nurse," Grey said. "But if the kidnapper has an ally inside the house—and he must . . . or she, I suppose," he added. "The boy did say he saw a witch."

"Ja, I see." Von Namtzen looked grim. One big hand fisted at his side, but then relaxed. "I will perhaps go and speak to the Princess. My men, I will have them come to guard the house. If there is a criminal within, he will not get out."

"I'm sure the Princess will be grateful." Grey felt all at once terribly tired. "I must take Bodger—the body—back to his regiment in the morning. Oh—in that regard . . ." He explained Sir Peter's wishes, to which von Namtzen agreed with a flip of the hand.

"Have you any messages for me to carry, to the troops at the bridge?" Grey asked. "Since I will be going in that direction, anyway." One English regiment lay to the south of the town, the other—Bodger's—to the north, between the town and the river. A small group of the Prussian artillery under Stephan's command was stationed a few miles beyond, guarding the bridge at Aschenwald.

Von Namtzen frowned, thinking, then nodded.

"*Ja,* you are right. It is best they hear officially of the—" He looked suddenly uneasy, and Grey was slightly amused to see that Stephan did not want to speak the word "succubus."

"Yes, better to avoid rumors," he agreed, saving Stephan's awkwardness. "Speaking of that—do you suppose Herr Blomberg will let the villagers exhume his mother?"

Stephan's broad-boned face broke into a smile.

"No," he said. "I think he would make them drive an iron rod through his own heart, first. Better, though," he added, the humor fading from his face, "if someone finds who plays these tricks, and a stop to it makes. Quickly."

Stephan was tired, too, Grey saw; his English grammar was slipping. They stood together for a moment, silent, listening to the distant hammer of the rain, both feeling still the chill touch of the graveyard in their bones.

Von Namtzen turned to him suddenly, and put a hand on his shoulder, squeezing.

"You will take care, John," he said, and before Grey could speak or move, Stephan pulled him close and kissed his mouth. Then he smiled, squeezed Grey's shoulder once more, and, with a quiet *"Gute Nacht,"* went up the stairs toward his own room.

Grey shut the door of his chamber behind him and leaned against it, in the manner of a man pursued. Tom Byrd, curled up asleep on the hearth rug, sat up and blinked at him.

"Me lord?"

"Who else?" Grey asked, made jocular from the fatigues and excitements of the evening. "Did you expect a visit from the succubus?"

Tom's face lost all its sleepiness at that, and he glanced uneasily at the window, closed and tightly shuttered against the dangers of the night.

"You oughtn't jest that way, me lord," he said reproachfully. "It's an Englishman what's dead now."

"You are right, Tom; I beg pardon of Private Bodger." Grey found some justice in the rebuke, but was too much overtaken by events to be stung by it. "Still, we do not know the cause of his death. Surely there is no proof as yet that it was occasioned by any sort of supernatural interference. Have you eaten?"

"Yes, me lord. Cook had gone to bed, but she got up and fetched us out some bread and dripping, and some ale. Wanting to know all about what I found in the churchyard," he added practically.

Grey smiled to himself; the faint emphasis on "I" in this statement indicated to him that Tom's protests on behalf of the late Private Bodger sprang as much from a sense of proprietariness as from a sense of propriety.

Grey sat down, to let Tom pull off his boots and still-damp stockings. The room he had been given was small but warm and bright, the shadows from the well-tended fire flickering over striped damask wallpaper. After the wet cold of the churchyard and the bleak chill of the Schloss's stone corridors, the heat upon his skin was a grateful feeling—much enhanced by the discovery of a pitcher of hot water for washing.

"Shall I come with you, me lord? In the morning, I mean." Tom undid the binding of Grey's hair and began to comb it, dipping the comb occasionally in a cologne of bay leaves and chamomile, meant to discourage lice.

"No, I think not. I shall ride over and speak to Colonel Ruysdale first; one of the servants can follow me with the body." Grey closed his eyes, beginning to feel drowsy, though small jolts of excitement still pulsed through his thighs and abdomen. "If you would, Tom, I should like you to talk with the servants; find out what they are saying about things." God knew, they would have plenty to talk about.

Clean, brushed, warmed, and cozily ensconced in night-shirt, cap and banyan, Grey dismissed Tom, the valet's arms piled high with filthy uniform bits.

He shut the door behind the boy and hesitated, staring into the polished surface of the wood as though to look through it and see who might be standing on the other side. Only the blur of his own face met his gaze, though, and only the creak of Tom's footsteps was audible, receding down the corridor.

Thoughtfully, he touched his lips with a finger. Then he sighed, and bolted the door.

Stephan had kissed him before—kissed innumerable people, for that matter, the man was an inveterate *embrasseur.* But surely this had been somewhat more than the fraternal embrace of a fellow soldier or particular friend. He could still feel the grip of Stephan's hand, curled around his leg. Or was he deluded by fatigue and distraction, imagining more to it than there was?

And if he were right?

He shook his head, took the warming pan from his sheets, and crawled between them, reflecting that, of all the men in Gundwitz that night, he at least was safe from the attentions of any roving succubi.

CHAPTER 3
A REMEDY FOR SLEEPLESSNESS

Regimental headquarters for the Fifty-second were in Bonz, a small hamlet that stood some ten miles from Gundwitz. Grey found Colonel Ruysdale in the central room of the largest inn, in urgent conference with several other officers, and indisposed to take time to deal with an enlisted body.

"Grey? Oh, yes, know your brother. You found what? Where? Yes, all right. See, um . . . Sergeant-Major Sapp. Yes, that's it. Sapp will know who . . ." The Colonel waved a vague hand, indicating that Grey would doubtless find whatever assistance he required elsewhere.

"Yes, sir," Grey said, settling his boot heels into the sawdust. "I shall do so directly. Am I to understand, though, that there are developments of which our allies should be informed?"

Ruysdale stared at him, eyes cold and upper lip foremost. "Who told you that, sir?"

As though he needed telling. Troops were being mustered outside the village, drummers beating the call to arms and corporals shouting through the streets, men pouring out from their quarters like an anthill stirred with a stick.

"I am a liaison officer, sir, seconded to Captain von Namtzen's Hanoverian foot," Grey replied, evading the question. "They are at present quartered in Gundwitz; will you require their support?"

Ruysdale looked grossly offended at the notion, but a captain wearing an artillery cockade coughed tactfully.

"Colonel, shall I give Major Grey such particulars of the situation as may seem useful? You have important matters to deal with . . ." He nodded around at the assembled officers, who seemed attentive, but hardly on the brink of action.

The Colonel snorted briefly and made a gesture somewhere between gracious dismissal and the waving away of some noxious insect, and Grey bowed, murmuring, "Your servant, sir."

Outside, the clouds of last night's storm were making a hasty exodus, scudding away on a fresh, cold wind. The artillery captain clapped a hand to his hat, and jerked his head toward a pot-house down the street.

"A bit of warmth, Major?"

Gathering that the village was in no danger of imminent invasion, Grey nodded and accompanied his new companion into a dark, smoky womb, smelling of pig's feet and fermented cabbage.

"Benjamin Hiltern," the Captain said, putting back his

cloak and holding up two fingers to the barman. "You'll take a drink, Major?"

"John Grey. I thank you. I collect we shall have time to drink it, before we are quite overrun?"

Hiltern laughed, and sat down across from Grey, rubbing a knuckle under a cold-reddened nose.

"We should have time for our gracious host—" He nodded at the wizened creature fumbling with a jug, "—to hunt a boar, roast it, and serve it up with an apple in its mouth, if you should be so inclined."

"I am obliged, Captain," Grey said, with a glance at the barman, who upon closer inspection appeared to have only one leg, the other being supported by a stout peg of battered aspect. "Alas, I have breakfasted but recently."

"Too bad. I haven't. *Bratkartoffeln mit Rührei,*" Hiltern said to the barman, who nodded and disappeared into some still more squalid den to the rear of the house. "Potatoes, fried with eggs and ham," he explained, taking out a kerchief and tucking it into the neck of his shirt. "Delicious."

"Quite," Grey said politely. "One would hope that your troops are fed as well, after the effort I saw being expended."

"Oh, that." Hiltern's cherubic countenance lost a little of its cheerfulness, but not much. "Poor sods. At least it's stopped raining."

In answer to Grey's raised brows, he explained.

"Punishment. There was a game of bowls yesterday, between a party of men from Colonel Bampton-Howard's lot and our lads—local form of skittles. Ruysdale had a heavy wager on with Bampton-Howard, see?"

"And your lot lost. Yes, I see. So your lads are—"

"Ten-mile run to the river and back, in full kit. Keep them fit and out of trouble, at least," Hiltern said, half closing his eyes and lifting his nose at the scent of frying potatoes that had begun to waft through the air.

"I see. One assumes that the French have moved, then? Our last intelligence reported them as being a few miles north of the river."

"Yes, gave us a bit of excitement for a day or two; thought they might come this way. They seem to have sheered off, though—gone round to the west."

"Why?" Grey felt a prickle of unease go down his spine. There was a bridge at Aschenwald, a logical crossing point— but there was another several miles north, at Gruneberg. Aschenwald was defended by a company of Prussian artillery; a detachment of grenadiers, under Colonel Bampton-Howard, presumably held the other crossing.

"There's a mass of Frenchies beyond the river," Hiltern replied. "We think they have it in mind to join up with that lot."

That was interesting. It was also information that should have been shared with the Hanoverian and Prussian commanders by official dispatch—not acquired accidentally by the random visit of a liaison officer. Sir Peter Hicks was scrupulous in maintaining communications with the allies; Ruysdale evidently saw no such need.

"Oh!" Hiltern said, divining his thought. "I'm sure we would have let you know, only for things here being in a bit of confusion. And truly, it didn't seem urgent; scouts just said the French were shining their gear, biffing up the supplies, that sort of thing. After all, they've got to go *somewhere* before the snow comes down."

He raised one dark brow, smiling in apology—an apology that Grey accepted with no more than a second's hesitation. If Ruysdale was going to be erratic about dispatches, it would be as well for Grey to keep himself informed by other means— and Hiltern was obviously well placed to know what was going on.

They chatted casually until the host came out with Hiltern's breakfast, but Grey learned no more of interest—save that Hiltern was remarkably *un*interested in the death of Private Bodger. He was also vague about the "confusion" to which he had referred, dismissing it with a wave of the hand as "bit of a muddle in the commissary—damn bore."

The sound of hooves and wheels, moving slowly, came from the street outside, and Grey heard a loud voice with a distinctly Hanoverian accent, requesting direction *"Zum Englanderlager."*

"What is *that*?" Hiltern asked, turning on his stool.

"I expect that will be Private Bodger coming home," Grey replied, rising. "I'm obliged to you, sir. Is Sergeant-Major Sapp still in camp, do you know?"

"Mmm . . . no." Hiltern spoke thickly, through a mouthful of potatoes and eggs. "Gone to the river."

That was inconvenient; Grey had no desire to hang about all day, waiting for Sapp's return in order to hand over the corpse and responsibility for it. Another idea occurred to him, though.

"And the regimental surgeon?"

"Dead. Flux." Hiltern spooned in more egg, concentrating. "Mmp. Try Keegan. He's the surgeon's assistant."

With most of the men emptying out of camp, it took some time to locate the surgeon's tent. Once there, Grey had the body deposited on a bench, and at once sent the wagon back to the Schloss. He was taking no chances on being left in custody of Private Bodger.

Keegan proved to be a scrappy Welshman, equipped with rimless spectacles and an incongruous mop of reddish ringlets. Blinking through the spectacles, he bent close to the corpse and poked at it with a smudgy exploratory finger.

"No blood."

"No."

"Fever?"

"Probably not. I saw the man several hours before his death, and he seemed in reasonable health then."

"Hmmm." Keegan bent and peered keenly up Bodger's nostrils, as though suspecting the answer to the private's untimely death might be lurking there.

Grey frowned at the fellow's grubby knuckles and the thin crust of blood that rimmed his cuff. Nothing out of the way for a surgeon, but the dirt bothered him.

Keegan tried to thumb up one of the eyelids, but it resisted him. Bodger had stiffened during the night, and while the hands and arms had gone limp again, the face, body, and legs were all hard as wood. Keegan sighed and began tugging off the corpse's stockings. These were greatly the worse for wear, the soles stained with mud; the left one had a hole worn through, and Bodger's great toe poked out like the head of an inquisitive worm.

Keegan rubbed a hand on the skirt of his already grubby coat, leaving further streaks, then rubbed it under his nose, sniffing loudly. Grey had an urge to step away from the man. Then he realized, with a small sense of startlement mingled with annoyance, that he was thinking of the Woman again. Fraser's wife. Fraser had spoken of her very little—but that reticence only added to the significance of what he *did* say.

One late night, in the Governor's quarters at Ardsmuir Prison, they had sat longer than usual over their chess game—a hard-fought draw, in which Grey took more pleasure than he might have taken in victory over a lesser opponent. They usually drank sherry, but not that night; he had a special claret, a present from his mother, and had insisted that Fraser must help him to finish it, as the wine would not keep, once opened.

It was a strong wine, and between the headiness of it and the stimulation of the game, even Fraser had lost a little of his formidable reserve.

Past midnight, Grey's orderly had come to take away the dishes from their repast, and, stumbling sleepily on the threshold in his leaving, had sprawled full length, cutting himself badly on a shard of glass. Fraser had leapt up like a cat, snatched the boy up, and pressed a fold of his shirt to the wound to stop the bleeding. But then, when Grey would have sent for a surgeon, had stopped him, saying tersely that Grey could do so if he wished to kill the lad, but if not, had best allow Fraser to tend him.

This he had done with skill and gentleness, washing first his hands, and then the wound, with wine, then demanding needle and silk thread—which he had astonished Grey by dipping into the wine as well, and passing the needle through the flame of a candle.

"My wife would do it so," he'd said, frowning slightly in concentration. "There are the wee beasties, called germs, d'ye see, and if they—" He set his teeth momentarily into his lip as he made the first stitch, then went on.

"If they should be getting into a wound, it will suppurate. So ye must wash well before ye tend the wound, and put flame or alcohol to your instruments, to kill the germs." He smiled briefly at the orderly, who was white-faced and wobbling on his stool. "Never let a surgeon wi' dirty hands touch ye, she said. Better to bleed to death quickly than die slow of the pus, aye?"

Grey was as skeptical of the existence of germs as of succubi, but ever afterward had glanced automatically at the hands of any medical man—and it did seem to him that perhaps the more cleanly of the breed tended to lose fewer patients, though he had made no real study of the matter.

In the present instance, though, Mr. Keegan offered no hazard to the late Private Bodger, and despite his distaste Grey made no protest as the surgeon undressed the corpse, making small interested "Tut!" noises in response to the postmortem phenomena thus revealed.

Grey was already aware that the private had died in a state of arousal. This state appeared to be permanent, even though the limbs had begun to relax from their rigor, and was the occasion of a surprised "Tut!" from Mr. Keegan.

"Well, he died happy, at least," Keegan said, blinking. "Sweet God Almighty."

"Is this a . . . normal manifestation, do you think?" Grey inquired. He had rather expected Private Bodger's condition to abate postmortem. If anything, it seemed particularly pronounced, viewed by daylight. Though of course that might be merely an artifact of the color, which was now a virulent dark purple, in stark contrast to the pallid flesh of the body.

Keegan prodded the condition cautiously with a forefinger.

"Stiff as wood," he said, unnecessarily. "Normal? Don't know. Mind, what chaps I see here have mostly died of fever or flux, and men what are ill aren't mostly of a mind to . . .

hmmm." He relapsed into a thoughtful contemplation of the body.

"What did the woman say?" he asked, shaking himself out of this reverie after a moment or two.

"Who, the woman he was with? Gone. Not that one might blame her." Always assuming that it had been a woman, he added to himself. Though given Private Bodger's earlier encounter with the gypsy, one *would* assume . . .

"Can you say what caused his death?" Grey inquired, seeing that Keegan had begun to inspect the body as a whole, though his fascinated gaze kept returning to . . . color notwithstanding, it really was remarkable.

The assistant surgeon shook his ringlets, absorbed in wrestling off the corpse's shirt.

"No wound that I can see. Blow to the head, perhaps?" He bent close, squinting at the corpse's head and face, poking here and there in an exploratory fashion.

A group of men in uniform came toward them at the trot, hastily doing up straps and buttons, hiking packs and muskets into place, and cursing as they went. Grey removed his hat and placed it strategically abaft the corpse, not wishing to excite public remark—but no one bothered to spare a glance at the tableau by the surgeon's tent; one dead man was much like another.

Grey reclaimed his hat and watched them go, grumbling like a miniature thunderstorm on the move. Most of the troops were already massed on the parade ground. He could see them in the distance, moving in a slow, disorderly mill that would snap into clean formation at the Sergeant-Major's shout.

"I know Colonel Ruysdale by reputation," Grey said, after a thoughtful pause, "though not personally. I have heard him described as 'a bit of a Gawd-'elp-us,' but I have not heard that he is altogether an ass."

Keegan smiled, keeping his eyes on his work.

"Shouldn't think he is," he agreed. "Not altogether."

Grey kept an inviting silence, to which invitation the surgeon acquiesced within moments.

"He means to wear them out, see. Bring them back so tired they fall asleep in their suppers."

"Oh, yes?"

"They been a-staying up all night, you see? Nobody wanting to fall asleep, lest the thing—a sucky-bus, is it?—should come round in their dreams. Mind, it's good for the tavern owners, but not so good for discipline, what with men falling asleep on sentry-go, or in the midst of drill . . ."

Keegan glanced up from his inspections, observing Grey with interest.

"Not sleeping so well yourself, Major?" He tapped a dirty finger beneath his eye, indicating the presence of dark rings, and chuckled.

"I kept rather late hours last night, yes," Grey replied equably. "Owing to the discovery of Private Bodger."

"Hmmm. Yes, I see." Keegan said, straightening up. "Seems as though the sucky-bus had her fill of him, then."

"So you do know about the rumors of a succubus?" Grey asked, ignoring the attempt at badinage.

"Of course I do." Keegan looked surprised. "Everybody knows. Aren't I just telling you?"

Keegan did not know how the rumor had reached the encampment, but it had spread like wildfire, reaching every man in camp within twenty-four hours. Original scoffing had become skeptical attention, and then reluctant belief, as more stories began to circulate of the dreams and torments suffered by men in the town—and had become outright panic, with the news of the Prussian soldier's death.

"I don't suppose you saw that body?" Grey asked, interested.

The Welshman shook his head.

"The word is that the poor bugger was drained of blood—but who's to know the truth of it? Perhaps it was an apoplexy; I've seen 'em taken so, sometimes—the blood comes bursting from the nose, so as to relieve the pressure on the brain. Messy enough to look at."

"You seem a rational man, sir," Grey said, in compliment.

Keegan gave a small, huffing sort of laugh, dismissing it,

and straightened up, brushing his palms once more against his coat skirts.

"Deal with soldiers for as long as I have, Major, and you get used to wild stories, that's all I can say. Men in camp, 'specially. Not enough to keep them busy, and a good tale will spread like butter on hot toast. And when it comes to dreams—!" He threw up his hands.

Grey nodded, acknowledging the truth of this. Soldiers put great store in dreams.

"So you can tell me nothing regarding the cause of Private Bodger's death?"

Keegan shook his head, scratching at a row of flea bites on his neck as he did so.

"Don't see a thing, sir, I'm sorry to say. Other than the . . . um . . . obvious," he nodded delicately toward the corpse's midregion, "and that's not generally fatal. You might ask the fellow's friends, though. Just in case."

This cryptic allusion made Grey glance up in question, and Keegan coughed.

"I did say the men didn't sleep, sir? Not wanting to give any sucky-bus an invitation, so to speak. Well, some went a bit further than that, and took matters—so to speak—into their own hands."

A few bold souls, Keegan said, had reasoned that if what the succubus desired was the male essence, safety lay in removing this temptation—"so to speak, sir." While most of those choosing this expedient had presumably chosen to take their precautions in privacy, the men lived in very close quarters. It was in fact complaints from more than one citizen of gross mass indecency by the soldiers quartered on his premises that had provoked General Ruysdale's edict.

"Only thinking, sir, as a wet graveyard is maybe not the place I'd choose for romance, was the opportunity to come my way. But I could see, maybe, a group of men thinking they'd face down the sucky-bus on her own ground, perhaps? And if Private . . . Bodger, you said was his name, sir? . . . was to have keeled over in the midst of such proceedings . . . well, I expect his comrades would have buggered off smartly, not hung about to answer questions."

"You have a very interesting turn of mind, Mr. Keegan," Grey said. "Highly rational. I don't suppose it was you who suggested this particular . . . precaution?"

"Who, me?" Keegan tried—and failed—to exhibit outrage. "The idea, Major!"

"Quite," Grey said, and took his leave.

In the distance, the troops were departing the parade ground in orderly fashion, each rank setting off in turn, to the clank and rattle of canteens and muskets and the staccato cries of corporals and sergeants. He stopped for a moment to watch them, enjoying the warmth of the autumn sun on his back.

After the fury of the night's storm, the day had dawned clear and calm, and promised to be mild. Very muddy underfoot, though, he noted, seeing the churned earth of the parade ground, and the spray of clods flying off the feet of the runners, spattering their breeches. It would be heavy going, and the devil of a sweat to clean up afterward. Ruysdale might not have intended this exercise principally as punishment, but that's what it would be.

Artilleryman that he was, Grey automatically evaluated the quality of the terrain for the passage of caissons. Not a chance. The ground was soft as sodden cheese. Even the mortars would bog down in nothing flat.

He turned, eyeing the distant hills where the French were said to be. If they had cannon, chances were that they were going nowhere for the moment.

The situation still left him with a lingering sense of unease, loath though he was to admit it. Yes, the French likely were intending to move toward the north. No, there was no apparent reason for them to cross the valley; Gundwitz had no strategic importance, nor was it of sufficient size to be worth a detour to loot. Yes, Ruysdale's troops were between the French and the town. But he looked at the deserted parade ground, and the troops vanishing in the distance, and felt a tickle between the shoulder blades, as though someone stood behind him with a loaded pistol.

"I should feel a little happier if an additional detachment could be sent to guard the bridge." Hicks's words echoed in memory. So Sir Peter felt that itch, as well. It was possible, Grey reflected, that Ruysdale *was* an ass.

CHAPTER 4
THE GUN-CREW

It was past midday by the time he reached the river. From a distance, it was a tranquil landscape under a high, pale sun, the river bordered by a thick growth of trees in autumn leaf, their ancient golds and bloody reds a-shimmer, in contrast to the black-and-dun patchwork of fallow fields and meadows gone to seed.

A little closer, though, and the river itself dispelled this impression of pastoral charm. It was a broad, deep stream, turbulent and fast moving, much swollen by the recent rains. Even at a distance, he could see the tumbling forms of uprooted trees and bushes, and the occasional carcass of a small animal, drowned in the current.

The Prussian artillery were placed upon a small rise of ground, concealed in a copse. Only one ten-pounder, he saw, with a sense of unease, and a small mortar—though there were sufficient stores of shot and powder, and these were commendably well kept, with a Prussian sense of order, tidily sheltered under canvas against the rain.

The men greeted him with great cordiality; any diversion from the boredom of bridge guarding was welcome—the more welcome if it came bearing beer, which Grey did, having thoughtfully procured two large ale-skins before leaving camp.

"You will with us eat, Major," said the Hanoverian Lieutenant in charge, accepting both beer and dispatches, and waving a gracious hand toward a convenient boulder.

It was a long time since breakfast, and Grey accepted the invitation with pleasure. He took off his coat and spread it over the boulder, rolled up his sleeves, and joined companionably in the hard biscuit, cheese, and beer, accepting with gratitude a few bites of chewy, spicy sausage as well.

Lieutenant Dietrich, a middle-aged gentleman with a luxuriant beard and eyebrows to match, opened the dispatches and read them while Grey practiced his German with the gun-crew. He kept a careful eye upon the Lieutenant as he chatted, though, curious to see what the artilleryman would make of von Namtzen's dispatch.

The Lieutenant's eyebrows were an admirable indication of his interior condition; they remained level for the first moments of reading, then rose to an apex of astonishment, where they remained suspended for no little time, returning to their original position with small flutters of dismay as the Lieutenant decided how much of this information it was wise to impart to his men.

The Lieutenant folded the paper, shooting Grey a sharp interrogative glance. Grey gave a slight nod; yes, he knew what the dispatch said.

The Lieutenant glanced around at the men, then back over his shoulder, as though judging the distance across the valley to the British camp and the town beyond. Then he looked back at Grey, thoughtfully chewing his mustache, and shook his head slightly. He would not mention the matter of a succubus.

On the whole, Grey thought that wise, and inclined his head an inch in agreement. There were only ten men present; if any of them had already known of the rumors, all would know. And while the Lieutenant seemed at ease with his command, the fact remained that these were Prussians, and not his own men. He could not be sure of their response.

The Lieutenant folded away his papers and came to join the conversation. However, Grey observed with interest that the substance of the dispatch seemed to weigh upon the Lieutenant's mind, in such a way that the conversation turned—with no perceptible nudge in that direction, but with the inexorable swing of a compass needle—to manifestations of the supernatural.

It being a fine day, with golden leaves drifting gently down around them, the gurgle of the river nearby, and plenty of beer to hand, the varied tales of ghosts, bleeding nuns, and spectral battles in the sky were no more than the stuff of entertainment. In the cold shadows of the night, it would be different—though the stories would still be told. More than cannonshot, bayonets, or disease, boredom was a soldier's greatest enemy.

At one point, though, an artilleryman told the story of a fine house in his town, where the cries of a ghostly child echoed in the rooms at night, to the consternation of the householders. In time, they traced the sound to one particular wall, chipped away the plaster, and discovered a bricked-up chimney, in which lay the remains of a young boy, next to the dagger that had cut his throat.

Several of the soldiers made the sign of the horns at this, but Grey saw distinct expressions of unease on the faces of two of the men. These two exchanged glances, then looked hurriedly away.

"You have heard such a story before, perhaps?" Grey asked, addressing the younger of the two directly. He smiled, doing his best to look harmlessly engaging.

The boy—he could be no more than fifteen—hesitated, but such was the press of interest from those around him that he could not resist.

"Not a story," he said. "I—we—" He nodded at his fellow. "—last night, in the storm. Samson and I heard a child crying, near the river. We went to look, with a lantern, but there was nothing there. Still, we heard it. It went on and on, though we walked up and down, calling and searching, until we were wet through, and nearly frozen."

"Oh, is that what you were doing?" a fellow in his twenties interjected, grinning. "And here we thought you and Samson were just buggering each other under the bridge."

Blood surged up into the boy's face with a suddenness that made his eyes bulge, and he launched himself at the older man, knocking him off his seat and rolling with him into the leaves in a ball of fists and elbows.

Grey sprang to his feet and kicked them apart, seizing the boy by the scruff of the neck and jerking him up. The Lieutenant was shouting at them angrily in idiomatic German, which Grey ignored. He shook the boy slightly, to bring him to his senses, and said, very quietly, "Laugh. It was a joke."

He stared hard into the boy's eyes, willing him to come to his senses. The thin shoulders under his hands vibrated with the need to strike out, to hit something—and the brown eyes were glassy with anguish and confusion.

Grey shook him harder, then released him, and under the guise of slapping dead leaves from his uniform, leaned closer. "If you act like this, they will know," he said, speaking in a rapid whisper. "For God's sake, laugh!"

Samson, experienced enough to know what to do in such circumstances, was doing it—elbowing away joking comrades, replying to crude jests with cruder ones. The young boy glanced at him, a flicker of awareness coming back into his face. Grey let him go, and turned back to the group, saying loudly, "If I were going to bugger someone, I would wait for good weather. A man must be desperate to swive *anything* in such rain and thunder!"

"It's been a long time, Major," said one of the soldiers, laughing. He made a crude thrusting gesture with his hips. "Even a sheep in a snowstorm would look good now!"

"Haha. Go fuck yourself, Wulfie. The sheep wouldn't have you." The boy was still flushed and damp-eyed, but back in control of himself. He rubbed a hand across his mouth and spat, forcing a grin as the others laughed.

"You *could* fuck yourself, Wulfie—if your dick is as long as you say it is." Samson leered at Wulf, who stuck out an amazingly long tongue in reply, waggling it in derision.

"Don't you wish you knew!"

The discussion was interrupted at this point by two soldiers who came puffing up the rise, wet to the waist and dragging with them a large dead pig, fished out of the river. This addition to supper was greeted with cries of approbation, and half the men fell at once to the work of butchery, the others returning in desultory fashion to their conversation.

The vigor had gone out of it, though, and Grey was about to take his leave, when one of the men said something, laughing, about gypsy women.

"What did you say? I mean—*was habt Ihr das gesagt?* He groped for his German. "Gypsies? You have seen them recently?"

"Oh, *ja,* Major," said the soldier, obligingly. "This morning. They came across the bridge, six wagons with mules. They go back and forth. We've seen them before."

With a little effort, Grey kept his voice calm.

"Indeed?" He turned to the Lieutenant. "Does it not seem possible that they may have dealings with the French?"

"Of course." The Lieutenant looked mildly surprised, then grinned. "What are they going to tell the French? That we're here? I think they know that, Major."

He gestured toward a gap in the trees. Through it, Grey could see the English soldiers of Ruysdale's regiment, perhaps a mile away, their ranks piling up on the bank of the river like driftwood as they flung down their packs and waded into the shallows to drink, hot and mud-caked from their run.

It was true: The presence of the English and Hanoverian regiments could be a surprise to no one; anyone on the cliffs with a spyglass could likely count the spots on Colonel Ruysdale's dog. As for information regarding their movements . . . well, since neither Ruysdale nor Hicks had any idea where they were going or when, there wasn't any great danger of that intelligence being revealed to the enemy.

He smiled, and took gracious leave of the Lieutenant, though privately resolving to speak to Stephan von Namtzen. Perhaps the gypsies were harmless—but they should be looked into. If nothing else, the gypsies were in a position to tell anyone who cared to ask them how few men were guarding that bridge. And somehow, he thought that Ruysdale was not of a mind to consider Sir Peter's request for reinforcement, though Grey had delivered it.

He waved casually to the artillerymen, who took little notice, elbow-deep in blood and pig guts. The boy was by himself, chopping green wood for the spit.

Leaving the artillery camp, he rode up to the head of the bridge and paused, reining Karolus in as he looked across the river. The land was flat for a little way, but then broke into rolling hills that rose to a steep promontory. Above, on the cliffs, the French presumably still lurked. He took a small spyglass from his pocket and scanned the clifftops, slowly. Nothing moved on the heights: no horses, no men, no swaying banners—and yet a faint gray haze drifted up there, a cloud in an otherwise cloudless sky. The smoke of campfires; many of them. Yes, the French were still there.

He scanned the hills below, looking carefully—but if the gypsies were there as well, no rising plume of smoke betrayed their presence.

He should find the gypsy camp and question its inhabitants himself—but it was growing late, and he had no stomach for that now. He reined about and turned the horse's head back toward the distant town, not glancing at the copse that hid the cannon and its crew.

The boy had best learn—and quickly—to hide his nature, or he would become in short order bumboy to any man who cared to use him. And many would. Wulf had been correct: After months in the field, soldiers were not particular, and the boy was much more appealing than a sheep, with those soft red lips and tender skin.

Karolus tossed his head, and he slowed, uneasy. Grey's hands were trembling on the reins, gripped far too tightly. He forced them to relax, stilled the trembling, and spoke calmly to the horse, nudging him back to speed.

He had been attacked once, in camp somewhere in Scotland, in the days after Culloden. Someone had come upon him in the dark, and taken him from behind with an arm across his throat. He had thought he was dead, but his assailant had something else in mind. The man had never spoken, and was brutally swift about his business, leaving him moments later, curled in the dirt behind a wagon, speechless with shock and pain.

He had never known who it was: officer, soldier, or some anonymous intruder. Never known whether the man had discerned something in his own appearance or behavior that led to the attack, or had only taken him because he was there.

He *had* known the danger of telling anyone about it. He washed himself, stood straight and walked firmly, spoke normally and looked men in the eye. No one had suspected the bruised and riven flesh beneath his uniform, or the hollowness beneath his breastbone. And if his attacker sat at meals and broke bread with him, he had not known it. From that day, he had carried a dagger at all times, and no one had ever touched him again, against his will.

The sun was sinking behind him, and the shadow of horse and rider stretched out far before him, flying, and faceless in their flight.

CHAPTER 5
DARK DREAMS

Once more he was late for dinner. This time, though, a tray was brought for him, and he sat in the drawing room, taking his supper while the rest of the company chatted.

The Princess saw to his needs and sat with him for a time, flatteringly attentive. He was worn out from a day of riding, though, and his answers to her questions were brief. Soon enough, she drifted away and left him to a peaceful engagement with some cold venison and a tart of mushrooms and onions.

He had nearly finished when he felt a large, warm hand on his shoulder.

"So, you have seen the gun-crew at the bridge? They are in good order?" von Namtzen asked.

"Yes, very good," Grey replied. No point—not yet—in mentioning the young soldier to von Namtzen. "I told them more men will come, from Ruysdale's regiment. I hope they will."

"The bridge?" The Dowager, catching the word, turned from her conversation, frowning. "You have no need to worry, Landgrave. The bridge is safe."

"I am sure it will be safe, madam," Stephan said, clicking his heels gallantly as he bowed to the old lady. "You may be assured, Major Grey and I will protect you."

The old lady looked faintly put out at the notion.

"The bridge is safe," she repeated, touching the religious medal on the bodice of her gown, and glancing pugnaciously from man to man. "No enemy has crossed the bridge at Aschenwald in three hundred years. No enemy will ever cross it!"

Stephan glanced at Grey, and cleared his throat slightly. Grey cleared his own throat and made a gracious compliment upon the food.

When the Dowager had moved away, Stephan shook his head behind her back, and exchanged a brief smile with Grey.

"You know about that bridge?"

"No, is there something odd about it?"

"Only a story." Von Namtzen shrugged, with a tolerant scorn for the superstition of others. "They say that there is a guardian; a spirit of some kind that defends the bridge."

"Indeed," Grey said, with an uneasy memory of the stories told by the gun-crew stationed near the bridge. Were any of them local men, he wondered, who would know the story?

"Mein Gott," Stephan said, shaking his massive head as though assailed by gnats. "These stories! How can sane men believe such things?"

"I collect you do not mean that particular story?" Grey said. "The succubus, perhaps?"

"Don't speak to me of that thing," von Namtzen said gloomily. "My men look like scarecrows and jump at a bird's shadow. Every one of them is scared to lay his head upon a pillow, for fear that he will turn and look into the night-hag's face."

"Your chaps aren't the only ones." Sir Peter had come to pour himself another drink. He lifted the glass and took a deep swallow, shuddering slightly. Billman, behind him, nodded in glum confirmation.

"Bloody sleepwalkers, the lot."

"Ah," said Grey thoughtfully. "If I might make a suggestion . . . not my own, you understand. A notion mentioned by Ruysdale's surgeon . . ."

He explained Mr. Keegan's remedy, keeping his voice discreetly low. His listeners were less discreet in their response.

"What, Ruysdale's chaps are all boxing the Jesuit and begetting cockroaches?" Grey thought Sir Peter would expire from suffocated laughter. Just as well Lieutenant Dundas wasn't present, he thought.

"Perhaps not all of them," he said. "Evidently enough, though, to be of concern. I take it you have not experienced a similar phenomenon among your troops . . . yet?"

Billman caught the delicate pause and whooped loudly.

"Boxing the Jesuit?" Stephan nudged Grey with an elbow, and raised thick blond brows in puzzlement. "Cockroaches? What does this mean, please?"

"Ahhh . . ." Having no notion of the German equivalent of this expression, Grey resorted to a briefly graphic gesture with one hand, looking over his shoulder to be sure that none of the women was watching.

"Oh!" Von Namtzen looked mildly startled, but then grinned widely. "I see, yes, very good!" He nudged Grey again, more familiarly, and dropped his voice a little. "Perhaps wise to take some such precaution personally, do you think?"

The women and the German officers, heretofore intent on a card game, were looking toward the Englishmen in puzzlement. One man called a question to von Namtzen, and Grey was fortunately saved from reply.

Something occurred to him, though, and he grasped von Namtzen by the arm, as the latter was about to go and join the others at a hand of bravo.

"A moment, Stephan. I had meant to ask—that man of yours who died—Koenig? Did you see the body yourself?"

Von Namtzen was still smiling, but at this, his expression grew more somber, and he shook his head.

"No, I did not see him. They said, though, that his throat was most terribly torn—as though a wild animal had been at him. And yet he was not outside; he was found in his quarters." He shook his head again, and left to join the card game.

Grey finished his meal amid cordial conversation with Sir Peter and Billman, though keeping an inconspicuous eye upon the progress of the card game.

Stephan was in dress uniform tonight. A smaller man would have been overwhelmed by it; German taste in military decoration was grossly excessive, to an English eye. With his big frame and leonine blond head though, the Landgrave von Erdberg was merely . . . eye catching.

He appeared to have caught the eye not only of the Princess Louisa, but also of three young women, friends of the Princess. These surrounded him like a moony triplet, caught in his orbit. Now he reached into the breast of his coat and withdrew some small object, causing them to cluster around to look at it.

Grey turned to answer some question of Billman's, but then turned back, trying not to look too obviously.

He had been trying to suppress the feeling Stephan roused in him, but in the end, such things were never controllable—they rose up. Sometimes like the bursting of a mortar shell, sometimes like the inexorable green spike of a crocus pushing through snow and ice—but they rose up.

Was he in love with Stephan? There was no question of that. He liked and respected the Hanoverian, but there was no madness in it, no yearning. Did he *want* Stephan? A soft warmth in his loins, as though his blood had begun somehow to simmer over a low flame, suggested that he did.

The ancient bear's skull still sat in its place of honor, below the old Prince's portrait. He moved slowly to examine it, keeping half an eye on Stephan.

"Surely you have not eaten enough, John!" A delicate hand on his elbow turned him, and he looked down into the Princess's face, smiling up at him with pretty coquetry. "A strong man, out all day—let me call the servants to bring you something special."

"I assure you, Your Highness . . ." But she would have none of it, and, tapping him playfully with her fan, she scudded away like a gilded cloud, to have some special dessert prepared for him.

Feeling obscurely like a fatted calf being readied for the slaughter, Grey sought refuge in male company, coming to rest beside von Namtzen, who was folding up whatever he had been showing to the women, who had all gone to peer over the card players' shoulders and make bets.

"What is that?" Grey asked, nodding at the object.

"Oh—" Von Namtzen looked a little disconcerted at the question, but with only a moment's hesitation, handed it to Grey. It was a small leather case, hinged, with a gold closure. "My children."

It was a miniature, done by an excellent hand. The heads of two children, close together, one boy, one girl, both blond. The boy, clearly a little older, was perhaps three or four.

Grey felt momentarily as though he had received an actual blow to the pit of the stomach; his mouth opened, but he was incapable of speech. Or at least he thought he was. To his surprise, he heard his own voice, sounding calm, politely admiring.

"They are very handsome indeed. I am sure they are a consolation to your wife, in your absence."

Von Namtzen grimaced slightly, and gave a brief shrug.

"Their mother is dead. She died in childbirth when Elise was born." A huge forefinger touched the tiny face, very gently. "My mother looks after them."

Grey made the proper sounds of condolence, but had ceased to hear himself, for the confusion of thought and speculation that filled his mind.

So much so, in fact, that when the Princess's special dessert—an enormous concoction of preserved raspberries, brandy, sponge cake, and cream—arrived, he ate it all, despite the fact that raspberries made him itch.

* * *

He continued to think, long after the ladies had left. He joined the card game, bet extensively, and played wildly—winning, with Luck's usual perversity, though he paid no attention to his cards.

Had he been entirely wrong? It was possible. All of Stephan's gestures toward him had been within the bounds of normalcy—and yet . . .

And yet it was by no means unknown for men such as himself to marry and have children. Certainly men such as von Namtzen, with a title and estates to bequeath, would wish to have heirs. That thought steadied him, and though he scratched occasionally at chest or neck, he paid more attention to his game—and finally began to lose.

The card game broke up an hour later. Grey loitered a bit, in the hopes that Stephan might seek him out, but the Hanoverian was detained in argument with Kaptain Steffens, and at last Grey went upstairs, still scratching.

The halls were well lit tonight, and he found his own corridor without difficulty. He hoped Tom was still awake; perhaps the young valet could fetch him something for the itching. Some ointment, perhaps, or—he heard the rustle of fabric behind him, and turned to find the Princess approaching him.

She was once again in nightdress—but not the homely woolen garment she had worn the night before. This time, she wore a flowing thing of diaphanous lawn, which clung to her bosom and rather clearly revealed her nipples through the thin fabric. He thought she must be very cold, despite the lavishly embroidered robe thrown over the nightgown.

She had no cap, and her hair had been brushed out, but not yet plaited for the night: it flowed becomingly in golden waves below her shoulders. Grey began to feel somewhat cold, too, in spite of the brandy.

"My Lord," she said. "John," she added, and smiled. "I have something for you." She was holding something in one hand, he saw; a small box of some sort.

"Your Highness," he said, repressing the urge to take a

step backward. She was wearing a very strong scent, redo-
lent of tuberoses—a scent he particularly disliked.

"My name is Louisa," she said, taking another step toward
him. "Will you not call me by my name? Here, in private?"

"Of course. If you wish it—Louisa." Good God, what had
brought this on? He had sufficient experience to see what she
was about—he was a handsome man, of good family, and
with money; it had happened often enough—but not with
royalty, who tended to be accustomed to taking what they
wanted.

He took her outstretched hand, ostensibly for the purpose
of kissing it; in reality, to keep her at a safe distance. What
did she want? And why?

"This is—to thank you," she said as he raised his head
from her beringed knuckles. She thrust the box into his other
hand. "And to protect you."

"I assure you, madam, no thanks are necessary. I did nothing." Christ, was that it? Did she think she must bed him, in
token of thanks—or rather, had she convinced herself that
she must, because she wanted to? She did want to; he could
see her excitement, in the slightly widened blue eyes, the
flushed cheeks, the rapid pulse in her throat. He squeezed her
fingers gently and released them, then tried to hand back the
box.

"Really, madam—Louisa—I cannot accept this; surely it
is a treasure of your family." It certainly looked valuable;
small as it was, it was remarkably heavy—made either of
gilded lead or of solid gold—and sported a number of crudely
cut cabochon stones, which he feared were precious.

"Oh, it is," she assured him. "It has been in my husband's
family for hundreds of years."

"Oh, well, then certainly—"

"No, you must keep it," she said vehemently. "It will protect you from the creature."

"Creature. You mean the—"

"Der Nachtmahr," she said, lowering her voice and looking involuntarily over one shoulder, as though fearing that
some vile thing hovered in the air nearby.

Nachtmahr. "Nightmare," it meant. Despite himself, a brief shiver tightened Grey's shoulders. The halls were better lighted, but still harbored drafts that made the candles flicker and the shadows flow like moving water down the walls.

He glanced down at the box. There were letters etched into the lid, in Latin, but of so ancient a sort that it would take close examination to work out what they said.

"It is a reliquary," she said, moving closer, as though to point out the inscription. "Of Saint Orgevald."

"Ah? Er . . . yes. Most interesting." He thought this mildly gruesome. Of all the objectionable Popish practices, this habit of chopping up saints and scattering their remnants to the far ends of the earth was possibly the most reprehensible. But why should the Princess have such an item? The von Lowensteins were Lutheran. Of course, it *was* very old—no doubt she regarded it as no more than a family talisman.

She was very close, her perfume cloying in his nostrils. How was he to get rid of the woman? The door to his room was only a foot or two away; he had a strong urge to open it, leap in, and slam it shut, but that wouldn't do.

"You will protect me, protect my son," she murmured, looking trustfully up at him from beneath golden lashes. "So I will protect you, dear John."

She flung her arms about his neck, and once more glued her lips to his in a passionate kiss. Sheer courtesy required him to return the embrace, though his mind was racing, looking feverishly for some escape. Where the devil were the servants? Why did no one interrupt them?

Then someone did interrupt them. There was a gruff cough near at hand, and Grey broke the embrace with relief—a short-lived emotion, as he looked up to discover the Landgrave von Erdberg standing a few feet away, glowering under heavy brows.

"Your pardon, Your Highness," Stephan said, in tones of ice. "I wished to speak to Major Grey; I did not know anyone was here."

The Princess was flushed, but quite collected. She smoothed

her gown down across her body, drawing herself up in such a way that her fine bust was strongly emphasized.

"Oh," she said, very cool. "It's you, Erdberg. Do not worry, I was just taking my leave of the Major. You may have him now." A small, smug smile twitched at the corner of her mouth. Quite deliberately, she laid a hand along Grey's heated cheek, and let her fingers trail along his skin as she turned away. Then she strolled—curse the woman, she *strolled* away, switching the tail of her robe.

There was a profound silence in the hallway.

Grey broke it, finally.

"You wished to speak with me, Captain?"

Von Namtzen looked him over coldly, as though deciding whether to step on him.

"No," he said at last. "It will wait." He turned on his heel and strode away, making a good deal more noise in his departure than had the Princess.

Grey pressed a hand to his forehead, until he could trust his head not to explode, then shook it, and lunged for the door to his room before anything else should happen.

Tom was sitting on a stool by the fire, mending a pair of breeches that had suffered injury to the seams while Grey was demonstrating saber lunges to one of the German officers. He looked up at once when Grey came in, but if he had heard any of the conversation in the hall, he made no reference to it.

"What's that, me lord?" he asked instead, seeing the box in Grey's hand.

"What? Oh, that." Grey put it down, with a faint feeling of distaste. "A relic. Of Saint Orgevald, whoever he might be."

"Oh, I know him!"

"You do?" Grey raised one brow.

"Yes, me lord. There's a little chapel to him, down the garden. Ilse—she's one of the kitchen maids—was showing me. He's right famous hereabouts."

"Indeed." Grey began to undress, tossing his coat across the chair and starting on his waistcoat buttons. His fingers were impatient, slipping on the small buttons. "Famous for what?"

"Stopping them killing the children. Will I help you, me lord?"

"What?" Grey stopped, staring at the young valet, then shook his head and resumed twitching buttons. "No, continue. Killing what children?"

Tom's hair was standing up on end, as it tended to do whenever he was interested in a subject, owing to his habit of running one hand through it.

"Well, d'ye see, me lord, it used to be the custom, when they'd build something important, they'd buy a child from the gypsies—or just take one, I s'pose—and wall it up in the foundation. 'Specially for a bridge. It keeps anybody wicked from crossing over, see?"

Grey resumed his unbuttoning, more slowly. The hair prickled uneasily on his nape.

"The child—the murdered child—would cry out, I suppose?"

Tom looked surprised at his acumen.

"Yes, me lord. However did you know that?"

"Never mind. So Saint Orgevald put a stop to this practice, did he? Good for him." He glanced, more kindly, at the small gold box. "There's a chapel, you say—is it in use?"

"No, me lord. It's full of bits of stored rubbish. Or, rather—'tisn't in use for what you might call devotions. Folk do go there." The boy flushed a bit, and frowned intently at his work. Grey deduced that Ilse might have shown him another use for a deserted chapel, but chose not to pursue the matter.

"I see. Was Ilse able to tell you anything else of interest?"

"Depends upon what you call 'interesting,' me lord." Tom's eyes were still fixed upon his needle, but Grey could tell from the way in which he caught his upper lip between his teeth that he was in possession of a juicy bit of information.

"At this point, my chief interest is in my bed," Grey said,

finally extricating himself from the waistcoat, "but tell me anyway."

"Reckon you know the nursemaid's still gone?"

"I do."

"Did you know her name was Koenig, and that she was wife to the Hun soldier what the succubus got?"

Grey had just about broken Tom of calling the Germans "Huns," at least in their hearing, but chose to overlook this lapse.

"I did not." Grey unfastened his neckcloth, slowly. "Was this known to all the servants?" More importantly, did Stephan know?

"Oh, yes, me lord." Tom had laid down his needle, and now looked up, eager with his news. "See, the soldier, he used to do work here, at the Schloss."

"When? Was he a local man, then?" It was quite usual for soldiers to augment their pay by doing work for the local citizenry in their off hours, but Stephan's men had been *in situ* for less than a month. But if the nursery maid was the man's wife—

"Yes, me lord. Born here, the both of them. He joined the local regiment some years a-gone, and came here to work—"

"What work did he do?" Grey asked, unsure whether this had any bearing on Koenig's demise, but wanting a moment to encompass the information.

"Builder," Tom replied promptly. "Part of the upper floors got the wood-worm, and had to be replaced."

"Hmm. You seem remarkably well informed. Just how long did you spend in the chapel with young Ilse?"

Tom gave him a look of limpid innocence, much more inculpatory than an open leer.

"Me lord?"

"Never mind. Go on. Was the man working here at the time he was killed?"

"No, me lord. He left with the regiment two years back. He did come round a week or so ago, Ilse said, only to visit his friends among the servants, but he didn't work here."

Grey had now got down to his drawers, which he removed with a sigh of relief.

"Christ, what sort of perverse country is it where they put starch in a man's smallclothes? Can you not deal with the laundress, Tom?"

"Sorry, me lord." Tom scrambled to retrieve the discarded drawers. "I didn't know the word for 'starch.' I thought I did, but whatever I said just made 'em laugh."

"Well, don't make Ilse laugh too much. Leaving the maid-servants with child is an abuse of hospitality."

"Oh, no, me lord," Tom assured him earnestly. "We was too busy talking to, er . . ."

"To be sure you were," Grey said equably. "Did she tell you anything else of interest?"

"Mebbe." Tom had the nightshirt already aired and hanging by the fire to warm; he held it up for Grey to draw over his head, the wool flannel soft and grateful as it slid over his skin. "Mind, it's only gossip."

"Mmm?"

"One of the older footmen, who used to work with Koenig—after Koenig came to visit, he was talkin' with one of the other servants, and he said in Ilse's hearing as how little Siegfried was growing up to be the spit of him—of Koenig, I mean, not the footman. But then he saw her listening and shut up smart."

Grey stopped in the act of reaching for his banyan, and stared.

"Indeed," he said. Tom nodded, looking modestly pleased with the effect of his findings.

"That's the Princess's old husband, isn't it, over the mantel-piece in the drawing room? Ilse showed me the picture. Looks a proper old bugger, don't he?"

"Yes," said Grey, smiling slightly. "And?"

"He ain't had—hadn't, I mean—any children more than Siegfried, though he was married twice before. And Master Siegfried was born six months to the day after the old fellow died. That kind of thing always causes talk, don't it?"

"I should say so, yes." Grey thrust his feet into the

proffered slippers. "Thank you, Tom. You've done more than well."

Tom shrugged modestly, though his round face beamed as though illuminated from within.

"Will I fetch you tea, me lord? Or a nice syllabub?"

"Thank you, no. Find your bed, Tom, you've earned your rest."

"Very good, me lord." Tom bowed; his manners were improving markedly, under the example of the Schloss's servants. He picked up the clothes Grey had left on the chair, to take away for brushing, but then stopped to examine the little reliquary, which Grey had left on the table.

"That's a handsome thing, me lord. A relic, did you say? Isn't that a bit of somebody?"

"It is." Grey started to tell Tom to take the thing away with him, but stopped. It was undoubtedly valuable; best to leave it here. "Probably a finger or a toe, judging from the size."

Tom bent, peering at the faded lettering.

"What does it say, me lord? Can you read it?"

"Probably." Grey took the box, and brought it close to the candle. Held thus at an angle, the worn lettering sprang into legibility. So did the drawing etched into the top, which Grey had to that point assumed to be merely decorative lines. The words confirmed it.

"Isn't that a? . . ." Tom said, goggling at it.

"Yes, it is." Grey gingerly set the box down.

They regarded it in silence for a moment.

"Ah . . . where did you get it, me lord?" Tom asked, finally.

"The Princess gave it to me. As protection from the succubus."

"Oh." The young valet shifted his weight to one foot, and glanced sidelong at him. "Ah . . . d'ye think it will work?"

Grey cleared his throat.

"I assure you, Tom, if the phallus of Saint Orgevald does not protect me, nothing will."

Left alone, Grey sank into the chair by the fire, closed his eyes, and tried to compose himself sufficiently to think. The conversation with Tom had at least allowed him a little distance from which to contemplate matters with the Princess and Stephan—save that they didn't bear contemplation.

He felt mildly nauseated, and sat up to pour a glass of plum brandy from the decanter on the table. That helped, settling both his stomach and his mind.

He sat slowly sipping it, gradually bringing his mental faculties to bear on the less personal aspects of the situation.

Tom's discoveries cast a new and most interesting light on matters. If Grey had ever believed in the existence of a succubus—and he was sufficiently honest to admit that there had been moments, both in the graveyard and in the dark-flickering halls of the Schloss—he believed no longer.

The attempted kidnapping was plainly the work of some human agency, and the revelation of the relationship between the two Koenigs—the vanished nursemaid and her dead husband—just as plainly indicated that the death of Private Koenig was part of the same affair, no matter what hocus-pocus had been contrived around it.

Grey's father had died when he was twelve, but had succeeded in instilling in his sons his own admiration for the philosophy of reason. In addition to the concept of Occam's razor, his father had also introduced him to the useful doctrine of *Cui bono?*

The plainly obvious answer there was the Princess Louisa. Granting for the present that the gossip was true, and that Koenig had fathered little Siegfried . . . the last thing the woman could want was for Koenig to return and hang about where awkward resemblances could be noted.

He had no idea of the German law regarding paternity. In England, a child born in wedlock was legally the offspring of the husband, even when everyone and the dog's mother knew that the wife had been openly unfaithful. By such means, several gentlemen of his acquaintance had children, even though he was quite sure that the men had never even thought of sharing their wives' beds. Had Stephan perhaps—

He caught that thought by the scruff of the neck and shoved it aside. Besides, if the miniaturist had been faithful,

Stephan's son was the spitting image of his father. Though
painters naturally would produce what image they thought
most desired by the patron, despite the reality—

He picked up the glass and drank from it until he felt
breathless and his ears buzzed.

"Koenig," he said firmly, aloud. Whether the gossip was
true or not—and having kissed the Princess, he rather thought
it was; no shrinking violet, she!—and whether or not Koenig's
reappearance might threaten Siggy's legitimacy, the man's
presence must certainly be unwelcome.

Unwelcome enough to have arranged his death?

Why, when he would be gone again soon? The troops were
likely to move within the week—surely within the month.
Had something happened that made the removal of Private
Koenig urgent? Perhaps Koenig himself had been in ignorance of Siegfried's parentage—and upon discovering the
boy's resemblance to himself on his visit to the castle, determined to extort money or favor from the Princess?

And bringing the matter full circle . . . had the entire notion of the succubus been introduced merely to disguise
Koenig's death? If so, how? The rumor had seized the imagination of both troops and townspeople to a marked extent—
and Koenig's death had caused it to reach the proportions of
a panic—but how had that rumor been started?

He dismissed that question for the moment, as there was no
rational way of dealing with it. As for the death, though . . .

He could without much difficulty envision the Princess
Louisa conspiring in the death of Koenig; he had noticed before that women were quite without mercy where their offspring were concerned. Still . . . the Princess had presumably
not entered a soldier's quarters and done a man to death with
her own lily-white hands.

Who had done it? Someone with great ties of loyalty to
the Princess, presumably. Though, upon second thought, it
need not have been anyone from the Schloss. Gundwitz was
not the teeming boil that London was, but the town was still
of sufficient size to sustain a reasonable number of crimi-
nals; one of these could likely have been induced to perform

the actual murder—if it was a murder, he reminded himself.
He must not lose sight of the null hypothesis, in his eagerness to reach a conclusion.

And further . . . even if the Princess had in some way contrived both the rumor of the succubus *and* the death of Private
Koenig—who was the witch in Siggy's room? Had someone
truly tried to abduct the child? Private Koenig was already
dead; clearly he could have had nothing to do with it.

He ran a hand through his hair, rubbing his scalp slowly to
assist thought.

Loyalties. Who was most loyal to the Princess? Her but-
ler? Stephan?

He grimaced, but examined the thought carefully. No. There
were no circumstances conceivable under which Stephan
would have conspired in the murder of one of his own men.
Grey might be in doubt of many things concerning the Landgrave von Erdberg, but not his honor.

This led back to the Princess's behavior toward himself.
Did she act from attraction? Grey was modest about his own
endowments, but also honest enough to admit that he possessed some, and that his person was reasonably attractive to
women.

He thought it more likely, if the Princess had indeed conspired in Koenig's removal, that her actions toward himself
were intended as distraction. Though there *was* yet another
explanation.

One of the minor corollaries to Occam's razor that he had
himself derived suggested that quite often, the observed result of an action really was the intended end of that action.
The end result of that encounter in the hallway was that
Stephan von Namtzen had discovered him in embrace with
the Princess, and been noticeably annoyed by said discovery.

Had Louisa's motive been the very simple one of making
von Namtzen jealous?

And if Stephan *were* jealous . . . of whom?

The room had grown intolerably stuffy, and he rose, restless, and went to the window, unlatching the shutters. The
moon was full, a great, fecund yellow orb that hung low

above the darkened fields, and cast its light over the slated
roofs of Gundwitz and the paler sea of canvas tents that lay
beyond.

Did Ruysdale's troops sleep soundly tonight, exhausted
from their healthful exercise? He felt as though he would
profit from such exercise himself. He braced himself in the
window frame and pushed, feeling the muscles pop in his
arms, envisioning escape into that freshening night, running
naked and silent as a wolf, soft earth cool, yielding to his
feet.

Cold air rushed past his body, raising the coarse hairs on
his skin, but his core felt molten. Between the heat of fire
and brandy, the nightshirt's original grateful warmth had become oppressive; sweat bloomed upon his body, and the
woolen cloth hung limp upon him.

Suddenly impatient, he stripped it off and stood in the
open window, fierce and restless, the cold air caressing his
nakedness.

There was a whir and rustle in the ivy nearby, and then
something—several somethings—passed in absolute silence
so close and so swiftly by his face that he had not even time
to start backward, though his heart leapt to his throat, stran-
gling his involuntary cry.

Bats. The creatures had disappeared in an instant, long before his startled mind had collected itself sufficiently to put
a name to them.

He leaned out, searching, but the bats had disappeared at
once into the dark, swift about their hunting. It was no wonder
that legends of succubi abounded, in a place so bat-haunted.
The behavior of the creatures indeed seemed supernatural.

The bounds of the small chamber seemed at once intolerably confining. He could imagine himself some demon of
the air, taking wing to haunt the dreams of a man, seize upon
a sleeping body, and ride it—could he fly as far as England?
he wondered. Was the night long enough?

The trees at the edge of the garden tossed uneasily, stirred
by the wind. The night itself seemed tormented by an

autumn restlessness, the sense of things moving, changing, fermenting.

His blood was still hot, having now reached a sort of full, rolling boil, but there was no outlet for it. He did not know whether Stephan's anger was on his own behalf—or Louisa's. In neither case, though, could he make any open demonstration of feeling toward von Namtzen, now; it was too dangerous. He was unsure of the German attitude toward sodomites, but felt it unlikely to be more forgiving than the English stance. Whether stolid Protestant morality, or a wilder Catholic mysticism—he cast a brief look at the reliquary—neither was likely to have sympathy with his own predilections.

The mere contemplation of revelation, and the loss of its possibility, though, had shown him something important.

Stephan von Namtzen both attracted and aroused him, but it was not because of his own undoubted physical qualities. It was, rather, the degree to which those qualities reminded Grey of James Fraser.

Von Namtzen was nearly the same height as Fraser, a powerful man with broad shoulders, long legs, and an instantly commanding presence. However, Stephan was heavier, more crudely constructed, and less graceful than the Scot. And while Stephan warmed Grey's blood, the fact remained that the German did not burn his heart like living flame.

He lay down finally upon his bed, and put out the candle. Lay watching the play of firelight on the walls, seeing not the flicker of wood-flame, but the play of sun upon red hair, the sheen of sweat on a pale bronzed body . . .

A brief and brutal dose of Mr. Keegan's remedy left him drained, if not yet peaceful. He lay staring upward into the shadows of the carved wooden ceiling, able at least to think once more.

The only conclusion of which he was sure was that he needed very much to talk to someone who had seen Koenig's body.

CHAPTER 6
HOCUS-POCUS

Finding Private Koenig's last place of residence was simple. Thoroughly accustomed to having soldiers quartered upon them, Prussians sensibly built their houses with a separate chamber intended for the purpose. Indeed, the populace viewed such quartering not as an imposition, but as a windfall, since the soldiers not only paid for board and lodging, and would often do chores such as fetching wood and water—but were also better protection against thieves than a large watch-dog might be, without the expense.

Stephan's records were of course impeccable; he could lay hands on any one of his men at a moment's notice. And while he received Grey with extreme coldness, he granted the request without question, directing Grey to a house toward the western side of the town.

In fact, von Namtzen hesitated for a moment, clearly wondering whether duty obliged him to accompany Grey upon his errand, but Lance-Korporal Helwig appeared with a new difficulty—he averaged three per day—and Grey was left to carry out the errand on his own.

The house where Koenig had lodged was nothing out of the ordinary, so far as Grey could see. The owner of the house was rather remarkable, though, being a dwarf.

"Oh, the poor man! So much blood you have before not seen!"

Herr Huckel stood perhaps as high as Grey's waist—a novel sensation, to look down so far to an adult conversant. Herr Huckel was nonetheless intelligent and coherent, which was also novel in Grey's experience; most witnesses to violence tended to lose what wits they had and either to forget all details, or to imagine impossible ones.

Herr Huckel, though, showed him willingly to the chamber where the death had occurred, and explained what he had himself seen.

"It was late, you see, sir, and my wife and I had gone to our beds. The soldiers were out—or at least we supposed so." The soldiers had just received their pay, and most were busy losing it in taverns or brothels. The Huckels had heard no noises from the soldiers' room, and thus assumed that all four of the soldiers quartered with them were absent on such business.

Somewhere in the small hours, though, the good-folk had been awakened by terrible yells coming from the chamber. These were produced not by Private Koenig, but by one of his companions, who had returned in a state of advanced intoxication and stumbled into the blood-soaked shambles.

"He lay here, sir. Just so?" Herr Huckel waved his hands to indicate the position the body had occupied at the far side of the cozy room. There was nothing there now, save irregular dark blotches that stained the wooden floor.

"Not even lye would get it out," said Frau Huckel, who had come to the door of the room to watch. "And we had to burn the bedding."

Rather to Grey's surprise, she was not only of normal size, but quite pretty, with bright, soft hair peeking out from under her cap. She frowned at him in accusation.

"None of the soldiers will stay here, now. They think the *Nachtmahr* will get them, too!" Clearly, this was Grey's fault. He bowed apologetically.

"I regret that, madam," he said. "Tell me, did you see the body?"

"No," she said promptly, "but I saw the night-hag."

"Indeed," Grey said, surprised. "Er . . . what did it—she— it look like?" He hoped he was not going to receive some form of Siggy's logical but unhelpful description, *"Like a night-hag."*

"Now, Margarethe," said Herr Huckel, putting a warning hand up to his wife's arm. "It might not have been—"

"Yes, it was!" She transferred the frown to her husband, but did not shake off his hand, instead putting her own over it before returning her attention to Grey.

"It was an old woman, sir, with her white hair in braids. Her shawl slipped off in the wind, and I saw. There are two old women who live nearby, this is true—but one walks only with a stick, and the other does not walk at all. This . . . thing, she moved very quickly, hunched a little, but light on her feet."

Herr Huckel was looking more and more uneasy as this description progressed, and opened his mouth to interrupt, but was not given the chance.

"I am sure it was old Agathe!" Frau Huckel said, her voice dropping to a portentous whisper. Herr Huckel shut his eyes with a grimace.

"Old Agathe?" Grey asked, incredulous. "Do you mean Frau Blomberg—the Buergermeister's mother?"

Frau Huckel nodded, face fixed in grave certainty.

"Something must be done," she declared. "Everyone is afraid at night—either to go out, or to stay in. Men whose wives will not watch over them as they sleep are falling asleep as they work, as they eat . . ."

Grey thought briefly of mentioning Mr. Keegan's patent preventative, but dismissed the notion, instead turning to Herr Huckel to inquire for a close description of the state of the body.

"I am told that the throat was pierced, as with an animal's teeth," he said, at which Herr Huckel made a quick sign against evil and nodded, going a little pale. "Was the throat torn quite open—as though the man were attacked by a wolf? Or—" But Herr Huckel was already shaking his head.

"No, no! Only two marks—two holes. Like a snake's fangs." He poked two fingers into his own neck in illustration. "But so much blood!" He shuddered, glancing away from the marks on the floorboards.

Grey had once seen a man bitten by a snake, when he was quite young—but there had been no blood, that he recalled. Of course, the man had been bitten in the leg.

"Large holes, then?" Grey persisted, not liking to press the man to recall vividly unpleasant details, but determined to obtain as much information as possible.

With some effort, he established that the tooth marks had been sizable—perhaps a bit more than a quarter inch or so in diameter—and located on the front of Koenig's throat, about halfway up. He made Huckel show him, repeatedly, after ascertaining that the body had shown no other wound, when undressed for cleansing and burial.

He glanced at the walls of the room, which had been freshly whitewashed. Nonetheless, there was a large dark blotch showing faintly, down near the floor—probably where Koenig had rolled against the wall in his death throes.

He had hoped that a description of Koenig's body would enable him to discover some connection between the two deaths—but the only similarity between the deaths of Koenig and Bodger appeared to be that both men were indeed dead, and both dead under impossible circumstances.

He thanked the Huckels and prepared to take his leave, only then realizing that Frau Huckel had resumed her train of thought and was speaking to him quite earnestly.

". . . call a witch to cast the runes," she said.

"I beg your pardon, madam?"

She drew in a breath of deep exasperation, but refrained from open rebuke.

"Herr Blomberg," she repeated, giving Grey a hard look. "He will call a witch to cast the runes. Then we will discover the truth of everything!"

"He will do *what*?" Sir Peter squinted at Grey in disbelief. "Witches?"

"Only one, I believe, sir," Grey assured Sir Peter. According to Frau Huckel, matters had been escalating in Gundwitz. The rumor that Herr Blomberg's dead mother was custodian to the succubus was rampant in the town, and public opinion was in danger of overwhelming the little Buergermeister.

Herr Blomberg, however, was a stubborn man, and most devoted to his mother's memory. He refused entirely to allow her coffin to be dug up and her body desecrated.

The only solution, which Herr Blomberg had contrived out of desperation, seemed to be to discover the true identity and hiding place of the succubus. To this end, the Buergermeister had summoned a witch, who would cast runes—

"What are those?" Sir Peter asked, puzzled.

"I am not entirely sure, sir," Grey admitted. "Some object for divination, I suppose."

"Really?" Sir Peter rubbed his knuckles dubiously beneath a long, thin nose. "Sounds very fishy, what? This witch could say anything, couldn't she?"

"I suppose Herr Blomberg expects that if he is paying for the . . . er . . . ceremony, the lady is perhaps more likely to say something favorable to his situation," Grey suggested.

"Hmmm. Still don't like it," Sir Peter said. "Don't like it at all. Could be trouble, Grey, surely you see that?"

"I do not believe you can stop him, sir."

"Perhaps not, perhaps not." Sir Peter ruminated fiercely, brow crinkled under his wig. "Ah! Well, how's this, then—you go round and fix it up, Grey. Tell Herr Blomberg he can have his hocus-pocus, but he must do it here, at the Schloss. That way we can keep a lid on it, what, see there's no untoward excitement?"

"Yes, sir," Grey said, manfully suppressing a sigh, and went off to execute his orders.

By the time he reached his room to change for dinner, Grey felt dirty, irritable, and thoroughly out of sorts. It had taken most of the afternoon to track down Herr Blomberg and convince him to hold his . . . Christ, what was it? His runecasting? . . . at the Schloss. Then he had run across the pest Helwig, and before he was able to escape had been embroiled in an enormous controversy with a gang of mule drovers who claimed not to have been paid by the army.

This in turn had entailed a visit to two army camps, an inspection of thirty-four mules, trying interviews with both Sir Peter's paymaster and von Namtzen's—and involved a further cold interview with Stephan, who had behaved as though Grey was personally responsible for the entire affair, then turned his back, dismissing Grey in midsentence, as though unable to bear the sight of him.

He flung off his coat, sent Tom to fetch hot water, and irritably tugged off his stock, wishing he could hit someone.

A knock sounded on the door, and he froze, irritation vanishing upon the moment. What to do? Pretend he wasn't in, was the obvious course, in case it was Louisa, in her sheer lawn shift or something worse. But if it were Stephan, come either to apologize or to demand further explanation?

The knock sounded again. It was a good, solid knock. Not what one would expect of a female—particularly not of a female intent on dalliance. Surely the Princess would be more inclined to a discreet scratching?

The knock came again, peremptory, demanding. Taking an enormous breath and trying to still the thumping of his heart, Grey jerked the door open.

"I wish to speak to you," said the Dowager, and sailed into the room, not waiting for invitation.

"Oh," said Grey, having lost all grasp of German on the spot. He closed the door and turned to the old lady, instinctively rebuttoning his shirt.

She ignored his mute gesture toward the chair, but stood in front of the fire, fixing him with a steely gaze. She was completely dressed, he saw, with a faint sense of relief. He really could not have borne the sight of the Dowager *en déshabille*.

"I have come to ask you," she said without preamble, "if you have intentions to marry Louisa."

"I have not," he said, his German returning with miraculous promptitude. *"Nein."*

One sketchy gray brow twitched upward.

"Ja? That is not what she thinks."

He rubbed a hand over his face, groping for some diplomatic reply—and found it, in the feel of the stubble on his own jaw.

"I admire Princess Louisa greatly," he said. "There are few women who are her equal—" And thank God for that, he added to himself. "—but I regret that I am not free to undertake any obligation. I have . . . an understanding. In England." His understanding with James Fraser was that if he were ever to lay a hand on the man or speak his heart, Fraser would break his neck instantly. It was, however, certainly an understanding, and clear as Irish crystal.

The Dowager looked at him with a narrow gaze of such penetrance that he wanted to take several steps backward. He stood his ground, though, returning the look with one of patient sincerity.

"Hmph!" she said at last. "Well, then. That is good." Without another word, she turned on her heel. Before she could close the door behind her, he reached out and grasped her arm.

She swung around to him, surprised and outraged at his presumption. He ignored this, though, absorbed in what he had seen as she turned.

"Pardon, Your Highness," he said. He touched the medal pinned to the bodice of her gown. He had seen it a hundred times, and assumed it always to contain the image of some saint—which, he supposed, it did, but certainly not in the traditional manner.

"Saint Orgevald?" he inquired. The image was crudely embossed, and could easily be taken for something else—if one hadn't seen the larger version on the lid of the reliquary.

"Certainly." The old lady fixed him with a glittering eye, shook her head, and went out, closing the door firmly behind her.

For the first time, it occurred to Grey that whoever Orgevald had been, it was entirely possible that he had not originally been a saint. Pondering this, he went to bed, scratching absentmindedly at a cluster of fleabites obtained from the mules.

CHAPTER 7
AMBUSH

The next day dawned cold and windy. Grey saw pheasants huddling under the cover of shrubs as he rode, crows hugging the ground in the stubbled fields, and slate roofs thick with shuffling doves, feathered bodies packed together in the quest for heat. Despite their reputed brainlessness, he had to think that the birds were more sensible than he.

Birds had no duty—but it wasn't quite duty that propelled him on this ragged, chilly morning. It was in part simple curiosity, in part official suspicion. He wished to find the gypsies; in particular, he wished to find *one* gypsy: the woman who had quarreled with Private Bodger, soon before his death.

If he were quite honest—and he felt that he could afford to be, so long as it was within the privacy of his own mind— he had another motive for the journey. It would be entirely natural for him to pause at the bridge for a cordial word with the artillerymen, and perhaps see for himself how the boy with the red lips was faring.

While all these motives were undoubtedly sound, though, the real reason for his expedition was simply that it would remove him from the Schloss. He did not feel safe in a house containing the Princess Louisa, let alone her mother-in-law. Neither could he go to his usual office in the town, for fear of encountering Stephan.

The whole situation struck him as farcical in the extreme; still, he could not keep himself from thinking about it— about Stephan.

Had he been deluding himself about Stephan's attraction to him? He was as vain as any man, he supposed, and yet he could swear . . . his thoughts went around and around in the same weary circle. And yet, each time he thought to dismiss them entirely, he felt again the overwhelming sense of warmth and casual possession with which Stephan had kissed him. He had not imagined it. And yet . . .

Embrangled in this tedious but inescapable coil, he reached the bridge by midmorning, only to find that the young soldier was not in camp.

"Franz? Gone foraging, maybe," said the Hanoverian Lieutenant, with a shrug. "Or got homesick and run. They do that, the young ones."

"Got scared," one of the other men suggested, overhearing.

"Scared of what?" Grey asked sharply, wondering whether,

despite everything, word of the succubus had reached the bridge.

"Scared of his shadow, that one," said the man he recalled as Samson, making a face. "He keeps talking about the child, he hears a crying child at night."

"Thought you heard it, too, eh?" said the Hanoverian, not sounding entirely friendly. "The night it rained so hard?"

"Me? I didn't hear anything then but Franz's squealing." There was a rumble of laughter at that, the sound of which made Grey's heart drop to his boots. *Too late,* he thought. "At the lightning," Samson added blandly, catching his glance.

"He's run for home," the Lieutenant declared. "Let him go; no use here for a coward."

There was a small sense of disquiet in the man's manner that belied his confidence, Grey thought—and yet there was nothing to be done about it. He had no direct authority over these men, could not order a search to be undertaken.

As he crossed the bridge, though, he could not help but glance over. The water had subsided only a little; the flood still tumbled past, choked with torn leaves and half-seen sodden objects. He did not want to stop, to be caught looking, and yet looked as carefully as he could, half expecting to see little Franz's delicate body broken on the rocks, or the blind eyes of a drowned face trapped beneath the water.

He saw nothing but the usual flood debris, though, and with a slight sense of relief he continued on toward the hills.

He knew nothing save the direction the gypsy wagons had been going when last observed. It was long odds that he would find them, but he searched doggedly, pausing at intervals to scan the countryside with his spyglass, or to look for rising plumes of smoke.

These last occurred sporadically, but proved invariably to be peasant huts or charcoal burners. The peasants either disappeared promptly when they saw his red coat, or stared and crossed themselves, but none of them admitted to having heard of the gypsies, let alone seen them.

The sun was coming down the sky, and he realized that he must turn back soon or be caught in open country by night.

He had a tinderbox and a bottle of ale in his saddlebag, but
no food, and the prospect of being marooned in this fashion
was unwelcome, particularly with the French forces only a
few miles to the west. If the British army had scouts, so did
the frogs, and he was lightly armed, with no more than a pair
of pistols, a rather dented cavalry saber, and his dagger to
hand.

Not wishing to risk Karolus on the boggy ground, he was
riding another of his horses, a thickset bay who went by the
rather unflattering name of Hognose, but who had excellent
manners and a steady foot. Steady enough that Grey could
ignore the ground, trying to focus his attention, strained
from prolonged tension, into a last look around. The foliage
of the hills around him faded into patchwork, shifting constantly in the roiling wind. Again and again, he thought he
saw things—human figures, animals moving, the briefly seen
corner of a wagon—only to have them prove illusory when
he ventured toward them.

The wind whined incessantly in his ears, adding spectral
voices to the illusions that plagued him. He rubbed a hand
over his face, gone numb from the cold, imagining momentarily that he heard the wails of Franz's ghostly child. He
shook his head to dispel the impression—but it persisted.

He drew Hognose to a stop, turning his head from side to
side, listening intently. He was sure he heard it—but what
was it? No words were distinguishable above the moaning of
the wind, but there *was* a sound, he was sure of it.

At the same time, it seemed to come from nowhere in particular; try as he might, he could not locate it. The horse
heard it, too, though—he saw the bay's ears prick and turn
nervously.

"Where?" he said softly, laying the rein on the horse's
neck. "Where is it? Can you find it?"

The horse apparently had little interest in finding the
noise, but some in getting away from it; Hognose backed,
shuffling on the sandy ground, kicking up sheaves of wet
yellow leaves. Grey drew him up sharply, swung down, and
wrapped the reins around a bare-branched sapling.

With the horse's revulsion as guide, he saw what he had overlooked: the churned earth of a badger's sett, half hidden by the sprawling roots of a large elm. Once focused on this, he could pinpoint the noise as coming from it. And damned if he'd ever heard a badger carry on like that!

Pistol drawn and primed, he edged toward the bank of earth, keeping a wary eye on the nearby trees.

It was certainly crying, but not a child; a sort of muffled whimpering, interspersed with the kind of catch in the breath that injured men often made.

"Wer ist da?" he demanded, halting just short of the opening to the sett, pistol raised. "You are injured?"

There was a gulp of surprise, followed at once by scrabbling sounds.

"Major? Major Grey? It is you?"

"Franz?" he said, flabbergasted.

"Ja, Major! Help me, help me, please!"

Uncocking the pistol and thrusting it back in his belt, he knelt and peered into the hole. Badger setts are normally deep, running straight down for six feet or more before turning, twisting sideways into the badger's den. This one was no exception; the grimy, tear-streaked face of the young Prussian soldier stared up at him, his head a good foot below the rim of the narrow hole.

The boy had broken his leg in falling, and it was no easy matter to lift him straight up. Grey managed it at last by improvising a sling of his own shirt and the boy's, tied to a rope anchored to Hognose's saddle.

At last he had the boy laid on the ground, covered with his coat and taking small sips from the bottle of ale.

"Major—" Franz coughed and spluttered, trying to rise on one elbow.

"Hush, don't try to talk." Grey patted his arm soothingly, wondering how best to get him back to the bridge. "Everything will be—"

"But Major—the red coats! *Die Englander!"*

"What? What are you talking about?"

"Dead Englishmen! It was the little boy, I heard him, and I dug, and—" The boy's story was spilling out in a torrent of Prussian, and it took no little time for Grey to slow him down sufficiently to disentangle the threads of what he was saying.

He had, Grey understood him to say, repeatedly heard the crying near the bridge, but his fellows either didn't hear or wouldn't admit to it, instead teasing him mercilessly about it. At last he determined to go by himself and see if he could find a source for the sound—perhaps wind moaning through a hole, as his friend Samson had suggested.

"But it wasn't." Franz was still pale, but small patches of hectic color glowed in the translucent skin of his cheeks. He had poked about the base of the bridge, discovering eventually a small crack in the rocks at the foot of a pillar on the far side of the river. Thinking that this might indeed be the source of the crying, he had inserted his bayonet and pried at the rock—which had promptly come away, leaving him face to face with a cavity inside the pillar, containing a small, round, very white skull.

"More bones, too, I think. I didn't stop to look." The boy swallowed. He had simply run, too panicked to think. When he stopped at last, completely out of breath and with legs like jelly, he had sat down to rest and think what to do.

"They couldn't beat me more than once for being gone," he said, with the ghost of a smile. "So I thought I would be gone a little longer."

This decision was enhanced by the discovery of a grove of walnut trees, and Franz had made his way up into the hills, gathering both nuts and wild blackberries—his lips were still stained purple with the juice, Grey saw.

He had been interrupted in this peaceful pursuit by the sound of gunfire. Throwing himself flat on the ground, he had then crept a little forward, until he could see over the edge of a little rocky escarpment. Below, in a hollow, he saw a small group of English soldiers, engaged in mortal combat with Austrians.

"Austrians? You are sure?" Grey asked, astonished.

"I know what Austrians look like," the boy assured him, a little tartly. Knowing what Austrians were capable of, too, he had promptly backed up, risen to his feet, and run as fast as he could in the opposite direction—only to fall into the badger's sett in his haste.

"You were lucky the badger wasn't at home," Grey remarked, teeth beginning to chatter. He had reclaimed the remnants of his shirt, but this was insufficient shelter against dropping temperature and probing wind. "But you said dead Englishmen."

"I think they were all dead," the boy said. "I didn't go see."

Grey, however, must. Leaving the boy covered with his coat and a mound of dead leaves, he untied the horse and turned his head in the direction Franz had indicated.

Proceeding with care and caution in case of lurking Austrians, it was nearly sunset before he found the hollow.

It was Dundas and his survey party; he recognized the uniforms at once. Cursing under his breath, he flung himself off his horse and scrabbled hurriedly from one body to the next, hoping against hope as he pressed shaking fingers against flaccid cheeks and cooling breasts.

Two were still alive: Dundas and a Corporal. The Corporal was badly wounded and unconscious; Dundas had taken a gun butt to the head and a bayonet through the chest, but the wound had fortunately sealed itself. The Lieutenant was disabled and in pain, but not yet on the verge of death.

"Hundreds of the buggers," he croaked breathlessly, gripping Grey's arm. "Saw . . . whole battalion . . . guns. Going to . . . the French. Fanshawe—followed them. Spying. Heard. Fucking succ—succ—" He coughed hard, spraying a little blood with the saliva, but it seemed to ease his breath temporarily.

"It was a plan. Got whores—agents. Slept with men, gave them o-opium. Dreams. Panic, aye?" He was half sitting up, straining to make words, make Grey understand.

Grey understood, only too well. He had been given opium

once, by a doctor, and remembered vividly the weirdly erotic dreams that had ensued. Do the same to men who had likely never heard of opium, let alone experienced it—and at the same time, start rumors of a demoness who preyed upon men in their dreams? Particularly with a flesh-and-blood avatar, who could leave such marks as would convince a man he had been so victimized?

Only too effective, and one of the cleverest notions he had ever come across for demoralizing an enemy before attack. It was that alone that gave him some hope, as he comforted Dundas, piling him with coats taken from the dead, dragging the Corporal to lie near the Lieutenant for the sake of shared warmth, digging through a discarded rucksack for water to give him.

If the combined forces of French and Austrians were huge, there would be no need for such subtleties—the enemy would simply roll over the English and their German allies. But if the numbers were closer to equal—and it was still necessary to funnel them across that narrow bridge—then yes, it was desirable to face an enemy who had not slept for several nights, whose men were tired and jumpy, whose officers were not paying attention to possible threat, being too occupied with the difficulties close at hand.

He could see it clearly: Ruysdale was busy watching the French, who were sitting happily on the cliffs, moving just enough to keep attention diverted from the Austrian advance. The Austrians would come down on the bridge—likely at night—and then the French on their heels.

Dundas was shivering, eyes closed, teeth set hard in his lower lip against the pain of the movement.

"Christopher, can you hear me? Christopher!" Grey shook him, as gently as possible. "Where's Fanshawe?" He didn't know the members of Dundas's party; if Fanshawe had been taken captive, or—but Dundas was shaking his head, gesturing feebly toward one of the corpses, lying with his head smashed open.

"Go on," Dundas whispered. His face was gray, and not

only from the waning light. "Warn Sir Peter." He put a trembling arm about the unconscious Corporal, and nodded to
Grey. "We'll . . . wait."

CHAPTER 8
THE WITCH

Grey had been staring with great absorption at his valet's
face for some moments, before he realized even what he was
looking at, let alone why.

"Uh?" he said.

"I *said*," Tom repeated, with some emphasis, "you best
drink this, me lord, or you're going to fall flat on your face,
and that won't do, will it?"

"It won't? Oh. No. Of course not." He took the cup,
adding a belated, "Thank you, Tom. What is it?"

"I told you twice, I'm not going to try and say the name of
it again. Ilse says it'll keep you on your feet, though." He
leaned forward and sniffed approvingly at the liquid, which
appeared to be brown and foamy, indicating the presence in
it of eggs, Grey thought.

He followed Tom's lead and sniffed, too, recoiling only
slightly at the eye-watering reek. Hartshorn, perhaps? It had
quite a lot of brandy, no matter what else was in it. And he
did need to stay on his feet. With no more than a precaution-
ary clenching of his belly muscles, he put back his head and
drained it.

He had been awake for nearly forty-eight hours, and the
world around him had a tendency to pass in and out of focus,
like the scene in a spyglass. He had also a proclivity to go intermittently deaf, not hearing what was said to him—and
Tom was correct, that wouldn't do.

He had taken time, the night before, to fetch Franz, put
him on the horse—with a certain amount of squealing, it
must be admitted, as Franz had never been on a horse before—and take him to the spot where Dundas lay, feeling
that they would be better together. He had pressed his dagger

into Franz's hands, and left him guarding the Corporal and the Lieutenant, who was by then, passing in and out of consciousness.

Grey had then donned his coat and come back to raise the alarm, riding a flagging horse at the gallop over pitch-black ground, by the light of a sinking moon. He'd fallen twice, when Hognose stumbled, jarring bones and jellying kidneys, but luckily escaped injury both times.

He had alerted the artillery crew at the bridge, ridden on to Ruysdale's encampment, roused everyone, seen the Colonel despite all attempts to prevent him waking the man, gathered a rescue party, and ridden back to retrieve Dundas and the others, arriving in the hollow near dawn to find the Corporal dead and Dundas nearly so, with his head in Franz's lap.

Captain Hiltern had of course sent someone with word to Sir Peter at the Schloss, but it was necessary for Grey to report personally to Sir Peter and von Namtzen, when he returned at midday with the rescue party. After which, officers and men had flapped out of the place like a swarm of bats, the whole military apparatus moving like the armature of some great engine, creaking, groaning, but coming to life with amazing speed.

Which left Grey alone in the Schloss at sunset, blank in mind and body, with nothing further to do. There was no need for liaison; couriers were flitting to and from all the regiments, carrying orders. He had no duty to perform; no one to command, no one to serve.

He would ride out in the morning with Sir Peter Hicks, part of Sir Peter's personal guard. But there was no need for him now; everyone was about his own business; Grey was forgotten.

He felt odd; not unwell, but as though objects and people near him were not quite real, not entirely firm to the touch. He should sleep, he knew—but could not, not with the whole world in flux around him, and a sense of urgency that hummed on his skin, yet was unable to penetrate to the core of his mind.

Tom was talking to him; he made an effort to attend.

"Witch," he repeated, awareness struggling to make itself known. "Witch. You mean Herr Blomberg still intends to hold his—ceremony?"

"Yes, me lord." Tom was sponging Grey's coat, frowning as he tried to remove a pitch stain from the skirt. "Ilse says he won't rest until he's cleared his mother's name, and damned if the Austrians will stop him."

Awareness burst through Grey's fog like a pricked soap bubble.

"Christ! He doesn't know!"

"About what, me lord?" Tom turned to look at him curiously, sponging cloth and vinegar in hand.

"The succubus. I must tell him—explain." Even as he said it, though, he realized how little force such an explanation would have upon Herr Blomberg's real problem. Sir Peter and Colonel Ruysdale might accept the truth—the townspeople would be much less likely to accept having been fooled—and by Austrians!

Grey knew enough about gossip and rumor to realize that no amount of explanation from him would be enough. Still less if that explanation were to be filtered through Herr Blomberg, whose bias in the matter was clear.

Even Tom was frowning doubtfully at him as he rapidly explained the matter. *Superstition and sensation are always so much more appealing than truth and rationality.* The words echoed as though spoken in his ear, with the same humorously rueful intonation with which his father had spoken them, many years before.

He rubbed a hand vigorously over his face, feeling himself come back to life. Perhaps he had one more task to complete, in his role as liaison.

"This witch, Tom—the woman who is to cast the runes—whatever in God's name that might involve. Do you know where she is?"

"Oh, yes, me lord." Tom had put down his cloth now, interested. "She's here—in the Schloss, I mean. Locked up in the larder."

"Locked up in the larder? Why?"

"Well, it has a good lock on the door, me lord, to keep the servants from—oh, you mean why's she locked up at all? Ilse says she didn't want to come; dug in her heels entire, and wouldn't hear of it. But Herr Blomberg wouldn't hear of her *not,* and had her dragged up here, and locked up 'til this evening. He's fetching up the Town Council, and the Magistrate, and all the bigwigs he can lay hands on, Ilse says."

"Take me to her."

Tom's mouth dropped open. He closed it with a snap and looked Grey up and down.

"Not like *that.* You're not even shaved!"

"Precisely like this," Grey assured him, tucking in the tails of his shirt. "Now."

The game larder was locked, but, as Grey had surmised, Ilse knew where the key was kept and was not proof against Tom's charm. The room itself was in an alcove behind the kitchens, and it was a simple matter to reach it without detection.

"You need not come farther, Tom," Grey said, low-voiced. "Give me the keys; if anyone finds me here, I'll say I took them."

Tom, who had taken the precaution of arming himself with a toasting fork, merely clutched the keys tighter in his other hand, and shook his head.

The door swung open silently on leather hinges. Someone had given the captive woman a candle; it lit the small space and cast fantastic shadows on the walls, from the hanging bodies of swans and pheasants, ducks and geese.

The drink had restored a sense of energy to Grey's mind and body, but without quite removing the sense of unreality that had pervaded his consciousness. It was therefore with no real surprise that he saw the woman who turned toward him, and recognized the gypsy prostitute who had quarreled with Private Bodger a few hours before the soldier's death.

She obviously recognized him, too, though she said nothing. Her eyes passed over him with cool scorn, and she turned away, evidently engrossed in some silent communion with a severed hog's head that sat upon a china plate.

"Madam," he said softly, as though his voice might rouse the dead fowl to sudden flight. "I would speak with you."

She ignored him, and folded her hands elaborately. The light winked gold from the rings in her ears and the rings on her fingers—and Grey saw that one was a crude circlet, with the emblem of Saint Orgevald's protection.

He was overcome with a sudden sense of premonition, though he did not believe in premonition. He felt things in motion around him, things that he did not understand and could not control, things settling of themselves into an ordained and appointed position, like the revolving spheres of his father's orrery—and he wished to protest this state of affairs, but could not.

"Me lord." Tom's hissed whisper shook him out of this momentary disorientation, and he glanced at the boy, eyebrows raised. Tom was staring at the woman, who was still turned away, but whose face was visible in profile.

"Hanna," he said, nodding at the gypsy. "She looks like Hanna, Siggy's nursemaid. You know, me lord, the one what disappeared?"

The woman had swung round abruptly at mention of Hanna's name, and stood glaring at them both.

Grey felt the muscles of his back loosen, very slightly, as though some force had picked him up and held him by the scruff of the neck. As though he, too, were one of the objects being moved, placed in the spot ordained for him.

"I have a proposition for you, madam," he said calmly, and pulled a cask of salted fish out from beneath a shelf. He sat on it, and, reaching behind him, pulled the door closed.

"I do not wish to hear anything you say, *Schweinehund,*" she said, very coldly. "As for you, piglet . . ." Her eyes darkened with no very pleasant light as she looked at Tom.

"You have failed," Grey went on, ignoring this digression. "And you are in considerable danger. The Austrian plan is known; you can hear the soldiers preparing for battle, can't you?" It was true; the sounds of drums and distant shouting, the shuffle of many marching feet, were audible even here, though muffled by the stone walls of the Schloss.

He smiled pleasantly at her, and his fingers touched the silver gorget that he had seized before leaving his room. It hung about his neck, over his half-buttoned shirt, the sign of an officer on duty.

"I offer you your life, and your freedom. In return . . ." He paused. She said nothing, but one straight black brow rose, slowly.

"I want a bit of justice," he said. "I want to know how Private Bodger died. Bodger," he repeated, seeing her look of incomprehension, and realizing that she had likely never known his name. "The English soldier who said you had cheated him."

She sniffed contemptuously, but a crease of angry amusement lined the edge of her mouth.

"Him. God killed him. Or the Devil, take your choice. Or, no—" The crease deepened, and she thrust out the hand with the ring on it, nearly in his face. "I think it was my saint. Do you believe in saints, Pig-soldier?"

"No," he said calmly. "What happened?"

"He saw me, coming out of a tavern, and he followed me. I didn't know he was there; he caught me in an alley, but I pulled away and ran into the churchyard. I thought he wouldn't follow me there, but he did."

Bodger had been both angry and aroused, insisting that he would take the satisfaction she had earlier denied him. She had kicked and struggled, but he was stronger than she.

"And then—" She shrugged. "Poof. He stops what he is doing, and makes a sound."

"What sort of sound?"

"How should I know? Men make all kinds of sounds. Farting, groaning, belching . . . pff." She bunched her fingers and flicked them sharply, disposing of men and all their doings with the gesture.

At any rate, Bodger had then dropped heavily to his knees, and still clinging to her dress, had fallen over. The gypsy had rapidly pried loose his fingers and run, thanking the intercession of Saint Orgevald.

"Hmmm." A sudden weakness of the heart? An apoplexy? Keegan had said such a thing was possible—and there was no evidence to belie the gypsy's statement. "Not like Private Koenig, then," Grey said, watching carefully.

Her head jerked up and she stared hard at him, lips tight.

"Me lord," said Tom softly behind him. "Hanna's name is Koenig."

"It is not!" the gypsy snapped. "It is Mulengro, as is mine!"

"First things first, if you please, madam," Grey said, repressing the urge to stand up as she leaned glowering over him. "Where *is* Hanna? And what is she to you? Sister, cousin, daughter? . . ."

"Sister," she said, biting the word off like a thread. Her lips were tight as a seam, but Grey touched his gorget once again.

"Life," he said. "And freedom." He regarded her steadily, watching indecision play upon her features like the wavering shadows on the walls. She had no way of knowing how powerless he was; he could neither condemn nor release her— nor would anyone else, all being caught up in the oncoming maelstrom of war.

In the end, he had his way, as he had known he would, and sat listening to her in a state that was neither trance nor dream; just a tranquil acceptance as the pieces fell before him, one upon one.

She was one of the women recruited by the Austrians to spread the rumors of the succubus—and had much enjoyed the spreading, judging from the way she licked her lower lip while telling of it. Her sister Hanna had been married to the soldier Koenig, but had rejected him, he being a faithless hound, like all men.

Bearing in mind the gossip regarding Siegfried's paternity, Grey nodded thoughtfully, motioning to her with one hand to go on.

She did. Koenig had gone away with the army, but then had come back, and had had the audacity to visit the Schloss, trying to rekindle the flame with Hanna. Afraid that he might succeed in seducing her sister again—"She is weak, Hanna," she said with a shrug, "she *will* trust men!"—she had gone to visit Koenig at night, planning to drug him with wine laced with opium, as she had done with the others.

"Only this time, a fatal dose, I suppose." Grey had propped his elbow upon his crossed knee, hand under his chin. The tiredness had come back; it hovered near at hand, but was not yet clouding his mental processes.

"I meant it so, yes." She uttered a short laugh. "But he knew the taste of opium. He threw it at me, and grabbed me by the throat."

Whereupon she had drawn the dagger she always carried at her belt and stabbed at him—striking upward into his open mouth, and piercing his brain.

"You never saw so much blood in all your life," the gypsy assured Grey, unconsciously echoing Herr Huckel.

"Oh, I rather think I have," Grey said politely. His hand went to his own waist—but of course, he had left his dagger with Franz. "But pray go on. The marks, as of an animal's fangs?"

"A nail," she said, and shrugged.

"So, was it him—Koenig, I mean—was it him tried to snatch little Siggy?" Tom, deeply absorbed in the revelations, could not keep himself from blurting out the question. He coughed and tried to fade back into the woodwork, but Grey indicated that this was a question which he himself found of some interest.

"You did not tell me where your sister is. But I assume that it was you the boy saw in his chamber?" *"What did she look like?"* he had asked. *"Like a witch,"* the child replied. Did she? She did not look like Grey's conception of a witch—but what was that, save the fabrication of a limited imagination?

She was tall for a woman, dark, and her face mingled an odd sexuality with a strongly forbidding aspect—a combination that many men would find intriguing. Grey thought it was not something that would have struck Siggy, but something else about her evidently had.

She nodded. She was fingering her ring, he saw, and watching him with calculation, as though deciding whether to tell him a lie.

"I have seen the Dowager Princess's medal," he said politely. "Is she an Austrian, by birth? I assume that you and your sister are."

The woman stared at him and said something in her own tongue, which sounded highly uncomplimentary.

"And you think *I* am a witch!" she said, evidently translating the thought.

"No, I don't," Grey said. "But others do, and that is what brings us here. If you please, madam, let us conclude our business. I expect someone will shortly come for you." The Schloss was at dinner; Tom had earlier brought Grey a tray, which he had been too tired to eat. No doubt the rune-casting would be the after-dinner entertainment, and he must make his desires clear before that.

"Well, then." The gypsy regarded him, her awe at his perspicacity fading back into the usual derision. "It was your fault."

"I beg your pardon?"

"It was Princess Gertrude—the Dowager, so you call her. She saw Louisa—that slut—" She spat casually on the floor, almost without pausing, and went on. "—making sheep's eyes at you, and was afraid she meant to marry you. Louisa thought she would marry you and go to England, to be safe and rich. But if she did, she would take with her her son."

"And the Dowager did not wish to be parted from her grandson," Grey said slowly. Whether the gossip was true or not, the old woman loved the boy.

The gypsy nodded. "So she arranged that we would take the boy—my sister and me. He would be safe with us, and after a time, when the Austrians had killed you all or driven you away, we would bring him back."

Hanna had gone down the ladder first, meaning to comfort Siggy if he woke in the rain. But Siggy had wakened before that, and bollixed the scheme by running away. Hanna had no choice but to flee when Grey had tipped the ladder over, leaving her sister to hide in the Schloss and make her way out at daybreak, with the help of the Dowager.

"She is with our family," the gypsy said, with another shrug. "Safe."

"The ring," Grey said, nodding at the gypsy's circlet. "Do you serve the Dowager? Is that what it means?"

So much confessed, the gypsy evidently felt now at ease. Casually, she pushed a platter of dead doves aside and sat down upon the shelf, feet dangling.

"We are Rom," she said, drawing herself up proudly. "The Rom serve no one. But we have known the Trauchtenbergs— the Dowager's family—for generations, and there is tradition between us. It was her great-great-grandfather who bought the child who guards the bridge—and that child was the younger brother of my own four-times-great-grandfather. The ring was given to my ancestor then, as a sign of the bargain."

Grey heard Tom grunt slightly with confusion, but took no heed. The words struck him as forcibly as a blow, and he could not speak for a moment. The thing was too shocking. He took a deep breath, fighting the vision of Franz's words— the small, round, white skull, looking out at him from the hollow in the bridge.

Sounds of banging and clashing dishes from the scullery nearby brought him to himself, though, and he realized that time was growing short.

"Very well," he said, as briskly as he could. "I want one last bit of justice, and our bargain is made. Agathe Blomberg."

"Old Agathe?" The gypsy laughed, and, despite her missing tooth, he could see how attractive she could be. "How funny! How could they suppose such an old fish might be a demon of desire? A hag, yes, but a night-hag?" She went off into peals of laughter, and Grey jumped to his feet, seizing her by the shoulder to silence her.

"Be quiet," he said, "someone will come."

She stopped, then, though she still snorted with amusement.

"So, then?"

"So, then," he said firmly. "When you do your hocus-pocus—whatever it is they've brought you here to do—I wish you particularly to exonerate Agathe Blomberg. I don't care what you say or how you do it—I leave that to your own devices, which I expect are considerable."

She looked at him for a moment, looked down at his hand upon her shoulder, and shrugged it off.

"That's all, is it?" she asked sarcastically.

"That's all. Then you may go."

"Oh, I may go? How kind." She stood smiling at him, but not in a kindly way. It occurred to him quite suddenly that she had required no assurances from him; had not asked for so much as his word as a gentleman—though he supposed she would not have valued that, in any case.

She did not care, he realized, with a small shock. She had not told him anything for the sake of saving herself—she simply wasn't afraid. Did she think the Dowager would protect her, for the sake either of their ancient bond, or because of what she knew about the failed kidnapping?

Perhaps. Perhaps she had confidence in something else. And if she had, he chose not to consider what that might be. He rose from the cask of fish and pushed it back under the shelves.

"Agathe Blomberg was a woman, too," he said.

She rose, too, and stood looking at him, rubbing her ring with apparent thought.

"So she was. Well, perhaps I will do it, then. Why should men dig up her coffin and drag her poor old carcass through the streets?"

He could feel Tom behind him, vibrating with eagerness to be gone; the racket of the dinner-clearing was much louder.

"For you, though—"

He glanced at her, startled by the tone in her voice, which held something different. Neither mockery nor venom, nor any other emotion that he knew.

Her eyes were huge, gleaming in the candlelight, but so dark that they seemed void pools, her face without expression.

"Let me tell you this. You will never satisfy a woman," she said softly. "Never. Any woman who shares your bed will leave after no more than a single night, cursing you."

Grey rubbed a knuckle against his stubbled chin, and nodded.

"Very likely, madam," he said. "Good night."

EPILOGUE
AMONG THE TRUMPETS

The order of battle was set. The autumn sun had barely risen, and the troops would march within the hour to meet their destiny at the bridge of Aschenwald.

Grey was in the stable block, checking Karolus's tack, tightening the girth, adjusting the bridle, marking second by second the time until he should depart, as though each second marked an irretrievable and most precious drop of his life.

Outside the stables, all was confusion, as people ran hither and thither, gathering belongings, searching for children, calling for wives and parents, strewing away objects gathered only moments before, heedless in their distraction. His heart beat fast in his chest, and intermittent small thrills coursed up the backs of his legs and curled between them, tightening his scrotum.

The drums were beating in the distance, ordering the troops. The thrum of them beat in his blood, in his bone. Soon, soon, soon. His chest was tight; it was difficult to draw full breath.

He did not hear the footsteps approaching through the
straw of the stables. Keyed up as he was, though, he felt the
disturbance of air nearby, that intimation of intrusion that
now and then had saved his life, and whirled, hand on his
dagger.

It was Stephan von Namtzen, gaudy in full uniform, his
great plumed helmet underneath one arm—but with a face
sober by contrast to his clothing.

"It is nearly time," the Hanoverian said quietly. "I would
speak with you—if you will hear me."

Grey slowly let his hand fall away from the dagger, and
took the full breath he had been longing for.

"You know that I will."

Von Namtzen inclined his head in acknowledgment, but
did not speak at once, seeming to need to gather his words—
although they were speaking German now.

"I will marry Louisa," he said, finally, formally. "If I live
until Christmas. My children—" He hesitated, free hand flat
upon the breast of his coat. "It will be good they should have
a mother once more. And—"

"You need not give reasons," Grey interrupted. He smiled
at the big German, with open affection. Caution was no
longer necessary. "If you wish this, then I wish you well."

Von Namtzen's face lightened a bit. He ducked his head a
little, and took a breath.

"*Danke.* I say, I will marry, if I am alive. If I am not . . ."
His hand still rested on his breast, above the miniature of his
children.

"If I live, and you do not, then I will go to your home,"
Grey said. "I will tell your son what I have known of you—
as a warrior, and as a man. Is this your desire?"

The Hanoverian's graveness did not alter, but a deep
warmth softened his gray eyes.

"It is. You have known me, perhaps, better than anyone."

He stood still, looking at Grey, and all at once, the relent-
less marking of fleeting time stopped. Confusion and danger
still hastened without, and drums beat loud, but inside the
stables, there was a great peace.

Stephan's hand left his breast, and reached out. Grey took it, and felt love flow between them. He thought that heart and body must be entirely melted—if only for that moment.

Then they parted, each drawing back, each seeing the flash of desolation in the other's face, both smiling ruefully to see it.

Stephan was turning to go, when Grey remembered.

"Wait!" he called, and turned to fumble in his saddlebag. He found what he was looking for, and thrust it into the German's hands.

"What is this?" Stephan turned the small, heavy box over, looking puzzled.

"A charm," Grey said, smiling. "A blessing. My blessing— and Saint Orgevald's. May it protect you."

"But—" Von Namtzen frowned with doubt, and tried to give the reliquary back, but Grey would not accept it.

"Believe me," he said in English, "it will do you more good than me."

Stephan looked at him for a moment longer, then nodded and, tucking the little box away in his pocket, turned and left. Grey turned back to Karolus, who was growing restive, tossing his head and snorting softly through his nose.

The horse stamped, hard, and the vibration of it ran through the long bones of Grey's legs. "Hast thou given the horse strength?" he quoted softly, hand stroking the braided mane that ran smooth and serpentlike down the great ridge of the stallion's neck. "Hast thou clothed his neck with thunder? He paweth in the valley, and rejoiceth in his strength: he goeth on to meet the armed men. He mocketh at fear, and is not affrighted; neither turneth he back from the sword."

He leaned close and pressed his forehead against the horse's shoulder. Huge muscles bulged beneath the skin, warm and eager, and the clean musky scent of the horse's excitement filled him. He straightened then, and slapped the taut, twitching hide.

"He saith among the trumpets, Ha, ha; and he smelleth the battle afar off, the thunder of the captains, and the shouting."

Grey heard the drums again, and his palms began to sweat.

Historical note: In October of 1757, the forces of Frederick the Great and his allies moved swiftly, crossing the country to defeat the gathering French and Austrian army at Rossbach, in Saxony. The town of Gundwitz was left undisturbed; the bridge at Aschenwald never crossed by an enemy.

THE SYMPHONY
OF AGES

ELIZABETH HAYDON

THE RHAPSODY TRILOGY:

The Symphony of Ages is written as a history in which the eras of time in the universe are recounted in seven distinct ages. The debut trilogy, *Rhapsody, Prophecy,* and *Destiny,* and the subsequent sequels, are set at the end of the Fifth Age, the age of Schism, and the beginning of the Sixth Age, the age of Twilight.

A giant tree stands at each of the places, known as the birthplaces of Time, where the five primordial elements—air, fire, water, earth, and ether—first appeared in the world. The oldest of these World Trees is Sagia, which grows on the Island of Serendair, the birthplace of ether. It is through the interconnected roots of Sagia that three people, all half-breeds, running from different pursuers, escape the cataclysm that destroys the Island and find themselves on the other side of the world, sixteen centuries later.

The three companions are initially antagonistic. Rhapsody, a woman of mixed human and Lirin blood, is a Namer, a student of lore and music who has learned the science of manipulating the vibrations that constitute life. She is on the run from an old nemesis, and is grudgingly rescued from his henchmen by two men. The Brother is an irritable and hideously ugly assassin with a bloodgift that makes him able to identify and track the heartbeats of any victim. His only friend, Grunthor, is a giant Firbolg Sergeant-Major with tusks, an impressive weapons collection, and a fondness for singing bawdy marching cadences. The two men are fleeing the demon of elemental fire who has control of the Brother's true name. Rhapsody accidentally changes the Brother's name to Achmed the Snake, breaking the control the demon has over him, and making his escape possible. The three make the trek along the roots of the World Trees through the belly of the Earth, passing through the fire at the center with the help of Rhapsody's ability to manipulate names. In the process, the distrustful adversaries become grudging friends. When they emerge on the other side they find themselves transformed; time appears to have stopped for them. In addition, they discover the story of their homeland's destruction and that refugees from Serendair, alerted to the impending cataclysm by a king's vision, traveled across the world to the place they have emerged, built a new civilization and destroyed it in war in the intervening centuries. Now the people from their homeland, knows as Cymrians, are hiding or quiet about their ancestry. It becomes clear to the three companions that a demon known as a F'dor accompanied the refugees away from the Island, and is clinging to an unknown host, biding its time and sowing the seeds of destruction. *Rhapsody* chronicles the journey of the Three as they cope with the loss of their world and build a new life in this new land, and the rise of the Firbolg, the demi-human nomads whom they eventually come to make a life with, and Achmed comes to rule, in the kingdom of Ylorc, the ruins of the Cymrian civilization carved into forbidding mountains. In *Prophecy,* the discovery of a dragon's claw in the ancient library of Ylorc leads Rhapsody to travel overland with Ashe, a man who hides his face, to find the dragon Elynsynos and return the claw before she destroys the Bolg in revenge. More of the F'dor's plot is uncovered, though its identity remains a mystery. Achmed discovers a child of living earth that slumbers endlessly in the ruins of a colony of Dhracians, tended to by the Grandmother, the only survivor of the colony. He realizes that the F'dor is seeking this Sleeping Child because her rib, made of Living Stone, would form a key like the one with which he opened Sagia—but in the demon's hand would be used to unlock the Vault of the Underworld and loose the remaining fire demons, who only seek destruction and chaos. *Destiny* follows the tale to its conclusion, the unmasking of the demon, the battle that ensues, and the re-formation of the Cymrian alliance.

The sequels, *Requiem* and *Elegy,* pick up the story three years later, and show the factors that eventually led to intercontinental war. With each new book, more of the history is laid bare, more of the secrets revealed, and more of the tale told in the style of a musical rhapsody.

The novella in this anthology is set in the Third Age, and chronicles the destruction of Serendair, telling the story of those who remained behind after the exodus.

THRESHOLD

ELIZABETH HAYDON

Two Ages ago, the doomed island of Serendair survived one cataclysm, when the burning star that came to be known as the Sleeping Child fell from the sky into the sea, taking much of the coastline, but sparing the middle lands. This time, as the Child that has slept beneath the waves for centuries signals its awakening, the earth and sea prepare for it to rise, and Gwylliam, the prescient king of the Island, foresees Serendair's obliteration in a vision of a second cataclysm.

Nearly everyone has left, the Nain of the northern mountains, the Lirin of the central forests and plains, and the humans, following their king in three great fleets to rebuild their civilization on another continent. The unbelieving, the foolish, the stubborn, the resigned, and a few truly abandoned souls remain, awaiting the end.

By the command of the king, a small detail of guards remains as well, to maintain order and protect those that stayed behind, and to keep some shred of the king's authority intact, just in case there is no second cataclysm. Condemned as they are, there is no way they could foresee what can happen when one pauses on the threshold between life and death.

This is their story, otherwise lost to history.

Hot vapor covered the sea, making it appear as calm and still as a misty morning.

There is more steam above the northern islands today,
Hector thought, shielding his eyes from the stinging glare of
the midday sun that blazed in rippling waves off the water,
blinding in its intensity. *Most definitely.*

He glanced to his right, where Anais stood, staring into the
impenetrable fog. The expression in his friend's silver eyes
was calm, contemplative, as always; it had rarely varied since
childhood. Hector knew he had made note of the thickening
as well.

He watched a moment longer as the plumes of mist ascended, then stood and wiped the sweat from his forehead
with the back of his sleeve, his gaze still affixed on the rising
steam.

"Still unable to make out the increase, Sevirym?" he asked
facetiously. He already knew the young soldier's answer.

"I see no difference from yesterday," Sevirym replied
rotely. "Or the day before."

Jarmon, older than the other men by twice over, took his
hand down from his eyes as well and exhaled in annoyance.

"And so he will continue to insist, until the waves fill his
mouth and the sea closes over his head," he said. "His eyes
work perfectly, but he is blind as a mole nevertheless. Do not
ask him any more, Hector. It sorely tries what is left of my
patience."

Sevirym spat into the sea and rose to follow Hector, who
had turned and now ambled away from the abandoned dock.

"I am not under false illusions, despite what you believe,
Jarmon," he muttered. "I just see no need to accept the in-
evitability of doom. Perhaps the king's vision was wrong, or
he misinterpreted it. Or perhaps the Sleeping Child *is* des-
tined to rise, but the sea won't consume the entire island; that
didn't even happen when the star fell to Earth in the first
place. Certainly we will lose some coastline, but if we go
to higher ground, as we have been telling all the others to
do—"

"I pray thee, cease," Cantha said.

The raspy dryness of her voice sliced through the wind,

causing Sevirym to fall immediately silent. Cantha used
words sparingly, as if doing so pained her. It was difficult not
to obey whatever she said.

Hector stopped, turning to look carefully for the first time
in as long as he could remember at his companions, four
completely different souls with one thing in common: they
had each willingly sacrificed whatever remaining time life
would have given them to stay behind on the Island, assisting
in his futile mission.

He was surprised by how much they had changed physi-
cally since the exodus of the Fleets, but was even more
shocked by the fact that he had failed until now to notice.
Jarmon's beard, a famous shade of burnt red all his life, had
gone gray enough to blend into the fog in which he stood;
Cantha's body, always thin and dark as a shadow, had withered to little more than a whisper on the wind. Her eyes
stared unflinchingly back at him from the haze; the strength
of her will was such that it held the space her physical presence had once taken in the air.

Sevirym was staring at the ground, the sting of Cantha's
words evident in his expression. Little more than a boy when
he had rashly thrown his lot in with Hector, he had aged a
score of years in the last five months, still maintaining an intermittent idealism that drove Jarmon to distraction. With
each disappointment, each rebuke from an elder, the life
seemed to seep a little more out of him, leaving him visibly
older.

Hector inhaled slowly, then caught the look of understanding aimed at him by Anais as if it were a ball tossed to
him. His closest friend, a brother in all but blood, Anais had
always understood his thoughts without needing to hear
them spoken aloud; perhaps it was their shared Lirin heritage
that made their minds one while granting them opposite
physical traits. Anais had been born with the traditional features of the Liringlas race, the silver eyes, the rosy skin, and
smooth hair that reflected the sun; Hector had favored his
mother's kin, dark of eye and hair, the crown of curls atop

his head reaching only to Anais's brow. Now they looked re-markably similar—both had faded, their features dulled to gray colorlessness by circumstance and exhaustion and the heat of the boiling sea.

He watched for a moment more, still in the thrall of the si-lence that Cantha had commanded, unable to feel anything about the changes he had noticed. Then he signaled word-lessly for them to head out.

That silence held sway for the duration of the walk along the rocky shore until the group reached the spot where the horses waited, oblivious to the changes in the morning wind. Then Anais cuffed Sevirym across the back of the head.

"I discern the reasons for your reluctance now!" he joked. "You wish to get out of sandbag duty."

Sevirym mustered a slight smile. "Can you blame me?"

"Certainly not," Anais said agreeably. "I just might form an alliance with you, Sevirym; we can mutiny and call for abandoning this mind-numbing task."

Hector chuckled as he mounted his roan. "A waste of time, that would be. The destruction of the Island may not be forgone, but sandbag duty remains as inevitable as death."

"You are decorating the wind, Hector," Jarmon said sourly. "But if it occupies your mind while we wait, I sup-pose there is nothing to be said against it."

Anais pulled himself into the saddle. "Speak for yourself. *I'll* gainsay it. If I had known this is how you were going to put us to use, I would not have stayed. It's one thing to agree to face certain death with one's best friend. It is altogether another to have one's carefully cleaned fingernails *ruined* playing in the dirt in the never-ending pursuit of useless sandbag fortifications. It is too onerous to be borne. You owe me a night of very expensive drinking, Hector."

Hector chuckled again and spurred the roan to a canter.

They rode without speaking down the northwestern shore-line to the outskirts of the abandoned fishing village and dismounted, to begin combing through what remained of the thatched huts and broken docks. Little effort had been needed to evacuate this place; fishermen knew the sea, and had been among the first to realize what was coming.

The five walked in silence through the packed-sand and crushed-shell streets, leading their mounts, the only sound the whine of the coastal wind, the cracking of thatch or the groaning of wood, the skittering of dock rats and the occasional snorting of the horses.

At the remains of each building one of the group peeled off from the others and poked through the fragments; little was left, as fishermen were practical people and had harvested whatever was usable in their village before packing their vessels and heading out in one of the earliest flotillas to the northern continent, the nearest haven.

On two earlier occasions they had found squatters, wild-eyed men, women, and children who had come from places inland, seeking passage off the Island after the Fleets had already gone. These lost souls had taken shelter in the shells of the huts that remained, praying for miracles or wandering in aimless dementia. Luck had it that places for them could be found on the few remaining rescue ships that came in the wake of the exodus of the Fleets. Hector himself prayed that he would never again have to tell a living soul that the time had passed when escape was possible; the wailing that resulted was too reminiscent of the sobbing he had heard upon breaking other such news.

As always, his mind wandered to Talthea and the children. If he closed his eyes he could almost see her, her belly great with child, her hand on the shoulder of his son—

"Body," Cantha called from within the ruins of the old salting shed.

Jarmon and Anais made their way over the litter of tin lantern shells and rusted iron hinges in the sand and opened the door. Cantha stood just over the threshold, her arms crossed, staring at the corpse, that of an old man who had curled up beneath what at one time had been the skinning table, its longboard missing. Flies swarmed in the heat.

"Wasn't here the last time we passed through—that was less than a fortnight ago, was it not, Hector?" Anais asked.

Hector only nodded, pulling forth his tinderbox as the others stepped out of the shed. He struck the flint against the steel and set the spark to the fragment of brittle twigs that remained in the roofing bundles.

"Whoever you are, I commit your body to the wind and your soul to the care of God, the One, the All," he said blandly, a chant he had intoned many times in the last few weeks. It was a Namer's benediction, but without a name.

Cantha, Kith by birth and thus a child of the aforementioned wind, blew gently on the sparks as she passed. They glowed brighter, then kindled, igniting a moment later into a thin flame.

When the remnants of the shed began to fill with smoke, and the flames had started to consume the roof, the group turned away and continued their task. Finding no one else in the empty village, they mounted again and rode south, not looking back at the billowing smoke and flames behind them.

The cobbled streets of Kingston, the great port city that lay south along the coast of the fishing village, introduced the element of noise back into the journey as the horses' hooves clattered loudly over the stones, echoing off the empty alleyways leading to the town square.

The stoicism that had beset the faces of the travelers seemed to wane somewhat whenever they returned to the capital city of the westlands, resolving into a quiet communal dismay. With each turn of the cycle, the shining jewel of the western seacoast looked more shabby, more broken, a desolate haven for ghosts and vermin that had once been a glistening city built by a visionary king centuries before.

Upon reaching the dry fountain in the square, the group dismounted. Sevirym's feet landed on the cobblestones first, followed by the muffled thuds from the others' boots.

"Damnation," he murmured, looking up at the place where the statue of that long-dead king riding a hippogriff had once towered over the mosaic inlaid in the fountain's bed. The figure had been battered savagely, the formerly outstretched wings of the king's mount shattered into marble shards that lay scattered in the dry basin. The statue's stone head had been smashed from its shoulders and now lay in the street just outside the capstones, the pupil-less eyes staring blindly at the hazy sky.

Jarmon had given a lifetime's service to the descendants of that king. He waded through the dust and gravel to the statue's base and numbly brushed the grit from the inscription:

> AN EMPIRE BUILT BY SLAVES CRUMBLES IN THE DESPOT'S LIFETIME; A CITY BUILT IN FREEDOM STANDS
> A THOUSAND YEARS.

"Fell short by half, Your Majesty," the elderly guard said softly, running his callused finger over the letters.

"What was the purpose in this?" demanded Sevirym of no one in particular. "What was the need? Did they not have enough to concern them that they had time for *this*? Is there not enough destruction coming that they needed more? Bloody *animals*."

"Peace," said Hector quietly. "It is but a statue. It doesn't matter now. The ideal remains."

Sevirym choked back a bitter laugh and seized the reins of his mount, leading the animal away from the dusty fountain.

"Must be hard on you westlanders, riding this continuous loop," Anais said after a moment, once Jarmon and Cantha had followed Sevirym away from the town square and were now combing through the remains of their assigned streets. "At least those of us who dwelt to the east beyond the Great River are spared watching the gradual destruction of our homelands."

Hector said nothing but clicked to his roan. He and Anais fell into routine, joining the others in their search through the empty city.

He walked numbly past the abandoned shops where as a child he had delighted to linger, maneuvering his horse around the mounds of broken glass and grit that had once been the window of the Confectionery; the shop had produced baked goods so exceptional that the populace believed them to be imbued with magic. He allowed himself to linger again, one last time, trying to recall the scent of the flaky pastries, the sight of the castles rendered entirely in cookies and sweetmeats, the chocolate carvings of winged horses and dragons with strawberry scales, but he could only see the hollowed shell of the building with patches of light on the floor sinking in from the holes in the roof, could smell only the odor of pitch and oil and destruction.

How long he had stood, staring futilely back into the past, he did not know, but when Anais's voice finally reached his consciousness, it was like a bell rousing him from a deep sleep.

"Nothing save for some stray dogs and a murder of crows that has taken refuge in the eaves of the old prelate's office."

"A murder of crows?"

Anais adopted an aspect of mock seriousness. "Aye, big uglies, too. One of them may have been the prelate's wife."

Hector smiled. "She certainly had quite a caw to her, but alas, none of the birds could be she. May God the One, the All, help my father—she sailed on his ship."

Anais shook his head in sympathy. "Poor MacQuieth. As if he did not have enough to contend with."

Hector nodded, abandoning the attempt to summon better memories of the Confectionery. "My father's greatest burden in the last days before the exodus was the irony of it all. He spent his youth fighting the Seren War to spare the Island from the fires of the Underworld, to keep the demons born of that fire from destroying Serendair. And now that the F'dor are defeated, the last of their kind sealed forever in the Vault of the Underworld, the Island is going to succumb to fire after all—fire from the sky long lodged in the sea."

"Somehow I doubt that the irony was your father's greatest burden," Anais said, kicking the broken storefront sign away from the cobbled street.

"Did you look in on the stable?"

"Aye."

"Are any of the horses still alive?"

"Remarkably, all of them are, the poor beasts. Most have withered to skin and bones. Cantha is feeding them the last of the hay."

Hector loosed a deep sigh. "I think we should deviate from our regular route, Anais. Before we leave here, let's take them out of the city to the fields at the crossroads and turn them loose. Surely it is kinder than leaving them in their paddocks, to be fed only when we come through. They can find grass and water there."

"Agreed," Anais said. "The human population is gone now. What's a delay in a route that guards no one, anyway?"

Hector looked back over his shoulder up the main street that led at its terminus to the entrance of the Gated City in the north of Kingston.

"Not all of the human population is gone," he objected quietly. "Only those who were free to leave."

Anais followed his gaze, then exhaled deeply.

As the sea wind blew through Kingston's desolate streets, whipping sand into their eyes, both men thought back to earlier days, after the exodus of the Fleets but before the rescue ships from other lands had stopped coming to Serendair. The young king, Gwylliam, newly crowned and the architect of the evacuation that had saved most of his subjects from death in the cataclysm that was still to come, had sailed on the last ship of the last Fleet, and so believed that every Seren citizen who wanted to leave had done so.

He had forgotten completely about the Gated City.

It was really not surprising that the City had been missed in the inventory of Gwylliam's conscious thought. Though it occupied geographical space in his realm, it was a world unto itself, a former penal colony of petty thieves and cutpurses that had evolved into its own entity, a dark and colorful society with layers of governance and threat that were incomprehensible to any but those who lived within its locked gates.

Despite the appearance of being contained, the Gated City clearly had as many tunnels out into the world beyond its fortifications as a beaver dam or a nest of rats. Even in the days prior to the Seren War that had ended two hundred years before, the City had been divided into the Outer Ring and the Inner Ring. The Outer Ring contained a flourishing market of exotic goods and eccentric services that citizens of the outside world could visit as long as they were checked through the gates.

They entered on the middle day of the week, known as Market Day, at the sound of the great brass bell, to shop in the bazaar, clutching the token that would allow them passage back out of the City again when the bell sounded at closing time, buying perfumes that could transport the mind to places beyond the horizons of reality, linens and silks of indescribable colors, jewels and potions and soothing balms and myriad other wares from the far corners of the earth. The mere existence of these exotic goods was a broad hint at how porous the thick walls of the Gated City really were.

The Inner Ring was even more mysterious, a dark place to which none but the permanent residents of the City had access. Within its windowless buildings, in its shadowy alleys, another sort of business was conducted that those who lived outside the Gated City could only imagine in the course of their nightmares.

When Hector and his companions first realized that the Gated City had been overlooked, they had sought to offer its residents refuge on the first of the ships that had come in the wake of the exodus. He had gone to the City himself—its massive gates no longer were guarded from the outside. He had sprung the lock and thrown the gates open wide, issuing an invitation to the startled population he found on the other side to flee, to save themselves from the destruction that was surely to come when the Sleeping Child awakened and rose, taking the Island of Serendair back beneath the waves of the sea with it, as the king had prophesied it soon would.

The Gated City was teeming with people then. They stared

at him as if he were mad, then turned away, averting their eyes, and went about their business as if he were not there.

The next day, when he returned to entreat them once again to reconsider, to explain once more the cataclysm that was coming, he found the gates closed again. A polite note was pinned to the outside, declining his offer with thanks and wishing him well.

The thought of the thousands of souls on the other side of those gates had haunted Hector for weeks afterward, as he and the others carefully packed the remaining stragglers that came from the lands east of the Great River, or had somehow missed the exodus, onto the last of the rescue ships. Ofttimes he found himself walking outside the City's walls, wishing he had a way to make whatever governing force was within them change its mind and spare its people.

After a while the point became moot. The ships stopped coming as the temperature of the sea over the gravesite of the Sleeping Child grew increasingly warmer, causing bilge-water to boil in the heat and some of the ships to burst at the seams. Hector no longer could summon the strength to think about those who might still be on the other side of the wall, condemned now to remaining on the Island to the end, just as the populations east of the Great River who had chosen to stay were condemned.

Just as he and his four companions were condemned.

It was far too late to worry about it now.

Hector blinked; the afternoon sun had shifted, blinding him. He shaded his brow and looked over at Anais, who nodded toward the docks.

"Come," his Liringlas friend said, his silver eyes glinting in the light.

Without a word, Hector clicked to his horse and followed.

Bonfires burned along the wharf, the ashes mixing with the steam from the sea. Cantha, Jarmon, and Sevirym must have found more bodies, human or otherwise, Hector knew, or something festering that warranted the spending of precious fuel in making the pyres.

The irony of the infernos no longer choked him. In the weeks since the last ship had come and departed, there had been many such bonfires along the route they traveled, a long south–north loop of the lands to the west of the Great River. They had only ventured into the eastern territories once—that wide expanse of land held the subkingdoms that had chosen to stay, either because they did not believe the king's vision, or, even in accepting it, preferred to remain in their birthlands to the end. Because the final departure of the Third Fleet had been launched from the port of Kingston, it was to the westlands that the stragglers had come late, and so it was this part of the realm that Hector had seen fit to guard, to maintain a futile sense of order in the last days. The rioting and looting had dwindled as starvation and disease had set in, and the western coast burned with cleansing pyres that would have made marvelous signal fires, beacons of distress, had there been any ship out on the sea to answer them.

The clouds of smoke swirled and danced, buffeted by the inconstant sea winds. Hector could see the black shadows of his friends moving silently in the haze, raking the ashes over, tossing driftwood onto the pyres.

On the docks a shade that must have been Anais beckoned to him.

Hector walked through the acidic mist, his eyes stinging from the smoke, to the end of the pier where his childhood friend waited and stood beside him, staring off into the lapping sea and the impenetrable fog. It was a ritual they both had observed many times since the Second Fleet had departed, this silent vigil. In standing there, together, as they had stood on that horrific day when together they bound over their wives and children into the hands of MacQuieth for safekeeping, for a moment there was a connection, a link back in Time, to the last place where life still held meaning for them.

"I no longer dream of them," Anais said, gazing into the steam. His voice was muffled by the whine of the wind.

"No?"

"No. You?"

Hector inhaled deeply, breathing in the salt and the heavy scent of ash, thinking of Talthea and their son, and their unborn child. "Yes. Each night." He broke his gaze away and looked down through the mist at the waves cresting under the pier. "Of nothing else." It was the only thing that made the day bearable, the knowledge that the night would come, bringing such dreams.

Anais nodded thoughtfully. "When awake, I can summon their faces if I try," he said, "but at night I dream of the World Tree."

Hector blinked and turned to face his friend. "Sagia?"

Anais nodded again. "And the forest Yliessan where I was born."

In the heat of the afternoon sun, Hector felt suddenly cold at his friend's mention of the great tree; it was the sacred entity of Anais's people, the Lirin, the children of the sky. Sagia was one of the five birthplaces of Time, where the element of Ether was born, and its power was the heart's blood of the Island.

"What do you see in these dreams, Anais?"

Anais inclined his head as if to facilitate recall of the vision. "I am standing in Yliessan at the base of the Tree, staring up its massive trunk to the lowest limbs that stretch out over the canopy of the other trees in the forest. Its silver bark is gleaming. Around the Tree are lines of Lirin of all strains, Lirindarc, the forest dwellers; Lirinved, the In-between, the nomads who live in both forest and field, making their home in neither; the Lirinpan from the cities—they are all waiting. The Liringlas, my own people, the skysingers, are at the end of the line, weaving flower garlands as they wait.

"One by one, they climb into the lowest branches, then higher, building shelters of sorts, nests, for lack of a better word. The Liringlas are adorning the trunk of Sagia with the floral garlands." Anais closed his eyes, concentrating on the vision. "They are singing. The Lirin are taking refuge in Sagia, awaiting the end in Her arms."

Sevirym's voice shattered the stillness of the docks.

"Hector! Hector! Ship! A ship is coming into port!"

The men at the dock's end turned in surprise and stared harder into the mist.

At the outer reaches of their vision they could see it after a moment, sails spilling wind as it approached the lower landing at the southern tip of the main jetty. Hector ran back down the pier, followed a moment later by Anais, where they met up with the other three.

Jarmon was shaking his head. "Fools," he muttered, watching the vessel as it disappeared into the steam rising off the seawall. "Must be lost. Can't be a ship's captain in the world who doesn't know the peril at this point."

Cantha shook her head too. "Not lost. Deliberate in its movements."

"Hoay!" Sevirym called, jogging toward the jetty and waving his arm in the swirls of floating black ash from the bonfires. "Hoay! Here!"

Nothing but the sea wind answered them.

They stood in the heavy mist for what seemed a half hour or more, until finally Anais spotted a dim light making its way over the waves in their direction, bobbing up and down near the water's surface.

"They've launched a longboat," he said, pointing out the approaching glow. "A lantern lights its prow, low to the water."

"The ship's a two- or three-masted schooner," Jarmon reported. "Brigantine, mayhap—I can't make it out. Big monster, she is. Must have dropped anchor just outside the seawall. Can't say as I blame her. Wouldn't want to navigate this harbor in the fog now that the light towers have gone dark."

"Sevirym, light a brand and wave it," Hector called as he walked to the end of the jetty. He strained to see through the smoke and mist, but caught only occasional sight of the tiny lantern that bobbed nearer on the wide bay.

"Madness," Jarmon muttered under his breath as Sevirym climbed to the top of the massive wall of sandbags that they had erected along the coastline and held the firebrand aloft for light. "It has been more than two full turns of the moon since the last one—why is a ship coming now? Can they not see the rising steam? It must reach well into the sky; how can they miss that from the open sea?"

"Perhaps they have the same sort of eyes as Sevirym," Anais suggested. "Let us wait and see."

They watched in impatient silence for a long while, then simultaneously made their way down the long pier through the brightness of the fog that had swallowed Hector, who waited at its end.

The light from the lantern on the longboat's prow was now in close sight, its radiance diffused by the glow of the sun in the steam that blanketed the coast. Over the sound of the waves slapping the pier they heard a ragged voice calling.

"Hoay!"

Farther out in the harbor, a score of voices picked up the hoarse cry.

"Hoay! Anyone there? Hoay!"

Before the eyes of the five companions, twinkling lights appeared, spread in an arrowpoint formation behind the first beacon. A longboat guided by a boatswain and steered by four rowers emerged from the fog, followed a moment later by five others that followed it.

In the first boat a man was standing; they could see his shadow begin to take on form and definition as the longboat neared the pier.

"Hoay! I am looking for Sir Hector Monodiere! Be any of you he?"

"I am he," Hector said, grasping the pylon and leaning out over the end of the pier to get a better look at the man in the longboat through the hazy light. "Why have you come here?"

The man shielded his eyes. "I am Petaris Flynt, captain of the *Stormrider,* sailing under the flag of Marincaer. I bear news; toss me a line."

Jarmon and Anais set about mooring the lead longboat, while Cantha went back to assist Sevirym in guiding the remaining ones to the pier with the firebrand. Hector offered the captain his hand and discovered upon pulling the man onto the dock how weak his grip had become, how much flesh had been lost from his arm.

The captain was a burly man, stout and barrel-chested, with a full gray beard and eyes as black as the depths of the sea. He looked up at Hector, half a head taller, then allowed his eyes to wander to the others and beyond to the empty wharf. He shook his head and sighed.

"Who could ever have imagined the great light tower of Kingston would go dark in my lifetime?" he mused. "I had thought the rising of the sun was more in doubt than the presence of that beacon. Alas and alack." He signaled to the sailors in the longboat to be at ease, then met Hector's eye again.

"We are here to take one last load, Sir Hector—whatever stragglers remain, whoever may have missed the last ship out—this truly *is* the final chance they will have. The sea above the Northern Isles is roiling in the heat; the bilge in any ship now boils within ten leagues of Balatron. We don't know if we will make it out ourselves—we sail with the tide at sunset, heading southwest as fast as the wind will carry us until we hit the Icefields, then looping back to the north. Anyone on board at sunset can come with us. All others remain—no exceptions."

"May God the One, the All, forgive my ingratitude, but why did you come here?" Hector asked incredulously. "The shipping lanes have been closed to this place for more than two months now. The exodus was completed three months before that; the Third Fleet left in midspring. There is no one left to save—everyone who was willing to leave is already gone."

Flynt's brow furrowed. "I came by the order of the king of Marincaer, who was asked to send me by Stephastion, one of the barons of Manosse."

"Manosse?" Hector glanced at Jarmon and Anais, who shrugged. Manosse was a great nation half a world away on the eastern coast of the Northern Continent, far from the lands to which the refugees who had refused to sail with the Fleets had fled.

"Aye," said Flynt. "It is from Manosse that the news comes as well. Your father's fleet landed there."

"In Manosse?" Hector asked in concern. "Why? What happened? That is not to where they were bound."

"Apparently they were beset by a great storm," Flynt replied, speaking rapidly. "Sundered at the Prime Meridian. Many ships were lost. Part of the surviving flotilla landed at Gaematria, the Isle of the Sea Mages, though it is a forbidden place to most. Your father led the remainder of the fleet back to Manosse, probably because he knew the weakened ships would not survive the rest of the voyage east to the Wyrmlands, where they were originally headed. They plan to stay there, I'm told."

Hector nodded. "What of the First Fleet? And the Third?"

The captain shook his head. "No word. But if they were going to the Wyrmlands, I fear there will never be word from them again. That place is not part of the Known World for a reason." He glanced around nervously.

"Do you have word of my family?" Hector asked.

"I am told your wife and son are safe in Manosse. And your daughter as well—your child has been born, safe and healthy, I am to tell you."

"Do you know what name she was given?"

"No, but your wife apparently said that you do."

"And my father—he is well? And his ship?"

Flynt looked away. "He survived the trip. His ship remained intact, I am told."

Hector and Anais exchanged a glance of relief; the news boded well for Anais's family, who had traveled with Hector's, though it was clear the captain was leaving something out.

"Tell me of my father, whatever it is you have not said," Hector asked. "Is he ill?"

"Not to my knowledge." The sea captain gestured nervously to the crew of his longboat, who took up oars and rowed toward the shore, then turned his attention back to the young man.

"Your father stands vigil in the sea, Sir Hector. Once what remained of the Second Fleet was docked, and his duty discharged, he went to the peninsula of Sithgraid, the southernmost tip of Manosse, and waded into the surf. It is said that he stands there, night into day into night again, refusing sustenance and company from any but your wife and son. When the baron asked your wife what he is doing, she merely said that he is waiting."

Hector absorbed the words in silence, gazing off to the eastern horizon. "Thank you."

Impatience won its battle for control of the sea captain. "All right, then, Sir Hector; I've delivered my news. As I have told you, I have come to take the last souls who wish to leave before the Island succumbs. Gather them."

As if hearing the words for the first time, Hector turned and looked intently at Flynt, then nodded.

"Very well."

"Open the gate, Sevirym."

The young soldier looked doubtful as his gaze ran up the massive entranceway to the empty guard towers on either side. He stared at the wall that encircled the Gated City, and, noting no one walking atop it, grasped hold of the rusted handle and pulled with all his strength.

The heavy wooden gate, bound in brass, swung open silently.

"Would you look at that," Jarmon muttered bitterly. "For four hundred years it took three men to spring those brass locks, seven to open that gate into this nest of thieves. Now it swings open like my mother's kitchen door. Truly I have lived too long."

Hector stepped through the entranceway past the thick walls reinforced internally with iron bars, trying to absorb the sight beyond them.

The Gated City was empty.

Or perhaps it only appeared that way. From every street corner, every boarded window and alleyway, he could sense the presence of shadows, could feel the weight of eyes on him, even though there was no one visible.

Through the silent thoroughfares they walked, stepping over the detritus of the bazaar that littered the streets, shreds of cloth and broken market carts, sparkling glass fragments and streaks of soot from long-cold roasting fires. At each street corner Hector stopped and peered into the recesses of the Outer Ring, but saw nothing; called, but received no answer.

Finally they came to the great well at the center of the Gated City, a place that a revered historian had described in his writings as the "upspout of a warren of Downworlders, people who lived entirely in the darkness beneath city streets, in lairs with more tunnels that a queendom of ants." Hector didn't know if he believed the lore of those mythical human rats, and didn't care; he only knew that sound in the well would reverberate throughout the city. He leaned over the edge and shouted.

"Hullo! Come out now, all you within the sound of my voice! I command you, in the name of Gwylliam, High King of Serendair, quit this place at once! The last ship that will ever come waits in the harbor, and sails with the tide at sunset. Come! The Sleeping Child rises in the northwest—save yourselves!"

His words resounded off the stones of the alleyways, echoed down the well and through the streets. Hector waited.

There was no answer.

"Anais," Hector said without turning, maintaining his watch on the streets and alleys before him, "go back to the gate and ring the Market Day bell."

"Are you certain it is there still?" Anais asked doubtfully. "Most of Kingston's bells were melted down for ship fittings when the exodus began."

"That bell was within the Gated City, which was overlooked in the planning of the exodus. It was too large to be taken by those who have already scurried out of here through whatever holes there may be in the walls. Keep ringing it until the walls start to give way."

Unconsciously the other three moved into a circle with their backs to Hector, watching at the compass points for signs of response. Aside from a shifting of shadows and a flutter here and there in the darkness, there were none.

They stood thus, crossbows nocked but pointed at the cobblestones, still as those stones, even as the great bell sounded loudly from atop the wall at the gate.

Waves of harsh brass sound rippled through the empty streets as Anais struck again and again. A wild flapping rose from the eaves of a boarded mudbrick building near the well; a flock of roosting pigeons started and took to the sky, squawking angrily.

For fifteen long minutes the great bell kept sounding, the clanging trailing off into silence after a few sustained moments, only to resume in its earsplitting furor again and again. Hector continued to stare into the darkened alleyways, enduring the cacophony without wincing, until finally a dark outline of a man appeared at the end of a street near the well. The man waited until Anais paused in his pounding of the bell, then shouted down the empty street.

"Have him stop immediately, or I will order him shot."

"It would be an unwise order to give," Hector shouted back, as the three who surrounded him leveled their crossbows, "and your last."

A ragged chuckle came from the bony figure, and the man at the alley's end came forward, limping slightly into the afternoon light as the bell began to crash once more.

"Hold, Anais," Hector yelled as the thin man stepped into the square the same moment the ringing paused again. He watched impatiently as the man leaned on his walking stick and turned his head to the south to scan the distant wall. The others did not lower their weapons.

"What, pray tell, do you think you are doing?" the ragged man asked in a mixture of annoyance and inquisitiveness. "Besides disturbing the pigeons and my afternoon nap."

"A final rescue ship has come into the harbor. I am here to

make one last attempt to save what remains of the king's people."

The bony man broke into a wide smile graced intermittently by teeth.

"Ah," he said smugly, running a thin hand over the gray stubble on his face. "Now the source of our misunderstanding is clear. You are merely confused." His tone turned conciliatory, with a hint of exaggerated condescension, as if he were speaking to children. "You see, these are not the king's people; they never were. The king forgot about this place long ago, just as his father and his grandfather before him did. I am king of this place now—well, they call me the Despot, actually—now that anyone with actual power has long ago left. These are *my* people. *I* say whether they come or go, live or die." He leaned forward on his walking stick, his patchy smile growing brighter. "And I say they are staying. So go about your business, sir knight; run along and board your ship. We do thank you for your kind offer, but respectfully, as king of those who remain, I decline."

"You are king of nothing," Jarmon shouted scornfully.

The Despot laughed. "Well, I have something in common with Gwylliam, then. How repulsive. I am more king than he ever was, he who frightened the people with his visions, his predictions of cataclysm, and then left them, a king who abandoned his birthright to save his own hide. At least I stayed with my people—held my post. Unlike Gwylliam, I am not a coward."

Jarmon's expression blackened and he raised his bow sight to his eye.

"Give the word, Hector," the old guard said angrily. "I want this one."

"There is no time for your games, your foolishness," Hector said tersely to the Despot, raising a cautionary hand to Jarmon.

"Then stop wasting what time you have left here," the Despot said, his tone flattening. "Do you not know the origins of this place? What is there here worth saving?"

Before answering, Hector sized him up. He had always been told that the city beyond the gates was full of tricks, but the scrawny man before him had no weapons he could detect, and he saw no open doors or windows that might conceal bowmen. He could not be certain that Anais's position was clear a block or so down.

"Them," he said simply, gesturing into the dark streets and alleyways. "Anyone who did not have the chance to choose life; anyone who was condemned as an afterthought. One man. One woman. One child. Any and all that want to leave, whatever their crimes, whatever their innocence. In the name of Gwylliam, the king, I am here to offer them that chance. Now, move aside! We have no time for this! We stand on the threshold of death."

The eyes of the Despot darkened as well, revealing a soulless depth.

"By all means, step over, then," he said icily. "It's rude to hover in doorways."

"After you, Your Majesty," Hector replied.

He dropped his hand.

Three bolts were unleashed simultaneously, piercing the ragged man in the eye, heart, and forehead, tearing through him as if he were parchment. The Despot fell back onto the broken cobblestones of the square with a thud, sending another bevy of pigeons skyward. The noise of his fall and their rise echoed through the empty streets, followed by a deafening silence.

"Anais, ring the bell thrice more," Hector called over his shoulder.

The metallic crashing resumed, then ceased, dying away slowly.

"Now, come!" Hector shouted into the Outer Ring. "Come with us if you want to live!"

For a long moment nothing answered him. Then, at the outer edges of his sight in the dark alleyways, Hector saw the shadows thicken a bit, then move.

Slowly, one and two at a time, figures began to move into the light of the square, like ghosts in the haze of the sun, squinting as if in pain. Thin men, emaciated women, and a few tattered children came forward, hovering close to one another, their eyes hollow and downcast. Hector loosed his breath; until this moment, he could not have been certain that there was anyone in the dark city left to save.

"Sevirym," he said to the young soldier, "lead these people to the pier and get them aboard the ship. Send Anais back when you pass through the gate; we will go quickly house to house, and into the Inner Ring."

Sevirym nodded curtly at the mention of the dark interior of the Gated City, then turned and gestured excitedly to the two dozen or so human shadows wandering slowly toward the gates.

"Come," he shouted. "Follow me to the ship—and to a chance at living another day."

Street after street, building after mudbrick building revealed no one living, only broken remains. There were decidedly more bodies in the Gated City than they had found elsewhere in the westlands, too many to burn or even pray over.

As they ran from lintel to lintel, from post to pillar, they called into the empty corridors and banged on the walls and stairs to rouse anyone in the upper floors or lofts, but only managed to disturb nests of rats, roosting birds, and packs of feral cats ripping out what little they could scrounge from the charnel.

Finally Anais, who had clambered from rooftop to rooftop through much of the city, climbed down and stood in the middle of the street before an interior wall that ran perpendicular to the rest of the buildings, sealing the Outer Ring from the dark streets that lay beyond it. A black wrought-iron gate shaped like a giant keyhole was broken off its hinges, the metal twisted with a savage ferocity. Anais bent over at the waist, panting from exertion and frustration.

"The Inner Ring must begin here," he said between breaths. "You are going to want to go in, aren't you, Hector?"

"Yes."

Anais sighed. "Of course. A waste of valuable air to have asked in the first place. Be so good as to allow me a moment to catch my breath. I am growing too old for this nonsense."

Hector said nothing. *What I would give if only you had the chance to grow old, Anais,* he thought.

"Sun's descending," Cantha said, shading her eyes with her long-fingered hand and staring into the all-but-impenetrable mist. "Two hours and 'twill be beyond the horizon."

"Right; thirty minutes' more search at most, then," Hector said, nodding his head at Jarmon to pull the twisted portal open. "And let us stay together in here. This was, in its day, a largely evil enclave, the closest place to the Vault of the Underworld that existed on this Island; we don't want to make a misstep."

Quickly they pulled themselves through the portal, avoiding the jagged metal, and stepped for the first time in any of their lives into the streets of the Inner Ring.

It was stunning in its dullness.

The buildings in what had once been one of the darkest corners of the world were no different than they had been in the Outer Ring, or even in the more populated parts of the westlands, for that matter. The streets here were, if possible, even quieter than they had been in the outside world, even more devoid of anything valuable left behind. The buildings stood, unmolested, appearing for all the world as pedestrian as the buildings of Kingston's residential area. The only discernible difference was the proximity of them; they crowded each other for space, squeezing next to each other on narrow streets. Ropes hung intermittently from windows, tying the streets closely together in the air above the ground as well.

Hector pulled aside a half door that hung from only one hinge and peered into the recesses of a dilapidated shop.

"My father walked these streets many times," he mused aloud. "He said there was a darkness that hung over the place, that was present in the very air itself. It must have been extant in the nefarious population that lived here; it appears they took it with them when they left."

"Good," Jarmon muttered. "Perhaps it obscured their path on the sea and they sank without a trace."

They combed each street, each alley, calling rotely as they had in the Outer Ring, but within this smaller, closer section of the Gated City their words were swallowed in the devouring silence that reigned here.

At one street corner halfway in, Cantha stopped and turned down the thoroughfare; the others followed her past a stand of dark buildings to a place where one appeared to be missing. A gray hole of cold ash held its place amid the otherwise unscathed structures, like a missing tooth in a dull smile.

The Kith woman inclined her head into the wind and inhaled.

"The Poisoner's," she said. It was the only building in the Inner Ring that had been razed.

"They took their secrets with them as well," said Anais.

"There's no one here, Hector," Jarmon called impatiently from farther up the street, his voice muted. "Can we quit this place now? We have searched as well as God, the One, the All, could possibly ask; let us be out of here before we set off a trap or discover some other sign of contempt left behind for the forces of His Majesty."

Hector glanced around at the desolate streets, the hollow buildings, silent witnesses to acts that would have defied description even if their stones could talk. *Another trove of mystery enters the annals of Time,* he thought bemusedly, then turned back to the others who watched him intently from farther up the street.

"Yes," he said at last. "We've searched enough. Let's be off."

The second longboat was preparing to depart when Hector and the others returned to the pier in Kingston's harbor.

Sevirym waved for the boatswain to wait and jogged back up the dock, looking behind his friends in the mist.

"Anyone else?"

"No one," Hector said flatly. "The City is empty."

The captain of the *Stormrider* came forward hastily out of the fog.

"We are not even two-fifths laden with this boatload," he said somberly. "Surely this is not all?"

"I'm afraid it is."

"Hardly worth the risk, the effort," Petaris Flynt muttered. "A score of ragged human rats—for this we chanced boiling and splitting?"

Hector's brow darkened in the dimming light of the setting sun.

"If you rescue but one soul, it will have been worth the effort," he said bitterly. "Would that I had the chance to do so. Take to your ship, captain, and set sail. Hurry home to whomever you love, bearing your human cargo. Quit this place while you can."

The captain nodded sharply. "Very well. Climb aboard, then, Sir Hector, and we'll be off for the Icefields."

Five pairs of eyes stared at him stonily through the mist.

"You misunderstand," Anais said finally after a long and awkward moment. "We are not leaving."

"I am sworn to stay here," Hector interrupted, waving Anais into silence. "By command of my king and lord, I am to remain to keep order in the last days, and hold the line of succession."

"Madness!" puffed Flynt. "The king is gone, Sir Hector; the exodus has passed, and passed successfully. There is nothing left to guard. Surely your king did not mean for you to remain to your death, now that your duty is fully discharged! Come aboard."

"I thank you, but I cannot."

"By the king's command?"

"By the king's command, yes."

"Then your king was a fool," said the sea captain contemptuously. "If there is nothing left to guard, to what end does a sovereign condemn good men to certain death standing watch over *nothing*? What sort of man, what sort of king, would do that?"

"My king," growled Jarmon, his eyes blazing in fury as he elbowed his way between Anais and Hector, stopping a hairsbreadth from the captain's face. "Our king. And you would be well advised not to gainsay him again, if you do not wish to face certain death yourself."

"Think of your family, man," the captain said desperately, ignoring the old guard and turning to Hector once more.

Hector leaned closer. "I do, with each breath," he said, gently pulling Jarmon back. "But I am sworn to my king, and they"—he nodded at the other four—"are sworn to me. I thank you for your concern, Captain Flynt, and for your heroic efforts on behalf of the remaining population of this land. But only one of us will be going with you."

The captain blinked; the tension that had run in the air like steel bands a moment before vanished, replaced with shock as the four others looked askance at each other, bewilderment on their faces.

Hector turned and signaled to his companions, nodding down the pier. Together they walked halfway back to the dock, shaking their heads, exchanging glances of confusion, until Hector stopped out of earshot of the captain, and pointed through the mist to shore, where the dark mountain of sandbags loomed.

"Cantha, Jarmon, walk on," he said softly. "You too, Anais."

"Me?" Sevirym shouted, too overwrought to catch the words before they exploded from his lips. "You are sending *me* away? No, Hector. I'll not leave."

Hector signaled again to his puzzled friends, urging them away from the pier.

"Yes, Sevirym," he said quietly, laying a hand on Sevirym's arm. The young soldier shrugged it off angrily. "Yes, you will."

"Why? Has my loyalty to you been any less than theirs? Have I dishonored you, failed you—"

"Never," Hector interrupted him, taking his arm again. "Hear me, Sevirym; time is short and words should be used sparingly, so that their meaning is undiluted. No man could have asked for a more loyal companion and a better friend than you have been to me, to the others—to this dying land. But I need you to go with the captain now, to guard the refugees, and to make certain they are not combative." Involuntarily he winced at the sight of the pain on his friend's face.

"I want to remain here, Hector."

Hector sighed. "Well, that makes one of us, Sevirym. I do not—but what I want is not at issue. Nor is what you want. We are both prisoners of what needs to be done, as decided by the one who commands us." His tone softened. "You are fulfilling the same order of the king that the rest of us are— 'keep my people safe in the last days.' These ragged refugees— they are the king's subjects as much as you or I. They need our protection. Get them out of here, Sevirym. Take them to safety."

Sevirym dropped his eyes, unable to maintain a calm mien anymore.

"You are commanding me to do this, against my will and my vow?" he said, his voice choked with anguish.

"Only if you force me to," Hector replied gently. "Rather, I am asking you to do this for me, as my friend and brother. You swore to stand by me, to help me in this task that was commanded of me. In leaving with the ship, you are helping me far more than by staying."

For a long moment, Sevirym continued to stare at the rotting planks of the pier, listening to the splash of the waves beneath the mist. Then finally he nodded.

In turn Hector nodded to the three standing on the docks and turned to walk with Sevirym back to the end of the pier. Anais raised his hand; Sevirym lifted his halfheartedly in return. Jarmon bowed his head, then turned away. Only Cantha remained still, her eyes staring sharply through the fog, her face expressionless.

"I am abandoning them, and you," Sevirym muttered as they walked back to where the longboats and the ship's captain waited. "I may live, but you are sentencing me to life as a coward."

Hector stopped suddenly, dragging Sevirym to a harsh halt by the arm.

"Damn your tongue if it utters such a thing again," he said sharply. "And damn your mind if it believes it. What I ask of you requires more bravery than staying behind, Sevirym; I am asking you to live. Dying is easy; any fool can do it—it's living that requires courage. Now get on that damned ship and do your duty to the king, to me, and to yourself."

After a moment Sevirym lifted his eyes and met Hector's. "Why me?" he asked softly. "I go, Hector, but I just want to know why you chose me, and not Anais, or Jarmon, or Cantha."

Hector exhaled. "Because you have never really believed that you were going to die, Sevirym. Unlike the rest of us, you kept hoping that the Island could be spared, that death was not inevitable—and perhaps that is a sign from God, the One, the All, that for you it is not."

Sevirym continued to stare at him for a long time, then finally nodded, acceptance in his eyes.

"I will find Talthea and your children, Hector, and guard them until my last breath."

Hector embraced him. "Thank you, my friend. Tell Talthea that they were in my thoughts until the last, and what happened here. Everything, Sevirym, tell her everything; do not spare her. She is stronger than any of us." His grip tightened. "I will say this to you, Sevirym, and it is something I have not said, nor will I say, to any other living soul." He leaned closer and whispered into his friend's ear.

"None of us should have had to stay."

Sevirym, unable to form words, nodded again.

They walked to the end of the pier, swathed in impenetrable vapor. The shade of the captain was waiting still. Hector watched as the boatswain lifted the lamp from the prow of the longboat to light Sevirym's way aboard, then raised a hand in final salute.

In the misty glow of the longboat's lantern, Sevirym held up his hand in return.

Hector stared, trying to keep his eyes focused until the shadow had slipped away into the sea mist, then turned to the captain again.

"Thank you," he said.

"Is that all, then?" Petaris Flynt said regretfully. "I cannot change your mind, Sir Hector?"

"That is all," Hector answered. "Can you take some of the horses from the livery? Those mounts served the king with their lives as well; if you have room for them, it would gladden my heart to see you spare them."

Flynt nodded dully. "Such a waste," he muttered. "A handful of human rats, some skeletal horses, and one soldier, while good men stay behind to their doom. Proffer my apologies for my insult to your elderly friend, Sir Hector; any king who inspires so much loyalty and devotion in such obviously true men must have been a very great king indeed."

Hector exhaled evenly. "He was our king," he said simply.

"I understand," said Flynt. He glanced toward the setting sun. "Have your companions round up those animals and get them into the longboats—we can only make one last trip back to the ship before we sail." The captain prepared to descend into the closest of the five remaining longboats.

Hector stopped him. "I have found that each life I spare saves my own a little bit," he said, shaking the man's hand. "Thank you for helping me in this way, Captain Flynt."

The captain nodded. "I'm sorry I won't have the chance to know you longer, Sir Hector," he said. Then he stepped into the longboat, shouted orders to the crew, and disappeared into the devouring fog.

As the sun slipped below the horizon, the four remaining companions stood atop the ramparts of sandbags, watching the dark masts of the *Stormrider* become part of the twilight beyond the heavy mist, listening to the crashing of the waves and the howling of the sea wind.

"That be it, then," said Jarmon finally when night took hold, casting the last of the light from the sky.

The others said nothing. Anais climbed down from the sandbag wall, handed Jarmon the firebrand, and jogged to the end of the pier, letting the fog swallow him. When he reached the edge he peered out into the blackness but saw nothing.

"Godspeed, Sevirym," he shouted into the wind. "Mind the ice!"

Hector descended from the wall as well. "I suppose we should put an hour or so into reinforcing the sandbags," he said, brushing the grit from his hands. "The burlap is long gone, but we can continue spading and packing around the base of the—" His words choked off as his eyes came to rest on the two shadows that hovered at the edge of the darkness behind them.

A woman was standing at the far end of the wharf that bordered the town, clutching the remains of a tattered shawl around her thin shoulders. More wraith than human, she said nothing, but stared out into the fog with hollow eyes.

Beside her was a child, a boy, it appeared, long of hair and slight, young enough to still warrant the holding of his hand, though he stood alone. Like his mother his eyes were large and appeared dark in the light of the brand, but unlike her he still showed signs of life behind those eyes.

The firelight flashed for a moment as Jarmon's hand quivered.

"Aw, *no*," he muttered. "No."

For a moment the only sound at the edge of the pier was the ever-present howling of the wind. A spattering of icy rain blew across the deserted wharf, stinging as it fell. Then Hector turned to the others, angrily brushing the hair from his eyes.

"Jarmon, Cantha—find me a longboat. There must be something still around here, a rowboat, a fisherman's skiff, something—"

"Hector—" Anais said quietly.

"Give me the brand," said Hector frantically, motioning to Jarmon. "I'll row them out quickly. The ship will see the light—"

"Stop it, Hector," Anais said more firmly.

The young knight's eyes held the bright gleam of desperation in the fireshadows.

"For God's sake, find me a bloody *boat*—"

"Cease," said Cantha. Her voice cut through the wind. The others turned to see her face impassive, her eyes glinting either from sympathy or, more likely, from the rivulets of cold water that were now insistently strafing her eyelashes. "Get them out of the rain."

The companions watched their leader silently, intently, oblivious to their increasingly sodden clothes and heads. Hector bent over at the waist and put his hands on his knees, as if suddenly winded. He stood thus for a long moment, then nodded, gulping for air.

"We will take shelter in the livery stable until the storm passes," Anais said, squeezing Hector's shoulder as he passed on his way to the woman and the child. "It's the only building left with most of a roof."

Hector nodded, still bent over.

"We will take them with us to the inn at the crossroads for the night," he said when he could speak again.

The woman did not move as Anais approached, but the child's eyes widened in fear and he dashed behind her. The Liringlas soldier stopped, then turned back to the others.

"Hector, you had best deal with this," he said, his voice flat in the wind. "I don't think he has seen one of my race before."

Hector straightened and shook the rain from his shoulders and head.

"I am part Liringlas too, Anais."

Anais gestured impatiently. "Aye, but you look more human, because you *are*. Come over here."

Hector exhaled deeply, then walked quickly to Anais's side. "Come with us," he said to the woman, but she did not appear to be listening; if she was not standing erect, he would have believed that the life had already fled her body. He crouched down and put out his hand to the child.

"Come with me," he said in the same tone he had used to coax his own son, only a year or so older than this one. "We will take you where it is dry."

The child stared out from behind the woman, water dripping from his hair.

Hector beckoned to him with his hand. "Come along," he said again.

The boy considered a moment more, then took the woman's hand and led her, still clutching her now sodden shawl, to where the men stood.

With a sizzle, the brand in Jarmon's hand extinguished in the rain.

The child slept all the way to the crossroads, leaning against Hector, sitting before him in the saddle. The woman, who rode behind Anais, slept as well, or at least seemed to; her hollow eyes remained open, glassy, and unfocused, but her breathing took on a more even rhythm after a mile or so.

Neither had spoken a word the entire time the six people had huddled in the livery. The insistent rainshower had given way quickly to a full-blown storm, tempestuous and drenching; the sheets of rain rattled what remained of the stable's roof and poured in small waterfalls through the openings.

"Well, at least the horses got out," Jarmon had observed sourly, shifting to avoid a new leak.

"Something to be grateful for," Anais had said. Hector had said nothing.

After the worst of the storm had passed, leaving great clouds of mist blanketing the cold ground, the travelers had taken to the road leading east out of Kingston, through the broken city archway that had once been an architectural marvel but now lay in pieces in the roadway. In the dark the destruction was not as apparent as it was by day, and once the city was behind them there was little indication that anything at all was wrong with the world on this rainy night. The horses trotted easily over the muddy roadway, seemingly invigorated, perhaps relieved to be away from the cleansing pyres and out in the cool mist of rolling fields again.

An hour's ride put them at the crossroads, where the legendary inn stood, abandoned and empty of most of its furnishings. The Crossroads Inn had been a place of historical impact beyond any a building should have a right to possess; a critical meeting place and refuge of blessed ground in the Seren War two centuries before and even after it, famous for its hospitality, safety, and the vast stone hearth where the fire was never extinguished. Now it was dark, hollow as the woman's eyes. Its door, once gilded with a golden griffin and said to be the talisman by which the inn remained untouched even in the times when enemies occupied the westlands, was missing, taken over the sea with the First Fleet. Its entrance yawned open like a dark cave.

The inn's hospitality may have been intrinsic, because it remained in the place even now, shell that it was. It was their favorite resting place, a refuge still, even in the absence of innkeeper, barkeep, household spirits, or door.

Jarmon dismounted, lit a brand, and went inside, scouting to ascertain whether anything had come to call since the last time they had been here. While he quickly checked the empty tavern and rooms, Cantha assisted Hector and Anais from their horses with their human cargo.

"Where did they come from?" Hector asked as the boy sleepily wound his thin arms around the knight's neck.

"From the market, I'd wager," said Anais, helping the woman down from the saddle.

"How could we have missed them?"

His friend shrugged. "I don't know that we did. They might have walked from east of the Great River, or a village along the river itself. We can't save everyone, Hector, though you certainly insist upon trying. Surely you must know that by now."

Hector passed his hand gently over the sleeping boy's back, thinking of another child like him. "I do, Anais."

Cantha strode off into the darkness; both men took note of her passing but did not comment. They had become accustomed to her nightly disappearances as she went to commune, as all members of her race did, with the wind.

"Clear inside," Jarmon called from within the flickering light of the inn.

"Good. Get a fire going, Jarmon. Anais, go below to the stores and bring up victuals if there are any left." He stepped through the dark opening and into the cold tavern.

Anais, following behind, nodded. "There should be, unless the vermin got to them. Sevirym laid in an estimable supply down there." He led the woman inside, then released her hand and crossed to the stairway, starting down to the hidden passage where the food was kept, chuckling softly. He turned in the dark on the stairs, his silver eyes twinkling. "Remember how he'd say that there was no point in surviving a cataclysm only to starve to death?"

Hector smiled slightly in return. "Yes."

"It was a good thing you did, sending him with the *Stormrider,* Hector," Anais called over his shoulder as he headed down the steps.

"I'm glad you think so, Anais," said Hector.

"Aye," agreed Jarmon sourly as he blew on the sparks of the hearth flame. "Now we can at least die in peace."

The boy woke when the tendrils of smoke that carried the scent of ham reached his nostrils; he was eating greedily in the flickering firelight by the time Cantha returned.

Anais ceased chewing long enough to prod her.

"Well, what does the wind have to say this night, Cantha?" he asked jokingly, pushing the plate they had saved for her nearer on the heavy table board. He waited for the withering stare that he alone in the group relished.

"Much," Cantha replied flatly, tossing her vest onto the hearth to dry and sitting down beside it. "None of it clear."

The eyes of the three men locked onto her as she picked up her plate and settled in to eating. They waited in pensive, almost tense silence to hear her elaborate, but the Kith woman merely finished her supper and took a deep draught of Sevirym's prized cider.

For a long time the only sound in the cavernous inn was that of the crackling fire. Finally Hector handed the boy his mother's untouched supper and silently urged him to convince her to eat.

"Cantha," he said, watching the woman take a piece of hard cheese from her plate and stare at it in her hand, "what did the winds say?"

Backlit by the hearth fire, Cantha's eyes were blacker than the darkness that surrounded them. The chestnut skin of her thin face glowed orange in the reflected light of the flames.

"Something comes," she said simply.

"What?" demanded Jarmon. "What comes?"

Cantha shook her head. "When the winds speak, most times they speak as one," she said, her raspy voice clear.

Then it changed, scratching against all of their ears. In it was the howling of many toneless voices, a cacophony of shrieks, rising and falling in intermittent discord.

"Now, they do not," she said, speaking in the discordant sound of the wind. "They moan wildly, as if in terror. What they say is like a maelstrom; unclear. But whatever is coming, the winds fear it."

The men exchanged a glance. In Cantha's voice they could hear the wail of sea winds, the rumblings of thunder, the nightmarish cadence of destruction as gusts in a gale battered buildings to their ruin. It was almost like the sound of battle, the confusion, the shouting, the utter sense of being lost in the fury of war. The wind was foretelling something dire, but that was not unexpected.

Anais wanted her to give voice to it anyway.

"So what, then, do you believe is coming?" he asked.

"The end," Cantha said.

Once the chill of emptiness had been driven from the great rooms of the inn by the steady hearth fire, the travelers began dropping off to sleep one by one. Jarmon first; as a lifelong member of the King's Guard, he had learned to stay awake and watchful for days on end, and thereby had learned to take his repose the instant it was offered him. His bedroll lay behind what had once been the tavernkeeper's bar as a courtesy to the others; Anais had once complained that Jarmon's prodigious snoring was causing his bow to warp and his sword to rust.

The woman, who still had not responded to a single salutation, had drifted off into unconsciousness soon after Jarmon. The boy had played a merry game of mumblety-peg with Anais and had spent more than an hour on Hector's lap, taking turns making shadow puppets on the wall in the firelight before finally curling up beside her under Hector's cloak.

Cantha eventually took her place near the open doorway where the wind could wash over her in her slumber, standing a watch of a sort, though there was little chance that even the brigands that still remained in the doomed land would approach the inn. Its reputation as a refuge of good and a bastion of those who defended it had survived the evacuation into these latter days.

After the others had fallen asleep, the two childhood friends passed a skin of wine between them, musing in mutual silence. Finally Anais looked up at Hector, who was staring pensively into the fire, and leaned forward, his silver eyes bright but solemn.

"A girl, then," he said softly.

Hector nodded.

"The twins must be happy with that," Anais said, thinking of his own daughters. "They were a mite put out when your Aidan turned out to be a boy."

"The three of them made fine playmates nonetheless," Hector said, leaning back and crossing his feet on the hearthstones. "It gives me comfort to know that our friendship has been passed along to another generation."

"What is her name? Flynt said you would know it."

Hector nodded again. "We agreed if the child were to be born a girl, and Talthea did not sense after seeing her that it was a misnomer, she would be named Elsynore."

Anais took another swig from the wineskin.

"A fine namesake," he said, lifting the skin in a comical

toast in the direction of the fire. "Elsynore of Briarwood. A fine Seren role model."

"Yes, but that is not the only thought behind the name," said Hector, watching the flames dance and pulse over gleaming coals in the old hearth. "The wyrm who opened her lands to the king and the refugees—"

"Ah, of course, Elynsynos, yes? You named your daughter to honor her."

"With the aid of a Liringlas Namer. We gave the child both names we had chosen, male and female, so that it could be named before birth."

Anais chuckled. "Were you expecting that giving her a name similar to the wyrm's own would give the dragon pause about eating her?"

Hector's eyes lost their warmth and he turned away, watching the shadows twist and writhe in the darkness behind them. He stared at the dark form of Cantha, sleeping on the open threshold, then glanced over to where the child and his mother slept. He could not see Jarmon, but the grinding snore that rose and fell in regular rhythm, almost like a marching cadence, signaled that he slept still.

"I confess that learning my father and the Second Fleet had been diverted to Manosse was heartening news for me," he said finally. "Manosse is an ocean away from the Wyrmlands; it is a long-civilized nation with a healthy shipping trade, an army, a mercantile—all signs that it is a stable place. Binding them over to his care when we all believed they would end up in uncharted lands beyond the known world, lands that are ruled by an ancient dragon whose hospitality is only attested to by Merithyn, was possibly the hardest thing I have ever had to do. Now at least I know they will be safe."

"As long as they stay in Manosse," Anais said seriously. "Each refugee pledged fealty to the king on the horn as they boarded, remember? They are charged with the duty to come should the horn ever sound, generation unto generation. If Gwylliam calls, they will have no choice but to set sail again for the Wyrmlands." He saw his friend's shoulders sag somewhat. "But it should reassure you that Merithyn believes the place to be a safe and bountiful paradise. When he set out with the king's other explorers to find a place for our people to emigrate to, no one had ever broached the Wyrmlands and lived to tell about it. As he was the only one of Gwylliam's explorers to return, and with a generous offer of asylum at that, I would hazard he knows about which he speaks."

"Who knows?" Hector said dully. "Who knows whether any of them made it to the Wyrmlands? Flynt said there had been no word whatsoever from the First and Third Fleets. Who knows? But God, the One, the All, has granted us a sweet boon in our final days. We know at least that our own families are safe in Manosse. When they left, I never expected to hear word of them again. And now, as Jarmon is so fond of saying, I can die in peace."

Anais rose from the hearth and stretched lazily. "Yes, but most likely not tonight," he said. "What are the plans now, Hector? Is there any reason to go back to our guard route? If, as Cantha believes, the end is what is coming, why not spend it here? There is food, and firewood, and shelter, and, above all else, ale. Seems like a good place to spend one's final days."

"Yes," Hector agreed. "I think there is wisdom in that, even though I suspect your love of fine ale might have more than a little to do with the suggestion." He glanced over at the woman and the boy. "And it would be folly to attempt to ride our regular watch with them. The woman is a walking corpse, and cannot properly care for the child alone. We may as well make them, and ourselves, as comfortable as we can." He shook out his own camp blanket and laid it, and himself, down before the hearth to sleep.

"And besides, we are close enough to town to do two shifts of sandbag duty daily."

Anais groaned and rolled over toward the fire.

And so they remained, wrapped in dreams of the World Tree and of faces they would never see again, still asleep before the coals, until the stillness was broken by the harsh metal sound of Cantha unsheathing her sword.

* * *

In one fluid movement that belied her age, the ancient Kith soldier rose, drew, and crossed the threshold to the doorstep of the inn, where foredawn had turned the sky to the smoky gray that signals morning is nigh.

"Halt and declare," she called sharply into the gloom.

The men were behind her a moment later. They peered through the doorway, drawn as she was, searching the semi-darkness for the sound that had summoned her attention.

At the crossroads a horse stood, dancing exhaustedly in place. Atop it a rider, bent with strain, was struggling to remain upright in the saddle.

"Help me," called an old man's voice. "I am Brann, from the village of Dry Cove on the northern seacoast at Kyrlan de la Mar. I seek the soldiers of the king."

"Jarmon, bring me a lantern," Hector ordered.

He stepped out into the cold gray air, watching closely as the rider slid from his mount, took a wobbly step, then collapsed in the center of the roadway. As the rider dropped, the horse took several steps away from him, which Hector took to be a sign of its poor training or the rider's lack of skill. Once he had the lantern in his hand, he signaled to Anais to wait with the boy and the woman, then beckoned to Cantha and Jarmon to follow him.

"What do you want?" he called as he approached.

"I—I seek the soldiers of—the king," the old man wheezed again.

Hector held up the lantern to better illuminate the man in the roadway. He was human, by the look of him in the shadows, and aged, with white hair that hung around his wrinkled face like dry leaves hanging from a dormant tree.

"I am Hector Monodiere, in the service of His Majesty, Gwylliam, High King of Serendair. What do you seek from me?"

"Your assistance, sir knight," the man croaked, waving away the water flask that Jarmon held out to him. "The Sleeping Child is awakening."

"I well know it. What would you have me do about it?"

The old man's eyes, bloodshot with exhaustion, held a desperate light that was visible even in the gray foredawn. "There may be a way to contain it—or at least to stem part of the flooding that is sure to come in its wake."

The three companions exchanged a glance, then Jarmon spat on the ground.

"Madness," he muttered as Hector reached behind the man's shoulder and helped him rise. "You rode all the way from the northern coast to tell us this? Why did you not flee with the rest to high ground in the east, or into the High Reaches?"

In the lantern light they could better make out the man's features. As they had seen a moment before, he was human, dark-eyed and aged, though much of that aging had clearly come from the hardship of life in the northern clime, a rough seascape of rocky beach and heavy surf where only the stoutest of heart continued to ply the rough waters near the Great River's mouth. He was dressed in the tattered oilcloth garb of a fisherman. Rot and decay clung to his clothing and breath, much as it did to the rest of the population they had encountered after the Fleets had left; it was beginning to cling to their own clothing and breath now as well. The man's malodor was particularly strong, coupled with the stale, fishy smell of a life on the sea that never completely washed clean of a fisherman's hands and clothes.

"My people are old," he said. "What you ask may seem simple, and perhaps it would be to those younger, haler of body. But we have lived at the sea's edge for a very long time, Sir Hector. We are frail. Fleeing would be an arduous undertaking, something many of us would not survive. If the Awakening is to determine our fate, we are ready to meet it."

"Then why have you come here?" Jarmon asked crossly. "There are others like you all across this doomed island— Liringlas, Bolg, Bengard, Gwadd, human—all who chose, for reasons of their own, to disregard the king's vision and stay behind. We cannot help you now. You were offered passage, all of you. You refused it. You have already sealed your own fate."

"Peace, Jarmon," said Hector quietly. He turned to the old man whose arm he was still supporting. "Come inside and warm yourself. We have food and drink that we are happy to share with you."

The old man shook his head. "No, no, Sir Hector. There is no time. You must help me—I—I believe—we have found a way—"

"Cantha, summon Anais," Hector said. He waited until the Liringlas soldier was within earshot, then asked again, "What would you have me do?"

From the center of the pool of illumination cast by the lantern, Brann pointed into the darkness to the southeast where the horizon was beginning to lighten.

"Go to the castle Elysian," he said, his voice stronger. "I know you guard the symbol of the king—his scepter, Sir Hector. I—have need of it."

Jarmon's arm shot out and grasped the man by the shirt, pulling him off the ground with little more resistance than the wind.

"Impudent *dog*," he snarled into the old man's face, his fury straining the limits of its bridle. "We stand on the brink of the death of this nation; we gave up all we had to stay behind with the imbeciles and the unbelievers who chose death over the life offered you by your king, and now you actually believe we would dishonor ourselves by yielding something like that to the likes of *you*?"

"Release him, Jarmon," Hector commanded angrily. "Get hold of yourself." The guard dropped the old man to the ground contemptuously. Hector crouched down next to the fisherman, who was now quivering in fright, and steadied the man by the shoulder. "What need? I ask you again, what is it you would have me do?"

For a moment the man's eyes darted around at the faces staring down at him. Finally he focused on Hector's, and seemed to be calmed by what he saw in it.

"From the highest point of our village, one has always been able to see across the strait that covers the grave of the Sleeping Child to the northern isles, on clear days, at any matter," he said haltingly. His words faltered; Hector nodded silent encouragement. "The sea now boils; much of the coastline has receded as the star awakens, gathering heat and power to itself. What was once the tidal basin of Dry Cove is now sand, sir knight. And as the sea has receded for the moment, it has revealed something vast, something dating back to another age of Time."

"What?" Anais asked.

The old man swallowed as his eyes went to the Liringlas soldier, then focused on Hector again.

"It appears to be an ancient mine, Sir Hector—silver, who knows, though in the First Age, the Day of the Gods, before the star fell to earth, there were mines of every sort delving into the crust of the world, where men of ancient races drew forth riches the way men now draw forth fish from the sea. This one's vastness cannot be described in words, at least not in my words, except to say that we can see the ridges and depressions that define some of its edges, but not all of them, revealed now by the drawing of water away from the tidal areas of the sea as the Child prepares to awaken. Those ridges and depressions stretch for as far as the eye can see."

Hector shrugged. "I still do not see what this has to do with me, or with the king's scepter."

The man named Brann spoke slowly, cautiously, his eyes nervously moving from soldier to soldier.

"It is said that in the days before the end of the First Age, much of what now rests beneath the sea was dry land. When the falling star Melita, now known as the Sleeping Child, struck Serendair from the sky, it took much of the Island with it, Sir Hector. What are now the northern isles, Balatron, Briala, and Querel, were mountaintops then; almost half of the tillable fields of the realm went into the sea in the flooding that ensued. For centuries Serendair was known as Halfland, so much of it was consumed by the ocean in the wake of the impact.

"In those days, before the first cataclysm, this mine, if that's what it is, once it was expended was probably locked by whatever king ruled the ancient race that quarried it. A mine of that size would be a hazard because of its vastness alone, but it may have been for other reasons as well—mines that are expended run with rivers of acid, and burn with fires that can only be extinguished by time; they contain treacherous precipices, deep shafts. One this size would have been an extremely dangerous place, and so it was shut, its great doors sealed and locked, seemingly forever." The old man's voice, hoarse from exertion, dropped low, and he leaned forward to be certain Hector could hear him. "We believe we have found those doors, Sir Hector."

"And you believe the king's scepter would unlock them?"

"Yes," said Brann, his dark eyes kindling with excitement. "In the hand of the king—or he who stands in his place. It could be the key—certainly it is the last remaining vestige of the king's authority here, the only symbol of his dominion that he did not take with him. Those doors face the Child's gravesite, and are bound more by a king's command than by a physical lock. Perhaps, as the king's regent, you could exercise his authority to bid them open. If you can throw open the doors before the Awakening, perhaps—and only perhaps—the mine can act as a natural levee of sorts, a dam, a dike—it is a mammoth underground cave at the sea's edge. Surely it is reasonable to think that some of the destruction may be averted if the swell of the sea is contained, or at least limited, by this great hole in the earth." The man fell silent, watching the knights intently as they stepped away from him to confer.

"Ridiculous," Jarmon muttered under his breath. "You can't hold back the sea with a hole in the ground any more than you can with a teacup."

"That's not necessarily so," said Anais, considering. "The fisherman is right in that what spared the Island the first time was the natural levees—mountains, reefs, low-lying areas—that ringed the larger Serendair. The sea took some of the coastline, but not all of it."

"You sound like Sevirym," Jarmon scoffed. "Please tell me, Anais, that the rigors of sandbag duty have not addled your brain that much." He turned to Hector to see their leader lost in thought. "You as well, Hector. This is folly—utter nonsense."

"What if it isn't, Jarmon?" Hector interjected. "What if, in these final days, God, the One, the All, has provided us with an answer? Is it so hard to believe, to hope, that we might be spared, or partially spared, by His grace?"

"Do you now doubt the king's vision?" Jarmon demanded, his voice agitated.

"The *king himself* doubted it," said Hector softly. "Had he been more assured that the cataclysm he foresaw on the day of his coronation meant the complete destruction of the Island, he would never have left us—left *me*—behind to maintain his line of succession on the throne." He looked to Cantha, whose eyes were narrow with suspicion. "Is that not correct, Cantha? I stand in the shadow of the king. I am of his line, and his regent, named so that his power over the land would hold sway. Should the Island survive the Awakening, because I remained here, in Gwylliam's name, his line of succession will have remained unbroken. He can return and reclaim the throne without contest."

"Aye," Cantha said curtly.

"So if the king himself entertained the possibility that complete destruction was not inevitable, is it so far beyond reasonability that we entertain it, too?"

Anais touched Hector's elbow. "Is it also possible that you are only now more willing to hope for it because of those who missed the *Stormrider*?" he asked in the Liringlas tongue.

Hector fell silent for a moment, then shrugged. "I no longer know my own motivations," he said bluntly. "I am not even able to ascertain what my father would do in these circumstances, and that has always been my touchstone, my guide. Like the wind that Cantha described last night, my senses are lost in a maelstrom of confusion. I have very little clarity anymore, Anais. I can only tell you that this possibility rings with promise in my head, probably because, if nothing else, it is doing *something*. As comfortable as spending the last days supping and imbibing in the inn might be, the thought does not sit well with me. The glory is in the trying. I would rather go to my death doing something futile, trying, than miss the chance to have saved what I could."

The other three fell silent, contemplating. Finally Anais spoke.

"Well, even in your confusion, you are still our leader, to whom we are sworn, Hector. If you wish to make the attempt, we are with you." He glanced at Cantha and Jarmon. "Are we not?"

"We are," Jarmon said. Cantha nodded imperceptibly.

Hector considered for a moment longer, then turned to the old man in the middle of the road.

"I will do as you ask," he said finally. "But let us be clear—the scepter does not leave my hand."

The man's face crumpled in relief. "Understood. None of my people would wish it any other way. And know, sir knight, that whether or not you are successful, the people of my homeland will be eternally grateful for whatever you attempt on our behalf."

Even Cantha, suspicious by nature, could hear the undeniable truth in the man's words.

It was full-sun, the moment the sun had just crested the horizon completely, when the group of seven set out into the east, following the brightening morning. Mist enveloped the ground, making it seem as if they were riding a golden pathway into the clouds.

The boy, who still had not spoken his name, sat before Hector in the saddle, drinking in the fresh breeze and the autumn splendor that was beginning to claim the countryside. A child of sooty city streets, he was transfixed by the sight of meadow wildflowers dried by the first signs of frost, of rolling fields that undulated in great waves like a grassy sea, of still-green trees along the roadway or in the distance, their leaves turning the color of fire.

Elysian castle lay to the southeast, across the Great River that bisected the western end of the Island from north to south. It stood perched atop high cliff walls that overlooked the southern seacoast ten miles away. On clear days the ocean was visible from its tallest towers, rolling gently to the leeward shores, in marked contrast to the angry, billowing breakers that battered the beaches in the north from whence Brann had come.

As they came within a league of the river, Anais and Hector exchanged a glance of confusion. The river was really a tidal estuary this far south, and roared grandly along its shores, swollen with the waters from the north sea joined by the runoff of every major river and stream on both sides of it. Its deep, abiding song could be heard for miles; now it was silent, the wind carrying no sound at all save the nervous twittering of birds and its own howl.

"The river was low the last time we crossed it, but I don't recall it being so quiet," Anais said, drawing the woman's arm more tightly around his waist when she tilted alarmingly to one side.

"It is all but dry now," Brann said, his voice thin with strain. "There are places along it where there are nothing but great muddy pools in the midst of a waterless, rocky bed. I rode the eastern shore on my way to you, and when I passed the stone mill at Hope's Landing, the wheel was still."

"The heat of the star is drawing the seawater back into its grave," Hector said, pointing out a circling hawk to the boy.

"The shoreline in the north has receded by more than a league, Sir Hector," said the fisherman. "Elsewise the doors would never have been revealed."

As soon as the words left his lips the ground rumbled.

The soldiers spurred their mounts on. Even before the exodus, the Sleeping Child had made its presence felt in this manner, loosing tremors through the earth as if stretching in slumber that was coming to an end. Those tremors were growing stronger.

They rode the rest of the way to the river in silence. The bridge at Pryce's Crossing was the largest in the land, and loomed before them, its timbers dark against the morning sun, now halfway up the firmament of the sky.

"Did you bring any bread for the trolls, Hector?" Anais asked jokingly as they slowed to cross. Tradition had long held that a scrap of biscuit or bread be tossed into the river for good luck to assuage the legendary beasts that lived beneath the centuries-old structure.

"No," Hector said, smiling slightly. "We should be saving every last crumb now, Anais. After all, there is no point in surviving a cataclysm only to starve to death."

"The trolls sailed with the Second Fleet anyway," said Jarmon. The fresh air of the open country seemed to have lifted his spirits.

"That would explain why the prelate's wife was on your father's ship," said Anais.

"To call the prelate's wife a troll is an insult to trolls," said Jarmon.

The horses' hooves clattered over the wooden planks that spanned the all-but-dry riverbed, drowning out the sound of their voices. As they passed out of the westlands for the last time, they looked over the edge of the Pryce's Crossing bridge; they could see the rocky bottom, normally more than a man's height in depth, tiny tributaries still running defiantly through the stony bed, as if to prove that the river was not quite dead yet.

The sun had reached the pinnacle of the firmament when the towers of Elysian castle came into sight. As many times as they had seen it, the soldiers could not help but slow to a halt for a moment to take in the distant majesty of it, white marble still gleaming against the blue of the autumn sky atop the crags from which it rose like a beacon, triumphant.

Hector had been born in that palace, as had his mother before him. He watched in silence for a moment, then urged his mount forward, cantering with a speed that delighted his small passenger.

It was not long before melancholy returned. They rode through the endless apple orchards that had once surrounded the castle's lands, now sparse and bare. The trees of the lowlands, west from Kingston across the Wide Meadows to Anais's birthplace, Yliessan, the Enchanted Forest in the east, had been harvested quickly and brutally to provide wood for the exodus. Even the apple trees, whose flesh was useless in the actual making of ships, had been stripped and used for chests, barrels, even firewood to stoke the forges that smelted steel for fittings, arrowheads, and thousands of other uses. Those few trees that remained bore a stunted crop, but it was worthy enough to merit a pause to be collected.

Harder to bear was the ride through Earthwood, the stone forest that had once led up to the base of the cliffs on which the palace stood. The ground from which the ancient trees had sprung was said to have been Living Stone, the pure element of earth left over from the Before-Time, the era prior to the first age of history, when the world was new. The seeds of the forest's trees had been scattered over the living earth, as the legend said, and had grown into mammoth redwoods, heveralts, and oaks, alive with magic. Those trees, their bark rich in shades of green, purple, vermilion, and gold, were as Living Stone themselves, and had never split or fallen in high wind, had never burned in fire, had never rotted with disease, but stood, stalwart and unchanging, their ancient saps coursing through their bark and leaves in an endless, mystical symphony of ages. Anais and Hector had spent their childhood in the stone forest, and so it was painful on a soul-deep level to see it razed to nothing more than broken stumps, its choice wood reaped to make hulls and masts and planks of ships that would not rot, nor burn, nor split in the high winds of a sea voyage.

Those ships bore our families to safety, Hector reminded himself as they passed the desolate forest ruin. *To safety.*

On the other side of Earthwood the ramparts of the castle walls could be seen, atop the three hundred steps that led up to them. Hector reined his horse to a halt, then looked to the others, observing the silent dismay on the face of the exhausted old fisherman.

"You needn't despair, Brann," he said reassuringly. "It's too much of a climb for most, now that the wagon-ramps are gone. Stay here, Jarmon, Anais. Cantha and I will return forthwith."

The two soldiers, one old, one young, inhaled deeply but said nothing.

For all the years he had spent in the palace, the design and construction of the place had been a constant source of fascination to Hector. As he and his father's oldest friend hurriedly climbed the stone steps hewn from the rock, passing through the empty gardens and loggias that had long beautified the terraces leading to Elysian, they both unconsciously glanced back at the ramparts hidden beneath them. In its time, more than ten thousand soldiers were routinely garrisoned within the palisaded battlements that scored, in ascending rings, the crags on which the palace stood. That they had been hidden so decoratively was tribute to Vandemere, the king who had designed and built the place as a shining monument to a new era of peace, knowing all the while that war loomed, ever watchful, in the distance.

The king riding the hippogriff whose broken statue was now rubble in the dry fountain bed of Kingston's square.

Hector's grandfather.

"Did you know him, Cantha?" Hector asked as they hurried over the granite walkways past beds of dried flora and dying topiary. "Vandemere?"

"Aye." The Kith woman kept her eyes focused directly on the great doors that marked the side entrance of the palace, now unguarded. One stood slightly open, a testament to the completeness of the evacuation. In its time, never fewer than a score of soldiers held watch over those doors.

Through the towering hallways they ran, keeping their eyes fixed on the corridors ahead of them, rather than see the emptiness of the once beautiful stronghold. Their footsteps echoed through the cavernous rooms, bare and dull in the dark.

Hector knew this place blind; it was only the urgency he had heard in the fisherman's voice and the stirrings of a long-denied hope that prevented him from taking the time to stop and gaze one last time at the rooms, alcoves, and nooks he had loved from childhood. Most of the tapestries still lined the walls; much of the art remained in place, unmolested by the looters and thieves who had picked the rest of the countryside clean. There was something sacred about Elysian that kept it sacrosanct; a power that protected it, even with no king on the throne.

Entering the corridor that led to the Great Hall, Hector realized what it was.

In a way, there was a king on the throne still. Gwylliam had named Hector the king's shadow, born of the same bloodline, and therefore, in a way, the king had not left, not completely.

"This was a remarkable place to spend time as a child," Hector said, passing the doors to the nursery where his mother and her siblings had played while their parents held court. "There were so many alcoves to explore, so many places to hide. The palace guards were more than once called out to find me. I had made a nest beneath the drape of a pedestal in the Hall of History, and had fallen asleep in there. It was great fun—until I had a child of my own and Aidan started doing it." He drew deeper breath. "I still don't know where that boy and his mother could have been secreted that allowed us to miss them."

"In the City's necropolis," Cantha said, her eyes fixed on the enormous mahogany doors of the Great Hall before them. "In one of the crypts."

"Why do you think so?"

"They had the smell of death about them." The Kith woman grasped the massive brass handle. "They still do, but it be different now."

The dark, cavernous room revealed the throne from which the unmarried last king had held court, a wide marble chair with blue and gold giltwork channels running up the arms to the back. Hector walked the long carpet to the foot of the dais, mounted the steps quickly, and sat down unabashedly in the king's seat. He took a moment to look up at Vandemere's motto, inscribed for the ages on the wall directly before his eyes, where each subsequent king was bound to see it at every moment while enthroned:

> HE WHOM ALL MEN SERVE BEARS THE GREATEST DUTY
> TO SERVE ALL MEN.

Then he stretched his hand out over the right arm of the throne.

"Traan der, singa ever monokran fri," he commanded softly, speaking in the tongue of the Ancient Seren, the mystical race of Firstborn beings born of the element of Ether, the first people of the Island. Come forth, in the name of the king.

The marble arm of the chair cracked open along a hidden fault, and split away. From beneath the dais a mechanical arm rose to an even height with the chair, the royal scepter of Serendair in its metallic grasp.

The symbol of state was simple in its design, a curved piece of dark wood the length of a man's thigh, gilt and inscribed with intricate runes. Beneath the golden overlay the thin striations of purple and green, gold and vermilion could still be vaguely made out, the colors of the stone trees in Earthwood, from which it had probably been harvested. Atop its splayed pinnacle a diamond the size of a child's fist was set; it gleamed dully in the darkness of the hall.

Hector stared at the scepter for a moment, encased within the mechanism of the king's design. Then he seized it, plucking it from the metal arm, pulling it free.

Cantha's dark eyes were watching with a gleam he had not seen before. He looked at her questioningly, inviting her to speak, and was surprised when she did. Cantha guarded her thoughts jealously.

"Had the crown passed to the first of Vandemere's children, rather than the last, this might have been a sight seen long ago; thee, Hector, on the throne as king."

Hector rose from the throne and started back out of the palace.

"I suppose that means I am foreordained to meet my end in this way, then," he said as they retraced their steps. "For if I had been king, I would not have left. You, however, Cantha, you and Jarmon, Anais, and Sevirym, would have been sent off with the others, to guard them in the new world, and live on. For that reason, and only that one, I am sorry that the line of succession did not fall to me."

The Kith woman said nothing.

They hurried from the palace in silence. At the brink of the battlements, Hector touched her arm.

"Tell me one thing, Cantha, now that the time for niceties is past, and there is nothing left to be gained in politeness," he said. "When you announced that the king of the Kith had decided you would stay behind as a representative of your race, I believe it was because you had volunteered to do so. You are my father's dearest friend. It was for him that you stayed with me, wasn't it?"

The Kith woman's eyes narrowed in displeasure. "MacQuieth would never have asked such a thing of me. Of anyone."

Hector smiled. "I know. But he didn't have to ask."

Cantha exhaled, frowning at him. Finally she assented.

"Nay," she said. "He did not have to ask. Aye, 'twas for him that I stayed, to stand with his son when he could not." She looked over the grassy fields, falling into shadows of gold as the sun began to set. " 'Twas as good a choice of end as any."

"Thank you," Hector said. "For staying, and for telling me."

The Kith woman merely nodded.

"I have one more boon to ask of you," Hector said as they descended the stone steps. "We will part company now. To take the woman and child north with us would only slow us down, and end any chance they have to survive. Elysian is the highest point on the southern half of the Island. If any ground is to be spared by the sea, it would be here. Stay with them, Cantha, in these last days; keep them safe, especially the boy. We will leave you supplies, and you can scavenge the orchards for fruit. If we succeed in containing the sea, and you run short of stores, you can go back to the inn." Cantha nodded, and Hector took her elbow, drawing her to a halt for a moment. "If the wave comes, though, get to the highest ground you can. I'd advise you stay near the vizier's tower." He nodded behind them to the tallest of the palace's spires, where Graal, the king's adviser and seer, had once dwelt. Cantha nodded again.

Jarmon had prepared the horses to leave as soon as Hector returned. As the men mounted, Hector heard a screech from below him.

"No," the child was screaming, struggling in Cantha's firm grasp. "No!" He turned to Hector, his eyes pleading. "No! Stay w'chyou! Stay w'chyou!"

The words echoed in Hector's mind; they were the same as the ones uttered by Aidan on the docks the day he bound his family over to his father for sailing.

Stay w'chyou! Da! Stay w'chyou!

His throat tightened, remembering Talthea, so strong and brave, dissolving into tears at the pain in their son's voice. He reached down and gently caressed the head of the writhing child, then nodded to Cantha. His last sight of the boy was seeing him struggling violently in her arms as she restrained him. He continued to kick and fight with a willfulness that finally collapsed into a visibly broken spirit once the horses were out of sight.

Just as Aidan had.

They rode north along the river now, following the mule road where barges had long traveled, laden with goods from the northern isles and distant ports that were traded at every crossing and village until the flat-bottomed boats finally reached Southport, the enormous city at the river's delta.

The rocks at the mule road's edge trembled as they passed; tremors in the north had intensified in strength and frequency, and viewing the sky above was now almost impossible through the mist. Patches of blue became fewer and farther between.

The men rode in silence. Each day that passed brought the mist down even more heavily, making first joking, then speaking, too weighty to bother with.

Finally they arrived in Hope's Landing, the largest mill town on the Great River, where the east–west thoroughfare had crossed. In its time Hope's Landing had been the heart of the river, a bustling city where the westlands met the east, with wagons lining up as far as the eye could see to unload grain for the mills, foodstuffs bound for markets in the south, and then were reloaded again with every kind of good imaginable from the barges. Now the city stood empty, the wheels of the great mills lodged in the mud or jammed by rocks where the water had once flowed freely.

Pratt's Mill had been the largest of all, spanning the river at its deepest and swiftest place. Bridges at one time had connected the east and west banks, with the mill between, an esplanade over which travelers could pass, observing the river's currents beneath them. The western span was gone, but the eastern bridge was still there, they noted, then rode past as the heat of the sun beat down from overhead, the only sign that it was now midday.

Just past the silent mill, where the roadway led off to the east, Hector signaled to the party to stop and let the horses graze. He scooped up a handful of smooth river stones, then beckoned to Anais, and together they walked to the banks of the Great River, dry now except for a thin stream that pooled and trickled in the wide riverbed.

"Remember when this river seemed a mile wide?" he mused, watching the water wend its way around the rocks and broken barrels that now lined its bed.

"Aye," Anais agreed. " 'Twas death to fall in up here. That millstone ground day and night; if you took a tumble north of it, you'd be bread the next day."

"And now we could cross easily, with feet barely wet. It's as if the river never divided the Island at all." Hector examined the stones in his hand. "My father once said something to me that is finally taking hold in my mind." He fell silent for a moment, trying to remember the words correctly. "He was a Kinsman, one of a brotherhood of soldiers whose patron was the wind, and thus had learned to pass through doors in the wind that would take him great distances in a short time. When I asked him by what magic this could happen, he said that it was not magic, but merely understanding that distance was an illusion.

"There are ties between us, Anais, all of us, friend and foe, that transcend what is normally seen as the space in the world. That distance, that space, is merely the threshold between one realm and another, one soul and another; a doorway, a bridge if you will. The stronger the connection between the two places, the smaller the threshold; the more easily crossed, anyway. The physical distance between the two becomes secondary. It was in making use of this that MacQuieth was able to win his greatest battle, his destruction of the fire demon, the F'dor Tsoltan. His hatred of that demon, and that primordial race, was a tie that could not be outrun. There was not enough space in the world to keep them apart." He sighed deeply. "I believe it is also the reason that my family is only as far away as my next breath, that I can see them in my dreams, see them as they are now, not as a memory. Why you dream of the World Tree, and the place where you were born."

Anais nodded, and they stood in companionable silence for a while, watching the trickling stream.

"How does the weather appear to be taking shape for the next few days?" Hector asked finally, tossing a stone into what was left of the water.

"Aside from the likelihood of catastrophic destruction, it looks to be a fine week," Anais answered jokingly. "Why do you ask?"

Hector lobbed another pebble into the stream. "I just

wanted to know how you would fare on your journey, if you would be dry or sodden with rain."

Anais's face lost its smile. "Journey?"

Hector exhaled and nodded. "I'm sending you home now, Anais. There is no need for you to go on with us from here. Either we will prevail in this undertaking or we will fail, but your being with us will not make that difference. The dreams you are having of Yliessan is Sagia calling to you to come home. If the World Tree is beckoning to you, it would be wrong to keep you from her."

His friend's silver eyes reflected sadness and understanding in the same gleam.

"I have come to accept many things I could not have fathomed would be possible a year ago, Hector, many tragic and horrific things, but until this moment, it had never occurred to me that I might not meet my end at your side."

Hector tossed the rest of the stones into the riverbed and wiped the grit from his hand on his shirt.

"We have lived in each other's company all our lives, Anais, and lived well," he said, his voice steady. "There is no need to die in each other's company, as long as we die well."

Anais turned away.

"Perhaps if Sevirym was right, or you prevail, we will not die at all," he said.

"Perhaps," Hector said. "But go home anyway."

Beneath their feet the ground rumbled, stronger than before, as if in confirmation.

On the way back to camp, Hector stopped his friend one last time.

"Know that wherever we are when the end comes, you will be with me, Anais," he said simply.

The Liringlas knight smiled. "Beyond the end, Hector. Not even death can separate you from me." He clapped his friend's shoulder. "You still owe me a night of very expensive drinking."

Once Anais had gone, the days and nights ran together.

In the distance, the sky had begun to glow yellow through

the mist above the northern isles. The rumblings had increased in sound and frequency, making the men nervous and edgy without respite. Sleep seemed a luxury that they could ill afford, and yet exhaustion threatened to drive them off course, bleary-eyed in the dense fog.

When at last the sea could be heard in the distance and splashing fire could be seen far away above the horizon, they determined they were near enough to Dry Cove and made camp for what they decided was the last time. Hector stirred the remains of their stores in a pot above their fire while the old fisherman and Jarmon tended to the horses before sitting down to a last meal at rest.

"Brann," Hector said, trying to break the awkward silence with conversation, "have you lived in Dry Cove all your life?"

The old man shook his head. "No. I was born there, but I had not been back until recently."

"Oh?" Jarmon asked, setting down his tankard. "That's odd for a fishing village, isn't it? It seems that most families in such places remain there for generations."

Brann nodded. "True. But long ago, I had the chance to leave, and I took it. I traveled the wide world, doing a variety of things, but my birthplace has never been far from my mind. When it became apparent that the Child was awakening, I wanted nothing more than to return home, to help in any way that I could."

"You do know the chances that we can do anything at all, let alone save your village, are very small?" Jarmon said seriously. "This is a fool's errand."

"No, it's not," Hector said quickly, seeing the light in the fisherman's eyes dim slightly. "It is a slim chance. But it is a chance, nonetheless. Trying is never foolish."

"That is all I ask, so that my people might live." Brann mumbled, drawing his rough burlap blanket over his shoulders and settling down to sleep.

When the old man's breathing signaled he had fallen into the deepest part of slumber, Jarmon took a well-used wallet of smoking blend from his pack and tamped nearly the last of it into his pipe.

Beneath them the earth trembled. It seemed to Hector that the quakes were lasting longer, and it was undeniable that they were coming more frequently. Anais had observed, just before he rode east, that even Sevirym would have been hard pressed to ignore it.

Hector looked up into the dark sky, missing the stars. "You and me, Jarmon; we are the last ones left," he mused, watching the clouds of thickening haze race along in the dark sky on the twisting wind.

"And Brann," the guard said, blowing out a great ring of smoke that blended with the mist around them.

"And Brann. Perhaps you should be kinder to him—he is obviously terrified of you."

The old guard smiled. "Good." He leaned forward over the fire coals. "I trust no one any more, Hector, especially those too stupid or selfish to have taken the chance they were given and now want to be saved in the last hour. Better that they fear me. They have reason to."

Hector turned the scepter of the king in his hands. "You needn't be on guard against him, Brann. The king's scepter is formed of an ancient element of power; it rings true in the hand of the one who holds it. I would be able to discern if the old fisherman was lying, and thus far he has told us nothing but the truth."

Jarmon shrugged. "What does it matter anyway?" he said nonchalantly. "You and he are the only ones who remain with something to lose." Hector signaled for him to explain, but the old guard just shrugged again.

"You say you believe that the glory is in the trying," Jarmon said, puffing contentedly on his pipe. "But in truth, you fear failure. You have all along—as if there was anything you could do to ward it off. This situation was doomed to failure from the beginning, Hector, but only you struggled with that. The rest of us are followers, not leaders. We know that even in inevitable failure, there is glory. In the end, to a soldier it matters not what the outcome of the battle is. What matters is how he fought, whether he stood his ground nobly, or whether, in the face of death, he faltered. A soldier does not decide who to fight, or when, or where. Deciding to remain behind with you was the only real choice I have ever made. It's a choice I do not regret.

"You have struggled in silence with the king's decision to leave you behind, and with our decisions to remain with you. You could cease that and live out your days in some semblance of peace if you were not born to lead. Unlike you, I know my opinion of His Majesty's decision doesn't matter. How I live between now and the end—that is what matters."

Hector stared out into the darkness. "I stand in the shadow of the king. I am of his line; I am his regent, named so that his power over the land would hold sway. His responsibilities are mine now. If I let go of them, then I have failed."

"Don't deceive yourself, lad," Jarmon said seriously, automatically stowing the wallet where it had come from. "The king's power that mattered left when he left—the Sleeping Child began its rise as his ship crested the horizon and sailed out of sight of Serendair. While I don't deny that his claim to the throne is in place because you are here, in the end it will mean nothing. The power that once reigned this land undisputed is broken. The protection it proffered is all but gone. There are holes in it, Hector, gaping holes that were once solid in the king's time, and that of all the rulers before him; an iron-strong dominion that is now rusted and pitted. You cannot plug those holes, no matter how much you struggle to. It's already been decided. You try to protect the Island in its last days by virtue of your vow, but your authority does not mean anything."

He took the pipe from his mouth and looked directly at the younger man. "But that doesn't mean your sacrifice was not worthy. You may never achieve greatness in itself, but when one has been groomed for greatness, to surrender the chance to prove it, now there's a sacrifice. On the word of your king to yield, give way in a battle you felt you could win, that's the most terrible sacrifice. It dwarfs all others." Jarmon settled down into a pile of leaves by the fire. "Except perhaps for having to serve sandbag duty."

On that last night Hector dreamed, as he always did, of Talthea and the children. The rocky ground beneath his ear burned with the rising heat from the north, making his night visions dark and misty where once they had been clear.

In his dreams he was holding his daughter, playing with his son, basking in quiet contentment with his wife when he felt a shadow beckon to him. When he looked up, the shade that was summoning him took form. It was the specter of a long-dead king, a forebear he had never known. The headless statue, broken in pieces in Kingston Square, whole once more. His grandfather.

Vandemere.

Wordlessly the king beckoned to him again. Hector looked down to find his arms empty, his wife and son gone.

He followed the shade of the king through a green glade of primeval beauty, back through Time itself. In this dream he trod the path of history, unspooling it in reverse as he walked deep into the silent forest through a veil of sweet mist.

All around him the world turned, undoing what had gone before as it did. The present, the third age in which history was now marked, unwound before his eyes. He could see the fleets returning to the docks from which they had been launched in anticipation of the second cataclysm, watched the disassembly of the new empire into the broken one that was the result of the Seren War, and the war itself. He saw bloody fields strewn with broken bodies turn green again, saw the ages slipping by, unhurried, remaking history as Time passed in reverse.

Hector looked ahead; the shade of the king was farther away now, disappearing into the mist.

He started to run, and as he did, the unspooling history sped back faster and faster. From the Seren War back to the racial wars that preceded it, the coming of the races of man to Serendair in the Second Age, Time hurried crazily back-

ward. He called to the king, or tried, but no sound came out
in this drowsy place, the misty vale of cool, rich green.

Racing now, compelled to find out the purpose of this visi-
tation or command, he barely noticed when the Second Age
slipped back to the First, the Day of the Gods, when the Elder
races walked the earth. From the corner of his eye Hector
saw the first cataclysm reverse itself, saw the waters that had
covered much of the island recede, the star rise back into the
sky, saw the Vault of the Underworld where the F'dor had once
been imprisoned sealed shut again, containing once more the
formless spirits that, upon its rupturing, had escaped and taken
human hosts, like Tsoltan, the one his father had vanquished.

With each undone event, the world through which he ran
grew greener, newer, more peaceful, more alive. It was in
watching the turning back of Time that Hector began to realize how much of the magic had been gone from the world he
had known, how much it had been present at one time, long
before, when the world was new.

As the First Age melted away into the Before-Time, the
prehistory, he saw the birth of the primordial races that
sprang from the five elements themselves—the dragons,
great wyrms born of living earth; the Kith, Cantha's race,
children of the wind; the Mythlin, water-beings who were
the forebears of humans, building the beautiful undersea
city of Tartechor; the Seren, the first of the races born, descended of the stars; and the F'dor, formless demons sprung
from ancient fire, destructive and chaotic, sealed by the four
other races into the Vault to spare the earth from obliteration
at their hands.

He saw the primeval world, glorious and unspoiled, and
quiet. And even that slipped from his view as he watched; the
land disappeared into the sea as the wind died away, leaving
the surface of the world burning with fire, until it was nothing more than a piece of a glowing star that had broken off
and streaked across the heavens on its own. That glowing
ball sped backward, joining the burning body from which it
had come.

Leaving nothing around him but starry darkness and the shade of the long-dead king.

Finally the shadow of Vandemere turned around and stared at him sadly.

What, Grandfather? Hector asked, no sound coming from his lips, but echoing nonetheless in the dark void around them. *What is it you are trying to show me?*

Eternity, the king said. His voice did not sound, but Hector heard the word anyway.

What of eternity? Hector asked, struggling to breathe in the heavy mist of the dark void.

The king's shadow began to fade.

There is no time in eternity. Vandemere's voice echoed in the emptiness. *In staying behind, you fought to give them more time. Instead, you should be fighting to keep from losing eternity.*

Hector woke with a start.

The ground beneath his head was splitting apart, a great fissure ripping the Earth asunder.

In a heartbeat he was on his feet, grasping the startled fisherman next to him and dragging the old man back from the brink of the chasm as Jarmon made a dive to untie the horses.

A roar like thunder shivered the scorched trees around them, and the fisherman shouted something that Hector could not hear. They backed away, pulling the frightened beasts with all their strength, running blindly north into the fire-colored mist, until the ground beneath their feet stopped shaking, settling into a seething rumble that did not cease.

"You all right, Brann?" Hector asked, trying to settle the roan and failing; the animal whinnied in fear and danced in place, her ears back and eyes wild.

The old man's eyes were as glassy as the horse's, but he nodded anyway.

"The Awakening—it's coming," he whispered, his voice barely audible above the rumbling ground. "There is no more time for sleep, Sir Hector. We are not that far away; if we hurry, we will be in Dry Cove before morning. Let us make haste, I beg you! My people await rescue."

"Your people are fools if they haven't quit the village by now, old man," Jarmon muttered. "The heat is searing from here. If they be closer, they have already cooked in the belching fire."

Hector took the trembling fisherman by the shoulders and helped him mount.

"We go," he said. "We will stop no more until we are there, or we are in the Afterlife."

Through the lowlands that had once been the towns and villages near the Great River's mouth they rode, the air thick with black smoke that obscured their vision of anything but the riverbed.

The horses, ridden ceaselessly and deprived of frequent stops for fresh water, began to show signs of faltering. When Brann's mount finally collapsed into a quivering mass on the mule road, Jarmon pulled the fisherman, gray of face from exhaustion and fear, behind him in the saddle and spurred his own mount onward.

"Sorry, Rosie, old girl," he muttered, patting the animal's neck. His hand was covered with flecks of sweat and horse sputum. "It will soon end, and then you can rest."

Finally the sound of the sea crashing in the distance broke through the screaming wind.

"Here! We are here!" Brann whispered, tugging roughly on Jarmon's sleeve. "The sea has drawn back a goodly distance, but you can hear it still."

Hector reined the roan to a halt. Off to the north sparks of molten flame, like iridescent fireflies, shot haphazardly into the wind above the sea, swirling in menacing patterns against the blackening sky. He strained to see through the smoke, and thought he made out the silhouettes of shacks and docks, charred timbers blending into the darkness.

They dismounted, abandoning the horses at the shoreline, and waded into the wet sand, every now and then passing what was probably once a body, now buried beneath a thick coating of ash.

Hector glanced at Brann, but the fisherman's gaze did not waver; rather, the old man shielded his eyes, trying to peer through the gray and black fog to where he had seen what he thought were the doors to the mammoth mine.

"This way," the fisherman said, his voice stronger now. "It was just north of that failed land bridge, past the tip of the peninsula, where once the water met on three sides."

As if to punctuate his words, the sandy ground shook violently.

"Lead onward," Hector shouted, following the fisherman into the sand bed.

Blindly they made their way across the tidal wasteland, where the sea had once swelled to the land, now nothing but a desert of ocean sand. The sea's retreat had laid bare the bones of ships, broken reefs, shells of every imaginable kind, broken and jagged in the wet grit where the water once broke against the shore.

A plume of fire shot into the black sky in the near distance, then fell heavily back into the sea.

Over the broken land bridge for a mile, then another, and another, the three men limped hurriedly across the wet sand, burning now through their boots. Finally, when they reached a place where the smoke blackened the air almost completely, Brann stopped near a small, intact fishing boat wedged in the seabed, dropped to his knees, and pointed beneath the low-hanging smoke down into the distance.

"There," he whispered.

Hector crouched down and followed the old man's arthritic finger with eyes that burned from the heat and ash.

At first he could see nothing save for the endless sand and black smoke. But after a moment, his eyes adjusted, and his breath caught in his raw throat.

They were standing on what appeared to be a great ridge in the seabed, a towering wall that led down into a crevasse a thousand or more feet deep, at the bottom of which the remnants of seawater pooled. Hector followed the perimeter with his eyes, and could not see its beginning, nor its end. The depression seemed to stretch to the horizon; the cliff wall beneath them made the seabed seem as if they were standing in a vast meadow atop a mountain. Whatever the actual dimensions of the ancient mine, it was clear that a man could not see all of it at once even in clear air; it stretched out beneath the sand, hidden for millennia by the sea, into the place to which the water had retreated. He finally now understood Brann's insistence that enough of the sea could be diverted into such a mammoth space that at least a part of the Island might be spared.

"Where are the doors?" he shouted over the thundering roar that came forth from within the sea to the north.

"At the bottom," Brann shouted in return, struggling to remain upright in the burning wind.

"Can we scale the cliff face, Hector?" Jarmon asked, looking for a foothold and finding none. "If we fall from this height there will be no stopping; 'twill be a quick end at least."

"There looks to be a path of a sort, or at least a place where the cliff wall slants," Hector said, ducking again so that he could see more clearly.

Brann was eyeing the sky nervously. "We must hurry!" he urged as liquid fire shot aloft again, spewing ash and making the ground lurch beneath their feet. He scurried over the rim and began sliding down the wall that Hector had indicated, followed a moment later by the two soldiers.

Down into the crevasse, running and slipping they ran, falling, sliding on knees or even on their backs, only to rise, driven by necessity and the imminence of the Awakening. The seabed was thick here, like rock beneath the sand, but absent of the debris that they had seen in the higher ground at the shoreline.

Finally, when they had fallen far enough down to have descended a small mountain, they found themselves at the base of a sheer cliff wall, their feet wet in the dregs of the sea that had covered this place a short time before, staring up at a solid wall of rock.

The wind howled and shrieked above them, but stayed at the level of the sea, venturing down into the canyon only long enough to whip sand into their eyes. "Where are the doors?" Hector asked again, his voice quieter in the near silence.

Brann pointed to a towering slab to the north. "There," he said, in a trembling tone.

Crawling now, the three men made their way over the scattered rock of the seafloor, scaling outcroppings, climbing over dips and hollows, until at last they stood where the fisherman had indicated.

Above them towered what appeared to be two massive slabs of solid earth, smooth as granite and white as the rest of the sea sand. There was a slash of thin darkness between them; otherwise they appeared in no way different from the rest of the rocky undersea hills.

Beneath their feet the ground trembled again, more violently than before. The winds atop the canyon screamed, rising into an atonal wail that fell, discordant. Distant fire shot into the sky, turning the clouds the color of blood.

From his pack Hector drew forth the scepter. It glowed brightly in his hand, the gilt shaft shining beneath the diamond, which sparkled almost menacingly.

Before them the slabs of stone seemed to soften. The three men watched, transfixed, as the sand that had covered them for time uncounted began to slide away, pooling at the base, revealing towering doors of titanic size bound in brass, with massive handles jutting from plates of the same metal, a strange keyhole in the rightmost one. The gigantic doors were inscribed with ancient glyphs and wards, countersigns and runes the like of which Hector had never seen before.

Brann was watching the northern sky nervously over his shoulder. "Make haste, sir knight," he urged.

Hector stared at the ancient key in his hand. It appeared different somehow than it had been a moment before; the dark shaft of once living wood that he thought was the branch of a stone tree now more closely resembled a bone, the diamond perched atop it on the rim of where a joint would connect. Carefully he held it next to the keyhole, trying to ascertain the angle which would fit it.

"Viden, singa ever monokran fri," he said. Open, in the name of the king.

The glyphs on the doors glowed with life.

The gilding began to fall from the scepter's shaft, sliding off in sandy golden flakes.

Hector pushed the key into the lock and slowly turned it counterclockwise.

Beneath his hand he more felt than heard an echoing thud. Ever so slightly the crack between the stone doors widened. Hector pushed on the rightmost of the two, but could only cause it to move infinitesimally. He attempted to look inside. He could see very little.

The darkness was devouring in its depth. Gingerly Hector pushed the door open a little farther, straining against the wedge of sand that had built up at the door's base over the ages. Brann took up a place beside him, adding the remains of his strength to the effort.

Behind him the flares of fire from the Awakening rose suddenly higher, burning more intensely, casting shadows into the black cavern beyond the doors. Hector peered through the crack.

The immensity of the place was more than Hector could fathom. From the small vista he had gained there seemed to be no border to it, no walls below limiting it to edges, but rather was more like opening a door into the night sky, or the depths of the universe.

"Again, sir knight," Brann whispered, pale with exertion. "We must open it wider. Hurry; there is no time left."

Jarmon leaned with all his strength against the door as well. With a groan that made Hector shudder, the rightmost of the two doors swung farther into the endless darkness.

Hector looked in again. At first he saw nothing, as before. Then, at the most distant edge of his vision, he thought he could make out tiny flames, perhaps remnants of the mine fires that could still be burning thousands of years later. But when those flames began to move, he felt suddenly weak,

dizzy, as his head was assaulted from within by the cacophony of a thousand rushing voices, cackling and screeching with delight.

Like fire on pine, the living flames began to sweep down
distant ledges within the mammoth pit, some nearer, some
farther, all dashing toward the door, churning the air with the
destructive chaos of mayhem.

Hector, his head throbbing now with the gleeful screaming
that was drawing rapidly closer, could only watch in horror
as the fire swelled, burning intensely, a legion of individual
flames scrambling down the dark walls toward the doors.

His mind reeled for a moment as the sickening realization
of what they had done crashed down on him. Time stood still
as the truth thundered around his ears, louder than the
tremors from the Sleeping Child.

He had just broken the one barrier that separated life from
void, that stood between the earth and its destruction, and
more.

That threatened even the existence of the Afterlife.

"My God," he whispered, his hand slick with sweat. "My
sweet God! Jarmon—This is the Vault! We've opened the
Vault of the Underworld!"

Jarmon's guttural curse was lost in the sound of oncoming
destruction and the orgiastic screaming of the approaching
fire demons, long entombed, now rushing toward freedom.

The soldiers seized the door handle and together they
pulled on it with all their strength. They succeeded in dragging the door shut most of the way, but they were able to
close it only as far as was possible with the obstacle of the
fisherman's body in the way.

Brann had interposed himself in the doorway, straddling
the threshold.

Jarmon reached over to shove the old man out of the way.
"Move, you fool!" he shouted. And gagged in pain when his
arm was crushed against the door, so that it was clasped in a
withering grip.

They looked at the old man. His face had hardened, had
become an almost translucent mask of undisguised delight.

Its wrinkled skin now was tight over a feral smile, above which a pair of dark eyes gleamed, their edges rimmed in the color of blood.

"I," Brann said softly. "I am what the winds forewarned you of, Sir Hector. I am what comes."

"No," Hector whispered raggedly. "You—you—"

The demon in the old man's body clucked disapprovingly, though his smile sparkled with amusement. "Now, now, Sir Hector," he said with exaggerated politeness. "This is a historic moment, one to savor! Let us not spoil it with recriminations, shall we?" He let go of Jarmon's arm.

The soldiers dragged on the heavy door again, but the F'dor only wedged himself in tighter, preventing it from closing with a strength that was growing by the moment. Hector pulled with all his might, but only managed to strip the skin from his sweating palms against the hot metal handles.

Jarmon stepped back angrily and drew his sword, but the fisherman merely gestured at him. Dark fire exploded from his fingers and licked the weapon; the blade grew molten in Jarmon's hand, melting away in a river of liquid steel. It drew a scream of agony from the guard, who fell heavily away into the sand.

"The scepter—" Hector choked.

"Would help you to discern the truth?" the demon asked solicitously, glancing at his approaching fellows, who were drawing nearer now. "Indeed, you were not wrong. Everything I told you was the truth. My people *have* lived at the sea's edge for a very long time; we *are* frail in body, though we are strong in spirit. Without a host, or someone to give us aid, we could never open the door alone. And I was most sincere when I assured you that none of my people would dream of touching the scepter; for one of our kind to touch an object of Living Stone crowned with a diamond would be certain death. That's why we needed you; we thank you for your service."

"Blessed ground," Hector whispered, pulling futilely at

the door and fighting off the screaming voices that swelled inside his head. "The inn is blessed ground—"

"I never broached the inn," said the F'dor. "Nor the palace, if you recall. No, Sir Hector, I never crossed the threshold of either place; you met me at the crossroads and left me at the foot of the castle. Kind of you." The demon laughed again. "And what I told you of my life was the truth as well. Long ago I had the chance to leave my birthplace—that was in the old days, during the first cataclysm, when the star first ruptured the Vault. Many of us escaped before it was sealed again, only to have been hunted throughout history, having to flee from host to host, hiding, biding our time. But now, once again, we will be out in the world, thanks to you, Sir Hector. You wished to rescue whomever you could from the cataclysm, and here you are! You have spared an entire race from captivity! And not only have you freed us from the Vault, but our master—the one who has long watched the doors, waiting for this day—you will be his host! What could be more edifying than that?"

The fire in the demon's eyes matched the intensity of that in the sky.

"When the old fisherman rowed out in his little boat to examine what the retreat of the sea had revealed, I was waiting, formless. I had come home when I heard of the upcoming Awakening, just as I said I had." The demon sighed. "A younger, stronger host might have been preferable, but one takes what one is offered in the advent of cataclysm. Isn't truth a marvelous thing? The art is in telling it so that it is interpreted the way one wishes to have it heard.

"Finally, I told you that we would be eternally grateful, sir knight. And we are. We are. Eternally."

Jarmon rose shakily to his feet and met Hector's eye.

"Hector," he said quietly, "open the door."

In his dizziness, the words rang clear. Hector's gaze narrowed a moment, then widened slightly with understanding.

With the last of his strength, he threw himself against the rightmost door of the Vault, shoving it open even farther than it had been before. His head all but split from the frenzied screaming of the demonic horde that was virtually within reach of the door; he tried to avert his eyes from the horror of the sight, but found his gaze dragged to the approaching fire that burned black with excitement as it rushed forward to freedom.

At the same moment, Jarmon threw himself into Brann and locked his arms around his knees. The frail form of the demon's host buckled in the strong arms of the guard and the momentum thrust both of them over the threshold and into the Vault.

Which gave Hector just enough time to drag the mammoth door shut before the multitude of F'dor that had been sealed away since the First Age crossed the threshold into the material world.

He pulled the key from the hole and tossed it behind him. Then he wrapped his arms through the huge brass handles, holding on with all the leverage he could muster as the gleaming doors darkened and settled back into lifeless stone once more.

Hector's mind buckled under the screaming he could hear and feel beyond those doors. The stone shook terrifyingly as the demons pounded from the other side, causing tremors that shook his entire body. He bowed his head, both to brace the closure and to try to drown out the horrifying sounds that scratched his ears. Within the demonic screeches of fury he thought he could hear Jarmon's voice rise in similar tone, the unmistakable sound of agony of body and soul ringing harshly in it.

As he clutched at the burning doors that seared the flesh from his chest and face, the sky turned white above him.

With a thundering bellow that cracked the vault of the heavens, the Sleeping Child awoke in the depths of the sea and rose in fiery rage to the sky.

The sound of the screaming on the other side of the door faded in the roar of the inferno behind him. All he could feel now was searing heat, heat that baked his body to the core from behind, and radiated through the stone doors before him, as molten volcanic fire rained down, sealing him eternally in an ossified shell to the brass handles.

As he passed over the threshold of death, from life to Afterlife, Hector finally saw what his father had told him of, and what he had relayed to Anais. Just beyond his sight, closer than the air of his last breath, and at the same time a half world away, he could see his friend in the branches of the World Tree, could see his father in knee-deep surf, standing vigil, Talthea and Aidan behind him on the shore, the baby in her arms. MacQuieth's eyes were on him, watching him from the other side of the earth, the other side of Time.

As his spirit fled his body, dissipating and expanding to the farthest reaches of the universe at the same time, Hector willed himself to hold for a moment to the invisible tether, paused long enough to breathe a final kiss on his wife and children, to whisper in his father's ear across the threshold over which they were bound to each other by love.

It's done, Father. You can cease waiting; go back to living now.

His last conscious thought was one of ironic amusement. As the sea poured in, sealing the entrance to the Vault once more beneath its depths, his body remained behind, fired into clay, forming the lock that barred the doors, vigilant to the end in death as he had been in life.

The key of living earth lay behind him, buried in the sand of the ocean floor, just out of reach for all eternity.

"Apple, Canfa, peez."

The daughter of the wind looked down solemnly into the earnest little human face. Then she smiled in spite of herself. She reached easily into the gnarled branches of the stunted tree that were beyond the length of his spindly arms and plucked a hard red fruit, and handed it to the boy.

She glanced to her left, where the woman sat on the ground of the decimated orchard, absently eating the apple she had been given a moment before and staring dully at Cantha's silver mare grazing on autumn grass nearby.

A deathly stillness fell, like the slamming of a door.

The winds, howling in fury as they had been for weeks uncounted, died down into utter silence.

And Cantha knew.

She stood frozen for a moment in the vast emptiness of a world without moving air, poised on the brink of cataclysm. And just before the winds began to scream, she seized the child by the back of the shirt and lifted him through the heavy air, bearing him to the horse as the apple fell from his hand to the ground.

She was dragging the startled woman to her feet and heaving her onto the horse as well when the sky turned white. She had mounted and was spurring the beast when the horizon to the northwest erupted in a plume of fire that shot into the sky like a spark from a candle caught by the wind, then spread over the bottom of the melting clouds, filling them with light, painful in intensity. Cantha uttered a single guttural command to the horse and galloped off, clutching the woman and the boy before her.

Even at the southern tip of the Island they could feel the tremors, could see the earth shuddering beneath the horse's hooves. Cantha could feel the child's sides heave, thought he might be wailing, but whatever sound he made was drowned in the horrifying lament of the winds. She prayed to those winds now to speed her way, to facilitate her path and her pace, but there was no answer.

At the foot of the battlements she pulled the humans from the horse's back, slashed the saddle girdings, and turned it loose, silently wishing it Godspeed. Then she seized the woman by the hand and tucked the boy beneath her arm as she began the daunting climb up the steps of the rock face.

She was halfway up, her muscles buckling in exertion, when the winds swelled, rampant, heavy with ash and debris. They whipped around her, dragging the air from her lungs, threatening her balance. Finally she had to let go of the woman lest she lose her grip on the boy.

"Climb!" Cantha shouted to the woman, but the woman merely stopped, rigid, where she was. Cantha urged her again, and again, pushing her futilely, finally abandoning her, running blindly up the steps as the sky turned black above her.

Through the dark halls and up the tower steps, two at a time, Cantha carried the child, in her arms now, clinging around her neck. The tower shuddered beneath them, swaying in the gale, the stone walls that had stood for five hundred years, stalwart, unmoving, buffeted by the winds of hurricanes and of war, trembling around them.

Finally they reached the pinnacle of the topmost tower, the dusty room lined with bookshelves and jars that had once been the abode of the royal vizier. Cantha, spent, set the boy down, took his hand, and ran through the study, throwing open the doors that already banged in the wind, running heedlessly through the shards of broken glass scattered across the stone floor, up the final flight of wooden steps, and pushed open the trapdoor to the utmost top of the parapets. She held tight to the boy as they stepped out onto the platform from which the vizier had once communed with the lightning, and stared down at the world below her.

Across the wide meadows and broken forests that surrounded Elysian dust was gathering in great spiral devils, loose earth driven upward by the chaos of the winds. In the distance she could see the silver horse running, galloping free, saddled no more. She looked around for the woman, but could not see the battlement steps.

Beside her she felt the boy move; she looked down to see him pointing north.

A wall of water the height of the tower was coming, dark gray in the distance, sweeping ahead of it a conundrum of debris that had once been towns and cities, bridges and mills.

It was but the forewave.

Behind it the real wave hovered, the crest of which Cantha could not see, rising to meet the dark sky.

Shaking, she reached down and lifted the child to her shoulders, mostly to give him as much height as possible, but also to avoid having to see again the expression in his eyes. Her own gaze was riveted on the vertical sea as it swelled forward across the Island, swallowing the river, the fields, the broken orchard as she watched. Just before it took the tower, sweeping forth to rejoin itself at the southern coast, she thought of the legends of enclaves of Lirin who had lived along the shore at the time of the first cataclysm, whose lands had been subsumed when the Child first fell to earth. The lore told of how they had transformed, once children of the sky, now children of the sea, coming to live in underwater caves and grottoes, building entire civilizations in the sheltering sands of the ocean, hiding in the guardian reefs, breathing beneath the waves. *If such a fairy tale be possible, may it be possible for thee, child,* she thought, patting the leg that dangled over her shoulder.

All light was blotted out in a roaring rush of gray-blue fury.

"Hold thy breath, child," Cantha said.

From the aft deck of the *Stormrider,* Sevirym watched the fire rise in the distance. The Island was so far away now, here at the edge of the Icefields at the southern end of the world, that at first he barely noticed; the Awakening resembled little more than a glorious slash of color brought on by the sunset. But as the clouds began to burn at the horizon, and the sea winds died at the same moment, he knew what he was beholding.

He was unable to tear his eyes away as the fire blazed, a white-hot streak in the distance brighter than the sun. And then, oblivious to the crew and passengers around him, staring east as well, he bowed his head and gave in to grief as the fire faded and disappeared into the sea.

The wave swelled to the outer edges of the Island, spilling over the charred land, swallowing the High Reaches in the north all the way down to the southeastern corner. It poured over what had once been great rolling fields and forests, largely blackened now or swollen with gleaming lava, all the way to Yliessan, where it seemed to hover for a moment above Sagia, her boughs adorned with flowers, sheltering the children of the sky who had sought final refuge there. Then it crashed down, meeting the sea at the land's edge on all sides.

As the tide rose to an even height, taking in the overflow, the crest of the waves closed above the Island, the first birth-place of Time, swallowing it from sight.

And then peace returned.

Hot vapor covered the sea, making it appear as calm and still as a misty morning.

SHANNARA

TERRY BROOKS

The time of the Shannara follows in the wake of an apocalypse that has destroyed the old world and very nearly annihilated its people as well. A thousand years of savagery and barbarism have concluded at the start of the series with the emergence of a new civilization in which magic has replaced science as the dominant source of power. A Druid Council comprised of the most talented of the new races—Men, Dwarves, Trolls, Gnomes, and Elves, names taken from the old legends—has begun the arduous task of rebuilding the world and putting an end to the racial warfare that has consumed the survivors of the so-called Great Wars since their conclusion.

But the wars continue, albeit in a different form. Magic, like science, is often mercurial, can be used for good or evil, and can have a positive or negative effect on those who come in contact with it. In *The Sword of Shannara,* a Druid subverted by his craving for magic's power manipulated Trolls and Gnomes in his effort to gain mastery over the other races. He failed because of Shea Ohmsford, the last of an Elven family with the Shannara surname. Shea, with the help of his brother and a small band of companions, was able to wield the fabled Sword of Shannara to destroy the Dark Lord.

Subsequently, in *The Elfstones of Shannara,* his grandson Wil was faced with another sort of challenge, one that required the use of a magic contained in a set of Elfstones. But use of the Stones altered Wil's genetic makeup, so that his own children were born with magic in their blood. As a result, in the third book of the series, *The Wishsong of Shannara,* Brin and her brother Jair were recruited by the Druid Allanon to seek out and destroy the Ildatch, the book of dark magic that had subverted the Warlock Lord and was now doing the same with the Mord Wraiths.

The story that follows takes place several years after the conclusion of *The Wishsong* and again features Jair Ohmsford, who must come to terms with his obsession with the past and his use of magic that his sister has warned him not to trust.

INDOMITABLE

TERRY BROOKS

The past is always with us.

Even though he was only just of an age to be considered a man, Jair Ohmsford had understood the meaning of the phrase since he was a boy. It meant that he would be shaped and reshaped by the events of his life, so that everything that happened would be in some way a consequence of what had gone before. It meant that the people he came to know would influence his conduct and his beliefs. It meant that his experiences of the past would impact his decisions of the future.

It meant that life was like a chain and the links that forged it could not be severed.

For Jair, the strongest of those links was to Garet Jax. That link, unlike any other, was a repository for memories he treasured so dearly that he protected them like glass ornaments, to be taken down from the shelf on which they were kept, polished, and then put away again with great care.

In the summer of the second year following his return from Graymark, he was still heavily under the influence of those memories. He woke often in the middle of the night from dreams of Garet Jax locked in battle with the Jachyra, heard echoes of the other's voice in conversations with his friends and neighbors, and caught sudden glimpses of the Weapons Master in the faces of strangers. He was not distressed by these occurrences; he was thrilled by them. They were an affirmation that he was keeping alive the past he cared so much about.

On the day the girl rode into Shady Vale, he was working at the family inn, helping the manager and his wife as a favor to his parents. He was standing on the porch, surveying the siding he had replaced after a windstorm had blown a branch through the wall. Something about the way she sat her horse caught his attention, drawing it away from his handiwork. He shaded his eyes against the glare of the sun as it reflected off a metal roof when she turned out of the trees. She sat ramrod straight astride a huge black stallion with a white blaze on its forehead, her dark hair falling in a cascade of curls to her waist, thick and shining. She wasn't big, but she gave an immediate impression of possessing confidence that went beyond the need for physical strength.

She caught sight of him at the same time he saw her and turned the big black in his direction. She rode up to him and stopped, a mischievous smile appearing on her round, perky face as she brushed back loose strands of hair. "Cat got your tongue, Jair Ohmsford?"

"Kimber Boh," he said, not quite sure that it really was. "I don't believe it."

She swung down, dropped the reins in a manner that suggested this was all the black required, and walked over to give him a long, sustained hug. "You look all grown up," she said, and ruffled his curly blond hair to show she wasn't impressed.

He might have said the same about her. The feel of her body against his as she hugged him was a clear indication that she was beyond childhood. But it was difficult to accept. He still remembered the slender, tiny girl she had been two years ago when he had met her for the first time in the ruins of the Croagh in the aftermath of his battle to save Brin.

He shook his head. "I almost didn't recognize you."

She stepped back. "I knew you right away." She looked around. "I always wanted to see where you lived. Is Brin here?"

She wasn't. Brin was living in the Highlands with Rone Leah, whom she had married in the spring. They were already expecting their first child; if it was a boy, they would name it Jair.

He shook his head. "No. She lives in Leah now. Why didn't you send word you were coming?"

"I didn't know myself until a little over a week ago." She glanced at the inn. "The ride has made me tired and thirsty. Why don't we go inside while we talk?"

They retreated to the cool interior of the inn and took a table at a window where the slant of the roof kept the sun off. The innkeeper brought over a pitcher of ale and two mugs, giving Jair a sly wink as he walked away.

"Does he give you a wink for every pretty girl you bring into this establishment?" Kimber asked when the innkeeper was out of earshot. "Are you a regular here?"

He blushed. "My parents own the inn. Kimber, what are you doing here?"

She considered the question. "I'm not entirely sure. I came to find you and to persuade you to come with me. But now that I'm here, I don't know that I have the words to do it. In fact, I might just not even try. I might just stay here and visit until you send me away. What would you say to that?"

He leaned back in his chair and smiled. "I guess I would say you were welcome to stay as long as you like. Is that what you want?"

She sipped at her ale and shook her head. "What I want doesn't matter. Maybe what you want doesn't matter either." She looked out the window into the sunshine. "Grandfather sent me. He said to tell you that what we thought we had finished two years ago isn't quite finished after all. There appears to be a loose thread that needs snipping off."

"A loose thread?"

She looked back at him. "Remember when your sister burned the book of the Ildatch at Graymark?"

He nodded. "I'm not likely to forget."

"Grandfather says she missed a page."

They ate dinner at his home, a dinner that he prepared himself, which included soup made of fresh garden vegetables, bread, and a plate of cheeses and dried fruits stored for his use by his parents, who were south on a journey to places where their special healing talents were needed. They sat at the dinner table and watched the darkness descend in a slow curtain of shadows that draped the countryside like black silk. The sky stayed clear and the stars came out, brilliant and glittering against the firmament.

"He wouldn't tell you why he needs me?" Jair asked for what must have been the fifth or sixth time.

She shook her head patiently. "He just said you were the one to bring, not your sister, not your parents, not Rone Leah. Just you."

"And he didn't say anything about the Elfstones either? You're sure about that?"

She looked at him, a hint of irritation in her blue eyes. "Do you know that this is one of the best meals I have ever eaten? It really is. This soup is wonderful, and I want to know how to make it. But for now, I am content just to eat it. Why don't you stop asking questions and enjoy it, too?"

He responded with a rueful grimace and sipped at the soup, staying quiet for a few mouthfuls while he mulled things over. He was having difficulty accepting what she was telling him, let alone agreeing to what she was asking. Two years earlier, the Ohmsford siblings had taken separate paths to reach the hiding place of the Ildatch, the book of dark magic that had spawned first the Warlock Lord and his Skull Bearers in the time of Shea and Flick Ohmsford and then the Mord Wraiths in their own time. The magic contained in the book was so powerful that the book had taken on a life of its own, become a spirit able to subvert and ultimately re-form beings of flesh and blood into monstrous undead creatures. It had done so repeatedly and would have kept on doing so had Brin and he not succeeded in destroying it.

Of course, it had almost destroyed Brin first. Possessed of the magic of the wishsong, of the power to create or destroy through use of music and words, Brin was a formidable opponent, but an attractive ally, as well. Perhaps she would have become the latter instead of the former had Jair not reached her in time to prevent it. But it was for that very purpose that the King of the Silver River had sent him to find her after she had left with Allanon, and so he had known in advance what was expected of him. His own magic was of a lesser kind, an ability to appear to change things without actually being able to do so, but in this one instance it had proved sufficient to do what was needed.

Which was why he was somewhat confused by Kimber's grandfather's insistence on summoning him now. Whatever the nature of the danger presented by the threat of an Ildatch reborn, he was the least well-equipped member of the family to deal with it. He was also doubtful of the man making the selection, having seen enough of the wild-eyed and unpredictable Cogline to know that he wasn't always rowing with all his oars in the water. Kimber might have confidence in him, but that didn't mean Jair should.

An even bigger concern was the old man's assertion that somehow the Ildatch hadn't been completely destroyed when Brin had gone to such lengths to make certain that it was. She had used her magic to burn it to ashes, the whole tome, each and every page. So how could it have survived in any form? How could Brin have been mistaken about something so crucial?

He knew that he wasn't going to find out unless he went with Kimber to see the old man and hear him out, but it was a long journey to Hearthstone, which lay deep in the Eastland, a draining commitment of time and energy. Especially if it turned out that the old man was mistaken.

So he asked his questions, hoping to learn something helpful, waiting for a revelation. But soon he had asked the old ones more times than was necessary and had run out of new ones.

"I know you think Grandfather is not altogether coherent about some things," Kimber said. "You know as much even from the short amount of time you spent with him two years ago, so I don't have to pretend. I know he can be difficult and unsteady. But I also know that he sees things other men don't, that he has resources denied to them. I can read a trail and track it, but he can read signs on the air itself. He can make things out of compounds and powders that no one else has known how to make since the destruction of the Old World. He's more than he seems."

"So you believe that I should go, that there's a chance he might be right about the Ildatch?" Jair leaned forward again, his meal forgotten. "Tell me the truth, Kimber."

"I think you would be wise to pay attention to what he has to say." Her face was calm, but her eyes troubled. "I have my own doubts about Grandfather, but I saw the way he was when he told me to come find you. It wasn't something done on a whim. It was done after a great deal of thought. He would have come himself, but I wouldn't let him. He is too old and frail. Since I wouldn't let him make the journey, I had to make it myself. I guess that says something about how I view the matter."

She looked down at her food and pushed it away. "Let's clean up, and then we can sit outside."

They carried off the dishes, washed them, and put them away, and then went out onto the porch and sat together on a wooden bench that looked off toward the southwest. The night was warm and filled with smells of jasmine and evergreen, and somewhere off in the darkness a stream trickled. They sat without speaking for a while, listening to the silvery sound of the water. An owl flew by, its dark shape momentarily silhouetted by moonlight. From down in the village came the faint sound of laughter.

"It seems like a long time since we were at Graymark," she said quietly. "A long time since everything that happened two years ago."

Jair nodded, remembering. "I've thought often about you and your grandfather. I wondered how you were. I don't know why I worried, though. You were fine before Brin and Rone found you. You've probably been fine since. Do you still have the moor cat?"

"Whisper? Yes. He keeps us both safe from the things we can't keep safe from on our own." She paused. "But maybe we aren't as fine as you think, Jair. Things change. Both Grandfather and I are older. He needs me more; I need him

less. Whisper goes away more often and comes back less
frequently. The country is growing up around us. It isn't as
wild as it once was. There is a Dwarven village not five miles
away and Gnome tribes migrate from the Wolfsktaag to the
Ravenshorn and back again all the time." She shrugged. "It
isn't the same."

"What will you do when your grandfather is gone?"

She laughed softly. "That might never happen. He might
live forever." She sighed, gesturing vaguely with one slender
hand. "Sometimes, I think about moving away from Hearthstone, of living somewhere else. I admit I want to see something of the larger world."

"Would you come down into the Borderlands, maybe?"
He looked over at her. "Would you come live here? You
might like it."

She nodded. "I might."

She didn't say anything else, so he went back to looking
into the darkness, thinking it over. He would like having her
here. He liked talking to her. He guessed that over time they
might turn out to be good friends.

"I need you to come back with me," she said suddenly,
looking at him with unexpected intensity. "I might as well
tell you so. It has more to do with me than with Grandfather.
I am worn out by him. I hate admitting it because it makes
me sound weak. But he grates on me the older and more difficult he gets. I don't know if this business about the Ildatch
is real or not. But I don't think I can get to the truth of it
alone. I'm being mostly selfish by coming here and asking
you to come to Hearthstone with me. Grandfather is set on
this happening. Just having you talk with him might make a
difference."

Jair shook his head doubtfully. "I barely know him. I don't
see what difference having me there would make to anything."

She hesitated, then exhaled sharply. "My grandfather was
there to help your sister when she needed it, Jair. I am asking
you to return the favor. I think he needs you, whether the
danger from the Ildatch is real or not. What's bothering him

is real enough. I want you to come back with me and help settle things."

He thought about it a long time, making himself do so even though he already knew what he was going to say. He was thinking of what Garet Jax would do.

"All right, I'll come," he said finally.

Because he knew that this is what the Weapons Master would have done in his place.

He left a letter with the innkeeper for his parents, explaining where he was going, packed some clothes, and closed up the house. He already knew he would be in trouble when he returned, but that wasn't enough to keep him from going. The innkeeper loaned him a horse, a steady, reliable bay that could be depended on not to do anything unexpected or foolish. Jair was not much for horses, but he understood the need for one here, where there was so much distance to cover.

It took them a week to get to Hearthstone, riding north out of Shady Vale and the Duln Forests, around the western end of the Rainbow Lake, then up through Callahorn along the Mermidon River to the Rabb Plains. They crossed the Rabb, following its river into the Upper Anar, then rode down through the gap between the Wolfsktaag Mountains and Darklin Reach, threading the needle of the corridor between, staying safely back from the edges of both. As they rode, Jair found himself pondering how different the circumstances were now from the last time he had come into the Eastland. Then, he had been hunted at every turn, threatened by more dangers than he cared to remember. It had been Garet Jax who had saved his life time and again. Now he traveled without fear of attack, without having to look over his shoulder, and Garet Jax was only a memory.

"Do you think we might have lived other lives before this one?" Kimber asked him on their last night out before reaching Hearthstone.

They were sitting in front of a fire in a grove of trees flanking the south branch of the Rabb, deep within the forests of Darklin Reach. The horses grazed contentedly a short distance off, and moonlight flooded the grassy flats that stretched away about them. There was a hint of a chill in the air this night, a warning of autumn's approach.

Jair smiled. "I don't think about it at all. I have enough trouble living the life I have without wondering if there were others."

"Or if there will be others after this one?" She brushed at her long hair, which she kept tied back as they rode, but let down at night in a tumbled mass. "Grandfather thinks so. I guess I do, too. I think everything is connected. Lives, like moments in time, are all linked together, fish in a stream, swimming and swimming. The past coming forward to become the future."

He looked off into the dark. "I think we are connected to the past, but mostly to the events and the people that shaped it. I think we are always reaching back in some way, bringing forward what we remember, sometimes for information, sometimes just for comfort. I don't remember other lives, but I remember the past of this one. I remember the people who were in it."

She waited a moment, then moved over to sit beside him. "The way you said that—are you thinking about what happened two years ago at Heaven's Well?"

He shrugged.

"About the one you called the Weapons Master?"

He stared at her. "How did you know that?"

"It isn't much of a mystery, Jair. You talked about no one else afterward. Only him, the one who saved you on the Croagh, the one who fought the Jachyra. Don't you remember?"

He nodded. "I guess."

"Maybe your connection with him goes farther back in time than just this life." She lifted an eyebrow at him. "Have you thought about that? Maybe you were joined in another life as well, and that's why he made such an impression on you."

Jair laughed. "I think he made an impression on me because he was the best fighter I have ever seen. He was so . . ." He stopped himself, searching for the right word. "Indomitable." His smile faded. "Nothing could stand against him, not even a Jachyra. Not even something that was too much for Allanon."

"But I might still be right about past lives," she persisted. She put her hand on his shoulder and squeezed. "You can grant me that much, can't you, Valeman?"

He could, that and much more. He wanted to tell her so, but didn't know how without sounding foolish. He was attracted to her, and it surprised him. Having thought of her for so long as a little girl, he was having trouble accepting that she was now full grown. Such a transition didn't seem possible. It confused his thinking, the past conflicting with the present. How did she feel about him, as changed in his own way as she was in hers? He wondered, but could not make himself ask.

In late afternoon of the following day, they reached Hearthstone. He had never been here before, but he had heard Brin describe the chimney-shaped rock so often that he knew at once what it was. He caught sight of it as they rode through the trees, a dark pinnacle overlooking a shallow, wooded valley. Its distinctive, rugged formation seemed right for this country, a land of dark rumors and strange happenings. Yet that was in the past, as well. Things were different now. They had come in on a road, where two years before there had been no roads. They had passed the newly settled Dwarf village and seen the houses and heard the voices of children. The country was growing up, the wilderness pushed back. Change was the one constant in an ever-evolving world.

They reached the cottage shortly afterward. It was constructed of wood and timber with porches front and back, its walls grown thick with ivy and the grounds surrounding it planted with gardens and ringed with walkways and bushes. It had a well-cared-for look to it; everything was neatly planted and trimmed, a mix of colors and forms that were pleasing to the eye. It didn't look so much like a wilderness cottage as a village home. Behind the house, a paddock housed a mare and a foal. A milk cow was grazing there as well. Sheds lined the back of the paddock, neatly painted. Shade trees helped conceal the buildings from view; Jair hadn't caught even a glimpse of roofs on the ride in.

He glanced over at her. "Do you look after all this by yourself?"

"Mostly." She gave him a wry smile. "I like looking after a home. I always have, ever since I was old enough to help do so."

They rode into the yard and dismounted, and instantly Cogline appeared through the doorway. He was ancient and stick-thin beneath his baggy clothing, and his white hair stuck out in all directions, as if he might have just come awake. He pulled at his beard as he came up to them, his fingers raking the wiry hairs. His eyes were sharp and questioning, and he was already scanning Jair as if not quite sure what to make of him.

"So!" He approached with that single word and stood so close that the Valeman was forced to take a step back. He peered intently into Jair's blue eyes, took careful note of his Elven features. "Is this him?"

"Yes, Grandfather." Kimber sounded embarrassed.

"You're certain? No mistake?"

"Yes, Grandfather."

"Because he could be someone else, you know. He could be *anybody* else!" Cogline furrowed his already deeply lined brow. "Are you young Ohmsford? The boy, Jair?"

Jair nodded. "I am. Don't you remember me? We met two years ago in the ruins of Graymark."

The old man stared at him as if he hadn't heard the question. Jair could feel the other's hard gaze probing in a way that was not altogether pleasant. "Is this necessary?" he asked finally. "Can't we go inside and sit down?"

"When I say so!" the other replied. "When I say I am finished! Don't interrupt my study!"

"Grandfather!" Kimber exclaimed.

The old man ignored her. "Let me see your hands," he said.

Jair held out his hands, palms up. Cogline studied them carefully for a moment, grunted as if he had found whatever it was he was looking for, and said, "Come inside, and I'll fix you something to eat."

They went into the cottage and seated themselves at the rough-hewn wooden dining table, but it was Kimber who ended up preparing a stew for them to eat. While she did so, directing admonitions at her grandfather when she thought them necessary, Cogline rambled on about the past and Jair's part in it, a bewildering hodge-podge of information and observation.

"I remember you," he said. "Just a boy, coming out of Graymark's ruins with your sister, the two of you covered in dust and smelling of death! Hah! I know something of that smell, I can tell you! Fought many a monster come out of the netherworld, long before you were born, before any who live now were born and a good deal more who are long dead. Might have left the order, but didn't lose the skills. Not a one. Never listened to me, any of them, but that didn't make me give up. The new mirrors the old. You can't disconnect science and magic. They're all of a piece, and the lessons of one are the lessons of the other. Allanon knew as much. Knew just enough to get himself killed."

Jair had no idea what he was talking about, but perked up on hearing the Druid's name. "You knew Allanon?"

"Not when he was alive. Know him now that he's dead, though. Your sister, she was a gift to him. She was the answer to what he needed when he saw the end coming. It's like that for some, the gift. Maybe for you, too, one day."

"What gift?"

"You know, I was a boy once. I was a Druid once, too."

Jair stared at him, not quite knowing whether to accept this or not. It was hard to think of him as a boy, but thinking of him as a Druid was harder still. If the old man really was a Druid—not that Jair thought for a moment that he was—

what was he doing here, out in the wilderness, living with Kimber? "I thought Allanon was the last of the Druids," he said.

The old man snorted. "You thought a lot of things that weren't so." He shoved back his plate of stew, having hardly touched it. "Do you want to know what you're doing here?"

Jair stopped eating in mid-bite. Kimber, sitting across from him, blinked once and said, "Maybe you should wait until he's finished dinner, Grandfather."

The old man ignored her. "Your sister thought the Ildatch destroyed," he said. "She was wrong. Wasn't her fault, but she was wrong. She burned it to ash, turned it to a charred ruin and that should have been the end of it, but it wasn't. You want to sit outside while we have this discussion? The open air and the night sky make it easier to think things through sometimes."

They went outside onto the front porch, where the sky west was turning a brilliant mix of purple and rose above the treetops and the sky east already boasted a partial moon and a scattering of stars. The old man took possession of the only rocker, and Jair and Kimber sat together on a high-backed wooden bench. It occurred to the Valeman that he needed to rub down and feed his horse, a task he would have completed by now if he had been thinking straight.

The old man rocked in silence for a time, then gestured abruptly at Jair. "Last month, on a night when the moon was full and the sky a sea of stars, beautiful night, I woke and walked down to the little pond that lies just south. I don't know why, I just did. Something made me. I lay in the grass and slept, and while I slept, I had a dream. Only it was more a vision than a dream. I used to have such visions often. I was closer to the shades of the dead then, and they would come to me because I was receptive to their needs. But that was long ago, and I had thought such things at an end."

He seemed to reflect on the idea for a moment, lost in thought. "I was a Druid then."

"Grandfather," Kimber prodded softly.

The old man looked back at Jair. "In my dream, Allanon's shade came to me out of the netherworld. It spoke to me. It told me that the Ildatch was not yet destroyed, that a piece of it still survived. One page only, seared at the edges, shaken loose and blown beneath the stones of the keep in the fiery destruction of the rest. Perhaps the book found a way to save that one page in its death throes. I don't know. The shade didn't tell me. Only that it had survived your sister's efforts and been found in the rubble by Mwellrets who sought artifacts that would lend them the power that had belonged to the Mord Wraiths. Those rets knew what they had because the page told them, a whisper that promised great things! It had life, even as a fragment, so powerful was its magic!"

Jair glanced at Kimber, who blinked at him uncertainly. Clearly, this was news to her as well. "One page," he said to the old man, "isn't enough to be dangerous, is it? Unless there is a spell the Mwellrets can make use of?"

Cogline ran his hand through his wiry thatch of white hair. "Not enough? Yes, that was my thought, too. One page, out of so many. What harm? I dismissed the vision on waking, convinced it was a malignant intrusion on a peaceful life, a groundless fear given a momentary foothold by an old man's frailness. But it came again, a second time, this time while I slept in my own bed. It was stronger than before, more insistent. The shade chided me for my indecision, for my failings past and present. It told me to find you and bring you here. It gave me no peace, not that night or after."

He looked genuinely distressed now, as if the memory of the shade's visit was a haunting of the sort he wished he had never encountered. Jair understood better now why Kimber felt it so important to summon him. Cogline was an old man teetering on the brink of emotional collapse. He might be hallucinating or he might have connected with the shades of the dead, Allanon or not, but whatever he had experienced, it had left him badly shaken.

"Now that I am here, what am I expected to do?" he asked.

The old man looked at him. There was a profound sadness mirrored in his ancient eyes. "I don't know," he said. "I wasn't told."

Then he looked off into the darkness and didn't speak again.

"I'm sorry about this," Kimber declared later. There was a pronounced weariness in her voice. "I didn't think he was going to be this vague once he had the chance to speak with you. I should have known better. I shouldn't have brought you."

They were sitting together on the bench again, sipping at mugs of cold ale and listening to the night. They had put the old man to sleep a short while earlier, tucking him into his bed and sitting with him until he began to snore. Kimber had done her best to hasten the process with a cup of medicated tea.

He smiled at her. "Don't be sorry. I'm glad you brought me. I don't know if I can help, but I think you were right about not wanting to handle this business alone. I can see where he could become increasingly more difficult if you tried to put him off."

"But it's all such a bunch of nonsense! He hasn't been out of his bed in months. He hasn't slept down by the pond. Whatever dreams he's been having are the result of his refusal to eat right." She blew out a sharp breath in frustration. "All this business about the Ildatch surviving somehow in a page fragment! I used to believe everything he told me, when I was little and still thought him the wisest man in the world. But now I think that he's losing his mind."

Jair sipped at his ale. "I don't know. He seems pretty convinced."

She stared at him. "You don't believe him, do you?"

"Not entirely. But it might be he's discovered something worth paying attention to. Dreams have a way of revealing things we don't understand right away. They take time to decipher. But once we've thought about it . . ."

"Why would Allanon's shade come to Grandfather in a dream and ask him to bring you here rather than just appearing to you?" she interrupted heatedly. "What sense does it make to go through Grandfather? He would not be high on the list of people you might listen to!"

"There must be a reason, if he's really had a vision from a shade. He must be involved in some important way."

He looked at her for confirmation, but she had turned away, her mouth compressed in a tight, disapproving line. "Are you going to help him, Jair? Are you going to try to make him see that he is imagining things or are you going to feed this destructive behavior with pointless encouragement?"

He flushed at the rebuke, but kept his temper. Kimber was looking to him to help her grandfather find a way out of the quicksand of his delusions, and instead of doing so, he was offering to jump in himself. But he couldn't dismiss the old man's words as easily as she could. He was not burdened by years and experiences shared; he did not see Cogline in the same way she did. Nor was he so quick to disbelieve visions and dreams and shades. He had encountered more than a few himself, not the least of which was the visit from the King of the Silver River, two years earlier, under similar circumstances. If not for that visit, a visit he might have dismissed if he had been less open-minded, Brin would have been lost to him and the entire world changed. It was not something you forgot easily. Not wanting to believe was not always the best approach to things you didn't understand.

"Kimber," he said quietly, "I don't know yet what I am going to do. I don't know enough to make a decision. But if I dismiss your grandfather's words out of hand, it might be worse than if I try to see through them to what lies beneath."

He waited while she looked off into the distance, her eyes still hot and her mouth set. Then finally, she turned back to him, nodding slowly. "I'm sorry. I didn't mean to attack you. You were good enough to come when I asked, and I am letting my frustration get in the way of my good sense. I know you mean to help."

"I do," he reassured her. "Let him sleep through the night, and then see if he's had the vision again. We can talk about it when he wakes and is fresh. We might be able to discover its source."

She shook her head quickly. "But what if it's real, Jair? What if it's true? What if I've brought you here for selfish reasons and I've placed you in real danger? I didn't mean for that to happen, but what if it does?"

She looked like a child again, waiflike and lost. He smiled and cocked one Elfish eyebrow at her. "A moment ago, you were telling me there wasn't a chance it was real. Are you ready to abandon that ground just because I said we shouldn't dismiss it out of hand? I didn't say I believed it either. I just said there might be some truth to it."

"I don't want there to be any. I want it to be Grandfather's wild imagination at work and nothing more." She stared at him intently. "I want this all to go away, far away, and not come back again. We've had enough of Mord Wraiths and books of dark magic."

He nodded slowly, then reached out and touched her lightly on the cheek, surprising himself with his boldness. When she closed her eyes, he felt his face grow hot and quickly took his hand away. He felt suddenly dizzy. "Let's wait and see, Kimber," he said. "Maybe the dream won't come to him again."

She opened her eyes. "Maybe," she whispered.

He turned back toward the darkness, took a long, cool swallow of his ale, and waited for his head to clear.

The dream didn't come to Cogline that night, after all. Instead, it came to Jair Ohmsford.

He was not expecting it when he crawled into his bed, weary from the long journey and slightly muddled from a few too many cups of ale. The horses were rubbed down and fed, his possessions were put away in the cupboard and the cottage was dark. He didn't know how long he slept before it began, only that it happened all at once, and when it did, it was as if he were completely awake and alert.

He stood at the edge of a vast body of water that stretched away as far as the eye could see, its surface gray and smooth, reflecting a sky as flat and colorless as itself, so that there was no distinction between the one and the other. The shade was already there, hovering above its surface, a huge dark specter that dwarfed him in size and blotted out a whole section of the horizon behind it. Its hood concealed its features, and all that was visible were pinpricks of red light like eyes burning out of a black hole.

—Do you know me—

He did, of course. He knew instinctively, without having to think about it, without having been given more than those four words with which to work. "You are Allanon."

—In life. In death, his shade. Do you remember me as I was—

Jair saw the Druid once again, waiting for Brin and Rone Leah and himself as they returned home late at night, a dark and imposing figure, too large somehow for their home. He heard the Druid speak to them of the Ildatch and the Mord Wraiths. The strong features and the determined voice mesmerized him. He had never known anyone as dominating as Allanon—except, perhaps, for Garet Jax.

"I remember you," he said.

—Watch—

An image appeared on the air before him, gloomy and indistinct. It revealed the ruins of a vast fortress, mounds of rubble against a backdrop of forest and mountains. Graymark destroyed. Shadowy figures moved through the rubble, poking amid the broken stones. Bearing torches, a handful went deep inside, down tunnels in danger of collapse. They were cloaked and hooded, but the flicker of light on their hands and faces revealed patches of reptilian scales. Mwellrets. They wound their way deeper into the ruins, into freshmade catacombs, into places where only darkness and death could be found. They proceeded slowly, taking their time, pausing often to search nooks and crannies, each hollow in the earth that might offer concealment.

Then one of the Mwellrets began to dig, an almost frantic effort, pulling aside stones and timbers, hissing like a snake. It labored for long minutes, all alone, the others gone elsewhere. Dust and blood soon coated its scaly hide, and its breath came in gasps that suggested near-exhaustion.

But in the end, it found what it sought, pulling free from the debris a seared, torn page of a book, a page with writing on it that pulsed like veins beneath skin . . .

—Watch—

A second image appeared, this one of another fortress, one he didn't recognize right away, even though it seemed familiar. It was as dark and brooding as Graymark had been, as thick with shadows and gloom, as hard-edged and rough-hewn. The image lingered only a moment on the outer walls, then took the Valeman deep inside, past gates and battlements and into the nether regions. In a room dimly lit by torches that smoked and steamed in damp, stale air, a cluster of Mwellrets hovered over the solitary book page retrieved from Graymark's ruins.

They were engaged in an arcane rite. Jair could not be certain, but he had the distinct feeling that they were not entirely aware of what was happening to them. They were moving in concert, like gears in a machine, each one in sync with the others. They kept their heads lowered and their eyes fixed, and there was a hypnotic sound to their voices and movements that suggested they were responding to something he couldn't see. In the gloom and smoke, they reminded him of the Spider Gnomes on Toffer Ridge, come to make sacrifice of themselves to the Werebeasts, come to give up the lives of a few in the mistaken belief that it was for the good of the many.

As one, they moved their palms across the surface of the paper, taking in the feel of the veined writing, murmuring furtive chants and small prayers. Beneath their reptilian fingers, the page glowed and the writing pulsed. It was responding to their efforts. Jair could feel the raw pull of a siphoning, a leaching away of life.

The remnant of the Ildatch, in search of a way back from the edge of extinction, in need of nourishment that would enable it to recall and put to use the spells it had lost, was feeding.

The image faded. He was alone again with Allanon's shade, two solitary figures facing each other across an empty vista. The gloom had grown thicker and the sky darker. The lake no longer reflected light of any sort.

In the aftermath of the visions, he had realized why the second fortress had seemed so familiar. It was Dun Fee Aran, the Gnome prisons where he had been taken by the Mwellret Stythys to be coerced into giving up his magic and eventually his life. He remembered his despair on being cast into the cell allotted to him, deep beneath the earth in the bowels of the keep, alone in the darkness and silence. He remembered his fear.

"I can't go back there," he whispered, already anticipating what the shade was going to ask of him.

But the shade asked nothing of him. Instead, it gestured and for a third and final time, the air before the Valeman began to shimmer.

—Watch—

"I knew it!" Cogline exclaimed gleefully. "It's still alive! Didn't I tell you so? Wasn't that just what I said? You thought me a crazy old man, Granddaughter, but how crazy do I look to you now? Hallucinations? Wild imaginings? Hah! Am I still to be treated as if I were a delicate flower? Am I still to be humored and coddled?"

He began dancing about the room and cackling like the madman that, Jair guessed, he was as close as possible to being while still marginally sane. The Valeman watched him patiently, trying not to look at Kimber, who was so angry and disgusted that he could feel the heat radiating from her glare. It was morning now, and they sat across from each other at the old wooden dining table, bathed in bright splashes of sunlight that streamed through the open windows and belied the darkness of the moment.

"You haven't told us yet what the shade expects of you," Kimber said quietly, though he could not mistake the edge to her words.

"What you have already guessed," he answered, meeting her gaze reluctantly. "What I knew even before the third image showed it to me. I have to go to Dun Fee Aran and put a stop to what's happening."

Cogline stopped dancing. "Well, you can do that, I expect," he said, shrugging aside the implications. "You did it once before, didn't you?"

"No, Grandfather, he did not," Kimber corrected him impatiently. "That was his sister, and I don't understand why she wasn't sent for, if the whole idea is to finish the job she started two years ago. It's her fault the Ildatch is still alive."

Jair shook his head. "It isn't anybody's fault. It just happened. In any case, Brin's married and pregnant and doesn't use the magic anymore."

Nor would she ever use it again, he was thinking. It had taken her a long time to get over what happened to her at the Maelmord. He had seen how long it had taken. He didn't know that she had ever been the same since. She had warned him that the magic was dangerous, that you couldn't trust it, that it could turn on you even when you thought it was your friend. He remembered the haunted look in her eyes.

He leaned forward, folding his hands in front of him. "Allanon's shade made it clear that she can't be exposed to the Ildatch a second time—not even to a fragment of a page. She is too vulnerable to its magic, too susceptible to what it can do to humans, even one as powerful as she is. Someone else has to go, someone who hasn't been exposed to the power of the book before."

Kimber reached out impulsively and took hold of his hands. "But why you, Jair? Others could do this."

"Maybe not. Dun Fee Aran is a Mwellret stronghold, and the page is concealed somewhere deep inside. Just finding it presents problems that would stop most from even getting close. But I have the magic of the wishsong, and I can use it to disguise myself. I can make it appear as if I'm not there.

That way, I can gain sufficient time to find the page without being discovered."

"The boy is right!" Cogline exclaimed, animated anew by the idea. "He is the perfect choice!"

"Grandfather!" Kimber snapped at him.

The old man turned, running his gnarled fingers through his tangled beard. "Stop yelling at me!"

"Then stop jumping to ridiculous conclusions! Jair is not the perfect choice. He might be able to get past the rets and into the fortress, but then he has to destroy the page and get out again. How is he to do that when all his magic can do is create illusions? Smoke and mirrors! How is he to defend himself against a real attack, one he is almost sure to come up against at some point?"

"We'll go with him!" the old man declared. "We'll be his protectors! We'll take Whisper—just as soon as he comes back from wherever he's wandered off to. Dratted cat!"

Kimber ran a hand across her eyes as if trying to see things more clearly. "Jair, do you understand what I am saying? This is hopeless!"

The Valeman didn't answer right away. He was remembering the third vision shown him by Allanon's shade, the one he hadn't talked about. A jumble of uncertain images clouded by shadowy movement and wildness, it had frightened and confused him. Yet it had imbued him with a certainty of success, as well, a certainty so strong and unmistakable that he could not dismiss it.

"The shade said that I would find a way," he answered her. He hesitated. "If I just believe in myself."

She stared at him. "If you just believe in yourself?"

"I know. It sounds foolish. And I'm terrified of Dun Fee Aran, have been since I was imprisoned there by the Mwellret Stythys two years ago on my way to find Brin. I thought I was going to die in those cells. And maybe worse was going to happen first. I have never been so afraid of anything. I swore, once I was out of there, that I would never go back, not for any reason."

He took a deep breath and exhaled slowly. "But I think that I have to go back anyway, in part because it's necessary if the Ildatch is to be stopped, but also because Allanon made me feel that I shouldn't be afraid any more. He gave me a sense of reassurance that this wouldn't be like the last time, that it would be different because I am older and stronger now—better able to face what's waiting there."

"Telling you all this might just be a way to get you to do what he wants," Kimber pointed out. "It might be a Druid trick, a deception of the sort that shades are famous for."

He nodded. "It might. But it doesn't feel that way. It doesn't feel false. It feels true."

"Of course, it would," she said quietly. She looked miserable. "I brought you here to help Grandfather find peace of mind with his dreams, not to risk your life because of them. Everything I told you I was afraid was going to happen is happening. I hate it."

She was squeezing his hands so hard she was hurting him. "If I didn't come, Kimber," he said, "who would act on your grandfather's dreams? It isn't something we planned, either of us, but we can't ignore what's needed. I have to go. I have to."

She nodded slowly, her hands withdrawing from his. "I know." She looked at Cogline, who was standing very still now, looking distressed, as if suddenly aware of what he had brought about. She smiled gently at him. "I know, Grandfather."

The old man nodded slowly, but the joy had gone out of him.

It was decided they would set out the following day. It was a journey of some distance, even if they went on horseback. It would take them the better part of a week to get through the Ravenshorn Mountains and skirt the edges of Olden Moor to where Dun Fee Aran looked out over the Silver River in the shadow of the High Bens. This was rugged country, most of it still wilderness, beyond the spread of Dwarf settlements and Gnome camps. Much of it was swamp and jungle, and some of it was too dangerous to try to pass through. A direct line of approach was out of the question. At best, they would be able to find a path along the eastern edge of the Raven-shorn. They would have to carry their own supplies and water. They would have to go prepared for the worst.

Jair was not pleased with the thought that both Kimber and Cogline would be going with him, but there was nothing he could do about that, either. He was going back into country that had been unfamiliar to him two years earlier and was unfamiliar to him now. He wouldn't be able to find his way without help, and the only help at hand was the girl and her grandfather, both of whom knew the Anar much better than anyone else he would have been able to turn to. It would have been nice to leave them behind in safety, but he doubted that they would have permitted it even if he hadn't had need of them. For reasons that were abundantly apparent, they intended to see this matter through with him.

They spent the remainder of the day putting together supplies, a process that was tedious and somehow emotionally draining, as if the act of preparation was tantamount to climbing to a cliff ledge before jumping off. There wasn't much conversation exchanged, and most of what was said concerned the task itself. That the effort helped pass the time was the best that could be said for it.

More often than he cared to admit, Jair found himself wondering how far he was pressing his luck by going back into country he had been fortunate to escape from once already. He might argue that this time, like the last, he was going because he had no choice, but in fact he did. He could walk away from the dreams and their implications. He could argue that Kimber was right and that he was being used for reasons that he did not appreciate. He could even argue that efforts at reviving the Ildatch were doomed in any case, its destruction by his sister's magic so complete that trying to re-create the book from a single page was impossible. He could stop everything they were doing simply by announcing that he was going home to ask help from his parents and sister. It would be wiser to involve them in any case, wouldn't it?

But he would not do that. He knew he wouldn't even as he was telling himself he could. He was just new enough at being grown up not to want to ask for help unless he absolutely had to. It diminished him in his own mind, if not in fact, to seek assistance from his family. It was almost as if they expected it of him, the youngest and least experienced, the one they all had been helping for so long. There was an admission of failure written into such an act, one that he could not abide. This was something he could do, after all. He had gone into this country once, and dangerous or not, he could go into it again.

His mood did not improve with the coming of nightfall and the realization that there was nothing else to be done but to wait for morning. They ate the dinner Kimber made them, the old man filling the silence with thoughts of the old days and the new world, of Druids past and a future without them. There would be a time when they would return, he insisted. The Druids would be needed again, you could depend on it. Jair kept his mouth shut. He did not want to say what he was thinking about Druids and the need for them.

He dreamed again that night, but not of the shade of Allanon. In his dream, he was already down inside the fortress at Dun Fee Aran, working his way along corridors shrouded in damp and gloom, hopelessly lost and searching for a way out. A sibilant voice whose source he could not divine whispered in his ear, *Never leavess thiss plasse.* Terrifying creatures besieged him, but he could see nothing of them but their shadows. The longer he wandered, the greater his sense of foreboding, until finally it was all he could do to keep from screaming.

When a room opened before him, its interior as black as ink, he stopped at the threshold, afraid to go farther, knowing that if he did so, something terrible would happen. But he could not help himself because the shadows were closing in from behind, pressing up against him, and soon they would smother him completely. So he stepped forward into the room—one step, two, three—feeling his way with a caution he prayed might save him and yet feared wouldn't.

Then a hand stretched toward him, slender and brown, and
he knew it was Kimber's. He was reaching for it, so grateful
he wanted to cry, when something shoved him hard from behind and he tumbled forward into a pit. He began to fall, unable to save himself, the hand that had reached for him gone,
his efforts at escape doomed. He kept falling, waiting for the
impact that would shatter his bones and leave him lifeless,
knowing it was getting closer, closer . . .

Then a second hand reached out to catch hold of him in a
grip so powerful it defied belief, and the falling stopped . . .

He woke with a start, jerking upright in bed, gasping for
breath and clutching at the blanket he had kicked aside in his
thrashings. It took him a moment to get out of the dream
completely, to regain control of his emotions so that he no
longer feared he might begin to fall again. He swung his legs
over the side of the bed and sat with his head between his
knees, taking long, slow breaths. The dream had made him
feel frightened and alone.

Finally, he looked up. Outside, the first patch of dawn's
brightness was visible above the trees. Sudden panic rushed
through him.

What was he doing?

He knew in that moment that he wasn't equal to the task
he had set himself. He wasn't strong or brave enough. He
didn't possess the necessary skills or experience. He hadn't
lived even two decades. He might be considered a man in
some quarters, but in the place that counted, in his heart, he
was still a boy. If he were smart, he would slip out the door
now and ride back the way he had come. He would give up
on this business and save his life.

He considered doing so for long moments, knowing he
should act on his instincts, knowing as well that he couldn't.

Outside, the sky continued to brighten slowly into day. He
stood, finally, and began to dress.

They departed at midmorning, riding their horses north out
of Hearthstone toward the passes below Toffer Ridge that
would take them through the Ravenshorn and into the deep

Eastland. A voluble Cogline led the way, having mapped out a route that would allow them to travel on horseback all the way to Dun Fee Aran barring unforeseen weather or circumstances, a fact that he insisted on repeating at every opportunity. Admittedly, the old man knew the country better than anyone save the nomadic Gnome tribes and a few local Trackers. What worried Jair was how well he would remember what he knew when it counted. But there was nothing he could do about Cogline's unpredictability; all he could do was hope for the best. At present, the old man seemed fine, even eager to get on with things, which was as much as Jair could expect.

He was also upset that Whisper had failed to reappear before their departure, for the moor cat would have been a welcome addition to their company. Few living creatures, man or beast, would dare to challenge a full-grown moor cat. But there was no help for this, either. They would have to get along without him.

The weather stayed good for the first three days, and travel was uneventful. They rode north to the passes that crossed down over Toffer Ridge, staying well below Olden Moor, where the Werebeasts lived, traveling by daylight to make certain of their path. Each night, they would camp in a spot carefully chosen by Cogline and approved by Kimber, a place where they could keep watch and be reasonably certain of their safety. Each night, Kimber would prepare a meal for them and then put her grandfather to bed. Each night, the old man went without complaining and fell instantly asleep.

"It's the tea," she confided in Jair. "I put a little of his medication in it to quiet him down, the same medication I used at Hearthstone. Sometimes, it is the only way he can sleep."

They encountered few other travelers, and there was an ordinariness to their journey that belied its nature. At times it felt to Jair as if he might be on nothing more challenging than a wilderness outing, an exploration of unfamiliar country with no other purpose than to have a look around. At such times, it was difficult to think about what was waiting at the end. The end seemed far away and unrelated to the present, as if it might belong to another experience altogether.

But those moments of complacency never lasted, and when they dissipated he reverted to a dark consideration of the particulars of what would be required when he arrived at Dun Fee Aran. His conclusions were always the same. Getting inside would be easy enough. He knew how he would use his magic to disguise himself, how he would employ it to stay hidden. Unlike Brin, he had never stopped using it, practicing constantly, testing its limits. So long as he remembered not to press himself beyond those limits, he would be all right.

It was being caught out and exposed once he was inside that concerned him. He did not intend for this to happen, but if it did, what would he do? He was older and stronger than he had been two years ago, and he had studied weapons usage and self-defense since his return to the Vale. But he was not a practiced fighter, and he would be deep in the center of an enemy stronghold. That his sole allies were a young woman and a half-crazed old man was not reassuring. Kimber carried those throwing knives with which she was so lethal, and the old man his bag of strange powders and chemicals, some of which could bring down entire walls, but Jair was not inclined to rely on either. When he wasn't thinking about turning around and going home—which he found himself doing at least once a day—he was thinking about how he could persuade Kimber and her grandfather not to go with him into Dun Fee Aran. Whatever his own fate, he did not want harm to come to them. He was the one who had been summoned and dispatched by Allanon's shade. The task of destroying the Ildatch fragment had been given to him.

His fears and doubts haunted him. They clung to him like the dust of the road, tiny reminders that this business was not going to end well, that he was not equal to the task he had been given. He could not shake them, could not persuade himself that their insistent little voices were lies designed to erode his already paper-thin confidence. With every mile traveled, he felt more and more the boy he had been when he had come this way before. Dun Fee Aran was a fire pit of terror and the Mwellrets were the monsters that stirred its coals. He found himself wishing he had his companions from before— Garet Jax, the Borderman Helt, the Elven Prince Edain Elessedil, and the Dwarf Foraker. Even the taciturn, disgruntled Gnome Slanter would have been welcome. But except for the Gnome, whom he had not seen since their parting two years earlier, they had all died at Graymark. There was no possibility of replacing them, of finding allies of the same mettle. If he was determined not to involve Cogline and Kimber as more than guides and traveling companions, he would have to go it alone.

On the fourth day, the weather turned stormy. At dawn, a dark wall of clouds rolled in from the west, and by mid-morning it was raining heavily. By now they were through the Ravenshorn and riding southeast in the shadow of the mountains. The terrain was rocky and brush-clogged, and they were forced to dismount and walk their horses through the increasingly heavy downpour. Cloaked and hooded, they were effectively shut away from one another, each become a shadowy, faceless form hunched against the rain.

Locked away in the cold dampness of his water-soaked coverings, Jair found himself thinking incongruously that he had underestimated his chances of succeeding, that he was better prepared than he had thought earlier, that his magic would see him through. All he had to do was get inside Dun Fee Aran, wait for his chance, and destroy the Ildatch remnant. It wasn't like the last time, when the book of magic was a sentient being, able to protect itself. There weren't any Mord Wraiths to avoid. The Mwellrets were dangerous, but not in the same way as the walkers. He could do this. He could manage it.

He believed as much for about two hours, and then the doubts and fears returned, and his confidence evaporated. Slogging through the murk and mud, he saw himself walking a path to a cliff edge, taking a road that could only end one way.

His dark mood returned, and the weight of his inadequacies descended anew.

* * *

That night they made camp below Graymark on the banks of
the Silver River, settled well back in the concealment of the
hardwoods. They built a fire in the shelter of oaks grown so
thick that their limbs blocked away all but small patches of
the sky. Deadwood was plentiful, some of it dry enough to
burn even after the downpour. Closer to Dun Fee Aran and
the Mwellrets, they might have chosen not to risk it, but the
most dangerous creatures abroad in these woods were of the
four-legged variety. This far out in the wilderness, they were
unlikely to encounter anything else.

Still, not long after they had cooked and eaten their dinner,
they were startled by a clanking sound and the sharp bray of
a pack animal. Then a voice called to them from the darkness,
asking for permission to come in. Cogline gave it, grumbling
under his breath as he did so, and their visitor walked into the
firelight leading a mule on a rope halter. The man was tall
and thin, cloaked head to foot in an old greatcoat that had
seen hard use. The mule was a sturdy-looking animal bearing a wooden rack from which hung dozens of pots and pans
and cooking implements. A peddler and his wares had stumbled on them.

The man tethered his mule and sat down at the fire, declining the cup of tea that was offered in favor of one filled
with ale, which he gulped down gratefully. "Long, wet day,"
he declared in a weary voice. "This helps put it right."

They gave him what food was left over, still warm in the
cooking pot, and watched him eat. "This is good," he announced, nodding in Kimber's direction. "First hot meal in a
while and likely to be the last. Don't see many campfires out
this way. Don't see many people, for that matter. But I'm
more than ready to share company this night. Hope you don't
mind."

"What are you doing way out here?" Jair asked him, taking advantage of the opening he had offered.

The peddler paused in mid-bite and gave him a wry smile.
"I travel this way several times a year, servicing the places
other peddlers won't. Might not look like it, but there are

villages at the foot of the mountains that need what I sell. I pass through, do my business, and go home again, out by the Rabb. It's a lot of traveling, but I like it. I've only got me and my mule to worry about."

He finished putting the suspended bite into his mouth, chewed it carefully, and then said, "What about you? What brings you to the east side of the Ravenshorn? Pardon me for saying so, but you don't look like you belong here."

Jair exchanged a quick glance with Kimber. "Traveling up to Dun Fee Aran," Cogline announced before they could stop him. "Got some business ourselves. With the rets."

The peddler made a face. "I'd think twice about doing business with them." His tone of voice made clear his disgust. "Dun Fee Aran's no place for you. Get someone else to do your business, someone a little less . . ."

He trailed off, looking from one face to the next, clearly unable to find the words that would express his concern that a boy, a girl, and an old man would even think of trying to do business with Mwellrets.

"It won't take long," Jair said, trying to put a better face on the idea. "We just have to pick something up."

The peddler nodded, his thin face drawn with more than the cold and the damp. "Well, you be careful. The Mwellrets aren't to be trusted. You know what they say about them. Look into their eyes, and you belong to them. They steal your soul. They aren't human and they aren't of a human disposition. I never go there. Never."

He went back to eating his meal, and while he finished, no one spoke again. But when he put his plate aside and picked up his cup of ale again, Kimber filled it anew and said, "You've never had any dealings with them?"

"Once," he answered softly. "An accident. They took everything I had and cast me out to die. But I knew the country, so I was able to make my way back home. Never went near them again, not at Dun Fee Aran and not on the road. They're monsters."

He paused. "Let me tell you something about Dun Fee Aran, since you're going there. Haven't told this to anyone.

Didn't have a reason and didn't think anyone would believe me, anyway. But you should know. I was inside those walls. They held me there while they decided what to do with me after taking my wares and mule. I saw things. Shades, drifting through the walls as if the stone were nothing more than air. I saw my mother, dead fifteen years. She beckoned to me, tried to lead me out of there. But I couldn't go with her because I couldn't pass through the walls like she could. It's true. I swear it. There was others, too. Things I don't want to talk about. They were there at Dun Fee Aran. The rets didn't seem to see them. Or maybe they didn't care."

He shook his head. "You don't want to go inside those walls again once you've gotten out of them."

His voice trailed off and he stared out into the darkness as if searching for more substantial manifestations of the memories he couldn't quite escape. Fear reflected in his eyes with a bright glitter that warned of the damage such memories could do. He did not seem a cowardly man, or a superstitious one, but in the night's liquid shadows he had clearly found demons other men would never even notice.

"Do you believe me?" he asked quietly.

Jair's mouth was dry and his throat tight in the momentary silence that followed. "I don't know," he said.

The man nodded. "It would be wise if you did."

At dawn, the peddler took his leave. They watched him lead his mule through the trees and turn north along the Silver River. Like one of the shades he claimed to have seen in the dungeons at Dun Fee Aran, he walked into the wall of early-morning mist and faded away.

They traveled all that day through country grown thick with scrub and old growth and layered in gray blankets of brume. The world was empty and still, a place in which dampness and gloom smothered all life and left the landscape a tangled wilderness. If not for the Silver River's slender thread, they might easily have lost their way. Even Cogline paused more than once to consider their path. The sky had disappeared into the horizon and the horizon into the earth, so that the land took on the look and feel of a cocoon. Or a coffin. It closed about them and refused to release its death grip. It embraced them with the chilly promise of a constancy that came only with an end to life. Its desolation was both depressing and scary and did nothing to help Jair's already eroded confidence. Bad enough that the peddler had chilled what little fire remained in his determination to continue on; now the land would suffocate the coals as well.

Cogline and Kimber said little to him as they walked, locked away with their own thoughts in the shadowy coverings of their cloaks and hoods, wraiths in the mist. They led their horses like weary warriors come home from war, bent over by exhaustion and memories, lost in dark places. It was a long, slow journey that day, and at times Jair was so certain of the futility of its purpose that he wanted to stop his companions and tell them that they should turn back. It was only the shame he felt at his own weakness that kept him from doing so. He could not expose that weakness, could not admit to it. Should he do so, he knew, he might as well die.

They slept by the river that night, finding a copse of fir that sheltered and concealed them, tethering the horses close by and setting a watch. There was no fire. They were too close to Dun Fee Aran for that. Dinner was eaten cold, ale was consumed to help ward against the chill, and they went to sleep sullen and conflicted.

They woke cold and stiff from the night and the steady drizzle. Within a mile of their camp they found clearer passage along the riverbank, remounted and rode on into the afternoon until, with night descending and an icy wind beginning to blow down out of the mountains, they came in sight of their goal.

It was not a welcome moment. Dun Fee Aran rose before them in a mass of walls and towers, wreathed in mist and shrouded by rain. Torchlight flickered off the rough surfaces of ironbound gates and through the narrow slits of barred windows as if trapped souls were struggling to breathe.

Smoke rose in tendrils from the sputtering flames, giving the keep the look of a smoldering ruin. There was no sign of life, not even shadows cast by moving figures. Nor did any sounds emanate from within. It was as if the keep had been abandoned to the gloom and the peddler's ghosts.

The three travelers walked their horses back into the trees some distance away and dismounted. They stood close together as the night descended and the darkness deepened, watching and waiting for something to reveal itself. It was a futile effort.

Jair stared at the keep's forbidding bulk with certain knowledge of what waited within and felt his skin crawl.

"You can't go in there," Kimber said to him suddenly, her voice thin and strained.

"I have to."

"You don't have to do anything. Let this go. I can smell the evil in this place. I taste it on the air." She took hold of his arm. "That peddler was right. Only ghosts belong here. Grandfather, tell him he doesn't have to go any farther with this."

Jair looked at Cogline. The old man met his gaze, then turned away. He had decided to leave it up to the Valeman. It was the first time since they had met that he had taken a neutral stance on the matter of the Ildatch. It spoke volumes about his feelings, now that Dun Fee Aran lay before them.

Jair took a deep breath and looked back at Kimber. "I came a long way for nothing if I don't at least try."

She looked out into the rain and darkness to where the Mwellret castle hunkered down in the shadow of the mountains and shook her head. "I don't care. I didn't know it would be like this. This place feels much worse than I thought it would. I told you before—I don't want anything to happen to you. This"—she gestured toward the fortress—"looks too difficult for anyone."

"It looks abandoned."

She gave him a withering look. "Don't be stupid. You don't believe that. You know what's in there. Why are you even pretending it might be something else?" Her lips compressed in a tight line. "Let's go back. Right now. Let someone else deal with the Ildatch, someone better able. Jair, it's too much!"

There was a desperation in her voice that threatened to drain him of what small resolve he had left. Something of the peddler's fear reflected now in her eyes, a hint of dark places and darker feelings. She was reacting to the visceral feel of Dun Fee Aran, to its hardness and impenetrability, to its ponderous bulk and immutability. She wasn't a coward, but she was intimidated. He couldn't blame her. He could barely bring himself to consider going inside. It was easier to consider simply walking away.

He looked around, as if he might be doing exactly that. "It's too late to go anywhere tonight. Let's make camp back in the trees, where there's some shelter. Let's eat something and get some sleep. We'll think about what to do. We'll decide in the morning."

She seemed to accept that. Without pursuing the matter further, she led the way into the woods, beyond sight and sound of the fortress and its hidden inhabitants, beyond whatever might choose to go abroad. The rain continued to fall and the wind to blow, the unpleasant mix chasing away any possibility of even the smallest of comforts. They found a windbreak within a stand of fir, the best they could expect, tethered and unsaddled their horses, and settled in.

Their stores were low, and Jair surprised the girl and her grandfather by bringing out an aleskin he told them he had been saving for this moment. They would drink it now, a small indulgence to celebrate their safe arrival and to ward against bad feelings and worse weather. He poured liberally into their cups and watched them drink, being careful only to pretend to drink from his own.

His duplicity troubled him. But he was serving what he perceived to be a greater good, and in his mind that justified far worse.

They were asleep within minutes, stretched out on the forest earth. The medication he had stolen from Kimber and

added to the ale had done its job. He unrolled their blankets,
wrapped them tightly about, tucked them in under the sheltering fir boughs, and left them to sleep. He had watched
Kimber administer the drug to her grandfather each night
since they had set out from Hearthstone, his plans already
made. If he had judged correctly the measure he had dropped
into their ale, they would not wake before morning.

By then, he would be either returned or dead.

He strapped on his short sword, stuck a dagger in his boot,
wrapped himself in his greatcoat, and set off to find out
which it would be.

He did not feel particularly brave or confident about what he
had decided to do. Mostly, he felt resigned. Even if Kimber
thought he had a choice in the matter, he did not. Jair was not
the kind to walk away from his responsibilities, and it didn't
matter whether he had asked for them or not. The shade of
Allanon had summoned him deliberately and with specific
intent. He could not ignore what that meant. He had traveled
this path before in his short life, and by doing so he had
come to understand a basic truth that others might choose to
ignore, but he could not. If he failed to act, it was all too
likely no one else would, either.

In his mind, the matter had been decided almost from the
outset, and his doubts and fears were simply a testing of his
determination.

He took some comfort in the fact that he had managed to
keep Kimber and her grandfather from coming with him.
They would have done so, of course, well meaning and perhaps even helpful. But he would have worried for them, and
that would have rendered his efforts less effective. Besides, it
would be all he could do to conceal himself from discovery.
To conceal two others while gaining entry into Dun Fee Aran
was taking on too much.

Mist and rain obscured his vision, and he was forced to
make his way cautiously, unable to see more than a few yards
in any direction. Ahead, the dull yellow glow of Dun Fee

Aran's torches reflected through the gloom as through a gauzy veil. Beneath his boots, the ground was spongy and littered with deadwood and leaves knocked down by the wind. The air was cold and smelled of damp earth and wet bark. The sharp tang of burning pitch cut through both, a guide to his destination.

Then the trees opened before him, and the massive walls of the fortress came into view, black and shimmering in the rain and mist. He slowed to a walk, studying the parapets and windows carefully, searching for movement. He was already singing, calling up the magic of the wishsong. Unlike Brin, he welcomed it as he would an old friend. Perhaps that had something to do with why he was the one who was here.

Ahead, the main gates to the keep loomed, thick oak timbers wrapped in iron and standing well over twenty feet high. A forbidding obstacle, but he had already seen the smaller door to one side, the one that would be used to admit a traveler on nights such as this when it was too dangerous to chance opening the larger gates. He walked toward that door, still singing, no longer cloaking himself in invisibility but in the pretense of being someone he wasn't.

Slowly, he began to take shape, to assume the form that would gain him entry.

When he reached the smaller doors, he sent a whispered summons to the sentry standing watch inside. He never doubted that someone was there. Like Kimber, he could feel the evil in this place and knew that its source never slept. It took only moments for a response. A slot opened in the iron facing, and yellow-slitted eyes peered out. What they saw wasn't really there. What they saw was another Mwellret, drenched and angry and cloaked in an authority that was not to be challenged. A decision was quickly reached, the door swung outward with a groan of rusted hinges, and a reptilian face appeared in the opening.

"Sstate what bringss . . ."

The sentry choked hard on the rest of what he was going to ask. The Mwellret he had expected was no longer there.

What waited instead was a black-cloaked form that stood seven feet tall and had been thought dead for more than two years.

What the sentry found waiting was the Druid Allanon.

It was a bold gamble on Jair's part, but it had the desired effect. Hissing in fear and loathing, the sentry stumbled backward into the gatehouse, too traumatized even to think to resecure the doors. Jair stepped through at once, forcing the Mwellret to retreat even farther into the small gatehouse. Belatedly, the ret snatched at a pike, but a single threatening gesture was sufficient to cause him to drop the pike in terror and back away once more, this time all the way to the wall.

"You hide a fragment of the Ildatch," the Druid's voice thundered out of Jair. "Give it to me!"

The Mwellret bolted through the back door of the gatehouse into the interior of Dun Fee Aran, crying out as he went, his sibilant voice hoarse before he reached the central tower and disappeared inside. He did not bother to look back to see if Allanon was following, too intent on escaping, on giving warning, on finding help from any quarter. Had he done so, he would have found that the Druid had vanished and the Mwellret he had thought to admit in the first place had reappeared. Cloaked in his new disguise, Jair pursued the fleeing sentry with an intensity that did not allow for distraction. When other rets scurried past him, bound for the gatehouse and the threat that no longer existed, he either stepped back into the shadows or gave way in deference, a lesser to superiors, of no interest or concern to them.

Then he was inside the main stronghold, working his way along hallways and down stairs, swimming upriver against a sudden flow of traffic. The entire fortress had come alive in a swarm of reptilian forms, a nest of vipers with cold, gimlet eyes. *Don't look into those eyes!* He knew the stories of how they stole away men's minds. He had been a victim of their hypnotic effect once and did not intend to be so ever again. He avoided the looks cast his way as the Mwellrets passed, advancing deeper into the keep, leaving behind the shouts and cries that now came mostly from the main court-yard.

He felt time and chance pressing in on him like collapsing walls. Where was the sentry?

He found him not far ahead, gasping out his news to an-other Mwellret, one that looked to be a good deal more capa-ble of dealing with the unexpected. This second ret listened without comment, dispatched the frightened sentry back the way he had come, and turned down a corridor that led still deeper into the keep. Jair, mustering his courage, followed.

His quarry moved with purpose along the corridor and then down a winding set of stairs. He glanced back once or twice, but by now Jair had changed his appearance again, no longer another Mwellret, but a part of the fortress itself. He was the walls, the floor, the air, and nothing at all. The Mwellret might look over his shoulder as many times as he chose, but he would have to look carefully to realize that there was something wrong with what he was seeing.

But what concerned Jair was that the ret might not be lead-ing him to the Ildatch fragment after all. He had assumed that the sentry would rush to give warning of the threat from Allanon and by doing so lead Jair to those who guarded the page fragment he had come to destroy. Yet there was nothing to indicate that the ret was taking him to where he wanted to go. If he had guessed wrong about this, he was going to have trouble of a sort he didn't care to contemplate. His ability to employ the magic was not inexhaustible. Sooner or later, he would tire. Then he would be left not only exposed, but also defenseless.

Torchlight flooded the corridor ahead. An ironbound door and guards holding massive pikes blocked the way forward. The Mwellret he followed signaled perfunctorily to the watch as he stepped out of the darkened corridor into the light, and the guards released the locks and stepped aside for him. Jair, still invisible to those around him, took advantage of the change of light, closed swiftly on his quarry at the entry, and slipped into the chamber behind him just as the door swung closed again.

Standing just inside, he glanced quickly at the cavernous, smoke-filled chamber and its occupants. Seven, no eight, Mwellrets clustered about a huge wooden table on which rested bottles, vials, and similar containers amid a scattering of old books and tablets. At their center, carefully placed on a lectern that kept it raised above everything, was a single piece of aged paper, its edges burned and curled. A strange glow emanated from that fragment, and the writing on its worn surface pulsed steadily. The aura it gave off was so viscerally repellent that Jair recoiled in spite of himself, a sudden wave of nausea flooding through him.

There was no question in his mind about what he was seeing. Forcing his repulsion aside, he gathered up the fraying threads of his determination and threw the bolt that locked the door from the inside.

Nine heads turned as one, scaly faces lifting into the light from out of shadowy hoods. A moment of uncertainty rooted the Mwellrets in place, and then the one the Valeman had followed down from the upper halls started back for the door, a long knife appearing in his clawed hand. Jair was already moving sideways, skirting the edges of the chamber, heading for the table and its contents. The Mwellrets had begun to move forward, placing themselves between the door and their prize, their attention focused on what might be happening outside in the hallway. All the Valeman needed was a few moments to get behind them and seize the page. He could feed it into one of the torches before they could stop him. If he were quick enough, they would never even realize he was there.

Stay calm. Don't rush. Don't give yourself away.

The Mwellret at the entry released the lock and wrenched open the door. The startled sentries turned in surprise as he looked past them wordlessly into the corridor beyond, searching. Jair had reached the table and was sliding along its edge toward the page fragment, a clear path ahead of him. The Mwellrets were muttering now, glancing about uneasily, trying to decide if they were threatened or not. He had only a few seconds left.

He reached the lectern, snatched up the page fragment, and dropped it with a howl as it burned his fingers like a live coal.

Instantly the Mwellrets swung around, watching their precious relic flutter in the air before settling back on the table amid the debris, steaming and writhing like a living thing. Shouts rose from its protectors, some snatching out blades from beneath their cloaks and beginning to fan out across the chamber. Furious with himself, terrified by his failure, Jair backed away, fighting to stay calm. Magic warded the Ildatch fragment as it had warded the book itself. Whether this was magic of the book's own making or of its keepers, it changed what was required. If he couldn't hold the page, how was he going to feed it into the fire? How was he going to destroy it?

He backed against the wall, sliding away from the searching rets, who were still uncertain what they were looking for. They knew something was there, but they didn't know what. If he could keep them guessing long enough . . .

His mind raced, his fading possibilities skittering about like rats in a cage.

Then one of the Mwellrets, perhaps guessing at his subterfuge, snatched up a round wooden container from the table, reached into it, and began tossing out handfuls of white powder. Everything the powder settled on, it coated. Jair knew what was coming. Once the powder was flung in his direction, he would be outlined as clearly as if a shadow cast in bright sunlight. The best he could hope for was to find a way to destroy the Ildatch fragment before that happened, and he was likely to get only one more chance.

He glanced over his shoulder to where a torch burned in its wall mount behind him. If he snatched it up and rushed forward, he could lay it against the paper. That should be enough to finish the matter.

Steady. Don't rush.

The Mwellrets were moving back around the table now, hands groping the empty air as they attempted to flush out their invisible intruder. The Mwellret with the powder continued to toss handfuls into the air, but he was still on the other side of the table and not yet close enough to threaten. The Valeman kept the wishsong steady and his concentration focused as he edged closer to his goal. What he needed was another distraction, a small window of opportunity to act.

Then the ret with the powder turned abruptly and began throwing handfuls in his direction.

The immediacy of the threat proved too much for the Valeman to endure. He reacted instinctively, abandoning the magic that cloaked him in the appearance of invisibility for something stronger. Images of Garet Jax flooded the room, black cloaked forms wielding blades in both hands and moving like seasoned fighters. It was all Jair could come up with in his welter of panic and need, and he grasped at it as a drowning man would a lifeline.

At first, it appeared it would be enough. The Mwellrets fell back in terror, caught off guard, unprepared for so many adversaries appearing all at once. Even the sentries who now blocked the doorway retreated, pikes lifting defensively. Whatever magic was at work, it was beyond anything with which they were familiar, and they did not know what to do about it.

It was the distraction Jair required, and he took immediate advantage of it. He reached for one of the torches set in wall brackets behind him, grasped it by the handle, and wrenched at it. But his hands were coated in sweat and he could not pull it loose from its fitting. The Mwellrets hissed furiously, seeing him clearly now behind his wall of protectors, realizing at once what he intended. Under different circumstances, they might have hesitated longer before acting, but they were driven by an irrational and overwhelming need to protect the Ildatch fragment. Whatever else they might countenance, they would not stand by and lose their chance at immortality.

They came at the images of Garet Jax in a swarm, wielding their knives and short swords in a glittering frenzy, slashing and hacking without regard for their own safety. The fury and suddenness of their onslaught caught Jair by surprise, and his concentration faltered. One by one, his images disappeared. The Mwellrets found not real warriors facing them, but men made of little more than colored vapor.

The Valeman gave up on his effort to free the recalcitrant torch and turned to face the Mwellrets. They were all around him and closing in, their blades forming a circle of sharp-edged steel that he could not get past. He had been too slow, too hesitant. His chance was gone. Despairing, he drew his own sword to defend himself. He thought fleetingly of Garet Jax, trying to remember the way he had moved when surrounded by his enemies, trying to imagine what he might do now.

And as if in response, a fresh image formed, unbidden and wholly unexpected. In a shimmer of dark air, the Weapons Master reappeared, a replication of the images already destroyed, black-cloaked and wielding one of the deadly blades he had carried in life. But this image did not separate itself from Jair as the others had. Instead, it closed about him like a second skin. It happened so fast that the Valeman did not have time to try to stop it.

In seconds, he had become the image.

Instantly, this hybrid version of himself joined to the Weapons Master vaulted into the Mwellrets with a single-mindedness of purpose that was breathtaking. The rets, thinking it harmless, barely brushed at it with their weapons. Two of them died for their carelessness in a single pass. Another fell on a lunge that buried his blade so deep it had to be wrenched free. Belatedly, the Mwellrets realized they were faced with something new. They slashed and cut with their own blades in retaliation, but they might as well have been wielding wooden toys. Jair heard sharp intakes of breath as his knives found their mark; he felt the shudder of bodies and the thrashing of limbs. Mwellrets stumbled, dying on their feet, stunned looks on their faces as he swept through them, killing with scythelike precision.

It was horrific and exhilarating, and the Valeman was immersed in it, living it. For a few stunning moments, he was someone else entirely, someone whose thoughts and experiences were not his own. He wasn't just watching Garet Jax—

he *was* Garet Jax. He was so lost to himself, so much a part
of the Weapons Master, that even though what he was expe-
riencing was dark and scary, it filled him with satisfaction
and a deep longing for more.

Now the ret guards rushed to join the battle, pikes spearing
at him. The guards were trained and not so easily dispatched.
A hooked point sliced through his sword arm, sending a flash
of jagged pain into his body. He feinted and sidestepped the
next thrust. The guards cut at him, but he was ready now and
eluded them easily. A phantom sliding smoothly beneath
each sweep of their weapons, he was inside their killing arc
and on top of them before they realized they had failed to
stop him.

Seconds later, the last of the rets lay lifeless on the floor.

But when he wheeled back to survey the devastation he
had left in his wake, he saw the young Valeman who had remained on the far side of the table. Their eyes met, and he
felt something shift inside. The Valeman was fading away
even as he watched, turning slowly transparent, becoming a
ghost.

He was disappearing.

Do something!

He snatched free a torch mounted on the wall behind him
and threw it into the powders and potions on the table. Instantly, the volatile mix went up in flames, white hot and
spitting. The Ildatch fragment pulsed at its center, then rose
from the table into the scorched air, riding the back of invisible currents generated by the heat.

Escaping . . .

He snatched the dagger from his boot and leapt forward,
spearing the hapless scrap of paper in midair and pinning it
to the wooden tabletop where the flames were fiercest. The
paper curled against his skin in a clutching motion and his
head snapped back in shock as razor-sharp pains raced up his
arm and into his chest. But he refused to let go. Ignoring the
pain, he held the paper pinned in place. When the inferno finally grew so intense that he was forced to release his death
grip on the dagger and back away, the Ildatch fragment was

just barely recognizable. He stood clutching his seared hand on the far side of the burning table, watching the scrap of paper slowly wither and turn to dust.

Then he walked back around the table and through the image of the Valeman and he was inside his own body again. Feeling as if a weight had been lifted from his shoulders, he looked over to where the shadowy, black-cloaked figure he had been joined to was fading away, returning to the ether from which it had come, returning to the land of the dead.

He fled the chamber, skittering through the sprawl of Mwellret bodies and out the door, hugging the walls of the smoke-filled corridors and stairwells that led to safety. His mind spun with images of what he had just experienced, leaving him unsteady and riddled with doubt. Despite having the use of the wishsong to disguise his passing, he felt completely exposed.

What had happened back there?

Had Garet Jax found a way to come back from the dead on his own, choosing to be Jair's protector one final time? Had Allanon sent him through a trick of Druid magic that transcended the dictates of the grave?

Perhaps.

But Jair didn't think so. What he thought was that he alone was responsible, that somehow the wishsong had given that last image life.

It was impossible, but that was what he believed.

He took deep, slow breaths to steady himself as he climbed out of Dun Fee Aran's prisons. It was madness to think that his magic could give life to the dead. It suggested possibilities that he could only just bear to consider. Giving life to the dead violated all of nature's laws. It made his skin crawl.

But it had saved him, hadn't it? It had enabled him to destroy the Ildatch fragment, and that was what he had come to Dun Fee Aran to do. What difference did it make how it had been accomplished?

Yet it did make a difference. He remembered how it had felt to be a part of Garet Jax. He remembered how it had felt to kill those Mwellrets, to hear their frantic cries, to see their stricken looks, to smell their blood and fear. He remembered the grating of his blade against their bones and the surprisingly soft yield of their scaly flesh. He hadn't hated it; he had enjoyed it—enough so that for the brief moments he had been connected to the Weapons Master, he had craved it. Even now, in the terrible, blood-drenched aftermath when his thoughts and body were his own again, he hungered for more.

What if he had not looked back at the last moment and seen himself fading away?

What if he had not sensed the unexpectedly dangerous position he had placed himself in, joined to a ghost out of time?

He found his way up from the prisons more easily than he had expected he would, moving swiftly and smoothly through the chaos. He did not encounter any more Mwellrets until he reached the upper halls, where they were clustered in angry bands, still looking for something that wasn't there, still unaware that the Druid they sought was an illusion. Perhaps the sounds had been muffled by the stone walls and iron doors, but they had not discovered yet what had happened belowground. They did not see him as he passed, cloaked in his magic, and in moments, he was back at the gates. Distracting the already distracted guards long enough to open the door one last time, he melted into the night.

He walked from the fortress through the rain and mist, using the wishsong until he reached the trees, then stopped, the magic dying on his lips. His knees gave way, and he sat on the damp ground and stared into space. His burned hand throbbed and the wound to his arm ached. He was alive, but he felt dead inside. Still, how he felt inside was his own fault. Wasn't bringing Garet Jax back from the dead what he had wanted all along? Wasn't that the purpose of preserving all those memories of Graymark and the Croagh? To make the past he so greatly prized a part of the present?

He placed his hand against the cool earth and stared at it.

Something wasn't right.

If it was the Weapons Master who had fought against the Mwellrets and destroyed the fragment of the Ildatch, why was his hand burned? Why was his arm wounded?

He stared harder, remembering. Garet Jax had carried only one blade in his battle with the Mwellrets, rather than the two all of the other images had carried.

Jair's blade.

His throat tightened in shock. He was looking at this all wrong. The wishsong hadn't brought Garet Jax back from the dead. It hadn't brought Garet Jax back at all. There was only one of them in that charnel house tonight.

Himself.

He saw the truth of things now, all of it, what he had so completely misread. Brin had warned him not to trust the magic, had cautioned him that it was dangerous. But he had ignored her. He had assumed that because his use of it was different from her own, less potent and seemingly more harmless, it did not threaten in the same way. She could actually change things, could create or destroy, whereas he could only give the appearance of doing so. Where was the harm in that?

But his magic had evolved. Perhaps it had done so because he had grown. Perhaps it was just the natural consequence of time's passage. Whatever the case, sometime in the past two years it had undergone a terrible transformation. And tonight, in the dungeons of Dun Fee Aran, responding to the unfamiliar urgency of his desperation and fear, it had revealed its new capabilities for the first time.

He hadn't conjured up the shade of Garet Jax. He hadn't given life to a dead man in some mysterious way. What he had done was to remake himself in the Weapons Master's image. That had been all him back there, cloaked in his once-protector's trappings, a replica of the killing machine the other had been. That was why he had felt everything so clearly, why it had all seemed so real. It was. The Garet Jax in the chambers of Dun Fee Aran was a reflection of himself, of his own dark nature, of what lay buried just beneath the surface.

A reflection, he recalled with a chill, into which he had almost disappeared completely.

Because risking that fate was necessary if he was to survive and the Ildatch to be destroyed.

Then a further revelation came to him, one so terrible that he knew almost as soon as it occurred to him that it was true. Allanon had known what his magic would do when he had summoned him through Cogline's dreams. Allanon had known that it would surface to protect him against the Mwellrets.

Kimber Boh had been right. The Druid had used him. Even in death, it could still manipulate the living. Circumstances required it, necessity dictated it, and Jair was sacrificed to both at the cost of a glimpse into the blackest part of his soul.

He closed his eyes against what he was feeling. He wanted to go home. He wanted to forget everything that had happened this night. He wanted to bury the knowledge of what his magic could do. He wanted never to have come this way.

He ran his fingers through the damp leaves and rain-softened earth at his feet, stirring up the pungent smells of both, tracing idle patterns as he waited for his feelings to settle and his head to clear. Somewhere in the distance, he heard fresh cries from the fortress. They had discovered the chamber where the dead men lay. They would try to understand what had happened, but would not be able to do so.

Only he would ever know.

After long moments, he opened his eyes again and brushed the dirt and debris off his injured hand. He would return to Kimber and her grandfather and wake them. He would tell them some of what had happened, but not all. He might never tell anyone all of it.

He wondered if he would heed his sister's advice and never use the magic again. He wondered what would happen if he chose to ignore that advice again or if fate and circumstances made it impossible for him to do otherwise, as had happened tonight. He wondered what the consequences would be next time.

The past is always with us, but sometimes we don't recognize it right away for what it is.

He got to his feet and started walking.